The Running Waves

T.M. Murphy
&
Seton Murphy

PublishingWorks, Inc.
Exeter, NH
2010

PublishingWorks, Inc.
151 Epping Road
Exeter, NH 03833
603-778-9883 603-772-7200
www.publishingworks.com

Distributed to the trade by Publishers Group West

Designed by Anna Pearlman

LCCN: 2009927778
ISBN-13: 978-1-935557-55-5

Printed in Canada.

In memory of Marc Steele and Peter Hurd

Silver Shores, Cape Cod

1994

—

ONE

It was an early June morning, twenty after eight to be exact, when nineteen-year-old Colin Brennan suddenly awoke from his dream. He tried to avoid it while lying in his bed wondering what that *fucking* sound was that had him feeling his hangover before his scheduled alarm. The high-pitched zinging clamor screamed into his window periodically. He tried to fight it by wrapping his pillow around his ears, but no luck.

"Are you fucking kidding me?" he said to the ceiling.

Colin knew that sound—landscapers. *I might even know the asshole behind that chainsaw massacre!*

Most of his buddies who stayed in Silver Shores, Cape Cod, were either manning leaf blowers or banging nails for a living. That was too much for him. He didn't like strenuous work unless he was competing, which now was a thing of the past.

His friends busted their asses during the week, only to blow their paychecks on the weekends on shitty beer and shittier weed. While shooting pool or downing shots, they'd try to convince him to come join them in their blue-collar world, but he was only willing to do that *after* the lawn and lumber trucks had been unloaded for the day. The last thing he wanted was *their* lives.

He did feel some guilt. *It's only Tuesday and I'm hung over. They're at least outside working.*

Colin flipped and flopped for another fifteen minutes before throwing his pillow, knocking one of his high school swimming trophies off his desk. He stared at the golden first-place man who was still doing the crawl, except now he was swimming on the hardwood floor. A flash of a memory came to him of his eleventh birthday when he got an Aquaman figure from his best friends, Matt Sweeney and Paul Hurley. After he had opened the gift, the three of them had snuck upstairs leaving the cake and ice cream and annoying pigtailed girls behind. Under Colin's bed, they had played with Aquaman for hours, pretending they were in an underwater cave searching for the lost city of Atlantis.

The memory left him as quickly as it had come, and he realized the golden man was just another meaningless trophy. He thought about getting up and retrieving it, but gritted his teeth and turned away.

Those days are long gone. He probably should box up all of that hardware anyway, or maybe should just throw it all away.

The chainsaw began buzzing hysterically again. "Ah, fuck it. You win!" He knew there was no way in hell he could ignore the commotion any longer and that sacred sleep was unachievable. His anger, plus curiosity, helped him to his feet, but he moved like a fallen boxer trying to rise from the canvas.

He was ragged and banged up. Both knees were scraped and spotted with dried blood. His right four knuckles looked even worse, swollen and raw.

My blood? Somebody else's? Both?

He didn't know, and not knowing made him nervous.

He shrugged. *Nothing I can do about it now.*

Any moment he was bound to get the phone call from his buddy, Dwayne. "Holy shit, man, that was some crazy shit you did," or if it had been really bad, he would stop by the shoe store and fill Colin in on the gory details. It was becoming a routine and he hated it. He'd laugh it off with his friends, but when he was alone there was no laughing. He moved gingerly toward the window to locate the asshole who woke him up so damn early. Stopping at his bureau, he gazed at his face. His shoulder-length blond hair was unkempt and shaggy and he hadn't shaved for two days.

"Wow, I look like hell," he spoke to his reflection. The dark circles under his blue eyes gave him a dangerous look, like an approaching thunderstorm. He rubbed his eyes, trying to make the circles disappear.

It was time for his morning ritual: emptying his pockets from the night before. As he littered the bureau with more than a dozen bottle caps of various brands, he gained clues about what kind of time he had had—Bud Light, Rolling Rock, Miller Light, and Otter Creek.

Otter Creek? He studied the cap.

The other beers he could account for, but for the Silver Shores crowd, Otter Creek might as well have been a foreign import since it was brewed in Vermont. And it wasn't cheap. Colin and his friends drank piss beer at poor man's prices, and they were quite all right with that. "A beer's a beer," they'd always say as they each fished through a cooler.

He reached into his right pocket to dig for more evidence.

"Ow!" His damaged knuckles grazed the inside of his shorts. He pulled out a Red Sox lighter, an empty pack of Marlboro Reds, and from his back pocket, a healthy half ounce of kind bud. "Wow." He unzipped the baggie to smell the skunked, green bud before taking it out for a quick inspection.

Where had he gotten this weed? This was the *chronic*, no townie brown crap. It was rare for him to smoke such good pot, but God how he loved kind bud. A smile came to his face. Things were looking up.

Deciding to finally unmask the noisemaker, he approached the window. Stevie Garrison and his enormous chainsaw had beaten and minimized a once-strong and dense oak tree. Stevie was five years older, but Colin knew him well. Garrison worked hard and had a decent business, but most of his commissions went into the drawer at *Pucky's Pub* or up his nose. He was a harmless townie who loved to party too much and then tell the most ridiculous, transparently fictitious stories. People laughed because he was always buying the next round. Stevie was more pathetic than cocky.

The tree that Colin had once used as a lookout when he was a kid to make sure no pirate ships were landing on Stirling Beach was now half the size, and a couple of Brazilians were dragging its cut limbs to a chipper truck.

"Poor bastards," he sighed.

Like Stevie, they were busting their asses, but unaware they were getting paid peanuts. The Brazilians flashed their grateful smiles and open palms on Friday afternoons.

"So they're finally cutting that goddamn tree down," he said softly, noticing his mother carrying a tray of lemonade and cookies across the street to the two Brazilians. The chainsaw paused.

"You're the best, Mrs. Brennan!" Colin heard Stevie call to his mom.

"Not a problem, Stevie. In this muggy weather you fellas have to stay hydrated," she greeted the men who rushed over with dirty hands to grab cookies and drinks. "Stevie, I haven't seen your mom in a while. Tell her to give me a call."

Colin didn't even know that his mom knew Stevie, let alone Mrs. Garrison, but he wasn't surprised. He watched her admiringly as she talked with the workers about what part of the country they came from and then she exited saying, "Well, you're all my saviors! Thank you so much."

"No. Thank you, ma'am." They toasted her with their half-eaten cookies.

Colin knew exactly what his mom meant by *saviors*. She wasn't only being sweet, she was also compensating them for being the reason she would now have a great view of Vineyard Sound from her kitchen window, something she had hoped for ever since she and her husband had bought the small Cape house twenty-five years ago on his modest teacher's salary. Colin didn't care one way or the other. He had been a lifeguard for three summers and had seen enough of the ocean.

Grabbing his towel off the doorknob, he headed for the shower. It was time to cleanse those wounds. It was only a matter of minutes before he'd bump into his parents on his way out the door to work, and the less they saw the better. *What they don't know can't hurt them.* He'd been living by that motto for a while, but he wondered if he could keep it flying now that his older brother, Dermot, would be back in the Shores for the summer. He stopped in his tracks. *Shit, is Dermot coming back today or tomorrow?* He couldn't remember. No sense in worrying about it now. He stepped into the stream and felt the burning flow needle into his wounds, making him groan. After his body acclimated to the temperature, he moved out of the stream to lather up, and then took on the shower again. The pain lessened, and the water felt good. Really good. Familiar. Colin closed his eyes to enjoy it, but then the dream came back to him. He shook his head from side to side, realizing even though he couldn't remember anything about the night before, he still could remember his dream. And now it poured over him with as much intensity as the hot water. He desperately wanted that water to drown the memory, but the faces in his dream floated in his thoughts.

In his dream he saw three ten-year-old boys dressed in their 1980s Ocean Pacific bathing suits with beach towels wrapped around their shoulders leaning on their BMX bikes. The vision was a happy one at first, but then he realized he was one of the boys, the one crying and pleading. He saw the strawberry blond-haired boy with the wondrous brown eyes. Those brown eyes. The thought of them made him want to turn off the shower. Colin had blue eyes, "like the ocean," he was told over and over again. But Paul's eyes were brown just like Matt's hair. Matt's curly brown hair. *God*, Colin thought, *he'd only get it cut when Augie's Barber Shop gave him the back-to-school deal.* Matt's eyes were also brown and always widened when Augie—known to nip an earlobe or two—grabbed for the clippers.

"Colin, you need to get going." Paul threw his bike down and pushed against Colin's chest.

"But I don't want to go. I want to stay with you and Matt."

"You can't stay with us. You need to stop crying, Colin. It's okay. You have to go," Matt urged while getting off his bike and walking over to them

"But I don't want to leave, Matt. I want to stay with you guys."

Paul and Matt pushed Colin along on his red BMX. He tried to take control of his bike screaming, "I can't get my feet on the pedals! I can't! They're going too fast! I don't want to leave!"

"It's okay. We'll be right behind you." Paul smiled and the dream faded.

With the dream now washed away and Colin back in the moment, he spat into the shower's fog, "Will you, Paul?"

TWO

Like a dying dog, the gray '84 Pontiac shitbox wheezed and clawed its way along the last stretch of highway passing the WELCOME TO SILVER SHORES, CAPE COD sign.

"You made it this far. Stay with me, baby. We're almost there." Dermot Brennan patted the dashboard, and the engine noisily growled back. He'd not driven the old car much since returning from Ireland on his "soul-searching" trip. Glancing in the rearview mirror, he spotted his second chin forming. *Oh, I found my soul all right—in bottomless pint glasses and greasy late night bags of fish and chips.* He brushed the thought aside and reassured himself that he would lose the chin this summer.

The highway merged into one lane where a red light halted him behind a station wagon. There was a little boy and girl peering through the backseat window making blowfish faces against the glass. They reminded Dermot of when he and his brother were kids, trying to entertain themselves on the long trips to their cousins' house in Canada. He laughed quietly as the vision of them puking their Ben and Jerry's ice cream all over the station wagon after the car had climbed up and down the winding Airline Road in Maine.

Man, I had forgotten all about that.

Now the children ahead of him must have grown emboldened by Dermot's attention and his smile. They both then picked their noses and pointed their findings at him.

"That's all you kids got?" he asked under his breath. He slowly placed his right index finger on the side of his nose pretending to dig for gold. Dermot pointed his finger at them, licked it, and smiled. "Um, um, good!"

Their bulging eyes were priceless as they fell back into their seats, and sprang back up. He could easily read their lips: "Eww, you're gross!"

He nodded. "I win!" His laughter grew as the light turned green. Spinning the wheel with his left hand while turning the radio dial with the other, he stopped when he heard the D.J. say, "Attention, Red Sox fans! Some very depressing news has just been reported to me. Many of you might think it's just talk that there's a baseball strike looming. Well, today an unnamed source from the players' union stated that the players do have every intention to picket some time in early to mid-August if an agreement isn't reached. Imagine that baseball fans? No fall classic! Of course, us Sox fans are used to having no fall classic! So, what else is new?" The D.J. laughed at his own joke and then spun into "U Can't Touch This" by M.C. Hammer.

"More like, *you* can't listen to this," Dermot grumbled, then turned the radio off and leafed through his tapes. There were around thirty scattered tapes titled by theme, but as his luck would have it, the one he blindly picked from the pile was Francesca's Mix.

The sight of the flowery, purple writing paralyzed him for a brief second, and he almost slammed into the Village Green's fence. They would listen to that tape, while riding in Francesca's dung-brown Volvo, singing along with Natalie Merchant or Sting. They never seemed to have a plan or a destination. Maybe, they'd go for ice cream. Maybe to the movies. Or maybe they'd park under the lighthouse where the blinking beam acted as *their* "fields of gold," revealing one another while they unfastened buckle and bra.

Dermot shook himself. He couldn't think about the brown Volvo because if he did, the *other* memory of what happened in that car would follow. He grabbed another tape and scanned the big block lettering: *CREW MIX*. This was the tape his crew would play at the *Island Ferry* parking lot. "Thank God. Bim will put me in the right mood," Dermot said, popping it in and turning the knob to full volume. The steady beat of Boston Ska legends Bim Skala Bim singing, "Wise Up" filled the car and did the job. His smile returned.

Summer is here, and it's time I move forward.

Unfortunately, Dermot's car didn't muster up the same enthusiasm as it inched along Main Street coughing up smoke.

"Please, just a couple miles longer, baby."

The irony was it actually gave him time to inhale. He may've been going down Main Street and taking in the smoke from his exhaust pipe, but there was also a hint of sea salt in the breeze telling him he was very close to home. It was the first time since his plane had touched down that he really breathed in and out, and when he did, he realized he was excited to be back.

"What's the good word, Tex?" he asked himself as he approached the yellow sign in front of Tex's Super Lube. Ever since he could read, he'd check the daily fortune cookie-style message underneath the prices for an oil change. Today the sign read, ENJOY WHAT YOU ARE! "Thanks, Tex, but I have no clue what that is anymore."

When he rolled past The Shoe Fort, he glanced over to see if he could spot Colin working, but the glare from the sun made the window a one-way mirror. He'd see him at dinner, anyway, but he'd hoped to catch a glimpse of his little brother now, as reassurance that all was well. From his parents' letters and cards there was ample reason to be worried about Colin. Yet in his Mom's last card, she wrote, "Colin is doing much better. I think he might be becoming his old self again. Remember, we always have to keep the faith." And after several months of playing overseas phone tag, Colin had left him a message on his roommate, Sandy's, answering machine. Sandy had played it moments before Dermot left for the Cape:

> Sandy, pass this on to Dermot. Big D, Mom says you'll be home on the seventh, which is cool 'cause word is out you're coming home and we've already been challenged. Their name is the Ferguson brothers. I set it up for the eighth. So put it in that notebook of yours. I'll meet you in front of The Shack on the eighth at ten forty-five. I already took the morning off that day so be there. Peace out.

"You've been *challenged* by the Ferguson brothers?" Sandy asked, looking utterly confused. "What the hell do you guys do down on the Cape, anyway? Are you going to fight these guys or something?" Sandy wasn't known as the brightest bulb on the tree, so Dermot threw him a serious squint followed by a pat on the back. "Believe, me, you don't want to know, Pony Boy. You really don't want to know."

"Pony Boy?"

Dermot's reference to *The Outsiders* went over Sandy's head, as most somewhat subtle jokes did. Dermot made sure Sandy would be doubly worried by intentionally rushing out of the apartment leaving his befuddled roomie on the stoop.

"If he only knew . . . that will bug the shit out of him all summer." He laughed again, turning onto Beach Street. After a hundred yards or so, he craned his neck to his right to see who was working at the *Island Ferry* parking lot. Easy Shift Molloy. Dermot smiled as he spotted middle-aged wanna-be playboy Gary Molloy leaning his chair against the parking lot shack sunning himself. He knew under those mirrored sunglasses Molloy was catching a late-afternoon nap. He also knew once the summer schedule started in a few days those naps for Molloy and every other parking lot crewmember would be few and far between, and Dermot would be one of them. "Pray for rain," was their mantra.

Dermot put the brakes on in the middle of the street and leaned on the horn, not only jarring Molloy awake, but sending him falling off his chair. "What *the* . . . ?" Molloy began as he jumped up, dusted himself off, and charged out of the lot onto the street before realizing it was Dermot.

"You asshole." Molloy's pearly whites shone as he headed toward the passenger door. "Hey, how was Irela—" Without letting him finish, Dermot peeled away, leaving behind a cloud of black smoke and a one-finger-waving Molloy. That was a double whammy: not only did he wake him up, but he didn't hang out and chat. Dermot chuckled. He knew Molloy would repeat the story of falling off the chair for the rest of the summer. He also knew he had around a hundred shifts to tell him about his trip to Ireland, and each time the stories would become a little more entertaining, and a little less true.

The Pontiac hit the final stretch and he had to make a choice. Take the quick left and head for home around the corner or drive straight ahead and loop around the hill and take in the view of the beach at the bottom. It wasn't really a hard choice. Even when he was little and had just played bike-chase with the rest of the neighborhood kids, he'd still pick the longer ride home. Shifting his bike to one speed, he would slowly make it to the top of the hill before flipping it back to ten and rocketing to the bottom as if on a rollercoaster. His car was about to turn the corner to climb Beach Hill Road when he wondered if he really *was* going to make it, and longed for his old blue Schwinn.

He passed St. Peter's Chapel overlooking the harbor on his right. He used to cross himself whenever he passed the chapel, but today his hands stayed on the steering wheel. He willed the car up the hill, reached the top, and coasted down where the scent of fried clams hit him—Pucky's Pub.

"Damn, it *is* summer and I *am* home," he said looking at the sea-worn shingled building at the bottom of the hill and then over at the ball field to his left. He expected to have that same giddy feeling he always got when the ocean came into view on his right, but he didn't. He gazed out into the ocean to the white marker bobbing from side to side with the red letters that he knew all too well: *No Swimming Beyond This Point.* The gruff and energetic voice of Dicky Barrett singing "Where'd You Go?" roused him. He had seen the Mighty Mighty Bosstones at The Channel in Boston one February evening, some years ago. "I think I got a phone number that night." He tapped the steering wheel to the song, but stopped when he saw two figures on the far end of the field playing Wiffle ball. The batter was tall and wiry, and the pitcher was short and stocky.

I would know those two jackasses anywhere.

In grade school, his dad, the movie buff, had dubbed them "Abbott and Costello." In high school, Dermot updated their names to "The Blues Brothers." Whenever he was pissed off at them, he'd just call them "Fat and Skinny." But whatever name he gave them, in the end, they would always be known as his two best friends—Tommy Keating and Benny "Clay" Pelligrini. Dermot parked beside the thorny, rose-covered wooden fence, *their* left field. He waited for a moment to see if either one of them would notice him, but they were too busy arguing with one another about balls and strikes.

"Dumb ass, we always play eight balls *is* a walk. And I'm telling you that was eight. God, you're such a jackass!" The thin batter, Tommy, barked and fired the ball wildly over Clay's head.

"Goddamn it," Clay replied, walking to retrieve the ball, "Can you ever get it right to me? And you know what, Tommy? *You're* the jackass!"

"You're one to talk! You're like goddamn Bob Stanley in Game Six or, maybe even worse, Calvin Schiraldi."

"How many times have you beaten me?" Clay shot back.

"That was then. This is now. I'm going to call you 'Mr. Eight Balls' from now on."

"That's eight more than you'll ever have. Next time get it to me."

"Yeah, I only throw it over your head so you can get some exercise, Mr. Eight Balls, you fat bastard."

"Well, I only needed two balls the other night with ah . . . your sister. And I got plenty of exercise with her," Clay said.

"That would be a great comeback if I even had a sister, dumbass. How long have I known you? Oh, wait a second, you were going to say with my *mother*, weren't you? That's five bucks to the jar." Mother jokes had been banned the day they all received their high school diplomas, but they were always slipping, and when you slipped with a mother joke it was five bucks in the drinking jar.

"No, I wasn't, and besides, I have to actually voice the shit to be fined."

Dermot had enough of their entertainment and turned the ignition back on. The Bosstones came back to life and this time it grabbed Tommy and Clay's attention.

"Bosstones?" Clay looked behind him. "Shit! Look who's back!"

Clay fired the Wiffle ball back at Tommy, then turned and did a half-run before slowing to a waddle and leaned against the chest-high fence. Dermot hopped out of the car and reached over the fence and gave him a hug.

"How are you doing, you ugly bastard?" Clay smiled.

"What do you think?" Dermot returned the smile. "I'm squeezing out another summer on the Cape."

"I hear you, brother."

Dermot then noticed Clay's shirt: FIREMEN CARRY THE BIGGEST HOSES.

"Real classy." Dermot pointed to the shirt. "Does that mean you're finally on the force?"

"Not even close, Derm. I'm still doing the weekend warrior bullshit. Haven't even put out a real fire yet. But my day is coming. Gotta lose some LBs though."

Dermot pointed to his own gut. "I hear you there."

Clay put his hands up. "Hey, no comment from me on that shit. All right, let's go unpack your stuff and have a few pops at The Shanty. I gotta hear about all the tail you got over there in Ireland."

"Sounds good to me. I've missed the ol' Sea Shanty," Dermot said thinking about his parent's garage that a few years earlier Tommy, the carpenter, had converted into the ultimate hangout.

Clay turned to Tommy who was waiting at home plate holding the bat and ball.

"Grab the chair and come say hi to your boy!" Tommy, who was pissed, folded the chair and headed over.

"He's got the lead?" Dermot asked.

"Yup, for once, but you know how that goes," Clay answered. "So are they hot over there?"

"The women?" Dermot asked.

"No, the goddamn sheep. Yeah, of course, the women!"

"Well, let's just say they drink over there for a reason."

"Ouch." Clay winced.

"Yeah, but I got some stories." Dermot paused. "I just can't remember them."

They both laughed.

"Your pops told me you were a big time newspaper man over there." Clay said.

Dermot chuckled. "So like my dad to pump me up. I was more like newspaper *boy*. I wrote for the paper and actually delivered them too."

"You mean you were like a paper boy?" Clay asked.

"Yeah, they gave me a bike and everything."

Clay laughed, "Geeze, bro. Don't go public with that one!"

"I hear you, man." Dermot laughed again as Tommy approached them.

"DB, I'm psyched you're back and all, but I got a six-two lead in the top of the fifth."

"Are you playing seven or nine?" Dermot asked.

"You know we always play nine," Tommy replied.

"Well, then you should know, TK, that I just saved your ass."

"Saved my ass? What are you talking about? I said I'm up six–two, and he just walked me."

Dermot laughed. "Yeah, and Clay would do his Robert Redford *Natural* act in the ninth and you'd be crying in your beer tonight."

"No, man," Tommy protested as Clay hopped over the fence and followed Dermot into the car. "I feel really good about this one. I know I can beat him this time."

Dermot waited while Tommy crammed into the back among his garbage bags of clothes and got settled. "Tommy, when are you going to learn Clay's secret?" Dermot looked at him through the rearview mirror.

Clay punched Dermot in the shoulder, "Shut up, man."

"Ow," Dermot said, "C'mon, Clay, it's getting a little ridiculous. Don't you think?"

"What secret?" Tommy leaned towards them.

"Clay always kicks your ass in the afternoon games. He's a lefty and the sea winds come off the beach around five and the wind on the whole field shifts." Dermot looked down at his watch before continuing. "In about ten minutes, he would've been hitting *SportsCenter* shots to right field."

Tommy's eyes widened like he had just heard the cure for cancer.

"Holy shit!" he said. "Are you serious? Wow . . . wait . . . yeah . . . oh, man. That's why you never play me in . . ."

"That's bullshit. I can't believe, Dermot, you still have that theory going," Clay said, but it was obvious to all of them he was trying not to laugh.

"And I can't believe I am just hearing it," Tommy said, stunned.

Dermot chuckled and shifted into gear, but stopped the car for a second and pointed at the Crescent Road sign behind the fence in center field.

"Do I even have to ask you guys?"

"That would be on the front page of the *Cape Cod Times* if someone had hit it," Clay said.

"Good, because I want to make something clear. This summer, I, Dermot Brennan, will hit the Crescent Road sign on the fly."

Tommy and Clay broke into hysterical laughter as Dermot turned the corner and headed down the road that led to his house.

"What?" he asked them.

They looked at one another, and Clay then pointed to Tommy. "You take it."

"Okay," he answered. "Well, Dermot, it's just that you've been saying that every fucking summer since we were eight. It's getting kind of old."

"This *fucking* summer is going to be different."

"Well, Mr. Confidence, Tommy and me figure that this is like our fifteenth year playing and not once has a Wiffle ball come close to hitting that sign."

"Whoa!" Tommy almost jumped over the seat. "Dude, that's not true. Remember that summer when we were like thirteen? I came only inches." He made the distance with his index finger and thumb.

"Yeah, inches. That's what she said." Clay laughed.

Tommy barked, "*She said* jokes should be part of this year's jar. Talk about old."

"Anyway," Clay continued, "Dermot, we're thinking of upping the ante to two kegs for whoever hits it."

Dermot became reflective as he pulled into the seashell driveway in front of The Shanty. He turned off the car and said, "I remember when it was just a case of soda of your choice and five dollars worth of penny candy."

"I know, man." Tommy patted him on the shoulder. "But the Fresca and Pop Rocks days are over. It's two kegs of your choice. And by looking at those Stay Puft Marshmallow chins you grew in Ireland, I'm thinking you're going to want those two kegs to be Guinness. Damn, you look like Clay if he wasn't such a little midget." Tommy roared with laughter before

Dermot hopped over into the backseat and pummeled him with leg shots. Clay reached over the passenger seat and also got a few shots in.

But then the fists turned on Dermot.

"Welcome back, jackass!" Clay said.

Yup, it's good to be home! Dermot thought.

THREE

The hefty orange sun kept the Atlantic Ocean lit, while Colin impatiently sparked a fat joint with his newly discovered Red Sox lighter. He sat comfortably in the driver's seat of his '87 Volkswagen Golf in the Silver Shores Harbor parking lot. It was early enough in the season that the sunset still belonged to the townies, which he and his passenger Dwayne Peters were going to take full advantage of. They both knew in two weeks there would be no way they'd be able to fishbowl without the chance of a baton tap on the window from a rent-a-cop or a knuckle from a tourist asking for a good place to get lobster.

"Damn, C-Dog, that shit is the chronic." Dwayne, also known as D, slowly turned his head toward Colin, looking as if he had forgotten where he was. "I'm really baked, man."

"Yeah, this is the two-hit quit, bro, but not tonight." Colin was just as burnt. His speech was slow. The haze had set in.

"You know what, D?" He studied his joint before continuing. "We need to cherish these highs because pretty soon it will be back to rolling blunts of that same brown seaweed."

He then took a monster hit before passing it off to Dwayne, who waited patiently, bearing that wide, white smile that grew ten times wider when he was stoned.

Colin met the nineteen-year-old Cape Verdean kid back in the fifth grade; a friendly one-on-one basketball game had ended up being a bloodthirsty, best two out of three. Dwayne had taken the third game on a jumper that seemed to roll around the cylinder for hours before falling in. Ever since that shot they had been tight, but even more so in the last year, since they both were *still* stuck in Silver Shores.

But, Colin knew they were heading down different roads. Dwayne had just finished his first year at Cape Cod Community College—aka Four C's—but there were no C's with Dwayne Peters.

A half hour before Colin picked him up, D got the word that he pulled a 3.7 GPA that now guaranteed him enrollment at Merrimack College, a four-year university outside of Boston. On top of that and his internship at a radio station, he DJ'ed weddings and parties, storing that green away for his one-way ticket off Cape Cod. That was what made him different from Colin and most kids who stayed in "The Shores" after graduation. Dwayne was steering his *own* ship. He didn't just talk shit. With today's news, the Silver Shores winters would be a thing of the past for him. Without them ever talking about it, Colin knew his buddy would soon be dropping the party scene, smoking a rare joint when he returned for the Thanksgiving game or the occasional summer cookout.

He even knew how to party right, always knowing when to exchange the beer and nips for Poland Springs. And when he was good to drive, he would sneak out some side door or tiptoe up and out of a dusty bulkhead when no one was looking, leaving the drunks asking, "Where's Dwayne at?"

I wish I knew when to leave a party. But as he smoked, Colin brushed that thought away and concentrated on the infectious, entertaining character beside him. A part of him didn't want the joint to burn out because it might also extinguish all of the fading memories. Colin held the smoke in before bursting into laughter.

"What's so funny?" D asked, also laughing, but not knowing why.

"Chooocolate Thunnnder . . ." Colin coughed a laugh and patted the steering wheel.

"Oh, Jesus. Chocolate Thunder," Dwayne repeated.

"You know, D, It's bad enough you took all of our women, but you also had to be a *black* man playing hockey."

"Shit, C–Dog. You, Matt, and Paul loved it. Let's not forget you guys gave me that nickname."

"Yeah," Colin said as he had a vision of the three of them huddled in that decrepit cold rink waiting for D to appear. Then they would all come alive when he skated onto the ice and Colin would lead the chant, "Chooocolate Thunnnder!"

"Remember Principal Norris got all politically correct and shit? Said it was racist and wanted you guys to stop that chant. Damn, who was it, you or Matt who asked him how many brothers he had for friends?"

"It was Matt." Colin focused on the big orange sun. *Tomorrow is going to be a great beach day.*

"Aw, shit. Of course, it was Matt. Shit, crazy kid . . ." His voice trailed off.

They sat silent while "Git up, Git Out" by Outkast played throughout the hatchback. The music pounded fiercely out of a pair of bazooka bass tubes Colin had stuffed away in the trunk. His eyes were still fixed on the ocean. It looked so blue, so tempting. That was the ocean he remembered. The ocean he missed. The ocean he now hated.

His friend's voice brought them both back to reality. "Yo, man, I hope this party is worth my time since I *am* passing up some good ass tonight." He made it sound like he was doing everyone a favor.

"Yeah, man. Of course it is." Colin turned away from the ocean and smiled at Dwayne. "Susan said a bunch of her UMass friends are gonna be down for the weekend. These are no Cape girls, bro. These are college girls done with finals looking to blow off some steam. And if things work out, maybe blow something else." He lit a cigarette and took a puff before continuing, "Plus the fact, D, the ass you're passing up tonight, and I mean, no offense to you, because you know I'm in awe of your gift and all, but that girl . . ." He finished the sentence without words as he held his hands far away from one another.

"Yeah, she does have a big ass." D laughed. "But it's all good."

"Bro, I think it might be all bad. I mean, it looks like she has a family of squirrels stuffed down the back of her pants. It's kind of nasty."

"A family of squirrels?" Dwayne laughed again. "Man, that's one visual I don't need."

"Yeah, but after a night of drinking, that's one visual you're gonna have," Colin replied while flicking his ash out the window. "I know how you operate. If there's no tail at this party you'll call that chick. She'll come all the way from *down* Cape, pick your drunk ass up, and drive you four miles back to your house. Then let you violate her like she's the underage Traci Lords. Then you'll pass out and when you wake up she's gone like a good girl. If that's what you need, you might as well save the poor girl the gas money and bang 'After Midnight.'"

"After Midnight" was Terry Handon, who was roommate of the party host Susan Bishop. Terry had played field hockey and softball in high school, but now all she did was drink, eat late-night subs, and screw whoever was willing to slide in between her gorilla-sized thighs. Colin had known Terry ever since the day they got in trouble for both eating paste in Mr. Rapoza's first grade art class. That day they became friends, and he protected her whenever the cliques teased Terry about her unfortunate appearance. He even went as far as taking her to the junior high semi-formal, so a part of him felt bad calling her that name. But he was high and he was going for the laugh.

D stared back at Colin and asked with a mixture of confusion and agitation, "Are you shitting me? Do you think I'd ever go there?"

Colin held the smile in as long as possible, but he was too stoned. "Of course, I'm kidding." He howled and patted Dwayne on the shoulder. "Relax, bro."

Dwayne wasn't amused. "That's not right to joke about that shit. After Midnight is one scary-looking female. I mean, I *think* she's a female, right?"

"Yup, that's what the unlucky ones say." Colin nodded, focusing on the *Island Ferry* heading out of the harbor. The moment was interrupted by an electronic beep coming from his pocket. He pulled out his pager.

"Aw, C-Dog, check it out." He pointed at it. "Looks like you got an anxious one on the hook. Reel her in, man." Laughing, Colin scanned it and saw his parents' number flash across the screen. "So, who's the lucky lady, C-Dog?"

Dermot is coming home today, Colin thought. "No one important. Let's jet, bro."

The chorus of the song rang out again, and even though it was already at the highest level, he still turned the knob up. Abruptly flicking the rest of his cigarette out the window, he shifted into reverse, turned out on the main road, and headed over the hill for the party.

Susan Bishop lived only a few blocks from Silver Shores Harbor. This meant he could take the beach way and avoid pre-summer traffic as well as five-O. He drove slowly as the music thumped throughout the small coupe, vibrating the back window, making the scene comical to any onlooker—his sound system was worth more than his car. He continued on as the ocean rolled in rhythm to the song.

All through his childhood, this road had been his bus route home. The bus with the hard, tight green plastic seats. The laughter and the freedom. Colin had never wanted the morning ride to end, and heading home was always an adventure. Another day gone was always another day closer to hanging out on the beach.

He remembered the last day of the fifth grade, racing out the barn-like doors of his school knowing he was free until autumn. It was beyond a good feeling. Heaven, really. He headed straight towards the tetherball pole where an eager Matt Sweeney and Paul Hurley stood waiting.

"Where's Mel?" Colin asked, referring to his best *girl* friend and Paul's *actual* girlfriend, Melissa Robertson. Of course, Matt and Colin never used that gross *girlfriend* word when describing her. To them, she was just one of the guys.

"Her parents sprang her early for winning that art award yesterday. So what took you so long, Aquaman?" Paul was aggravated because he wanted to know either yes or no to the question, so the three then could go on with their summer vacation.

Colin was also visibly annoyed, but for another reason. "Miss Shannon was warning me to behave and get my act together." He rolled his eyes. "Last day of school and she was still yelling at me, but she doesn't scare me." Miss Shannon was the principal of Silver Shores Elementary/Middle School. She had served in the army and brought a certain type of old-world discipline to the school. Everyone feared her, and Colin was no exception, but he never let it show. His defense was to play like he didn't care. But the truth was, ever since kindergarten, Miss Shannon calling him "stupid" and saying things like, "Why can't you be nice and smart like your older brother Dermot?" paralyzed him whenever he was called to the chalkboard. It was Matt and Paul, and even Mel, who always rescued him, who always made him feel safe.

"Whatever she said this time, C, don't listen to her. Miss Shannon is a witch," Paul said.

"Yeah, Colin, take away the *W* and put a *B* in the front of *witch* and that's what you get. Miss Shannon!" He howled and Colin and Matt joined in, but then their laughter died.

The three stood in a semi-circle looking into one another's eyes. Another year had passed and here they were again.

Colin started to open his report card and then abruptly stopped. "You know what? I always go first. Let's switch it up."

Paul and Matt looked at one another and then back at Colin.

As always, Matt took the lead. He was the stronger of the two. Whatever he said or did, Paul followed. He tore the report card envelope open, skipped what his folks would find important—his grades—and looked straight at the bottom of the thin pink sheet.

"Mrs. Toleson . . . oh, man, that stinks! I hear she's really strict." His disappointed expression moved from the paper and up to his two friends who were chuckling together.

"What the heck is so funny?"

"I'm sorry, Matt," Paul replied, "but yeah, I hear her name rhymes with *witch*, too! All the sixth-graders say that she always gives homework on the weekends and every Monday she has pop quizzes."

Colin chimed in, "Yeah, man. I hear she's terrible. And she's ugly too. I'm not so sure I want to be in your class *after all*."

"Cut the crap, you guys. Someone else go," Matt ordered, trying to suppress his pain.

Paul stood there with his famous, mischievous smile drawn while his long strawberry-blond hair changed styles in the wind. He was such a character with a flair for the dramatics. Still smiling, he took his time opening the envelope.

"Could this be the year, gentlemen?" he asked with the same cheesy game-show-host voice he had first used in the second grade when they began their routine.

"Hurry up, Paul." Matt was annoyed.

Paul opened his report card, and his big brown eyes moved right to the bottom, hopping over his High Honor achievements. He studied the name and announced in shock, "Mrs. Toleson . . . Mrs. Toleson . . . holy crap!" He turned to Matt and they high-fived. "That's awesome!"

Matt exclaimed, "This is so cool, Paul! This summer is going to be amazing!"

The two of them continued their celebration as Colin jealously watched. Matt abruptly put an end to the party as he turned to Colin. "All right, Aquaman. It's your turn. Go for it. . . ."

As Colin's car rounded the hill that hugged his neighborhood, the smell of fried clams blanketed his vehicle. He turned to D and they both said, "Pucky's Pub."

He drove by the aged and beaten seafood bar and grille and thought of how he and Dermot always knew summer was around the corner when the stoves of the seasonal pub were fired up. He smiled briefly and then looked in his rearview mirror and caught the last of the sun setting in the horizon. Colin drove for a few more minutes before taking a left on Steel Toe Lane where a long stretch of parked cars seized the street.

"I told you this party was gonna be hoppin', D." He hit him on the shoulder and pointed.

Dwayne inspected the scene closer. "What can I say, C-Dog? That's why I roll with you."

After Colin parked, they jumped out and headed toward the front door. As they got closer they heard "Cannonball" by The Breeders mixed with rowdy, drunken teenager voices screaming from the windows.

They strolled into the house and into a sea of familiar faces and were greeted with shouts of "C-Dog," "D," and "Chocolate Thunder." They were like celebrities slapping hands with the well-wishers. They were making their way to the back porch where they knew a keg was waiting for them, when Susan Bishop, the owner of the house, accompanied by an unknown beautiful girl cut them off.

"Hey, you two! So glad you're finally here!" Susan was visibly buzzed, sporting an early summer sunburn that helped her usual pale complexion. She had to holler to be heard over the music and voices.

"I want you to meet my friend, Lizzie, from UMass," she shouted in Colin's ear. Lizzie was tall, blonde, and sexy, with eyes like giant chestnuts. She was wearing short jean shorts and a white t-shirt tied in a knot revealing her belly-button ring that gave Colin heart palpitations. He shook her hand.

"Very nice to meet you," he scanned her over.

"Yeah, nice to meet you, too." She gave him a courtesy smirk and then moved her attention over to Dwayne. "And you are?"

"My name is Dwayne and I gotta say you are fine!"

Lizzie responded with a nervous laugh, and the two shook hands longer than necessary. Drunk and annoying, Susan chimed in, "You'll like this, Lizzie. His nickname is Chocolate Thunder!"

"Oh, wow! Chocolate Thunder. Does that mean you bring the boom-boom?" She asked with a "do me" look on her face.

"Only if you let me, girl!"

Their flirtations were beginning to irritate Colin. "Susan, where are your other college friends?" Waiting for her answer, he anxiously looked around the packed room.

"Oh, only Lizzie came. Everyone else is with their boyfriends or home for the summer. Lizzie's going to be staying on the Vineyard for a few days. So she'll be just a boat ride away, isn't that awesome?" Susan directed her answer to Dwayne.

There was an awkward silence and Colin looked uncomfortable until D spoke up. "Lizzie, you look real thirsty. Let's you and me go see how that keg is flowing." He extended his hand, and she gladly took it.

"Great idea." She smiled and the two slid through the mob of kids toward the deck.

"She *loves* black guys." Susan was in Colin's face.

"That's great, Susan. That's just great."

"Hey, C-Dog, I have a shitload of Jell-o shots in the freezer. If you want you can . . ."

He didn't even wait for her to finish as he bee-lined toward the kitchen. He wanted to meet a woman at the party, but he was really only there for one thing—to get drunk. He was excited now as he elbowed his way through the crowd. When he got to the kitchen, he heard a voice.

"C-Dog. My main fucking man. Have some of these Jell-o shots, bro." Chucky "He's All" Dunn smiled with bits of green Jell-o stuck in between his slightly brown-stained teeth. Dunn was a classic. Sporting a black crew cut and no neck, he was built like a pit bull. His red wife-beater, highlighting his muscles on muscles, showed everyone he *was* a pit bull because the guy was an animal. He was kept back twice as a kid, which enabled him to drop out halfway through his junior year of high school. He had already been to rehab three times, kicked out of his parents' house, and now he changed oil at Tex's Super Lube during the day and drank his face off at night. His favorite pastime: destruction of private property. The previous Christmas he was found passed out on the beach holding baby Jesus whom he had kidnapped from the Village Green display.

"I love Jell-o shots. I guess I just love booze," Chucky thought out loud as he ingested several Dixie cups.

"I hear you."

"You know, C-Dog, we haven't partied since this past winter when you . . ."

"Yeah, I know," Colin broke in. "But I'm back out there. So how ya doing, Mother Chucky? How's the lube business?" Colin began devouring some of the fruity-liquored treat.

"It's okay." He paused for a while. "Work is work. It's starting to get real hot in that garage. Good thing I have tomorrow off or else I'd be screwed. Being hung over in that pit is no fucking picnic."

"Oh, yeah?"

"Yeah. Shit, you might get a smelly foot now and then at your job but me, man . . ." He tongued a shot. "Last week I was draining an old van, late-seventies model. Those are the worst because you got no room to work. I was hurting real bad from the night before." He was animated and his eyes were blood red from being stoned. "The engine was so goddamn hot. I had oil splashing on me and shit because I was still drunk. Next thing I know

I'm heaving my 7-Eleven burritos all over my boots. For the rest of the day the pit smelled like puke." He laughed and patted Colin on the back. "I'll tell you, bro, I won't be drinking gin anytime soon. That shit does make you sin!"

Colin laughed along with Chucky, who caught his breath. "Guess what I bought today?"

"What, man?" Colin asked.

"Lollapalooza tickets, and one has your name on it."

"Not so sure about that one. I would've been down for it if Kurt Cobain didn't off himself." Colin reached in his pocket for a cigarette.

"Yeah, I hear you. It blows. No Nirvana. But dude—the Beastie Boys, Smashing Pumpkins, A Tribe Called Quest and shit. George Clinton is gonna be there, too. Plus"—he put a lighter to Colin's cigarette while flashing a dangerous grin—"I think I'm gonna be scoring some mushrooms, motherfucker."

His eyes widened. "'Shrooms. Well, that changes everything."

"I knew it would. Imagine seeing Parliament while tripping your balls off. How sweet would that be?"

Colin smiled and followed Chucky out to the back deck and joined a group of friends who were sucking down funnels. Chucky, as he always did, made his presence known. "Hey, let me get that funnel so me and the C-Dog can show you bitches how it's really done."

The others handed it over, and Chucky was all business. Colin plugged the plastic tube with his thumb while Chucky filled the funnel with keg beer.

"Shit, C-Dog, this is a three-beer funnel. We're gonna get you good and drunk tonight, brother!"

"That's what I do best, Mother Chucky."

Chucky filled the funnel to the top. "I got a lot of foam here. Give me a minute." He then swiped the sides of his nose with his right index finger and placed it directly into the suds.

"Aw, man." Colin winced.

"Nothing a little nose grease can't fix." He winked at Colin and began to stir. The froth evaporated instantly and the funnel filled to the top with beer.

"Am I the fucking man or what?"

"I'm not sure if poor hygiene defines you as the man, but whatever." Colin laughed.

"Ah, fuck you. Are you ready?"

Colin nodded and on the crowd's count of three, Chucky raised the funnel over his head. With his mouth on the tube, Colin kneeled down on the deck. In about four seconds, the entire funnel was drained.

"Hell yeah! That's how you do a funnel. Not one drop of beer hit the deck. That's my boy!" Chucky broadcasted to the party pointing to Colin. "Nobody can touch this fucking kid!"

In victory, Colin raised his hands and then wiped his mouth clean before lighting a cigarette.

"More like nobody can get in touch with this kid." Colin felt a hand on his back.

He turned and saw his friend Josh Baker from his high school swim team. Years ago, Josh was known as his archrival at the annual town beaches swim meet, but that all changed in high school when they swam together for one of the best teams in the state. They had become better swimmers and friends by pushing one another. But Colin didn't want to be pushed anymore.

"Hey, what's up, Josh?" He turned on his smile.

"What's the deal, Colin? A whole year and you don't come and visit me?"

"Ah, come on, man. You know I love you." He brushed off the question and then yelled out, "Yo, Chucky, we got our next victim."

Chucky's eyes lit up as he got everything ready. Colin walked away leaving Josh confused as the funnel was being shoved down his throat. He avoided Josh for the rest of the night by talking with other friends he hadn't seen since the previous summer. It was good to catch up, but better to have a drink in his hand while doing it. Laughter to memories came easier. And with each joke came another beer, and before he knew it, the party had wound down. But he refused to let sleep kill his buzz. Trying to fight the inevitable, he sprawled out in a lawn chair and sipped on a beer between taking puffs on his cigarette. His heavy eyes gazed at the lone Tiki torch flame dancing in front of him and then he was back in front of the tetherball pole where a restless Matt and Paul waited for him to open his report card.

"You're taking way too long. Just go for it," Matt encouraged him with a smile.

Colin stood there, frozen, motionless.

"C, just open it . . . it's cool," Paul reassured.

Colin looked back at the envelope and slowly tore it open. He took a deep breath and pulled the sheet out and was greeted with that smell that always turned his stomach. It was the fresh ink smell of grades and that scent usually brought bad news. He wasn't concerned with that right now. Just as Matt and Paul had done, he skipped his marks and scanned the bottom, and, in disbelief, read out loud, "Mrs. Toleson." He then looked up at his friends and said the name again, this time in joy, "Mrs. Toleson, you guys! I got Mrs. Toleson!"

Matt grabbed the sheet from him to see for himself and yelled with exhilaration, "Oh my God! Mrs. Toleson! Mrs. Toleson!"

Paul shouted at the top of his lungs, "Mrs. Toleson! Mrs. Toleson!"

The three friends danced in a circle happily shouting the worst sixth-grade teacher's name. After their celebration, they sprinted to the bus and spent the whole ride home plotting how they would make it a terrible year for the meanest teacher in Silver Shores.

"That was the best bus ride ever," Colin said to himself as his eyelids fought to stay awake. The flames were blocked by a large figure, and Colin opened his eyes and saw her standing in front of him. He cracked a crooked smile and barely was able to utter, "'Member the paste in art class?"

She talked, but he couldn't understand her because he couldn't understand anything. He was fading in and out of sleep. *What time is it?* His blurred eyes looked around the yard. Other than a few stragglers, the party had cleared out, so it was definitely late, but he still had no idea of the time until Terry Handon grabbed his arm and led him into the house to her bedroom. That's when a distant voice in Colin's head told him that it was well after midnight.

FOUR

The Sea Shanty, named as a tribute to The Pogues song, was decorated like the average college dorm room with pictures of the Boston sports teams along with posters of bands ranging from U2 to The Cult, to Echo and The Bunnymen. Exotically labeled beer bottles standing beside the occasional Pabst Blue Ribbon, Keystone, or Miller Lite lined the shelves that had been originally designed for Dermot's favorite novels. But there was only one book that had survived the beer bottle collection—a yellowed, dog-eared copy of *Old Man and The Sea*, the first book he had ever read from cover to cover, appropriately stranded behind an empty Rogue Shakespeare Stout.

In the window were a couple of neon beer lights—Guinness and Corona—that Eddy Monahan, a college buddy who worked for a beer distributor and did promotions all over Cape Cod, had given him. Of course, Eddy was hammered the night he grabbed the signs from his truck, and always remarked as he entered, "Hey, nice lights. Where'd you get those?"

Pushing aside what he dubbed "the Greg Brady beads" and walking into the room that contained a bathroom, bar, dartboard, and the almond and black spray-painted refrigerator meant to resemble a pint of Guinness, Dermot would ignore the question. He'd open the door and toss Eddy a cold one and the question about the signs would be gone with the first sip. But in his friend's honor, whenever the string was pulled that flickered the signs to life, the boys always made it a point to make their first toast of the evening to "the generous Eddy Monahan."

They all knew there was something special, maybe even magical, about the signs. The lights transformed the place from just a fun, renovated two-car garage into the famous after-hours watering hole. On more than one occasion the signs served as a beacon for the not-so-bright female tourists who'd tap on The Shanty screen door asking, "Is this that Pucky's Pub place our boyfriends have been talking about?" Unfortunately, Dermot and his friends never got lucky with any of the lost travelers, but it was always a great way to jumpstart their night of drinking with the imagine-what-would've-happened-if-those-chicks-*weren't*-meeting-their-boyfriends scenarios.

The Shanty also had a pull-up ladder leading to a loft and a queen-size air mattress. But as the early morning birds—almost knowingly and happily—serenaded his hangover, Dermot woke up rubbing his brow, realizing he wasn't lying on his air mattress. Instead, he had passed out on one of the three couches that semi-circled the quarters game coffee table. He and his boys usually spent their pre- and post-game drinking sessions at the table. They'd huddle around it and philosophize or bullshit.

Why am I down here and not up in the loft?

Then he remembered why. Someone tossed a comforter on him before they left. *Was it Tommy or Clay? Yes, it had to be Tommy. He's the responsible one*, he thought, massaging his arm, slightly bruised from wrestling. *What an asshole I am.*

He had vowed to his friends that he'd never again sleep up in that "fucking loveless" loft. The loft equaled Francesca, which equaled memories. He didn't want memories, and it suddenly dawned on him he was no longer excited to be home. The euphoria had actually begun to dwindle the moment he drove into town. Hiking the comforter up over his head, he tried to hide his face from the golden sun that, like a laser, had found its target—the hung-over guy.

He recalled the events of the evening. Clay and Tommy had helped him carry his garbage bags of clothes into The Shanty. It was all laughs with Clay, but when it came to Tommy, something seemed different. His sarcasm seemed to have a little more bite than usual. At first, Dermot thought it might have just been his imagination, so he brushed off Tommy's behavior and began unpacking his stuff as Clay went into the other room.

"Dermot, Tommy, come in here and check this out," Clay hollered.

"What?" Dermot asked as he walked through the beaded doorway.

"That." Clay pointed to a note taped to the Guinness fridge.

Dermot pulled the note off the fridge and with it came some of the almond paint.

"That fridge needs a fresh coat of spray paint. It's been a couple of years," Clay pointed out.

"Yup." Dermot looked down at the paper with block handwriting on it and read out loud, "Dear Dermot, I dropped off some American beer so you can get back into the swing of things. Come by and tell me about your time in Ireland. Pucky."

Clay opened the fridge to reveal a twelve pack of cold Miller Lite. He grabbed three beers and handed one to Dermot, threw another to Tommy, and popped open the last one and pressed it against his head.

"Aw, goddamn it that feels good." Clay exhaled.

"That Pucky is a hell of a guy," Tommy added, after taking a swig.

"Crazy bastard." Clay laughed. "But cool. And he loves the shit out of you, Dermot. What's that all about?"

"It's the old movies," Dermot replied after taking a long chug. "On slow nights at Pucky's, he'll put on old movies and I'll go get drunk and we'll just talk old movies all night and about writing and shit like that."

Tommy shook his head. "Jesus, man, you're so 1940s. So, alright, let's get to it. So how *was* Ireland?"

"Wet." Dermot laughed and took another sip.

"The weather or the women?" Clay smirked.

"I bet you'd like to know, you dirty bastard," Dermot said, getting a big laugh from Clay, but nothing from Tommy.

"I'm serious, Dermot. I mean you're gone all winter and we don't even get a postcard with a fucking donkey or some shit on it," Tommy barked.

"What is it about you guys and fucking donkeys?" Dermot tried to joke, but Tommy didn't laugh, and now he knew it was no longer his imagination. Tommy *was* pissed about something.

"I told you, Dermot, I'm serious. I mean, for a guy who goes on and on about wanting to be a writer, you sure didn't do much writing to us. In fact, you didn't do any."

"Take it easy, TK," Clay said and patted his shoulder.

Tommy glared at him. "That's so like you, Clay. All winter you bitched to me like a little girl about not hearing from DB, and now you're the first one to defend him. Grow a pair, will you?"

Dermot watched the guilty expression appear on Clay's face, and knew Tommy was right. He had blown them off. "Look . . . Tommy, Clay, I'm sorry I didn't write to you guys. I just . . . I just wanted to escape and forget about things for a while."

"You mean Francesca?" Tommy pushed, and now it was Clay who was pissed.

"Tommy I can't fucking believe you, man! We *also* talked about *this*. The guy isn't back ten minutes and you're already bringing up the *F* word. What the hell kind of shit is that?"

"I'm just saying . . . he *did* say he wanted to forget about things."

"He said *things*, not Fra—" Clay stopped before continuing, "I mean you-know-who."

Dermot forced a smile. "It's okay, Clay. Really, it is. Don't worry about it. I know I was a little crazy there for a bit around Christmas, but then I left. And being away was good for me. I'm completely over her."

"Completely?" his friends asked.

"Yup. And even if I wasn't, her old man sent her off to Italy for the summer, anyway. So you guys don't have to worry because I'm not going to let her ghost haunt me this summer. I'm totally over her."

Tommy moved closer to Dermot. "So you're saying if I were to look through your things I wouldn't find any pictures of her?"

Dermot ignored the question by opening the fridge and grabbing three more beers, which he passed around. He opened his, took a sip, and realized they were both looking at him.

"What?" Dermot asked.

"Pictures, Dermot," Tommy stressed. "If I looked through your stuff would I find any pictures?"

"No, man. Course not. I didn't forget our ex-girlfriend rule. I burned every one of them."

Clay jumped in. "How about letters?"

"Ripped them to shreds. I told you, I'm totally over her."

"See, that would be all well and good if we believed you." Tommy put his beer on the counter.

"Man, Tommy, why are you being such a dick?" Dermot shook his head.

"You might call it being a dick, but I call it tough love, bro. And you need plenty of it. I'm going to look out for you for two reasons. One, last summer you fell for that bit—" Tommy caught himself. "Chick. And basically to you, Clay and I fell off the face of the earth."

"That's not true. We used to . . ."

Tommy put up his hands. "No, that's cool. We knew what was going on. You were getting your noodle wet living in one of those John Hughes movies you always say you want to write. We were happy for you, but then bang! Out of nowhere, she busts your balls, man."

"I think you're being a little dramatic here," Dermot said.

"Am I right, Clay? Did she bust his balls or what?"

Clay nodded and said, "Dermot, I gotta say, it was more than busting. 'Shredded them' to use your words. Actually, it was more like she de-balled you and then threw your balls into Pucky's Frialator and then served them back to you. And you were like, 'Mm, good. I like my balls.'"

"All right. All right. I get it. So what's your point?" Dermot turned to Tommy.

"My point is my original question. Did you burn the pictures?" Tommy asked.

"Yes, Mike Wallace, I burned the pictures."

Tommy shook his head in disappointment and pulled a stack of about a dozen photographs out of his back pocket and threw them on the counter. The smiling faces of the dark Italian beauty and the pale-skinned Irish man stared up at them. Posing at the beach, riding bikes, making funny faces, eating ice cream, laughing at the county fair.

"Wow," Clay said to Dermot in disbelief. "You lied. We never lie to each other. Never."

"I can't believe you went into my stuff." Dermot tried to retrieve the pictures, but both Clay and Tommy stepped in front of the counter blocking him.

"I didn't go through your stuff, Derm. I accidentally kicked open your shoebox when we were wrestling in the car. Oh, and by the way, Clay, he also has letters from her. Tons of them. So, you know what this means?"

"What?" Dermot asked, knowing the answer.

"Tonight, we get you good and drunk and you burn every last picture, letter, and card. We do this now, the first night you're back and then you can move on. You'll wake up tomorrow feeling great that you finally got your balls out of that Frialator."

And that's what they did. They got him liquored up, while they both took turns putting pictures or letters into the candle's flame. Of course, they had to hold him down, feeding him whiskey like he was a cowboy having a bullet removed.

The next day the bullet was gone, but the wound remained—Francesca Giordano. Burning pictures and letters wasn't going to heal that wound, and he wasn't quite sure about his balls, but his head sure felt like it had just been dipped into Pucky's Frialator.

He pushed the comforter off and looked up at the wall clock. It was 10:16 a.m. *We said 10:45. I still have time. That is, if he even shows up.*

"Maybe an outdoor shower will make me feel better," he said to himself, rising from the couch. He stripped down to his boxers, grabbed a towel, slid out the side door, and headed for the outdoor shower behind his parents' house.

After a ten-minute shower, Dermot dried off in the wooden enclosure and was feeling refreshed, but he still had a sick feeling swimming around in his gut. He knew it had nothing to do with the booze, although he also knew the seven shots of Wild Turkey to signify his months with Francesca certainly hadn't helped. The feeling came from something else, something his mother had said the evening before when they had dinner, before he met up with Tommy and Clay and got so totally shitfaced. He thought about it as he wrapped the towel around his waist, opened the shower door, and walked past his mother's Twelve Step Meditation Garden.

His dad had been grilling some marinated steaks while his mom set the picnic table, bobbing her head and singing to "Moondance" by Van Morrison, which floated out the kitchen window. Dermot grabbed the spatula and took over the grill duties as his dad twirled his mother and serenaded her with his awful but lovable voice.

"Jim, honey, I love you dearly, but you've got a voice for lip-sync." Mrs. Brennan grinned.

"But I certainly don't have a face for radio. One of my students told me I look like Tom Cruise," Mr. Brennan responded.

"More like she saw you *with* Tom Cruise in *Rain Man*," Dermot added, and his mother took her hand off his father's shoulder and high-fived Dermot.

The laughter, innocent jokes, and joy among them made Dermot feel like the old days were back, and he was actually excited to see his brother because then the jokes would really start flying around the picnic table. But Colin had not shown up. Mrs. Brennan called his pager to see where he was, hoping for a message saying he was running a little late. But nothing came. After an hour she took away Colin's place setting and said, "Let's enjoy our dinner and not take it on."

There was a significant pause before Mr. Brennan spoke. "How can we not take it on?" His voice cut like the knife he was working. "Margaret, we're losing him."

"Losing him?" Dermot jumped in. "Mom, you said in your letters Colin was doing much better."

"Well, he is . . . sort of. Dermot, I wanted you to enjoy your trip. I didn't want to triangulate."

"Triangu—what?"

"It's your mom's word from the Program, meaning get in the way or something. I think it means having an excuse not to help out."

"Jim, that's not fair! We've talked about this, and we need to be on the same page. Colin has to find his way on his own. When he is ready, he will come to us. I just know it. I just know he will."

"And what if he ends up . . ." Mr. Brennan couldn't finish the sentence because the phone rang.

Dermot ran into the kitchen and picked it up expecting to hear his brother crack a joke, but instead it was some crying woman named Lilly Garrison who "needed to talk to Margaret." Mrs. Brennan took the phone from him, put her palm on the receiver, and mouthed lightly, "Stevie Garrison's mom. Her husband is an alcoholic. She needs someone to talk to." Shaking his head, Dermot went back to the table, where his dad was refilling both glasses with iced tea.

"Since when has Mom been buddies with Stevie Garrison's mom?"

"You know your mom," was all his father said on the subject. "So, Derm, do you think there will really be a baseball strike in August?"

Dermot couldn't remember how he had answered his dad, but now, the next morning, as he continued from the garden to The Shanty, he was thinking of his brother.

Are we losing him?

Something seemed different, so he stopped walking and looked across the street. He realized why so much sun had spilled into The Shanty's window. The big tree in the Sullivan's yard had been cut down giving him a clear view of the ocean. His eyes followed two squirrels that raced out of the Meditation Garden across the street and stopped where the tree had been. The squirrels almost looked human as they turned their heads to face one another. They were clearly confused about which way to go now that their home had been cut down.

I know the feeling.

FIVE

A thick, salty wind crept through the Venetian blinds in Terry Handon's room, slapping Colin's worn face.

"*I* might as well bang After Midnight?"

Colin picked his heavy head up from the pillow to see Dwayne standing at the edge of the bed looking down at him with a stunned expression.

"Not now, D," Colin responded, stretching and scratching his brow. "I feel like I got hit by a bus. God, my brain is throbbing."

"Fine, I'll bust your balls later. Let's just get you the hell out of here." Dwayne pulled the sheets off the bed, exposing Colin's half-naked body— blue boxers, no shirt. "Yo, man, these sheets are a little damp." Dwayne eyed his hand and then winked. "I can't believe you and After Midnight got all sweaty and shit between the sheets. Man, I gotta say, that makes me want to puke, but I guess we all make mistakes. But I'll take my girl with the family of squirrels over After Midnight any day. Shit, C-Dog, I guess you're going to have to change her nickname now to 'a.m.' considering . . ."

"All right. All right." Colin forced a grin and began to rise from the bed, but stopped when Dwayne, his eyes bulging, pointed at the large, moist circle where Colin's waist had been.

"What the . . . ?" Dwayne moved closer to the bed, still pointing, "What *is* that? No . . . Did you . . . Did you piss the bed, homey?"

The dread pumped through Colin's veins and then he glanced down at his crotch area. "Oh man! Oh, shit . . . Yeah, I did . . . God, I hate that shit!"

"Damn, C-Dog! Oh, man, and I touched that shit." Dwayne looked at his hand like it was diseased.

"You mean *piss*."

"Huh?"

"You touched piss, not shit."

"Not funny, man."

"All right, but D, you gotta help me hide the evidence." Colin's eyes searched the room.

"Wait, let me get this straight. You honestly pissed yourself? What are you, eight years old?" he asked, while wiping his hands on one of Terry's shirts.

"Once again, D, not now!" Colin ripped the sheet off and then flipped the mattress. Only a small amount of urine had made it to the other side. "Good. That's not too bad"

He knew he had to work fast. The room had a musty, rank smell, like an old cellar, so he ran to the window and opened it as much as it would allow, pulling the cord for the Venetian blinds and sending them screaming to the top of window.

Colin snapped his fingers and pointed to the bureau. "D, grab that perfume and start spraying the sheets."

"What?"

Colin didn't bother repeating himself and sighed before darting to the dresser, grabbing a bottle of Avon Serenade, and spraying the sheets with one hand while pulling the covers onto the bed with the other.

"Goddamn, these sheets *are* wet!"

"No, shit." Dwayne looked on, arms folded.

Colin ignored him and scanned the room until he saw it—a blow-dryer hanging by the mirror. "Sweet!" He grabbed it, plugged it in, and attempted to dry the stain. "Oh yeah, man. I think we're gonna be okay."

"*We*?" Dwayne stressed above the noisy dryer.

"Where's Terry?" Colin asked.

"I can't believe this. You're asking me that question *now*?"

"Yeah, D, where the fuck is she?"

"In the shower." He thumbed behind him beyond the door.

"Good." Colin fumbled with the controls. "I need a little more time. This blow-dryer is a piece of shit. It doesn't seem to get as hot as most of them."

"Most of them? Since when do you blow-dry your hair?"

"How many times do I have to say, 'Not now'?" He leaned down over the bed and waved the dryer above the sheet. He resembled a sweeper on a curling team as he intensely worked the area.

"Colin, I'm sure she already knows. Did you see the size of that stain? Man, she's probably washing your piss off her as we speak."

He ignored the comment. "I got another plan."

Colin switched the blow-dryer off and hung it back around the mirror. He removed the sheets from the bed and crumpled them up before grabbing a beer bottle off the nightstand, and pouring the remains of it on the mattress. He then strategically placed the bottle under his pillow.

"Are you fucking serious, man?" Dwayne asked with disgusted amusement.

"Bro, she was so drunk she won't know." Colin laughed. "I'll tell her we got all kinky and shit and poured beer on each other."

"I hate to break it to you, but After Midn—I mean Terry—had just finished work. She wasn't drunk at all. *You* were the one who was drunk." He pointed to the spot. "Really drunk."

Colin tossed him the car keys. "Just get the car and pick me up out front."

"Whatever." Dwayne left the room shaking his head.

That one word stung him, but he tried to ignore it. He picked up his jeans, smelled them, and said, "Thank God."

Opting to "go cowboy," he pulled off his rancid underwear and put on his jeans. He shoved his damp boxers in his back pocket, and rubbed his swollen eyes. The throbbing in his head intensified. Reality brought exhaustion and shame. *After Midnight . . . What the hell was I thinking?*

His depression was interrupted by his pager vibrating. He looked down and saw the number of The Shanty flash across the screen.

"Dermot. Oh great!" He was still putting his head through his polo shirt as he fled the crime scene. The screen door slammed behind him as he sprinted to his car, jumped into the passenger seat, and ordered, "Let's bolt!"

Dwayne hit the gas, and they were off. It was an odd feeling being in the passenger seat since he had never sat shotgun in his own car before. While they headed towards Dwayne's house, he chucked his soiled boxers out the window. Neither spoke for a while until Dwayne finally broke the ice.

"You want to talk about last night? It's only a matter of time before everyone else does." His tone was measured, serious, and he kept his hands on the wheel and his eyes on the road.

"Shit, you're not gonna sell me out, are you, D?"

He threw Colin a hard stare. "I would never sell you out. You know that. How can you even ask me that, man?"

"Sorry."

"But you know, Terry will probably go squawking about it all over town."

The pager beeped again. It was The Shanty again, this time with 911 following the number.

"Just don't bring it up again. It will all go away," he said to Dwayne, but was really talking to himself.

Colin reached over and turned the volume up, and allowed the soothing voice of Shannon Hoon of Blind Melon to relax and take him to a place where he could escape for at least the remainder of the ride.

Dermot kicked some stray seashells back onto the driveway as he waited for Colin outside The Shanty. Would he show up? He had no idea. The thought worried him. In the past, it wouldn't even be a question. They were supposed to meet at 10:45. He checked his watch for a third time—11:09—and then moved his eyes to the street directly in front of him.

Come on, man. Get your ass here. Now he was getting nervous. He waited. Still nothing. *He didn't call or show up for dinner last night. Why would he show up for this?* Dermot knew there was a one-word answer to the question: tradition.

Throughout childhood, they had, of course, fought and given each other the silent treatment, but their fights always took a backseat to an outside challenge. In the end, they were brothers. Pride also played a part in resolving their arguments because everyone in Silver Shores knew the Brennan brothers were the best. It was that simple. So no matter how pissed off they were at one another, they were always able to put aside their differences to defend their title.

"But I'm twenty-three now, so maybe those days are over?" As the question left his lips, he heard a car approaching. "Or maybe not." His grin froze instantly when a brown Volvo pulled into the driveway, sending a few seashells shooting back onto the grass.

Francesca? Dermot wanted to sprint to the car, pull her out, and kiss her all over, but the reality was he couldn't move. His heart was pumping overtime, and the blood shot to his pale face, giving him an adrenaline burn. It didn't seem right. Her car was *right* there in his driveway. It was exactly how he had imagined it every night before falling asleep in Ireland. The scene didn't seem real. And then he realized it *wasn't* real. A woman in her late sixties opened the driver's door, got out, and walked over to him.

"Excuse me, young man, I'm a little lost. I think I took a wrong turn or something. I'm looking for the *Island Ferry* Parking Lot." She smiled.

"Huh?"

"The *Island Ferry* Parking Lot? You know the lot for the boat to the Vineyard?"

"Ah . . . yeah. Yeah, I ah . . . know it."

"Well, could you tell me where it is then?"

"Ah, yeah." Dermot somehow directed the woman, but the whole time his mind was shouting, *Of all the kinds of cars in the world that could pull into my driveway, why did it have to be a brown Volvo?*

Then he remembered the philosophy his mother constantly lived by. She always preached to her boys, "Look for signs from the universe because they are meant to teach you. Sometimes they can be right in front of you and you might not even notice them. Be aware because God is sending those signs to help guide you in life." Dermot saw this sign a mile away. What the fuck did it mean? Was it there to remind him how incredibly cruel God can be? He didn't need a refresher course on that fact of life.

He finished giving the woman directions and watched her walk back to her car, hop in, and rev up the engine. While adjusting her rearview mirror, she stopped and stared him in the eye. Then she quickly rose, popped her head through the sunroof, and hollered, "Thanks, again. Oh, and cheer up and enjoy this beautiful day!"

"You gotta be . . ." He couldn't get the curse out of his mouth as he watched the brown Volvo putt away.

Only a few hours earlier, the ex-girlfriend exorcism had ended. He had been so determined to forget her. The moment the woman stood up through the sunroof, he knew he didn't have a prayer, and a vision of Francesca from the previous summer overtook him. Francesca was at the wheel as they drove down the hill and passed Stirling Beach. She wore a green tank top and white shorts that accentuated her tanned legs. Her long, black hair rode the wind. She giggled, flashing a sparkling smile at him.

"What's so funny?" he asked.

She turned the radio up. "I was just wondering. You seem to know the words to every song. I was curious if you knew this one."

Dermot listened for a second, smiled, and then began serenading her with "Lost In Love," by the soft rock duo Air Supply.

She put her hand out laughing. "Okay, honey. I believe you. You know the song."

"Babe, that's an easy one. Back in the fifth grade, I sang that to Amy Cutrona. Can you believe it didn't work on her?"

"What I can't believe is how it works on me. Dermot Brennan, you are so cheesy!" She laughed, easing on the brake, and waited behind a parked ice cream truck while it finished with its last customer.

"I'm cheesy? Should I take that as a compliment?"

She gave him a playful punch. "Of course. Your cheesiness is one of the reasons I love you, you dumb jerk."

Instantly, Dermot leaned over and turned off the radio. "Babe, did you hear what you just said?"

"What? That you're a dumb jerk?"

"No, that you loved me. That's the first time you've ever said that to me."

"I'm sure I've said it before." She laughed lightly and switched her focus back on the road since the ice cream truck was moving again.

"No, you haven't told me that. I've said it to you four times, but I know you haven't said it to me yet. I know because I've been hoping you would. You see, I've never heard that word from anyone other than my parents and Colin. Wow, I can't believe you just said it. God, I hope you mean it, because I really love you, baby. By the way, that's five times."

"Dermot, I really think I've said it before, but I'm not going to argue because I *do* love you. You are so unlike the other guys I've dated. You listen to me, you're sweet, and I always feel comfortable with you. Yes, I love you, Dermot Brennan! But just so you know how serious I am, take the wheel."

"Huh?"

"Take the wheel, Dermot," Francesca said again. She put the car on cruise control and stood up, popping her head out of the sunroof.

"What are you doing?" He kept his left hand on the wheel while watching her.

She looked down at him. "You'll see." She cupped her hands and yelled to the crowded beach, "Hey everyone! Listen up! I just want everyone to know that I, Francesca Giordano, love Dermot Brennan! I love Dermot Brennan! I love Dermot Brennan!" Francesca yelled it over and over to the point that the sunbathers actually craned their necks to follow her voice and laughed with amusement at the romantic scene.

Dermot had never felt better in his life, but the ice cream truck's next pause pulled him out of his reverie. "The brake! The brake!"

"Huh?" Francesca saw where Dermot was pointing. Jumping back down into her seat, she slammed on the brake, stopping only inches from the ice cream truck. She then turned to him, "Did I make my point?"

He didn't reply. He just leaned over and kissed her for a very long time until a car horn behind them beeped.

And just like a segue in a movie, a beeping horn and blaring music brought Dermot into the present. He looked up as a blue Volkswagon Golf barreled into the driveway. The driver flicked a cigarette out of the window. Dermot knew that at last his little brother had arrived.

SIX

Dermot expected Colin to jump out of the car and apologize for being late, but instead his brother stayed seated, bobbing his head and tapping his hands against the steering wheel to the pounding music. "Goddamn, it," Dermot said under his breath. He planned on staying pissed off at Colin, so he bit the side of his mouth to suppress the smile he felt forming. Sometimes he couldn't resist his little brother's mischievous grin, and when he saw it, his jaw loosened, and he headed over to the driver's side window.

"What are you grinning at, you ghost?" he asked, wondering if Colin would guess the movie quote.

Colin snapped his fingers. "Ray Kinsella to Shoeless Joe Jackson in *Field of Dreams.*"

"I'm impressed. Very good, bro."

"I learned from the best."

"Thanks."

"I meant Dad."

"Oh, yeah. So are you getting out of that car sometime today, jackass?"

Colin's grin expanded as he turned the radio up and hollered over the music, "You know who this is?"

Dermot hadn't been listening, but he took in the song and liked the beat instantly. He waited for the lyrics and when they kicked in he too smiled. "Shit, new Beasties?"

"You got it, bro," Colin answered and continued to nod his head along till the song ended. "It's called 'Sabotage,' off their album *Ill Communication*. And it is *ill*, bro. You should see the video too. Coolest thing on MTV since the early days when they made videos that actually told stories like 'Take On Me' and the Tears For Fears videos and shit like that."

"Damn, where the hell have I been? I didn't know The Beastie Boys had a new album out."

Colin turned the radio off, got out of the car, and patted him on the shoulder. "Maybe, *you're* the ghost, Ray."

"You really want to go there?" Dermot eyed his brother.

"Go where?"

"Talking about ghosts 'cause you were one last night."

"Last night?"

"You didn't show for dinner."

"Oh, yeah, that. My goddamn beeper wasn't working. It's all good though."

"Well, actually, it's not. Mom and Dad were . . ."

"Hey, bro," Colin interrupted, pointing to The Shanty. "I know we're running late, but I'm going to freshen up a bit. It'll take me not even two minutes."

Dermot didn't feel like arguing, so he dropped it with one last shot. "Yeah, you do look like shit, but make it quick. We're already late, and I don't know these Ferguson brothers. Who knows if they're even still there?"

"Trust me, Derm, they're still there," Colin said before stepping inside The Shanty screen door.

When he walked in, Colin was instantly hit with the familiar smell of stale booze and burnt ash. Crushed beer cans and empty bags of Cape Cod Potato Chips littered the red pavement floor making the place resemble last call at Pucky's Pub.

"Wow," he said, spotting a broken chair in one corner of the room along with several smashed beer bottles. It reminded him of the day after rowdy city punks invade Stirling Beach for the Fourth of July fireworks. There was no question some heavy partying had taken place.

Clay and Tommy must've thrown Dermot a little welcome home bender.

On his way past the quarter's table, he spotted a dismembered teddy bear nailed to a beam that looked like it had endured some bizarre, sadistic ritual.

"What the . . . ?"

The bear looked familiar. He knew it from someplace but couldn't remember from where and took a closer look. Stuffing from the bear rested on top of burnt pictures and half-smoked cigars that had been extinguished in candle wax. In the center of the table, positioned like a trophy, was an empty bottle of Wild Turkey. He picked up one of the pictures and as he peered closer, he could make out the half face of Francesca Giordano staring up at him. He turned back to the teddy bear and now remembered where he had seen it, and he also knew it was no welcome-home party the boys had thrown for his brother.

Well, it's about time Dermot burned those memories. Maybe that's what I should do with mine?

He shrugged off the thought and, feeling thirsty, pushed through the beads to get to the bar. He opened the Guinness fridge, and his trembling hand passed over the large bottle of spring water and grasped a Miller Lite. Like a little kid stealing a cookie, he looked around to see if the coast was clear, then stuffed the beer bottle into his pocket and headed for the bathroom. He opened the door and felt something crunch beneath his sneakers. There were pieces of glass decorating the tacky, seventies-style orange tile. There was also glass covering the sink, all of which had showered down from the overhanging Jim Beam mirror.

Wow, the boys weren't kidding around.

He opened the top drawer and grabbed some aspirin. Dumping four tablets into his palm, he cupped them, and washed them down with his beer.

"Hair of the dog." It was all he needed. The aching head subsided, at least that's what he made himself believe, as he downed it with one more gulp. He peeked out the bathroom window to check on Dermot who, with a vacant expression, was looking up at the cloudless blue sky. *What was he thinking about?*

With his index finger, he worked some toothpaste along his teeth, rinsed, and gazed into the cracked mirror. His broken reflection mirrored the same vacant look his brother had. *Dermot must be thinking about her. I wonder if losing Francesca is all he ever thinks about.* The water ran on his hand until it numbed his testing palm, and then he splashed his face alive, trying to shake the pounding that had returned in his head. He took a breath realizing the pain had probably never left. After washing the dried piss off his crotch area, he closed his eyes, leaned on the counter, and took a deep breath. "All right, no puking. Keep your shit together, C-Dog."

He threw on a pair of his brother's boxers, shorts, and a Sox T-shirt and hurried outside, but he realized Dermot had already started walking across the street and was heading around the corner for the field.

Maybe I have time for another beer then?

Dermot called, "Come on, man! We have a title to defend!"

"All right. All right. I'm coming." Colin jogged until he caught up to his brother and then they continued on, walking side by side to the park.

"So, what the hell happened in The Shanty last night?" Colin did not expect a truthful answer.

"Oh, yeah, that." Dermot paused. "Tommy and Clay got hammered and like a couple of jackasses wrestled, and as a result, broke a lot of shit."

"Yeah, like that cool *Jim Beam* mirror in your bathroom for one."

"Oh, yeah, they were rolling all over The Shanty." Dermot answered. *Shit, I forgot they made me bust the mirror too.*

"Why were they wrestling?" Colin asked, trying to make his brother sweat a little. He had also become a master liar, so it was a great feeling for him to put the shoe on someone else's foot.

"Well, as I just said, they were hammered, pie-eyed really, but I think it all started yesterday when they were playing Wiffle ball. They were arguing about Clay being a lefty and playing in the afternoon and all." Dermot continued his lie, and now felt confident in it, pointing over at the far corner of the field where two guys were playing a one-on-one wiffle ball game.

"Oh, you mean how the sea winds shift in the afternoon?"

"Yeah, exactly. They were already fighting when I rolled in. God, they were bitching like an old married couple. Archie and Edith Bunker, as Dad would say. I just poked them with a stick by mentioning the wind in the afternoon games. Tommy freaked 'cause he never figured it out."

"Really? Tommy never knew that?"

"Nope."

"Man, those two really are a couple of clowns sent to amuse you, huh, Derm?" Instead of calling his brother out on the lie, he referenced Pesci's line from *Goodfellas* and smiled.

Dermot laughed. Colin had chosen the right tactic. He knew if he had pried further into the Francesca Giordano exorcism, Dermot would only shine the interrogation lights right back on him.

When they arrived to the part of the field that was known to the townies as Crescent Sign Alley, the men who were playing Wiffle ball weren't men at all. They were actually two kids around twelve and fourteen years old. The kids had matching red crew cuts and were covered in freckles from head to toe. The pitcher who looked to be the older of the two stopped in mid-throw, said something to the batter, and they both glared over at the Brennan brothers.

"Sorry guys." Dermot put an apologetic hand up and then grunted to himself.

"Ah, man. I knew we were late. The Ferguson brothers must've taken off, and even if they come back, we've lost the field."

He turned to walk back home, but Colin grabbed his shoulder and laughed. "No, bro, we're right on time for the main event."

"Huh?"

"Don't those kids look like brothers to you?"

"Yeah, but . . ." Dermot began while Colin cupped his hands and gave a good-natured shout, "Hey Fergusons! Gonzy at the shoe store said that you guys put out the challenge, so here we are. The question is, are you sure you're ready to take on the Brennan brothers, *the* Wiffle ball legends of Silver Shores?"

The kid standing in front of the pitcher's mound, made up of two pairs of white Air Jordans, motioned with the ball in his hand. "That's right. We're the ones. So bring it on, Grandpa!"

"Grandpa?" Dermot looked at Colin and they both burst into laughter, realizing how crazy the situation was.

"Colin, bro, you can't be serious." Dermot was still laughing. "We can't play them. They're just . . . just little kids."

"*Little kids* who are going to beat your motherfucking asses!" spat the kid at home plate who was the size of an elf, pointing his bat at Dermot.

Colin rushed forward. "What did you say?"

"You heard my little brother." The pitcher didn't back down. "We're going to kick your motherfucking asses."

"Yeah, that's what I thought you said." Colin shook his head, ready to explode. "You have to understand something. This field is sacred ground. We don't talk that way here."

"Yeah, guys," Dermot added. "You see, we've been playing for years on this field and when we were your age we didn't swear. Really . . . Let's just have a fun game of Wiffle ball with a few harmless laughs. Sure, we can talk a little trash with one another, but we don't have to take it to that level, okay?"

Now the elf was the one who edged closer. While giving a practice swing with his bat, he sneered. "It's 1994, puss-ays! We'll talk any way we want. So, are you motherfuckers going to play us or are you two going to play hide the pickle with each other all day?"

"Why you little piece of . . . " Colin reached out to grab the kid, but Dermot pulled him back.

"Take it easy, bro. Remember, they're just a couple of punks," Dermot whispered to him and then turned to the kids. "Let's all calm down for a minute, okay?"

"Whatever," they answered with unfazed expressions.

Dermot rolled his eyes and gritted his teeth. "You kids are absolutely right. You can talk any way you want, but I promise you one thing, you won't be doing much squawking after our game. So give us the ground rules, assholes!"

"All right, I like that. The man wants to get down to motherfucking business." The pitcher smiled. "We play nine. Two outs a team. We got last bats. It's straight home run derby, so you don't have to catch it for it to be an out. Meaning if the ball stays in the park, it's a fucking out. We're not playing any of that singles shit, okay?"

"Okay. What about walks? I don't want to be here all day." Colin was still staring him down.

The elf tapped his bat on the beach chair. "I hear you. You have to rotate pitchers every inning, but we also don't want to deal with any bullshit pitching either. So, eight balls and you walk. We use this chair as the strike zone. You hit any part of it and it's a strike. The foul poles are . . ." He motioned over to the rosebush-covered wooden fence that enclosed the field.

Colin snapped, "We know. We've been playing here forever, remember?"

"Well, here's something you don't know," the pitcher replied, pointing to center field. "If you hit it over the fence and it goes off any part of that Crescent Road sign, it's an automatic grand slam."

"Yeah, we also know the sign. All of us old guys in the Shores have been gunning for that sign since we were your age," Dermot said.

"No shit." The pitcher's smile widened and he turned to his brother. "Willy, didn't I tag that motherfucker last week?"

"Yeah, Dickie hit it right on the C part," the elf named Willy agreed.

Colin started laughing and couldn't stop. The kids and Dermot looked at him confused.

"What's so funny?" Willy asked.

"I was just thinking. I'm Colin, and this is my brother Dermot."

"Yeah," Dickie said, "what's so fucking funny about that?"

"Nothing's funny about our names, but your names are Willy and Dickie. That's just too easy."

"What do you mean?" Willy asked.

"I was just thinking how appropriate those names are for you guys."

Dermot joined in his brother's laughter. "Hey, Col, I bet I know who named them?"

"Who, Derm?"

"It would have to be their mother."

"Fuck you, assholes. Let's play some ball." Willy slammed the Wiffle ball bat to the ground and headed to play the field.

The first pitch was thrown and Colin unleashed on it, hitting a laser beam over the fence. He felt something he hadn't felt in a very long time: joy. He was genuinely having a good time.

At one point in the game, after Dermot had struck out Willy, he looked over his shoulder and winked at his brother, and Colin replied with his best *Ferris Bueller* impression: "Hey, batter, batter, batter, ah swing batter . . ."

Dermot smiled. "I love that movie. Remember when dad said it was one of his favorites?"

"Yeah, he surprised us all."

Dermot chuckled. "That move alone made him the coolest dad in the neighborhood, huh?"

"Yeah," Colin nodded. "I remember Matt and Paul thought he was a god. They actually told everyone at school I had the coolest dad in the world."

Dermot chuckled again.

"What's so funny?" Colin yelled over.

Dermot turned around. "Remember when you were like seven or eight and that guy at that store in Canada gave us free ice cream because he thought you were Ricky Schroder?"

Colin broke into laughter. "That was all Dad, too, telling the guy I was shooting a sequel to *The Champ*."

"Don't forget Mom was also guilty. She was actually worse. Remember she had you do the impression of Ricky Schroder trying to wake up the Champ after he died. You actually made that poor ice cream guy cry."

"Yup, how could I forget?" Colin morphed into a child's voice, "The Champ always comes through . . . Champ. Champ. Champ. Wake up. Wake up. Don't sleep now. You gotta go home. You gotta go home, Champ. Georgie! Georgie, don't cry."

"Geez," Dermot waved his hand. "Stop or you're going to make me ball my eyes out. You used to do the best fake crying when you did that impression, but no tears today, huh?"

"Nope. It's been a long time." Colin shrugged, wondering, *when was the last time I cried?*

"Hey, assholes," Dickie interrupted, "could we play sometime today?"

They went back to playing the game, but Colin stood in the outfield and no longer had a bounce in his step. The first few innings it seemed he had escaped back to his youth. The song "Sunshine Superman" by Donovan was running around in his brain while memories of driving around town with his dad listening to his old eight track tapes also played. But when Dermot mentioned *Ferris Bueller* and then the death scene from *The Champ*, it put Colin back to the place he now lived—a place where the only emotions he ever showed were anger or apathy.

Colin's mood darkened and his game began to suffer. The Fergusons, who were being blown out, suddenly inched their way back into the game, and now had a chance in the final frame.

"That's ball seven," Willy said, moving away as Colin's pitch flew over the chair.

Colin put his hand out and barked, "No, shit! Just throw it back."

Dickie picked it up and threw it back to him. "It's thirteen to eleven, you guys, but we have a guy on. One more ball and it's a walk."

"Again, no shit! But don't forget one more out and we win."

Dermot cupped his hands and yelled from the outfield, "Take it easy, bro. Just throw strikes."

Colin nodded, turned, and threw the Wiffle ball, and again it missed the chair.

"Goddamn it!" he yelled.

Willy handed the bat to Dickie and then went to retrieve the ball.

"Shit, we're hanging tough like the New Kids! We might be down by two, but with one swing of the bat we win." Dickie took a practice swing.

"Just shut the hell up and throw me the ball." Colin motioned with his hand and Willy threw it.

Dermot ran to the mound. "Colin."

"What?" he snapped.

"Take it easy, man. Just throw strikes and let them hit it. I'll be out there for you. Don't worry. I promise. I'll be there for you."

"Will you?"

"Of course. I told you 'I promise.'"

Colin nodded and Dermot gave him a pat on the back.

"All right, you ready?" Colin asked Dickie.

"Yeah, ready to end this game."

Colin peered in, aimed, and lobbed a rainbow that hit the center of the chair.

"Striiiiiike one!" Dermot yelled.

"That was such a fucking meatball. Why didn't you swing?" Willy yelled at his older brother.

"He just threw about ten fucking balls before that. I had to take it. Don't worry, I'll fucking end this shit now," Dickie growled over his shoulder and then dug into his batting stance.

Colin took a deep breath and lobbed it again, but this time Dickie unloaded on it, sending a towering shot to center field.

"Ah, shit." Dermot scampered as fast as he could go, trying to track the ball down.

"Yes!" Dickie celebrated, raising the bat over his shoulders, assuming the ball was well out of the park. But at the last possible second, Dermot went flying through the air and swatted the ball back onto the field before tumbling over the thorny rose-covered fence.

"Yes! Yes! We did it! We win!" Colin fell to his knees and pumped his fists into the sky, but then he realized his brother was still lying on the ground on the other side of the fence. He bolted over and looked on the other side, only to see his big brother pulling thorns out of his forearm and smiling up at him.

"I told you I'd be there for you, bro."

"Thanks." Colin reached over the fence, and Dermot accepted his hand as he helped him up.

The Fergusons left the field trying to one up one another with four letter words, while the Brennan brothers walked home laughing and recounting every pitch. "You thirsty? I bet Mom's got some of her lemonade waiting for us," Dermot said as they were about to cross the street to their yard.

"Yeah, sounds good."

"Hey, maybe we could go for a swim after we . . ." Dermot began, but couldn't finish because a blue BMW pulled up to them beeping its horn.

"C-Dog, hop in, man," the driver hollered.

"Where the hell did you get this ride?" Colin asked Chucky "He's All" Dunn.

"Some guy went to the Vineyard and left it at the shop. He won't be back till tomorrow. What he doesn't know . . . Oh, hey, Dermot."

"Hey, Chucky." Dermot's voice was soft, his disapproval of Chucky obvious. Colin turned to Dermot and patted him on his cut arm. "Hey, bro, let's have a rain check on that lemonade. I gotta roll."

Before Dermot could reply, Colin was in the passenger seat and out of reach.

SEVEN

Six forty-five on a Monday morning and Dermot was already in his work uniform: a pair of beige khakis and a white polo. ISLAND FERRY appeared on the shirt's right pocket in green cursive lettering and a blue wave of stitching ran underneath the logo in an attempt to give the boat's name that extra touch of sea worthiness. This would be Dermot's ninth year working in the parking lot and *not* on the boat. After barfing up his breakfast bagel on Captain Stansfield six years earlier, he had discovered *his* sea legs weren't exactly worthy.

Working in the lot didn't bother him, even though he was earning a dollar-an-hour less than deck hands. The lot gave him more time to observe characters and acquire stories. He didn't have to be to work until 7:45, so he thought about those stories for a moment. He put his legs up on the oak desk his mom had surprised him with the day before and wondered if he would ever write any of the stories down. Actually, he wondered if he'd ever write *anything* down. He'd been screwing around for a couple of years now saying he was taking notes in his writer's journal and was "planning" on writing the "Great American Novel" soon. But that was bullshit. Nothing grabbed him and for some reason he couldn't find the discipline to just sit down and write. His mind liked to wander off the page to that far away land of Francesca Giordano, and before he knew it, hours would pass and there wouldn't even be a damn smudge mark on the paper. In college, he'd been motivated, writing short stories till four in the morning instead of his assigned term papers. It was an ability, or maybe hindrance, because he would write during his math classes, leading to an extra semester at Northeastern.

Deep down, Dermot knew he had set himself up for failure in the writing business because all eyes were now watching him. At his graduation party, he had pronounced he was going to be a writer. But when nothing was produced after two years, everyone began whispering. The whispers got louder and turned into questions, and that's why the trip to Ireland had been a wonderful diversion. But now he was back. Time was running out and if he didn't come up with something to write about soon, he would have to break down and finally learn how to tie a tie, something he had vowed never to do in his life. Massaging his neck, it suddenly felt like that tie was already there strangling his dreams, but then he remembered that the summer had just begun.

"I still have time. I'll think about it later." He allowed a smile and searched for his *Island Ferry* baseball hat, before remembering, with a laugh, that his hat was now in Japan. He had given his hat to a beautiful Japanese tourist named Natuski after talking her ear off about Francesca in a pub on the Aran Isles. Later that night he walked Natuski along a path back to the youth hostel under a moonlit sky. She had given Dermot the international sign for romance by lingering in the doorway for several minutes, laughing and talking to him in broken English, but he didn't act on her flirtations. Like a pitcher who has had eight strong innings, but suddenly buckles in the ninth, instead of leaning in for a kiss, he ended up hugging Natuski and giving her his *Island Ferry* hat to remember him by.

What a loser I was! What a loser I am!

The next morning in the breakfast line, one of her traveling comrades, a guy named Kaz, whispered to him, "'Merican friend bad . . . bad to Natuski last night."

"What do you mean *bad*? I didn't do anything bad."

"No. No. Not bad that way . . . I talk to Natuski. You understand this. Women same everywhere. Don't want hear about girl you miss. Want you talk about new girl. Look Natuski."

Kaz pointed over at the table where she was seated beside Dermot's bunkmate, an Australian model-type named Luke. She was showing Luke the *Island Ferry* hat and laughing with him as he tried it on and posed for her cackling in his Outback brogue.

"Oh, my God," Dermot said. It was bad enough the Aussie kept him awake snoring all night, but now he was wearing *his* hat and stealing *his* new girl. Dermot slammed his tray down on an empty table and was about to storm over and confront the newlyweds when Kaz grabbed his arm and ushered him to sit down.

"Chance over for you, 'Merican friend. Lurke's turn. Resson for my friend, Derm-ent. Woman no time for man who cries in drink."

"Yeah, yeah, I know. You're right," Dermot agreed, angrily spooning his oatmeal into his mouth.

"We eat. Then go to pub. Talk about bad girlfriend. I am on trip for same reason. I had bad girlfriend . . . bad girlfriend . . . are what you 'Merican's say . . . *bitches*. It will be good. We go to pub. We talk about bitches. You cry in drink with Kaz. We get drunk!"

He smiled and made a drinking motion, and then shook his head from side to side like a crazy person causing Dermot to burst into laughter and spit his oatmeal onto the table.

And boy, did we get drunk, Dermot laughed to himself as he left The Shanty, ducked around the corner, and headed down the street for the four-minute walk to work. *It makes a great story, but I will have to slightly alter it when I tell the crew, for entertainment purposes, of course.* In the new version he would not be too hooked on Francesca to miss his chance with Natuski.

A teenager around fifteen or sixteen in a pristine *Island Ferry* uniform waited outside the locked parking lot gate. The kid wore a just-out-of-the-box, straight-billed *Island Ferry* hat over his curly brown hair and looked at Dermot with his brown eyes. He seemed nervous. Something about the kid's appearance seemed familiar.

"Excuse, me, are you Dermot Brennan?"

"Yeah, I'm Dermot, and you must be the new guy."

"Yes, Mr. Brennan. How did . . ."

"The clean uniform for one, and I've been working here for like forever."

"Oh, yes, sorry."

"Nothing to be sorry about, man. So what's your name?"

"Oh, ah, Er—" he answered in a whisper.

"I can't hear you. What is it?"

"Eric."

"Eric what?"

"Eric Chance."

"Okay, Eric Chance, let's open this lock and get you started." Dermot fiddled with the combination.

"Yes, sir."

After he unlocked the gate, he turned to the kid. "Eric, this summer we'll be sitting outside that shack sometimes up to fourteen hours a day. We're going to get to know more about one another than we'll probably want to know, so let's get something clear. That will be the last time you call me 'sir.' My name is Dermot. Or Derm, or D.B, or sometimes I bet it will even be 'that Jackass I work with,' but it will never be 'sir' again, okay?"

Eric cracked the thinnest of smiles and replied, "Yes, Dermot, I'm just a little nervous, I guess, first day and all."

Dermot nodded and headed to unlock the parking lot shack.

That afternoon, Dermot hopped up the step into the parking lot shack, opened his small dorm refrigerator, and grabbed a Coke. On the shelf above the fridge, the digital clock flicked *4:46*.

"Long day," he muttered and opened the can, took a swig, and fell onto the worn green plaid Lay-Z-Boy. Listening through the window, he heard Molloy trying to get the new kid to talk.

Good luck.

Dermot hoped it was just first-day jitters that caused Eric Chance to answer every question with a *yes* or *no* or one simple line. Molloy had just arrived and was going through the same routine.

"So are you from *Silver Shores?*"

"No."

Silence.

"So your family moved here then?"

"Yes."

Silence.

"When?"

"This year."

Silence.

"So where are you from?"

"Allston."

"Why did you move here?"

"My Mom liked the Cape."

"Dermot! Get your ass out here! I need to hear more about Ireland," Molloy hollered and a knowing smile crossed Dermot's lips. The new kid was striking out when it came to providing Gary Molloy his afternoon entertainment. When asked why he worked at the *Island Ferry* parking lot, Molloy claimed the reason he had the second job was for the stories he couldn't find climbing phone poles for the Sea Shore Cable Company from seven to three every day. That may have been one reason, but Dermot knew there was another, but he always kept it to himself.

He finished the last of his Coke, went outside, and sat in the white plastic lawn chair in between Molloy and Eric. "All right, so what do you want to know, Easy Shift Molloy? Oh, Eric, by the way, that's what we call Molloy 'cause he only works the afternoon shifts and, as you see, they're pretty easy compared to all the running around we did this morning. We'll probably sell only about twenty-five spots this afternoon compared to the three hundred and ten we did before that ten-thirty boat."

"All right," Molloy interrupted "Enough of that shit. The kid will see it for himself. So, I want to get back to your winter, Dermot. Where were we? Oh yeah, so first, the guinea chick dumps your pale Mick ass. Now was that before or after Christmas?"

"Before."

"Well, that's good. At least, that means you didn't have to give the I-talian bitch any gifts, right?"

"Right," Dermot quickly answered, but looked over and saw the horrified expression on Eric's face. He couldn't help but laugh. "Something you'll get used to, Eric. The only way Molloy knows how to talk is with racist and sexist remarks. Believe me, it took me almost half my first summer to get used to it. I tried changing him, but it's useless; that's his lovable way. Although, Molloy, you don't claim you're racist, right?"

"That's right, kid." Molloy leaned over to Eric and grinned. "I hate *everybody* equally. Anyway, Dermot, what was the reason the Ginzo broad dumped you? Was she tired of you being hung like an Irish field mouse?"

"Nope. It was her father. He found out I wanted to be a writer and decided he wouldn't pay her tuition if she continued seeing me. I think he wants her to marry a lawyer or doctor or something. I guess I just wasn't good enough for his little girl."

"You're not fucking serious, are you?" Molloy shot up from his chair.

"Dead serious. I guess he actually paid for her to go to Italy for a few months instead of coming back to the Cape, just so she wouldn't see me."

"Fuck that wop! And fuck her, too! You don't need her. They'll be plenty of tail for you in the tag-and-release program this summer. You just gotta get out there. I bet it's not stopping Fran-chest-hair. I bet she's getting back at her old man right now by riding some don in a villa in Sicily. Yup, what goes around comes around, and I bet she's *getting* around. She might not marry a doctor, but she'll end up needing one for all the diseases she'll pick up. Mark my words: her old man will be sorry he chased you off. So, cheer up."

"That's your idea of cheering me up? Molloy, you're talking about the girl I love . . . d . . ."

"Seriously, Dermot, I *am* trying to cheer you up. Believe me, I know how much you liked that bitch." Molloy paused as if there was actually a thought running through his head. "Remember when she would come by and bring us iced coffees? That was pretty nice of her. I have to say, she always had a smile on her face, and man did she love you and all your romantic bullshit."

"Geez, Molloy, that's even worse. I'd rather you be your abrasive, asshole self than to let me know that Francesca actually made you feel human emotions." Dermot shook his head, got out of the chair, and was about to wait on a gray Saab when he noticed three women in the car.

I need some entertainment for myself.

He turned around. "Hey, Eric, why don't you take this one?"

Eric hopped to attention and went over to the car while Dermot sat back down next to Molloy and smiled. After the transaction, Eric settled into his chair and they all watched the Saab head off and park on the hill in the back of the lot.

Molloy flashed his white teeth. "So, Chance? Are we talking seven, eight, nine, or ten?"

"Huh?" the kid replied.

"Molloy wants to know if they were hot," Dermot translated.

"Oh, I don't know."

"What do you mean, you don't know?" Molloy asked, almost offended.

"I guess I wasn't looking. They seemed nice."

"Aw, shit." Molloy shook his head and turned to Dermot. "This kid reminds me of you when you started working here."

"And what's wrong with that?" Dermot asked.

"If you don't know by now . . . We'll check those chicks out when they walk by us and I want ratings from you, Chance."

Eric didn't answer because he was chasing after a blue truck with KEATING AND SON CONSTRUCTION painted on its side, which sped past all three of them and parked in an employee parking spot.

"Excuse me, sir, but you can't park there," Eric said to Tommy Keating, who got out of the truck and continued walking toward Dermot and Molloy.

Tommy thumbed behind him at Eric. "Who the fuck's the new kid?"

Dermot jumped in. "Eric, don't worry about it. That rude asshole is a buddy of mine. He's just doing his daily ten-minute pop-in."

Eric nodded and was about to go back to his chair, when Tommy sat in it and turned to Molloy. "Hey, big dog, you divorced yet?"

"Nope. I'll never get a divorce. Too expensive, Tommy. She's still cheating on me, having oral relations with vodka bottles."

"Real classy, Molloy. I don't know why a woman married to you would *ever* drink. Speaking of drinking, Derm, I feel like getting my drink on tonight."

"I don't think so, Tommy."

"Why not?"

"I think I'm going to try and do some writing tonight."

"You and that writing shit. You can write any night."

"I can drink any night, too." Dermot glared at Tommy. He hated how his friends never took his dream seriously.

"Wait, here they come." Molloy snapped his fingers at Eric and pointed over to the three girls. The girls looked to be in their early twenties; they were carrying overnight bags and headed towards the men. They were all blonde, busty, and had sweatshirts tied around their waists.

"Okay, Eric, get ready for your first test," Molloy warned.

"Yes, Mr. Molloy."

"Excuse me, sir, but where does the boat dock?" Sweatshirt Girl #1 asked Molloy.

He got out of his chair, pointed down the street, and said in a honey-laden voice, "Oh, ladies, it's just a hundred-and-fifty-yard walk up the street. It'll take you two minutes."

"Thank you."

"No problem."

All three girls smiled and walked out of the lot and headed down the street. When they were out of sight Molloy turned to Eric. "Okay, Chance, in your opinion, are those girls good looking?"

"What, Mr. Molloy?"

"Aw, shit, kid. Do you need Miracle-Ear? It's a simple question. Are they good looking?"

"Yes. Yes. They are pretty."

"In twenty-five years will they still be *pretty*?"

"I suppose."

Molloy gestured to Tommy. "Dermot's useless on this topic, so help me on this one TK."

Tommy got up out of the chair and gestured for Eric to sit in it. When he did, Tommy paced back and forth and then turned to him. "Kid, it's like seventy-five degrees out and all three of those girls had sweatshirts tied around their waists. Don't you find that a little strange?"

"A little, I guess. I was wondering, since it's so hot and all."

Molloy took over. "Eric, that's what we call 'the sweater trick.' In this case, it's 'the sweatshirt trick.' It's an age-old tradition among women who have monster asses. They think if they tie something around their waist, they're fooling us. Some guys do fall for it, but not our crew. From now on, look for it, because you'll see it everywhere you go."

"Another thing to watch out for is fankles," Tommy pointed out.

"Yeah," Molloy added. "If she has fankles, you can put it in her, but don't buy her dinner."

"What are fankles?" Eric asked, as Dermot sat in the background, shaking his head, knowing this would set off Tommy and Molloy.

"Fat ankles," Tommy said.

"I know them as cankles. When the calf and ankle are one. You know, cattle ankles," Molloy said.

"You guys are terrible," Dermot said.

"I'm still kind of confused, what's the big deal about cankles and fankles?" Eric asked.

It was the longest sentence Eric had uttered all day, and both Molloy and Tommy wanted to tackle the question, but Tommy jumped in first.

"Let me put it this way for you. I'm a builder. If I'm building a small house I will need a small foundation. If it's a big house I'll need to build a big foundation. It's the same with women, but the foundation is already there. Small ankles. Nice small house. Big ankles. A big-ass house will end up on that foundation. Does that make sense?"

"So, you're saying the next time I go on a date with a girl, I should bring a tape measure with me to see how wide her ankles are?" Eric asked, looking for a laugh and he got it. Both Molloy and Tommy erupted and Eric joined in feeling accepted.

"Geez, Eric, don't become one of those guys," Dermot said.

Molloy, still laughing, pointed at Dermot, "No, Eric, don't listen to 1940s over there. That's what we call Dermot because he thinks he's goddamn Jimmy Stewart, an old romantic and shit like that. He does the whole dating thing wrong. He's too honest with chicks. Dermot, this summer do me a favor and lie to the women a little. Just a little, okay? And Eric, stick with me kid and I'll get you laid."

Eric's laughter hiccupped a bit, and he blushed. He may've felt good because Molloy had just accepted him into the fold, but Eric was still a quiet, innocent sixteen-year-old. Regardless of how funny Molloy and Tommy's BSing was, Dermot knew he had just witnessed a bit of that innocence stolen from Eric. At that point, he decided that every chance he could, he'd make sure that he'd look out for the new kid. After all, when he saw the red face, Dermot realized that Molloy was right. Eric Chance was a lot like him on Dermot's first day of work at the *Island Ferry* parking lot.

EIGHT

Halfway out his front door, Colin turned back to answer Dwayne's page. He grabbed the kitchen phone and dialed. After one ring, Dwayne answered, "Peters residence. Can I help you?"

"Hootie Hooo . . . "

"Yeah, hey, what's up, Colin? Just returning your page from this morning. What's the good word?"

"'Peters residence. Can I help you?' What the hell is that, D?"

"Summer season, kid. I have a lot of customers calling me."

"Yeah . . . well . . . all right. So are we gonna blaze at sunset tonight or what?"

"Wish I could, C-dog, but I'm DJing a wedding tomorrow."

"So?"

"So, I got to be on my game for these summer folks. Potential customers will be there, man. It's at the Silver Shores Yacht Club, so we're talking big dollars, and you know I can't afford to look like an amateur in front of those no-sock wearin' cats."

Colin laughed. "I have to have to say, Dwayne, you sound like one of *those* cats . . . soft. You're telling me that you're gonna skip sunset because you have a wedding *tomorrow*? Damn, that's weak. I don't like it, bro."

"Well, I'm sorry to disappoint you, but I don't plan on being a townie my whole life."

The statement hit Colin squarely in the gut, and there was an uncomfortable silence as he bit hard on the side of his mouth.

Dwayne must have sensed said it, because he added, "Here's a thought: why don't you drop the party scene for a night and we'll catch a movie? I know that movie *Speed* is playing at the mall with your boyfriend Keanu Reeves. Shit, I'll even buy your ticket."

"Keanu Reeves . . . my boyfriend . . . that's some real funny stuff, D. Nah . . . it's summer, bro . . . I'm straight . . . In more ways than one. But for real, I'm picking up Chucky in a couple of hours, and we're hitting a beach party in East Shores. I know for a fact it's supposed to be filled with summer girls. You say the word and I'm at your house in *no* time."

This time, the line went silent on Dwayne's end.

"You there, D?"

"Chucky? Chucky Dunn?" Dwayne asked.

"Yeah . . . What other Chucky do you know?"

"Jesus, man. Why are you hanging out with that deadbeat?"

"What's wrong with Chucky?"

"What's wrong with Chucky? What's *right* with Chucky is more like it. The kid is a lifetime loser. Big-time trouble. He has no redeeming qualities whatsoever."

"He's not that bad."

"I'm telling you, hanging out with him is like playing Russian roulette with a full barrel. You can't win, man."

"Aren't you being a bit dramatic?"

"Trust me, Col, with all the shit Dunn gets into, the kid will bring you down with him and you're going to get caught in that undertow of shit."

Colin pulled the receiver away from his ear for a second before returning it, thinking Dwayne was finished. He wasn't.

"Colin, you keep hanging with him, and you're the one who is going to be 'all done.'"

"Ah, man, all right. All right. Why you gotta be like that? Remember it's summertime, D. It's all about partying, letting loose, warm weather, girls . . . damn!"

"You don't get it, do you? Why are you hanging out with assholes that don't give a shit about you? All they want is a drinking buddy."

"I hang out with you. Is that what *you* are? A drinking buddy."

"Nah, man. You know I'm not that. That's why I'm telling you this shit. I've been wanting to say it for a while. You're hanging with guys you never wanted to be like and now it's like you're becoming best friends with them. Honestly, you need to drop some of that luggage, man."

There was a long pause.

"Okay. I've said my peace," Dwayne ended.

Colin now knew where he stood with his friend. It shook him up. He had sensed it coming on, but he thought he'd at least get the summer with him before the Dwayne-game officially began. I'll give it one last cast he thought, and said, "Here's the story. I'm going to this party and I'm picking up Chucky. Either you're in or you're out."

"You *really* don't you get it? I'm out. I don't want to go to the party, and I don't think you should go, either. Chucky is bad news, straight up. And, by the way, I thought you said to me a few weeks back that you never wanted to be in the paper again?"

"That's a low blow, D. Ease up, will ya?"

"Colin, I just don't want to see you go down, that's all."

Colin wanted to yell, "Fuck you, Dwayne!" Instead, he pulled the phone away and called out to no one, "I'm on the phone!" to cover his escape route. Colin raised his voice. "What? Oh, okay. I'll be right there. Yeah . . . Yeah . . . Okay, Mom." To Dwayne, he said breezily, "Yo, D, my mom is calling me. You know her. Wants me to move some summer furniture or something. I'll catch up with you tomorrow."

"Yeah, okay, man, just be caref—"

Colin slammed the receiver down. It was bad enough other people treated him like a child or a pariah. But not Dwayne. He didn't need his shit.

From across the kitchen his eyes saw something had been added to the much adorned refrigerator. He walked over to it. Underneath the *You Can't Heal What You Can't Feel* slogan magnet was a note left by his father. He squinted and whispered the message to himself.

Colin and Derm, the Sox are on at 7 o'clock. Who knows how many of these games are left?! I was thinking the three of us could get some Paul's Pizzas and some Cokes and make a night of it. Hope to see you later. Love, Dad.

"Sorry. Not tonight, Dad," he said, walking out of the kitchen and grabbing the Island Ferry baseball hat off the coat-rack in the entry way. He stuffed it into his back pocket before pushing open the screen door and heading around the corner for Stirling Beach. He cut through the park where the smell of freshly cut grass permeated the air. As he passed the basketball court, he wondered when he would be lacing up his high-tops again, if ever. He missed the freedom of a simple basketball game, but lately he didn't have the energy to even play a game of HORSE. A loud howl cut into his thoughts.

"Hey, a little help, man?"

Turning around he noticed his buddy from high school, John Forcellese, standing at mid-court.

"Oh hey, C-Dog. I didn't know that was you. Can you throw me the rock?" He clapped his hands and waited for the pass.

Colin bent down, picked up the ball that had rolled away from the game, and tossed it back to John.

"There you go, big man. Hope you're working on that weak jump shot of yours," he jabbed.

John laughed. "Always. You know that. Thanks, C-Dog. Hey, stick around. You can have next. And *then* I can show you how much I really have been working on my jumper."

"Another day, man. I got shit to do."

"You say that every time. Hey, C-Dog," he gave one more shout. "Thanks for hooking my brother up with that discount."

He put his hand up to acknowledge John, but kept on walking straight for the beach. After exiting the park, he looked over to Pucky's Pub and noticed the dinner crowd shuffling in. He crossed the street, dodging traffic, and headed over to the seawall along Stirling's. He slipped off his sneakers and socks, placed them neatly on top of the concrete barricade, and jumped down to the sand.

When he was a kid he would get in a racing stance at the street, and then sprint to the edge of the wall, and using his towel like a cape, he would soar through the air pretending he was Superman landing feet first into the hot sand. The staircase was always an afterthought, except the year Paul sprained his ankle skateboarding. Matt and Colin had spent that summer on either side of Paul assisting him down the stairs while pretending they were the Secret Service escorting President Regan down from Air Force One.

"One for all and all for one, Mr. President," Matt and Colin would say as they'd settle him onto his towel.

On the heels of that memory, Colin headed towards his favorite jetty and with each sinking step, he thought about getting drunk. He promised himself to hold off for the time being. As he searched through his pockets for cigarettes, he noticed a father and son ahead of him down by the edge of the shoreline. The blond boy, who looked to be about four years old, was in the final stages of sandcastle construction and stood up and looked over at a man standing on dry sand, apparently his father. The man pointed behind the boy at the surf, and when he turned and saw that the water was rushing in, he frantically began building a barrier to protect his castle. It was a futile effort.

The boy then stood up and in defiance, with his little palm facing the sea, he screamed. "Stop, ocean! Stooooop!" The boy looked again to his father, this time for a solution.

"Mother Nature doesn't pick favorites, buddy!" his father hollered.

As the waves slowly began pulling the castle to the ocean, the father walked over to his son's side and got on one knee, letting the water drench his pants. He put his right hand on the boy's shoulder. The child began to cry.

Although Colin couldn't hear what the father was saying as he hugged his son, he could see the boy was listening intently, and whatever he said obviously worked. Finally the father let go of the boy, who nodded, wiped his tears, and sat next to his creation in silent acceptance, watching the water slowly erase his castle from existence.

Colin continued onto his jetty, and when he got there, he smirked at the KEEP OFF THE ROCKS sign some lazy lifeguard had forgotten to grab. He knew that by the end of the night, there was a pretty good chance that sign would be gone and end up as a backdrop next fall in a dorm room or frat house. But it wasn't his concern anymore. He was no longer a lifeguard, and that warning did not apply to him. How many times as kids did he, Paul, and Matt test the boundaries and stand on the rocks during beach hours, hoping to catch a lifeguard napping?

He felt for his cigarettes, pulled the pack out, and held it tightly in his hand. Like a tightrope walker, he made his way gingerly along the clammy surface to the end of the jetty to what Matt had dubbed, "The Fighting Chair." The Chair was actually a rock, resting on another rock, and it was the best spot to fish from, especially in the dead of night. Buckets and buckets of striped bass had been reeled in from that spot over the years.

Whenever they went fishing, the three of them would play Rock, Paper, Scissors to see who got the sacred honor to be Quint from *Jaws* for the night. "Hoooop-ah!" Colin could still envision Paul doing the best impersonation of the crotchety shark hunter.

He fired up a cigarette, took a long drag, and inhaled deeply. It had been a long time since he had looked at the ocean from this view, and it was the first time that he had sat in the "Chair" sober with no one beside him. Beyond him, the Vineyard was a stone's throw away. The *Island Ferry* was returning, crowded with day-trippers, headed for the inlet beside the Silver Shores lighthouse, a timeless reference landmark that commanded the hill overlooking the sea. He didn't want to think of the lighthouse, but his thoughts moved to Dwayne and what he had said. He didn't exactly want to think about that, either.

The light blue water crashed around him, and even though the beach was practically empty except for the little boy on his father's shoulders walking back to their truck, there was a lingering scent of tanning lotion in the early evening air.

God, I love that smell!

He pulled out Eric Chance's hat from his back pocket and began sculpting it as he observed the marble surface of the Sound. Earlier that day, after he got off work at the Fort, Colin had stood patiently in line at Coffee Mania, waiting for the annoying foreigners in front of him to hurry up and order. The European couple stood out like a sore thumb with their thick accents. Carrying an unpleasant odor, the two wore Birkenstocks with black socks and sported spandex shorts that did not compliment their plump figures. Watching the pair sort through their pleather fanny packs for their American money had amused him. He had a quick picture of the Von Trapp family, dancing on a mountaintop in *The Sound Of Music*, and desperately wanted to crack a do-re-me joke, but as he half turned he remembered, awkwardly, that he was alone.

So instead he browsed the customers who crammed the cozy hangout. "Nutshell" by Alice in Chains echoed through a pair of speakers. The usual quiet group of kids studying had been replaced with laughter and elation—signaling the school year was almost done. At one table a young couple played footsies. The teenage girl twirled her curly auburn hair through her fingers while she stared deeply into her boyfriend's eyes. Appearing to be completely in love, the two ignored their melting iced coffees and centered their attention on one another. Beyond them at a corner booth, a group of teens wearing all black sat. The girls with thick eyeliner exchanged giggling stories while the boys compared their skateboards and scars.

He had witnessed the scene thousands of times, so maybe that's why the boy writing furiously in a notebook and sitting alone at a table drew his curiosity. Something about him seemed familiar. The boy was staring right at Colin, but when their eyes met, he looked down and continued scribbling in his notebook.

Colin turned his attention back to the foreign couple, who hadn't made any progress with their U.S. coin collection. They were now trying to calculate their change, which they had dumped out of their packs onto the countertop.

His eyes wandered to his left and he studied the wall decorated with paintings, drawings, and photographs by local artists. (The manager of Coffee Mania, Jeff, an aspiring musician, was great for using the shop to promote artists from town and always picked the best work the locals had to offer.) Then he saw it. It stood out from the rest. He knew *that* style. *Those* colors. The eerie painting of the Silver Shores Lighthouse literally made his heart pump faster, and he could feel his face flush. The purple and white watercolor portrayed the lighthouse in a rainstorm, surrounded by the breaking Atlantic. He knew the scene well; it was an image that flashed continually across his mind before he fell asleep. A sharp pain pierced his stomach, and he wiped sweat from his brow. He knew the answer to the question, but he had to ask it anyway.

"Hey, Jeff, who did . . . ah, that one?" he managed, while pointing at the painting.

"Oh." Jeff looked up while helping the foreigners with their money. "Great painting, huh? That's one of Mel's. I haven't been able to put her label and info up yet. We're going to have an art exhibit here in a couple of days, and she's going to be our featured artist. I knew that art school in Colorado was the right place for her. Have you run into her? You know, she's back in town."

Colin was fixated on the lighthouse and answered under his breath, "No, I haven't."

Of course, he knew it would only be a matter of time before he would. He hadn't seen or talked to her since Christmas break and that meeting was more than a little foggy. He did remember consoling her at some bender while she cried in the bathroom. That night he had promised he would visit her, but that was only to stop her tears so they both could get back to drinking.

Frozen by the painting, he stood motionless viewing the picture until he was snapped from his trance by the loud scream of skateboarders standing behind him,

"Aquaman!"

"What did you say?" he asked not believing what he had just heard.

"Sorry, dude. I'm talking to my buddy," the kid replied and said to the kid beside him, "Dude, I'm telling you, Aquaman is one of the six original members."

The other wasn't convinced until one of the girls behind them chimed in, "C.J. is right, Damien. Aquaman is one of them, but that gives us only five. Who's the last one?"

Aquaman! Aquaman!

Colin felt like he was suffocating when finally the foreigners moved aside, leaving the tip jar still empty and making room for him at the counter. He read the chalkboard featuring its daily trivia question and what the kids were talking about suddenly made sense.

"FIVE CENTS OFF IF YOU CAN NAME THE ORIGINAL SIX MEMBERS OF THE JUSTICE LEAGUE."

The pain in his stomach intensified. *God, they are everywhere!*

"Colin . . . Colin." He rubbed his dry eyes and then looked over at the exotic, young girl standing behind the counter next to Jeff.

"Oh . . . sorry, Natalie. I'm out of it. Been a long day."

"That's okay." She gave that wide smile of hers. "Hot chocolate?"

"Of course. Nothing like it." He returned her smile while wishing he was sixteen again.

"Isn't it a little warm for hot chocolate?" she asked.

"Isn't it a little warm for coffee?"

"You make a good point. How is the Shoe Fort?"

"Busy as hell. School is almost out, so kids are everywhere. I can't tell you how many sandals I've sold in the past two days. It's like an Apostles convention. Okay, lame joke, but anyway, it's been ridiculous." He laughed. "How are you? How's the writing going?"

"To be honest, a little slow, but I'll get back to it."

"That's good. Don't waste your talent. You only live once." He wagged his finger at her.

"Thanks, Colin. Have a great day!" She handed him his hot chocolate, her smile never fading, her cheeks pink.

"You too, Natalie. Keep smiling."

The pink turned red as Colin headed for the side door. He noticed the kid who had been staring at him before was doing it again. When he threw him a look, the kid quickly buried his head back in his notebook. Colin noticed the writing on the boy's hat: *Island Ferry.*

His curiosity mounted. He walked behind the kid and looked over his shoulder at the notebook and silently mouthed the lines:

I see her stare

with Sea blue eyes

under long black hair

no matter what I try

her eyes like tumbling waves have crashed my shores . . .

He looked up from the notebook and followed the kid's gaze to Natalie and realized the poem was about her. Chuckling to himself, he noticed the writing on the top right page.

COFFEE MANIA CHARACTERS, GOOD FILLERS FOR A STORY

1. FOREIGNERS WHO DON'T TIP WEARING BIKE SHORTS THAT MAKE THEM BOTH LOOK LIKE THE MICHELIN MAN.

2. SKETCHY GUY WITH BLOND HAIR ORDERS A HOT CHOCOLATE IN MID-JUNE. LOOKS TIRED AND SAD. WHAT'S HIS STORY?

Colin couldn't help himself. "Sketchy guy?"

The kid swiveled around in shock. "Huh?"

"You heard me, Hemmingway. Who's the sketchy guy?"

"No, it's not what you think. I just like to jot down nonsense, honest." He nervously backed up.

The kid's description of Colin perturbed him and he felt like playing with the kid. His day at the Fort was done, and he had already heard of three different parties for the night, so he knew he would be drunk soon and his adrenaline was jumping.

"Well, I'm just a little curious." He looked down, making eye contact. "Do I really look tired and sad, and why am I sketchy? Tell me, Shakespeare, how is my story going so far?"

"No, sir. It's not that you're . . ."

Colin quickly halted him with his free hand. "Sir?"

The kid looked at him, not knowing how to respond.

Colin then threw his head back, laughing. "So, not only am I tired, sad, and sketchy, but I'm also an old man to you? Kid, I'm only nineteen. Don't call me 'sir.' Do you have any other compliments for me?"

"I'm sorry. I don't want problems with you." The teen quivered, and his body recoiled, making Colin suddenly feel guilty. He knew what it was like to be on the receiving end of a bully. Seeing the boy's pale complexion turn burgundy made him realize the fun should be over.

"Hey, relax, man, I'm just kidding around. You know I'm just giving you a little shit. Anyway, I guess I'd rather look tired, sad, and sketchy than look like the Michelin Man, right?" He pointed over at the foreigners and the kid smiled.

"So, you work at the *Island Ferry*?" Colin asked, tapping the boy's hat.

"Yes. It's my first year."

Colin examined him from head to toe.

"Nice shell-toes," he said pointing to his sneakers. "So you're from the city?"

"Well, yeah, just outside the city. Allston."

Colin nodded. "You a summer kid?"

"No, but I did summer down here one year when I was like eight or nine." He scratched his hat. "I don't quite remember. But now I live in town, moved here last fall."

"Prep school or high school?"

"High school. I'm going into my junior year at Silver Shores High."

"What's your name?"

"Eric. Eric Chance."

Colin extended his hand. "Well, it's nice to meet you, Eric Chance. I'm Colin."

Eric's hand met his. "It's nice to meet you, too." He seemed still to be wary of Colin's motives.

"So, Eric, why did you move to the Shores?"

"My mom needed a change. Well . . . we both needed a change. And I really like the ocean, so we figured Cape Cod would be the best place to escape the hustle and bustle of the city."

"Well, I gotta be honest with you about something."

"What's that?"

"If you really want to be a true Cape Codder, the first thing you need to do is fix that hat."

"What do you mean? What's wrong with it?" Eric began caressing the top of his hat. "It's brand new."

"Exactly. That's my point. The brim is so damn straight. It looks like you just grabbed it off the shelf. That's how all the old retirees wear them.

You're not moving to Florida, are you?" He laughed as Eric made a closer inspection of it. "I could probably balance my hot chocolate on that thing. May I?"

"Put your hot chocolate on my hat?"

"No, man." Colin laughed again. "Let me check out what you're working with."

Eric reluctantly handed it over to Colin who began studying it. "Yeah, same model as last year's. This is a cardboard brim. Don't get me wrong. It definitely has potential, but you'll need to put it through the dishwasher and rubber band the brim for a couple of nights. Maybe even shove it under your mattress for a day or two."

Eric was lost. "Dishwasher?"

"Apparently you have never broken in a hat before, my friend." Colin slapped him good-naturedly on the shoulder. "You should treat a hat like a baseball glove. Think about it, Eric. You don't go buy a glove and then expect to play shortstop the same day. Same thing with a hat. No offense, but right now you shouldn't be wearing that in public." He smiled and winked and then lowered his voice. "Especially in front of a beautiful woman with long black hair and sea blue eyes that have crashed your shores."

Eric's eyes widened, and he shut his notebook. "God, what the hell? What are you Superman with X-Ray vision or something?"

"No, Superman is overrated. Actually, my friends used to call me Aquaman, but then it became C-Dog. Double meaning, with the ocean and my first initial and all. Don't worry, man, your observations about Coffee Mania will stay in that notebook. I've sat where you sit. But as someone who has been there, you gotta learn a few things, and one is a man's hat is his signature." He handed it to Eric who looked at it and then gave it back to Colin.

"I don't think I would know how to explain to my mom that I need to put my hat in the dishwasher," Eric said. "Can you do it?"

"I'd be happy to," he answered as he worked the brim. "Just give me a couple of days."

Eric pointed to Colin's shirt. "Should I come to the Shoe Fort?"

Raising his brow and shaking his head, Colin smiled. "No. Don't worry. I know where to find you, Eric Chance."

There was now a connection between the two and their conversation flowed freely. They spent the next fifteen minutes talking about the possible baseball strike, and then Colin gave Eric tips on the best jetties in town to catch "keepers," and he even told him about The Fighting Chair. It was refreshing for Colin to have a conversation with someone who didn't know him. It felt innocent and genuine, and somehow familiar.

"What's up, C-Dog?"

Colin peered over his shoulder. "Oh shit. Chucky, what's up?"

Normally, the two would slap hands or maybe even exchange a hug, but Chucky was in his lube uniform covered head to toe in grease, with the smell of oil and marijuana blowing off his body. He was his usual unstable self. "Shit, did you hear the news?"

"What news?"

"About OJ Simpson's wife?"

Colin shook his head. "No man, what happened?"

Chucky's bloodshot eyes bulged. "She's all dead up, man. She was murdered along with some other guy. They got stabbed to death. Grisly crime scene. Her fucking throat was all slashed and shit. Probably looks like a goddamn Pez dispenser. It's all over the fucking news, bro."

"No, way," Colin said, stunned.

"Yeah, man. Where the hell have you been? This thing is wild. They're trying to find the Juice to tell him the bad news. I guess he's out of town or something. It's crazy. I just heard it on the radio." Chucky looked around the room. "Of course, why would you know? This fucking coffee shop needs a TV. Bunch of fucking hippies don't wanna spend the money. Serious shit goes down and these guys are too busy shoving coffee beans up each other's asses."

In his head, Colin saw his old Buffalo Bills Topps card and managed, "Poor OJ."

"Yeah, no kidding. I mean you see him all over the TV running in airports and in movies and smiling and shit . . . You just never know. It's a tough break. L.A. is fucking crazy. Riots and murders." Chucky laughed and screeched, "Welcome to the jungle!"

"So what brings you here, Axl?"

"Nothing, man. Just popping in to get myself a coffee and, who knows, maybe pop Natalie's cherry while I'm at it." His greasy finger pointed over to Natalie who was behind the counter making some iced coffees. "I mean, Damn! She is one sexy bitch! Damn, I wanna hit that so bad. I think she's like Greek or Russian. Ten bucks says she's a screamer. If not, I'll make her one! Ouch!"

Colin glanced at Eric who was now staring down at the floor, deflated.

"Hey, Chucky, cut the shit man. She's a good kid, and she's only sixteen, dude. Don't talk that way about her."

"Whoa, easy, C-Dog, we can share if you want. You know how the song goes. Tag team! Back again! Whoop, there it is!" He laughed it off.

Colin gave Chucky a long scowl. "I'm fucking serious. I don't want to hear that kind of talk, all right?"

"C-Dog, relax, man, I'm only kidding around. You sound like our principal back in the day, Miss Shannon. Remember that bitch? I just changed her oil. Still a miserable, old hag. Hey, you're still going to roll with me tonight to that beach party, right? Gonna be a lot of summer sluts."

Colin's grimace slowly changed to a smile. "Shit, after the day I had, it would be the perfect remedy."

"See, that's why you're my boy. I was thinking, we could prime up at my place, maybe do some funnels and then make our way to sunset and blaze a fatty. Maybe even start a party train with whoever is down there and make our way to the party. Of course, you'll have to drive. Can't get that second DUI," he said and laughed.

"Yeah, I figured as much. Drop me a page in a little bit and we'll get on this. I have to do a couple of things when I get home, but it won't take long."

"Word." The two high-fived, and Chucky sauntered his way to the counter to flirt with Natalie.

Colin turned to Eric, who still had his eyes fixed on the floor. He rubbed the grease off his hand and said, "That's Chucky. He's got a big mouth, but he's harmless."

"Yeah," Eric looked up at him and laughed sarcastically. With a little more bite in his voice he responded, "Harmless if he doesn't get that second DUI, right?"

Eric kept his eyes on Colin, who finally replied, "Ah, yeah. Well, I gotta roll, Eric." He waved the hat. "I'm gonna take care of this for you."

"Thanks, Colin." They shook hands and parted ways.

Colin walked out, got in his car, and before turning the engine on, looked in his rearview mirror, and that's when he realized what was familiar about Eric Chance: he reminded him of himself, just three years ago.

A tennis ball suddenly slapped the ocean to his right, and Colin's thoughts came back to the present. Looking over, he watched two black Labrador retrievers fiercely swimming after it. The bigger of the two easily snatched it and then the pair fought the current and swam back to their owner, who stood at the shoreline. The dogs' owner tossed the ball back into the ocean and called out, "Hey, stranger!"

"Hey, what's up?" Colin said, realizing it was his old teammate from his high school swim team, Josh Baker. He was probably the last person on earth Colin wanted to see. He made his way off the jetty back onto the sand.

"Reminiscing about the old days?" Josh pointed to the end of the jetty.

"Not really."

"You know I don't think I ever beat you on this beach. Well, actually, I'm not sure if *anyone* has ever beaten you here? The C-Dog 'owns' Stirling Beach. That's what we always said at my beach." He looked Colin dead in the eye. "You were so damn strong, man."

"Yup. So what's up, Josh? Nice," Colin said, pointing to Josh's T-shirt that read in bold red lettering: U.S. COAST GUARD ACADEMY SWIM TEAM.

"Oh, thanks. You know you could have one of these, too. Let's face it. SATs take a back seat to how Colin Brennan swims. At least, that's the whisper I heard at the Academy. Anyway, Coach said you still have that scholarship if you want it. He also said he tried calling you over the winter to see how you were doing and you never called him back."

"Well, I was busy with work and stuff."

"Yeah, dealing with smelly feet all day must take a lot out of you."

Colin laughed. "Yeah."

He was pissed and wanted to tell Josh to fuck off along with everyone else, but held it in.

The two dogs emerged from the ocean, and the big one dropped the ball at Josh's feet. Then they both shook their heavy coats. With their tails wagging and tongues hanging, the pair waited for another throw. Colin picked the ball up and hurled it as far as he could. Josh followed the line of the ball and when he turned around, Colin was already walking up the stairs.

He yelled out to him, "Yeah, real cool, C-dog! Walk away like you always do. You know you're throwing your life away!"

Determined not to look back, Colin ignored him and continued up the stairs.

"Cross that damn bridge and call Coach back! He's not going to wait forever."

NINE

Dermot had spent the next couple of nights sitting at his new desk staring at the blinking white cursor on the screen of his Brother word processor. So, the symbolic gesture of unplugging and replacing it with the small black and white TV was not lost on him. At a work site earlier that day, Tommy had snagged the TV from a construction trailer and brought it over so they could watch game five of the NBA Finals. Being a Celtics fan, Dermot didn't like the Rockets and he, of course, despised the Knicks, but it *was* the finals, and that meant it was a great excuse for not spending his night trying to write.

He suddenly didn't have any guilt for his decision because after popping a second beer, the scene in front of him took on a bizarre, or as the sportscaster Bob Costas was describing it, "surreal twist." He knew he and Tommy were now watching something that everyone would be talking about for years to come, and it had nothing to do with the game.

"I can't believe this shit. It's like a movie. It's actually better than a movie. Basketball on one side and real-life drama on the other side of the screen," Tommy said, pointing to the split-screen images. "Derm, do you think OJ will off himself or is he setting up some hopeless insanity defense case 'cause that guy driving didn't sound too worried when he was talking on the phone. I mean, I'd be shitting my pants wondering if the Juice would blow my brains on the dash first."

"I don't know about that Cowlings guy not being worried, TK. He sounded pretty damn tense to me. Think about it. He also said he's buddies with OJ. So, he's probably just trying to keep him calm. I mean he did say the Juice had a friggin' gun to his head and was going to kill himself. He's probably worried he'll take him out first. But don't worry, TK, I want you to know if I'm ever in that situation and you're driving me around, I won't take you out with me. I'll leave you behind to tell the story. I mean, someone has to get some of that post-funeral sympathy sex."

"Thanks, man, you're the best," Tommy said, shaking his empty. "You know what? That deserves another beer."

"Nah, I just opened this one."

Tommy slinked through the Brady beads into the other room, opened the fridge, and brought back two beers.

"Take the nipple off that one and drink up. You're one behind." He handed the beer to Dermot, who accepted it as he downed his other and then licked his lips.

"So, back to your question," Dermot said, opening the fresh Miller Lite and then tossing the bottle cap into the large Beer Nuts bucket that contained thousands of caps. "It's obvious now that the asshole killed his wife and that waiter dude, so at this point, killing himself might be his best way out of this shit. Think about it. If he kills himself on live TV, he'll be remembered forever. And if he doesn't, he'll just be remembered for fucking up game five of the NBA Finals." He focused back on the TV, intently trying to process what he was witnessing.

On one side of the screen Hakeem Olajuwon was posting up on Patrick Ewing, while on the other side a white Bronco driven by some guy named AC Cowlings and carrying OJ Simpson was traveling slowly down a freeway followed by a few dozen LAPD cruisers.

"Maybe OJ will make a run for it. But wait . . . Canada's the other way, right?" Tommy asked.

"Yup, TK, I think Mexico would be the better bet for him."

"I was never good in geography." Tommy laughed and added, "Damn, this whole thing would already be over if Ponch and John were still on the force."

"Yeah, followed with some real bad, cheesy joke at the end of the chase scene like, 'I guess we scored a touchdown on this one, John.'" Dermot joined in, but then shook his head from side to side. "Goddamn it. Molloy's going to give me so much crap when I see him."

"Why's that?"

"I spent all yesterday afternoon on my soap box telling him how I thought OJ was innocent."

"Yeah, well, if it makes you feel any better, I thought that too when I first heard about it, but this chase now seals the deal. Guilty as fucking sin. But Derm, you know what sucks most about this whole thing?"

"No, what?"

"We can never watch *The Naked Gun* the same way again."

"Shit, you're right."

"Damn, remember the time your parents went on that trip to Bermuda and you had to take care of Colin for the week, so we rented a bunch of movies? I remember the first one was *Naked Gun* and we watched it with him, Matt, and Paul."

Dermot chuckled. "Yeah, the best part was right before we put it on, Clay told them *Naked Gun* was a gay porno."

"Yeah, their eyes practically popped out their heads. But man, did we all laugh our asses off that night . . . really . . . we all laughed that whole week eating junk food and watching movies. God, *Naked Gun* was a classic and now fucking OJ Nordberg has ruined it for future generations."

Dermot sighed. He took a sip from his beer and stayed transfixed on the set for as long as the drama lasted. On the other side of the screen, Houston pulled away 91–82 and not one person outside of Texas cared. The chase ended with OJ surrendering by handing over his gun to the cops and collapsing in grief on his doorstep.

Clay knocked on the door. "Did you hear about OJ?" Tommy asked him, excited to break the story.

Clay glanced over at the TV and said, "Oh, he finally pulled over and surrendered?"

"Wait," Dermot said, "you mean to tell me you didn't watch the whole chase."

"What's wrong with you, man?" Tommy added.

"I watched some of it, but I was in a hurry. I had to get here before you two walked over to Pucky's or something. I need you guys to do me a favor."

"What?" Dermot asked.

"Wait," Tommy broke in, "Why the hell are you wearing those hideous khakis and that nasty T.J. Maxx wanna-be polo shirt? And I might add, you smell like the fucking sailor from that Old Spice commercial."

"Screw you, TK. It's Nautica, man. It's good stuff. And yes, you might have an argument with the pants, but this polo shirt is the real-deal, Holyfield. I need to look good tonight 'cause I was invited to a party, and I came here for my wingmen."

"Aw, Clay, I'm not in the mood," Dermot said.

"Don't listen to him. Where's it at?" Tommy jumped in.

"In a minute. Let me tell you who invited me first. Do you remember Meri Nazarian?"

Dermot and Tommy exchanged glances and said, "Ah, no."

"Wait," Dermot snapped his fingers. "Nazarian? Her dad, Noah, owns Coffee Mania. I like him. Knows his movie trivia. Good man."

"Yeah," Clay replied excitedly, "and her little sister Natalie works there."

"Oh, yeah, I know Natalie. She likes to write. I didn't know that was Noah's daughter. Anyway, she's cool. Knows everyone's order. Pretty girl and a nice kid, too. But I have no memory of a Meri." Dermot shook his head.

"Okay … moving on. Do you remember senior year when I kept buying Girl Scout cookies at the booth outside the Silver Shores Supermarket."

"Yeah, we thought you just had a thing for thin mints, but then we found out you had a crush on that little eighth-grader," Dermot began.

"Yeah, the one with the long black hair who was always there. Talk about a cradle robber," Tommy added.

"I *do* love thin mints and I didn't have a crush on her. I just said she was cute once, just like Dermot just said about her sister and you guys were all over me."

"Whatever, Clay," Tommy said. "You'd always find a way to mention her every time you bought those cookies. Shit, if we turned your perverted ass in back then, you'd probably be wearing the silver bracelets with OJ right now playing 'honey hide the football.'"

"Anyway, Meri no longer has long hair. It's short now and she's no longer a little girl. And I might add, she's no longer cute."

"Okay, so if she's no longer cute, what's your point?" Dermot asked the question for both of them.

"My point is . . ." Clay paused and smiled. "She's not cute. She's fucking hot. I mean smoking hot, *and* a few hours ago, she invited me to a party."

"Whoa, I need another beer for this story. You guys in?" Tommy pointed at them.

"Yeah, sure." Dermot nodded.

"None for me. I'm going to drive you guys there," Clay said.

"Wow, Clay is actually volunteering to be the D.D. This Meri chick must be a friggin' ten if Mr. 'I have only three dollars to my name' is actually going to use his own gas!" Tommy exclaimed.

Clay ignored him and turned to Dermot, "She *is* a ten but, Derm, I know you'll appreciate this story. This morning I was running along the bike path when . . ."

"Wait a second!" Tommy hollered from the other room and then appeared with the beers.

"What?" Clay asked.

"I already don't believe you. *You* were running. Come on, Mr. Clayhead, that alone is Fantasy Island. I'm Mr. Roarke and you're little Tatoo, and Tatoo's not supposed to have any fantasies that come true." Tommy patted Clay's stomach, then flipped the beer cap off and took a swig.

"Stop being a dick and could you just shut the fuck up and let me tell the story, asshole?"

"Yeah, come on, Tommy. Let him talk," Dermot said.

Tommy put his surrender hands up and said, "All right, Mr. Eight Balls, go ahead."

"Okay, well anyway, I *have* been running a lot, so I can lose those LB's and hopefully get full-time status on the department. So I was running along the bike path and who comes rollerblading my way wearing a Silver Shores Lifeguard half-shirt, red spandex shorts, and a baseball cap, but the girl I used to buy Girl Scout cookies from. But like I mentioned . . ."

"*As* I mentioned." As the son of an English teacher, Dermot couldn't help himself.

Clay looked at him annoyed. "*As* I mentioned, she's all grown up now and looks absolutely amazing."

"Can one of you guys tell me what it is about a girl in a baseball hat that turns me on so much?" Tommy interrupted.

"That's easy, TK. Think about it," Dermot replied. "The two greatest loves of men are women and baseball; if you put a woman in a baseball hat it's like having the two best worlds collide, so it's natural for you to be turned on. I know it turns *me* on."

"Wow," Tommy said. "That's so true. Of course, Dermot, I don't think your theory still flies if the chick wearing the hat is a four-hundred-pound lesbian softball player or something like that."

"Okay, Seinfeld and Kramer, can I continue?" Clay asked.

"Go ahead, George," they both answered without missing a beat.

"At this point, I just think it's a hot girl, but then the closer she gets, I realize it's the Girl Scout girl. So I turn my Walkman to low as I jog toward her, and I say hi, and she smiles and mouths *hi*. But it looks like she's really into her music, so I just blurt out as I pass, 'God, why can't I get a girl like you?' But then I continue on. Story over, right?"

"Usually," Dermot and Tommy said in unison.

"Exactly, but about five minutes later, I'm listening to my Walkman and I have to admit I could only get that new goddamn soft rock station. So, you know, I'm running by the ocean, and I start humming to a song and pretty soon I'm singing along to it. Okay. I'm going to admit this. It was 'Sailing' by Christopher Cross."

"The guy who sings 'Arthur's Theme'?" Dermot screeched.

"Yeah, it's not really a bad song. I mean, especially since I was running by the ocean. I gotta say, the guy does capture the feel of it all."

"Jesus, Mary, and Joseph, as Grandma Keating would say!" Tommy said, crossing himself.

Clay laughed. "I know, TK, I hear you, and it gets worse. I actually got into the song, so I was singing it pretty loud. You know that song, 'Sailing.' He began singing.

"Yeah, we know the song." Tommy gave a stop sign with his left hand.

"Yeah, so as I ran along looking at the ocean singing it and actually dreaming about the girl I just saw, I feel the tap on my shoulder. I look behind me and it's her, Meri, my Girl Scout girl!"

"Oh shit! How friggin embarrassing. So what did she want? For you to shut the fuck up?" Tommy asked.

"Now, I have your attention." Clay smiled at him. "Well, of course, I'm really frazzled because I'm thinking she probably just heard me. But instead, she pointed at my shirt."

Dermot interrupted. "Please don't tell me that FIREMEN CARRY THE BIGGEST HOSES shirt actually worked on her?"

"No, the Chief told me to stop wearing that one, but that's another story. I was wearing a Silver Shores Firefighter Reserves T-shirt. So she says to me, 'Hi again, I don't mean to interrupt you, but as I was rollerblading by I noticed your T-shirt.' 'Oh, yeah,' I say back to her thinking thank God she didn't hear me singing. 'So, you're a firefighter?' she asks me. And I stumbled through my answer, saying that I was in the guard and I'm not officially one yet, but I'm in training and all that shit. Well, it turns out she thinks that's the coolest thing in the world because her uncle is a firefighter in New York City and when she was little, she would always go there for the Paddy's parade and he'd let her ride on the fire engine and all that kind of stuff. So I tell her how my uncle let me do the same thing when I was a kid, but I'd go up to Southie."

"I don't get it. Your Italian uncle is a firefighter in Southie?" Tommy asked.

"Yeah, I thought your uncle was a big time Wall Street guy like Gordon Gekko?" Dermot's brow raised.

"He is." Clay smiled.

"Well, it's good to see you and this girl are starting out in an honest relationship," Dermot said sarcastically.

Clay brushed off the comment and continued. "So after we talked some more, she tells me her name is Meri Nazarian."

"Did you tell her your real name or why we nicknamed you *Clay?*" Dermot asked.

"No, man. I hate Benny. I just told her my name is Clay. Too early for why you assholes call me that. Anyway, Meri then invites me to a party at her parents' house tonight, but the best part of the story is right as I was jogging away she yells real sweet and cute to me, 'Hey, Clay,' and I turn and say, 'What,' and she smiles and yells, 'I just wanted you to know that I love Christopher Cross, too, and you have a real lovely singing voice.' Can you believe that shit? She actually heard me singing that song and she was being all cute with me. I mean, Dermot, I knew you'd appreciate that. That's a 100 percent movie stuff there, man."

"It is. That's a good story, Clay man." Trying not to remember his first encounter with Francesca, Dermot sipped his beer.

"So, guys, that's why I'm here. I gotta go to this party, but I need my wingmen or this will end up a one-and-done story. You know it's true. It's mid-June and you know by the end of the month she'll have guys flying to her like . . ."

"Moths to a bug zapper." Dermot filled in the sentence.

"Exactly. If I don't strike while the iron is hot, she'll probably end up dating some Tom Cruise bottle-tossing bartender, or worse, one of those muscle-head Cape League ballplayers. Sorry, Tommy, but you know what I'm talking about with that one."

"Huh?" Tommy faked ignorance.

"Remember a few summers ago when that fat catcher stayed for the summer at your parents' house and he ended up stealing that girl you were seeing."

"The term is *dating*. I was *dating* her. And gee, no, Clay, that whole traumatic episode in my life somehow slipped my mind. Thanks for reminding me."

"What was that guy's name again?" Dermot thought out loud.

"Craig George," Tommy spat.

Dermot remembered their old saying and snapped his fingers. "That's right. Never trust a guy with two first names."

"Yeah, Derm, like I . . . I mean *as* I told you the other night we all have our battle wounds. God, I remember how that prick drove into town in his flashy red Dodge Stealth blasting "I Wanna Sex You Up" by Color Me Badd. He was draped in thick, gold chains, and wearing neon green

Hammer-time pants straight from his high school Chess King collection. At first, since he was staying at our house for free, he was all cool to me and my parents, saying we were like family to him and he'd remember us all when he made it to the show. But then he hit a few homeruns, and the next thing I know he's grand slamming my girl behind the Silver Shores Pirates concession stand."

"Day-night doubleheader is what I heard," Dermot said.

"Yeah, the bitch," Tommy growled.

"It was that waitress from The Sand Bar. Her name was Addison or Adrienne or something like that, right?" Dermot asked.

"Yeah, it's Adrienne, but now the ho is known as Mrs. George, the wife of the fat catcher with the bad knees who bats seventh with a buck eighty-two average for the Tigres Capitalinos."

"Who are they?" Clay asked.

"They're in the Mexican League," Tommy replied.

"Well, at least you're not keeping tabs on her. Damn, TK, too bad the Juice *didn't* drive to Mexico!" Dermot laughed.

"Believe me. I was hoping that earlier." Tommy sighed.

"Okay, TK's situation is a terrible reality, but that is also my point. If I don't act now, some fat catcher is going to block home plate and tag my girl! That's why I need help. Are you guys in?" Clay pleaded.

Tommy looked at Dermot and answered, "It's not even a question, bro."

"We're your boys, of course we're in." Dermot smiled.

TEN

The laughter echoed as Clay, Tommy, and Dermot sang and tapped along to DaDa's "Here Today, Gone Tomorrow." How could there not be laughter? Clay had allowed Tommy and Dermot to bring road sodas and was driving them to a party where *supposedly* a bunch of drunken chicks were waiting. The '88 black Cadillac Fleetwood, an aging high school graduation gift from Clay's Wall Street uncle, rolled slowly along Bell Buoy Avenue in search of Meri Nazerian's parents' house. Even though they were a little lost, their spirits were high because if the worst case scenario occurred and it *did* turn out to be a "sausage fest," Tommy reminded Dermot they were still armed with the ultimate icebreaker for what few women were there.

"All we say to them is, 'Did you see that shit with OJ tonight?' Either way, we're in. Derm, to use the Juice's terminology, how can we *not* score a touchdown with that approach?"

"So, Tommy," Dermot leaned over the front seat, "let me get something straight. You want us to use a vicious double homicide, which also involved the downfall of an American icon, as our lead-in to get laid tonight?"

Tommy paused. "Well . . . since you put it that way . . ." And then he laughed. "Ab-so-fucking-lutely . . . That doesn't make me a bad guy, does it?"

"You're ridiculous." Dermot chuckled as Tommy grinned. "Hey Clayhead, there's a line of cars in front of that big-ass blue house up ahead. That's gotta be it."

"Yup, I see it." Clay nodded and continued on, while Dermot looked over at the cars and didn't like what he saw.

"Ah, shit. Look at all the Jeeps," he said.

Clay eyed the backseat from the rearview mirror. "What's wrong with Jeeps?"

Tommy answered for Dermot. "All the little rich summer punks drive Jeeps, playing their fucking Jimmy Buffet and acting like they were the ones who discovered him. It's a Cape Cod tradition."

"Yeah, and most of them are lifeguards. This better not be a lifeguard party, Clay. Lifeguards are the worst," Dermot added.

"Your brother's a lifeguard and he's a fucking great kid," Clay said.

"*Was* a lifeguard. And he *was* a fucking great kid. Not so sure anymore. I've heard the whispers his shit continued while I was away." Their silence confirmed what he didn't want to know.

Clay parked behind a gray Jeep covered in Phish and MITCH BUCHANON FOR PRESIDENT bumper stickers.

Finally Tommy found a reason to perk up. "Jeez, look at that. Mitch Buchannon? Isn't that who Hasselhof plays on *Baywatch*?"

"Yup," Clay said. "Okay, Derm is right. I gotta admit that's pretty gay. Not P-town gay. Just gay."

"Almost as gay as a guy who wears a shirt that says FIREMAN CARRY THE BIGGEST HOSES. You never did say why the chief told you to stop wearing it," Tommy said.

"Yeah, what *did* he say?" Dermot jumped in, back in the moment.

"Bring your empties," Clay ordered as they got out of the car. "Well, first the chief said until I put out a real fire I have no right wearing that shirt."

"Well, he's got a point," Tommy said.

"Yeah, I know, he's right, but then the asshole added, in front of all the other guys, that even if I put out one bigger than the friggin Chicago fire of 1871, I still shouldn't wear that shirt."

"Why?" Dermot asked.

"Because he said he's seen me in the shower."

Tommy, who was downing his last sip, sprayed it onto the road, as Dermot and he broke into hysterical, contagious laughter. They kept laughing as they walked across the lawn to the front door.

"Yeah, he's a dick." Clay laughed in spite of himself before walking up the front step.

Two lanky kids around nineteen or twenty wearing popped-collar polo shirts and matching white shorts stood with their arms folded, looking like wannabe bouncers, minus the muscles.

"Sorry, guys." The one wearing the blue polo stopped them. "This is a private party."

Clay stepped forward. "Yeah, I know. We were invited."

"By who?" Red Polo asked.

"By Meri."

The two bouncers looked at one another for a second and then Blue Polo took the lead. "I think you're at the wrong party, guys."

"We're at the right place. Just go tell Meri that Clay is here."

"Meri's in the backyard. She doesn't have time to come check on everybody who tries to crash her party."

"This is fucking bullshit," Tommy said.

Clay tried to stay calm. "Look, man, she invited me personally."

"I don't know about that. I've never seen you before. What's Meri's last name and I might believe you?" Blue Polo asked.

"*Might* believe me." Clay laughed and turned to Dermot and Tommy. "Can you believe this shit?"

"Actually, I can," Dermot said.

"What's that supposed to mean?" Red Polo asked in a threatening tone, moving forward.

Dermot didn't back down. "It means he's a dick and so are you."

Red Polo thumbed over his shoulder. "Look. Graham and I are rolling with six deep for backup in there. You keep it up, I'll call my boys and we'll be popping some heads in no time."

Dermot wasn't fazed. He wanted the conflict. "It seems, Country Club, the only thing you can pop is that collar."

"Fuck you."

"Yeah, fuck me. Great." Dermot continued, "By the way, while you're popping heads, you might also want to try to pop some of the ones on your face!"

Tommy laughed and pointed at the kid's dotted face. "You're right about that, Derm. He looks like the before picture in an Oxy commercial."

Instinctively, Red Polo put his hand to his face while the Blue Polo named Graham gave a "calm down" gesture with his hands.

"Hey, guys, take it easy. We were asked to watch the door and collect for the keg. That's all. We don't want any trouble. You say you know Meri, so that's cool with us." He turned behind him and grabbed three cups off a small table by the door and handed the cups to them.

"That's thirty bucks."

"What?" Clay gasped.

"Thirty bucks?" Dermot and Colin echoed.

"Our parties are about class. First rule of business. You charge ten bucks a keg cup, you'll weed out the riffraff. Isn't that right, Myles?" Graham turned to his buddy.

"Damn straight." Myles nodded.

"This is ridiculous," Dermot said. "Let's cut bait while we can and get a few pints at Pucky's. I still haven't been there this summer, and I'm sure Pucky's pissed about that."

"Yeah, I'm with you, Derm. I mean, for ten bucks each we should be getting free table dances with our drinks," Tommy added.

"Hey, I'm not forcing you fellas to stay." Graham smiled and reached to retrieve the cups.

"Wait a second," Clay said to him and turned to the boys. "Come on. I don't ask much. I need you guys."

Tommy and Dermot looked at one another, still trying to decide.

"C'mon," Clay pleaded. "She approached me. Remember? She thought it was cute that I was singing Christopher Cross. Dermot, I thought you'd at least appreciate that considering your Air Supply moment with Francesca last summer."

"Jesus, Clay!" Tommy snapped.

"It's okay. Really, it's okay. In the end it will be his funeral." Dermot reached into his pocket and pulled out a twenty to hand to Graham. "You got change?"

"Actually," Clay interrupted, "Derm, can you cover me?"

Dermot laughed. "Yeah, let me guess, you only have three dollars to your name?"

"Five." Clay smiled. "I'll get you back."

Tommy followed by hastily handing over a ten to Graham and said, "Clay, you owe me ten, too. Whatever happened to five dollars and two kegs in the woods behind the movie theater?"

"Like I said, fellas, we're about class."

"*As* I said." The three corrected Graham.

"Yeah, whatever. Now put your hands out."

Not thinking, all three extended their right hands and Myles pressed a blue stamp on them.

Dermot looked down. "What's this symbol?"

"It's a parrot," Myles answered.

"Oh, is the blue parrot from the restaurant in *Casablanca*?" Dermot asked.

"What? No, man. It's in honor of Buffet. Buffet rules!" Myles howled.

"This is a lifeguard party, huh?" Tommy said as he headed into the house.

"Damn straight," Graham replied.

"So, I guess we're damn straight then," Tommy mocked and then turned to Clay. "You seriously owe us, man."

They walked through the living room and couldn't help but stop and watch the scene in front of them. Three guys barely twenty, blitzed out of their minds, using golf clubs as makeshift guitars or microphones. All three were screaming along to "Two Princes" by The Spin Doctors, which was blaring on the stereo. Clay cupped his hands and yelled, "Where's Meri?"

The lead singer, who had a clove cigarette dangling from his mouth, didn't answer; he just pointed his club to the door in front of him.

"That scene was wrong on so many levels," Dermot said, before following Clay and Tommy through the doorway.

Tommy and Clay nodded in agreement before continuing on to face what was on the other side of the door. A laughing group of four guys and three girls sitting around the table were playing the drinking game Hi or Low. They stopped their game, looking up at Dermot and his crew as if they were aliens invading their planet.

"Is Meri around?" Clay asked.

"Well, yeah, it *is* her house." One of the girls snapped her gum at them.

"Yeah, I know. Could you tell me where she is?"

"She's out back, dude." A much friendlier guy pointed at the sliding door leading to the sundeck.

"Thanks, man," the three of them responded and headed for the deck.

"Hey, are you Colin Brennan's brother?" he asked.

In dread, Dermot turned around. "Yeah, why?"

"No reason, really. I was a guard with the C-Dog last year. He's a great guy. Probably the best swimming teacher on the Cape."

"Really?"

"Oh, yeah. The kids loved him, especially the little ones. He was always so patient with them."

"Yeah?"

"Oh, yeah, man! He was like a god to them. Anyway, when you see him tell him his boy Billy McCarthy said to quit that shoe store job and get his ass back to the beach. That's where he belongs."

"I will . . . Hey, it was cool to meet you, Billy."

"You too, Dermot."

Dermot looked at him surprised. "How'd you know my name?"

"Aw, shit, man, the C-Dog talked about you all the time. Says you're going to be a famous writer someday." Billy turned to the girls. "See this guy. He's got some serious talent. He even had a few of his stories published in a big time magazine up in Boston."

The table now seemed to look at Dermot differently, and he tried to suppress a grin. *The Beacon*, the so-called "big time magazine," was a monthly seven-page underground newspaper run by some old-school hippie Dermot had met at a poetry slam at the Middle East in Cambridge. He had even helped distribution by skipping classes, hopping on the T, and hocking the paper. He had hoped that his stories on war is bad, homelessness is bad, racism is bad, etc., would change the views of those rare businessmen who'd flip him a quarter. He quickly realized most of them were only buying *The Beacon* so that they could have something to rest their Dunkin Donuts' coffees on in order to keep their suits clean.

Feeling like a celebrity, Dermot nodded good-bye to Billy and the whole table waved as he headed outside to the jammed sundeck and backyard. Clay led them through the crowd with Tommy making comments under his breath about the surprisingly promising ratio of girls to guys. Dermot wasn't listening, though; he was now thinking about his brother. Colin had never directly spoken to him about the articles in *The Beacon*, but he now knew Colin had talked to others—like a proud brother. That knowledge alone made him feel really good. What made him feel great was what Billy said about Colin. But that was *then*, and this was *now*, and now meant his brother was no longer motivating little kids to swim the crawl to the marker and back. Instead, he was hastily lacing up their sneakers before taking smoke breaks in the back alley behind the dumpster.

The last time he had tried counseling his brother was just before he had left for Ireland. Dermot had been walking along the cold, winter beach late at night listening to "Tomorrow" by U2, wallowing in his own melancholic thoughts when he heard someone shouting from the jetties. He turned off the Walkman and hurried to the jetties. When he got close, he realized it was Colin, blind drunk, shouting incoherently at the sea.

"Dermot! Dermot!"

"Oh, ah, yeah." He looked up to see Clay, Tommy, and a beautiful girl with dark hair and darker eyes all staring at him. He went from one trance to another as he checked her out. She was wearing a white tank top that complemented her "look at me" breasts and Nantucket red shorts that highlighted her long, tanned legs.

Clay snapped his fingers in Dermot's face. "Are you with us?"

"Oh, yeah." He nodded. "Yeah, sure."

"Well, *as* I was saying, this is Meri." Clay moved his eyes down to her outstretched hand and back up to Dermot and gave him a "dumbass, shake her hand" look.

"Oh, yeah, sorry." He put his hand out, and Meri took it.

"Nice to meet you." She smiled and put her keg cup back in her right hand and then took a sip.

"I know your sister. We hang out now and then," Dermot blurted.

"Isn't she a little young for you?" Meri laughed.

"Huh? Oh, I mean I know her from the coffee shop."

"No, I'm kidding. I know you do. She says you're real nice and you guys talk about writing a lot. You see." She turned her smile back to Clay. "I've done a little research on you and your crew, Mr. Pelligrini."

"You have, have you?" Clay smiled.

"Oh, yes, I have, *Benny*."

"Benny? Classic!" Tommy laughed, clapping his hands.

"Yes, I found out his real name," she said to Tommy and then turned to Clay, "but my sources failed me when I wanted to know why everyone calls you Clay."

"Busted." Tommy laughed again.

"Aw, geez. You might not get this, because you're a little younger than us," Clay said, "but when the three of us were kids, there was a show on Sunday mornings called *Davey and Goliath*. And . . ."

"Oh, my God! The show with the claymation people?" she interrupted.

"Yeah," all three of them answered.

"I used to love that show. Oh, wow. I haven't thought about it for years. Do you remember the Easter episode?" she asked.

Again, all three answered at once, "When Davey's Grandmother dies."

"Yeah, that was so sad. I had major waterworks!" Meri said and took another sip from her cup.

"Yeah, they still show it at like five in the morning on Easter and every time I still bawl my eyes out. I probably shouldn't admit that, huh?" Clay said while Dermot bit his lip, thinking, *Or if you do say it, at least give me the credit!* It wasn't an original statement. A few Easters before Dermot had admitted that same fact line for line to his boys and got a good laugh.

Meri's voice lowered, "Vulnerability is a very attractive quality."

Of course it is attractive when it comes to everybody else! But when it comes to me it's pathetic! Dermot kept his smile and tried not to let his anger show.

"But from that story, I still don't understand how you got the name Clay."

With his right hand, Clay gave Tommy the go-ahead to finish the story. Tommy stepped forward. "Well, Meri, back when we were kids, his hair looked just like Davey's hair. It still does, kind of. It was so flat and matted down, so I started calling him *Clayhead*."

Meri laughed.

"Yeah, Benny hated his name, so, of course, like the good friends we are, we kept calling him Clayhead, but eventually, we got lazy and over the years it shortened to Clay. In the long run, I actually think the nickname has worked out for the bastard."

"Yeah, I definitely like *Clay* better than *Benny*." She nodded in agreement.

"Yeah," Dermot said, "it's also been good for us, too, because when we were kids Clay's mom used to call us Benny and the Jets, like the Elton John song, and of course she would always have to sing it."

"What does his mom call you guys now? The Clayheads?" she asked.

"Nope. She only calls us when she wants to . . ." Tommy put the brakes on his mother joke just before it was fineable and turned to Dermot. "Okay, hey, let's leave these two kids to chat and hit that keg."

"Sounds good to me," Dermot said and followed him off the deck to a barrel that rested against a tree. They filled up their cups and were tempted to join the Name Game being played beside them, but when it got to the *D*'s and the name Danny Pintauro, former costar of *Who's The Boss?* was thrown out, they decided there was a more-pressing matter to investigate: Clay hanging out with a hot chick. They settled into two lawn chairs within earshot of Clay and Meri's conversation and homed in.

They had grown up watching Clay constantly strike out with girls, and they could hardly believe their eyes and ears. Meri was all over him. She'd say something. He'd reply with a not-so-funny line, but she'd tilt her head back, howl, and give him a lover's tap.

Clay's beeper suddenly went off. He scanned it and jumped to his feet. Dermot and Tommy couldn't hear what he said to Meri, but whatever it was caused her to plant a kiss on the side of his face. He smiled and walked over to them.

"What the hell was that?" Tommy pointed at Clay's cheek.

"Oh, the kiss." He looked over and waved to Meri as she walked off toward the name-gamers. "She said I'd get a real one on the lips tomorrow, but for now, that is something for me to dream about. Turns out she had her Walkman off when she rollerbladed by and heard me say all that shit about why can't I get a girl like her. She thought it was real sweet and genuine. Plus, she had seen my shirt. I don't know what it is, but she really has a thing for firefighters, and as luck would have it, boys, my beeper just told me I have my very first fire to go put out. So I gotta burn."

"Shit, I hope not," Dermot said, and they laughed.

"I hear you there, Derm. I hate to leave you guys without a ride, but seriously, I gotta go."

"No, problem. Be careful, bro." They both gave him handshakes, and he was gone in seconds.

Dermot and Tommy were still mystified by what they had just witnessed.

Tommy finally spoke. "I don't get it. I know he's our boy and all, but she's like a ten."

"I know. I know. Maybe it's like one of those evil teen movies where she has to date him to get into a sorority or some shit."

"You got that right, man. It *is* like a movie. Derm, maybe that's something you could write about."

"But no one would believe it. Not even John Hughes."

"Shit, you got that one right, too."

They both laughed, but then Dermot felt a tap on his shoulder.

"Excuse me. Did you say John Hughes?"

"Huh?" Smiling, he turned, but the smile instantly became a dropped-jaw expression when he saw the face behind the interruption. If Meri had been a ten, the girl he was now looking at was that times two, and add one for exclamation. It was impossible to process all of her beauty casually because the first thing he noticed was her curly, blonde hair. Probably due to past rejections, Dermot had never been into blondes, but that curly blonde hair that she twirled like a schoolgirl at a sock hop followed with the coy smile she threw at him gave her an old-fashioned look.

Old fashioned, Dermot thought, *like Marilyn Monroe wrapped in a bed sheet.*

"I'm sorry but I thought you were talking about John Hughes as in the guy who did *Pretty In Pink*?"

It was appropriate she was talking about pink, considering she was wearing a pink tank top and licked her pink lip gloss like it was cotton candy dissolving in her mouth.

A quick memory about cotton candy tried to force its way into Dermot's consciousness, but he was able to shut it out by focusing on her emerald eyes.

"Oh, yeah," he finally managed. "And don't forget he also did *Sixteen Candles.*"

"Yeah, he did them all in the eighties. *Breakfast Club, Ferris Bueller's Day Off,* but my all-time favorite was *Some Kind Of Wonderful.* I love that scene at the end when Eric Stoltz realizes his true love was right in front of him all along. It's so romantic."

He managed a quick glance at her long, tanned legs that matched her tan shorts before answering.

"Yeah, but let's face it, in real life Eric Stoltz's character would've gone for his friend Watts two minutes into the movie."

"And he probably would've lasted only two minutes," Tommy jumped in, breaking up the moment.

Dermot expected embarrassment, but the girl laughed for a minute before putting her hand out to Dermot. "My name is Tabitha and my friend coming over here is Jessica." As if she had been waiting in the wings, a-six-beer girl with dark brown hair came over to them.

What Jessica lacked in looks she tried to make up for by wearing an open, low-cut blue blouse displaying her cleavage. She reminded Dermot of a secretary ripped straight out of the pages of a Mickey Spillane book. He laughed, thinking how much his dad, the English teacher, would've liked that over-the-top description.

"What's so funny?" Tabitha asked.

"Oh, nothing," he said, finally letting go of her hand.

"So, are you going to tell me?"

"Tell you what?"

"What your name is."

"Oh, sorry, I've had a few. I'm Dermot and this is my buddy Tommy."

"Yeah, I'm Tommy, and I'm thirsty. You girls need another."

"I'm all set for now." Tabitha kept her eyes on Dermot.

Jessica wiggled her empty cup. "Actually, I'll go with you."

Tommy gave her a quick survey. "Works for me."

When it came to trying to split up couples for alone time, "Who needs another beer" was one of the oldest lines in the book, but it worked. Tommy and Dermot suppressed their smiles and nodded, "Later," to one another, knowing they both had women on their hooks, and it was time to reel them in. That was always the hardest part for Dermot and, because of it, he froze, bringing an uncomfortable silence to the scene.

"So I heard your friend talking. He mentioned something about writing. Are you a writer?" Tabitha served the first volley.

"Ah, yeah."

"Do you write books?"

"Well, ah no, not yet."

"Oh, so are you like a journalist or something?"

"Well, I did work this winter for a newspaper in Ireland."

"In Ireland! How cool! Was it tough work?"

"Well . . ." He paused, but then Gary Molloy's voice screamed in his head. *This summer do me a favor and lie to the women a little. Just a little.* "Well, yeah, it was tough work. I was in charge of writing most of the articles. I was also in charge of making the distribution process run effectively. There are some serious topics to cover over there and sometimes I actually met up with the subjects I was covering."

"Wow, that must've been dangerous!" She moved closer.

"At times, it *was* dangerous."

Dermot wasn't exactly lying to Tabitha. He *did* work for a paper for two months writing articles. As far as helping the distribution process run effectively, he used a rickety, old black bike that had a wicker basket to hold the papers. He'd ride along the cobblestone streets tossing the latest edition into subscribers' yards. Technically, Dermot was also telling the truth about meeting the subjects he covered. He met the menacing Mr. Cork in a dark alley just a day after he wrote the article about him being on the loose. The County Commissioner's missing cat, Mr. Cork, clawed Dermot's face before taking him on a high-speed bike chase through town. It looked hopeless until Dermot was able to corral him with the help of a tenacious Australian sheepdog with the highly unoriginal name of Lassie. It had made a great headline, though: "Lassie Returns To Save Cork."

"Yes." He tried to sound edgy and reflective. "At times it really *was* dangerous. But, now I'm home working my old job at the *Island Ferry* parking lot and spending the summer figuring out my next move. How about you?"

"I'm just waiting tables down here for the summer. I'm actually going to be a senior at Emerson. I major in theatre, but I like to write, too, but my thing is screenplays. It's my minor. You know, like movie scripts."

"No, way." Dermot waved his hands in excitement. "I've thought of that myself. I love movies."

"Even old ones? 'Cause those are my favorites."

He thought he was going to faint.

Holy shit! This is my dream girl!

"I was brought up on old movies. My dad teaches English, but in the summer he teaches a film appreciation class at Cape Cod Community College. He has practically fed my brother and me movies like they were cereal."

"So what kind of old movies do you like, Dermot?"

Hearing her say his name, Dermot knew that he was actually doing well. *Don't blow it!*

"I like them all," he said. "From John Wayne to Hitchcock to everything in-between."

"Even the romantic ones?"

"Of course, *Casablanca* is one of my all-time favorites."

"Everyone loves that one. I'm talking about the ones people forget like *The Philadelphia Story.*"

Okay, I really am in heaven!

Without missing a beat, he said, "Katherine Hepburn, Cary Grant, and Jimmy Stewart. Here's one for you, Tabitha. *September Affair.*"

"What a movie! I wish they could've stayed on Capri forever . . . let me think here. Who was in that? Um, Joan Fontaine, Jessica Tandy, and the guy from *Citizen Kane.* What was his name?"

"Joseph Cotton," Dermot answered.

"Wow." She looked at him wide-eyed. "I'm impressed."

"You're impressed? I've never met . . ."

"Tabby! Tabby!" one of the name-gamers yelled over.

"What, Liz?"

The girl gave the hand signal for smoking and said, "I need smokes and rolling papers. Can you drive me to 7-Eleven?"

Tabitha rolled her eyes at Dermot and turned to her friend. "Sure."

"Oh, and we gotta still pick up Randy, too."

"Oh, yeah, that's right." Tabitha put her hand on Dermot's forearm. "Are you still going to be here in about an hour or so?"

Of course I am!

"Ah, yeah, I think so."

"Oh, good. We'll finish up where we left off. I'll meet you by the keg in an hour or so." She smiled and followed her friend through the crowd, leaving Dermot glowing with hope.

He was about to take a victory sip from his keg cup and then thought better of it. *I can't get drunk! I refuse to drink myself out of the game!* After emptying the beer onto the grass, he tossed the cup into a barrel and headed for the mixed-drinks table to grab a Coke, but stopped when he saw the manager of Coffee Mania, Jeff, with his guitar serenading a double-fisted girl. The girl seemed to be in a trance, and as she stared at Jeff, she took turns drinking from each of her cups. The sight intrigued Dermot because he wasn't sure if it was the booze or Jeff's singing that caused her hypnotic state, so he stopped and lingered in the background to listen.

Jeff strummed away and after a minute of listening, Dermot decided it was a little bit of both, because the manager did sing a pretty decent version of R.E.M.'s melodic "Night Swimming."

When the song ended, Jeff leaned in to the girl and said smoothly, "That one was for you."

"Oh, my God!" the girl shrieked. "That was like so awesome! Is that like an original?"

"Well . . ." Jeff paused and looked around to see if anyone was listening, and when his eyes met with Dermot's, they begged, *Please, don't sell me out!*

Dermot responded with a thin smile and walked away. In the distance, he could hear Jeff saying, "Yeah, of course it's an original. Why? Do you think it's okay?"

When Dermot got to the table, he heard a voice call his name. He turned around and it was fifteen-year-old Natalie Nazerian. He tried not to check her out in her blue sundress swaying in the breeze, but his eyes finally won out, and he glanced quickly up and down. His brain screamed, *Pervert!* Fortunately, Natalie had no clue, or if she did, she didn't let on.

"What are you doing here?" he asked.

"Well, I do *live* here." She laughed, but added as he looked at her keg cup, "Don't worry. This is just caffeine. I thought I'd need it, considering this party looks like it's not going to end any time soon. It's *so* like my sister not to give me a heads up so I could sleep over a friend's house. But never mind me. I have to say I'm very upset with you, Mr. Brennan."

"Why's that?"

"We had some great chats last winter before your trip to Ireland, and now you're back and you haven't been into Coffee Mania to tell me about it. So, how was it? Did you leave a pen at James Joyce's grave for good luck? Did you see any shows at The Abbey Theatre? How about Newgrange? I know you wanted to hit there."

"Well, you got a half hour?" He laughed.

She looked around and said, "With all these drunks lurking about I have all night."

For the next forty minutes or so, Dermot told Natalie every story he could remember without embellishments. She was an active participant, listening and then asking meaningful questions. The girl had an old soul. Dermot was in the middle of his "How I Gave My Island Princess Baseball Hat to the Japanese Girl" story when he was interrupted by a drunken Tommy.

"Hey, sorry to interrupt, but I need to talk to Derm."

"That's okay." Natalie smiled. "I probably should try to get some sleep. See you later, Dermot. It was great talking with you."

"You too, Natalie."

When Natalie left, Tommy said, "Ah, fuck, man. I cock-blocked you."

"How?"

"With the girl." Tommy pointed at Natalie walking away.

"Man, that's Natalie from the coffee shop."

"Oh, shit, then I saved your ass from being a registered sex offender."

"No, you hammered dumb-ass, we were just talking."

"Okay, Derm." Tommy gave him a sarcastic pat on the shoulder. "Anyway, I'm heading out. You're going to have to get your own ride home, man."

"Why are you taking off? I thought you were hanging out with Tabitha's friend."

"I am. *Jessica*, I think that's her name, didn't come with your girl, so maybe you have a shot at a ride home, too," Tommy answered, but had his attention on making another Captain and Coke.

"No, shit. That Jessica chick is driving you home."

"After we go for a midnight swim."

"Dude, you've been drinking."

"Don't worry, man. I'm going to do the-party-guy-in-*Jaws*-who-falls-down-on-the-beach routine. You know that's my patented move."

"Yes, it is. Wow, first Clay and now you. And guess what, that Tabitha girl totally blew me away. She's so cool, and Tommy, she loves the old movies. I mean, what is going on here? There is no way all three of us could find women the same night."

Tommy waved his left hand as he drank for a second. "All right, slow down, cowboy. Don't question it. If you start to question it, she'll start to question it, and you'll fucking blow it! Remember, just give her a piece of bread."

"What?"

"A piece of bread, man, and not the whole fucking loaf. I better not hear shit that you told her how she blows you away and she's different from the rest, just 'cause she likes old movies. I'm sure she likes to do other shit, too. Promise me you don't do any of that. That was your problem with Francesca this time last year. You met her and got on great, talking about *Brady* fucking *Bunch* reruns and then you became this fucking die-hard romantic. Don't blow it by being so honest. They say they want that, but that's bullshit!"

Dermot just stared at him.

"Ah, shit, I shouldn't have brought up the F-word. Derm, I'm sorry. I just want you to get laid for a change."

"I know. I know. It's okay. I won't get all 1940s on her. I promise. I'm here to have fun tonight."

"Good." He squeezed Dermot's shoulder. "It's good to see you back in the game, kid. And remember, Derm, whether you like it or not, it *is* a fucking game. She's no different from any of the others. Now go get your drink on 'cause I gotta go and unleash Justine's party balloons."

"Jessica," Dermot corrected.

"Oh, shit, yeah, Jessica. I gotta remember that. I know that is one thing they *do* get pissed about. All right, later, bro." Tommy stumbled off into the crowd.

Dermot knew it was time to head over to the keg and find Tabitha. He also knew that Tommy was right. There is only one thing worse than drinking yourself out of the game and that is *talking* yourself out of the game, and Dermot knew he had done that too many times before. Inside he was psyching himself up, but outwardly, while heading toward their meeting place, Dermot kept his composure like a relief pitcher slowly walking from the pen to save Game 7.

While he weaved through the couples and clusters of partygoers, he heard a radio blare a rap song, but didn't pay much attention to it. He had one thing on his mind, so he continued on and finally spotted the curly, blonde hair and backside of Tabitha. She was exactly where they had planned to meet, standing by the keg with a group of three other people. A smile crossed his face. *She came back!*

He picked up his pace and when he got closer, he realized the music was coming from a radio that the 7-Eleven smoker, Liz, was holding over her shoulders for all to hear. His smile changed to confusion when he saw Tabitha shaking the cigarette in her right hand, rapper-style, gyrating and singing along to one of the dirtiest rap songs he'd ever heard, "Gangster of Love" by The Geto Boys.

After Tabitha finished screaming the filthiest verse, she spread her arms open and tilted her head to the heavens and professed to the world, "I fucking love this song! Motherfuckers! Yeah!" Then she turned toward

Dermot's direction and yelled, "Oh, my God! You made it! You made it!"

He was still in shock and didn't know how to react, but quickly realized something. He didn't have to react because Tabitha wasn't talking to him. She blew past him and literally jumped into the arms of another guy, blocking his face from Dermot. The two made out for several seconds before finally coming up for air. When they did resurface, Dermot couldn't believe what he had witnessed, but his eyes got even wider when he saw the guy's face.

"Hey, Dermot, how are you doing, you motherfucker?" The guy patted him on the back and headed to the keg, followed by Tabitha, who added, "Oh, babe, you know him? He's a nice guy."

"Yeah, I've been partying with his brother a lot lately. Crazy bastard, that C-Dog! We were rolling before I got here, but he got caught up at another party. Anyway, let's get fucking blitzed, bitch!" Chucky ordered two guys to hold his legs while he did a handstand on the keg, and, like a newborn, he readied himself for the beer nozzle.

ELEVEN

Waiting for Dwayne alone in Dermot's Shanty, Colin sat anxiously swigging a beer. Like so many other times, he watched his brother drive off before sneaking in and making himself comfortable. But tonight he wasn't comfortable. Far from it. How could he be? He was going to see Melissa tonight for the first time since . . . *When was that?*

He took another sip and suddenly remembered the last time he talked to her was in a bathroom at a party. They must have spent at least two hours in there, Colin drinking from a flask he had "just in case," while Melissa sobbed heavily on his shoulder. *But whose party was that? It was around Christmas.* Thinking back to the worst Christmas of his life, he chased the faded memory around in his head, trying to remember when and where—a difficult task for someone who was notorious for blacking out.

His eyes widened as he perked up, remembering where he had been that night.

"Dwayne's bathroom!" It was a night he shouldn't have forgotten and now that he had grabbed the memory, he wanted it back, so the events of that evening began to play.

It had started out with Colin in the driver's seat, Melissa beside him, and Dwayne in the back aimlessly circling town, and just like senior year there was no destination in sight. Listening to A Tribe Called Quest's "Midnight Marauders," they puffed on a joint and bullshitted with one another. But it was Melissa and Dwayne doing all the talking. The main topic: Melissa's soon-to-be first semester in Colorado.

"I feel like we are sheltered here on the Cape, and I know I've kind of used that as a crutch to avoid the future. It took me a while, but I'm now ready to move on and grow. I'm really looking forward to going to Boulder. Really, I know I'm ready now. I'm ready to enjoy life again." She paused and then laughed, while she exhaled. "I just want to pick up a brush and go crazy."

"You're going to do awesome, Mel. I know it. Life is all about change and adapting to it. And, you're right. It's impossible to grow when you're stuck forever in the same damn place with the same damn people. I'm hoping I only have a semester left at Four C's and then I can fly the coop, too. The plan is if I get the grades I'm off to Merrimack."

"Dwayne, if anyone is going to make it big, it's going to be you. I have so much admiration for your dedication and drive. When I heard clips of your radio show with that silky voice and the smooth lines I thought I was hearing Barry White."

D laughed and spread his Barry White impression on thick, "Thanks, baby. You know, baby, I've been thinking about you and me."

She laughed. "I'm serious. You're such a talented guy. Not to sound like your mother, but I gotta say, I'm proud of you."

She passed the joint to the backseat and D accepted in his normal voice. "Thanks, Mel. But I don't think my mom has ever passed me a joint. But seriously, you know how I feel about you." He patted her on the head. "You're the strongest girl I know. There's only one Melissa Robertson."

She turned around and flashed a "thank you" smile.

Colin remained silent. He had nothing to contribute because their conversation about the future was indirectly taking shots at his recent choices, and it was pissing him off. With clenched teeth, he gripped his hand tightly around the wheel and turned up the radio. As he drove slowly through town, he tried to concentrate on the "street poetry" that pumped from his speakers. And as much as he was trying to stay focused on the lyrics, he couldn't help but wonder what it would have been like to be a part of their conversation. Their hopes. Their dreams. Their future. *Will I ever get out of Silver Shores?*

He was about to circle through town again when Dwayne chimed in from the back seat laughing, "Yo, C-Dog. I really hope you're not going to bust the Portuguese Five Hundred *again*. I almost feel like I'm gonna get seasick with this same route."

Colin tried to sound lighthearted. "What do you have in mind, Miss Daisy? It's January on Cape Cod."

"Well, my parents *are* out of town," D stopped and pondered for a minute. "Fuck it. Let's go to my house and throw an impromptu going away party for Mel and everyone else who's going back to college. We'll have a mini-bender. Hell, it beats the shit out of lighting a fire by the power-lines and freezing our asses off."

"Looks like someone's high." Colin perked up and flipped his blinker.

Melissa added, "Oh that sounds awesome! Can we go skating on Pearson's Pond first?"

"Babe, we can do anything you want. Tonight is your night, girl. I'll make some calls when we get back."

Colin glanced in the rearview mirror. "Hmm, no ladies this evening, Chocolate Thunder?"

Dwayne laughed, knowing what he was referring to and winked. "I could use a break. I'm a little worn out lately."

Mr. and Mrs. Peters had gone away on a "romantic weekend," leaving Dwayne, who had three older siblings all married, home alone.

"But I'm not Macaulay Culkin, kid, I'm gonna pimp this house out like my girl Heidi Fleiss," was his joke earlier when finding out he would have the place to himself. But now Dwayne wasn't concerned with getting a piece of *strange*. Like the good friend he was, sending Melissa off with a happy memory was his top priority.

After a couple of hours of night skating with a group of a dozen or so friends, D provided a warm house to continue the partying. Of course, the old rule applied, "If you're drinking at Dwayne's, you're sleeping at Dwayne's." Everyone always agreed, giving them an excuse to push the limit, and that night was no different.

Colin briefly pressed the pause button on the memory, and opened the other beer he had stuffed in his cargo shorts. It was his fifth of the night and he drank it deep down hoping for the liquid courage that would allow him to face the rest of the winter memory. His buzz sharpened, and his mind turned it back on.

After hours of bong hits in Dwayne's bathroom and funnels on the frozen front lawn, the night was finally winding down. Colin found himself at the Peters' kitchen table playing the card game Asshole. For the time being, everything was in its right place.

"Blue Sky" by The Allman Brothers Band played on WMVY, the Vineyard station. As the music roared through the speakers, the card players began singing along, but not Colin. He became stiff. Rubbing his moist palms together, he desperately tried focusing on the game, but as his heart raced, his thoughts raced faster. He didn't want to go to the memory, but it was too late. It was there. He couldn't shake it.

It had been six months ago, that he, Melissa, Matt, and Paul had been chasing the *Island Ferry's* wake on Paul's fifteen-foot skiff, *Plato's Paradise*. After wave jumping, they anchored off Stirling Beach and cast their rods into the indigo sea like so many other summer days. It was calm and peaceful, prime for fishing.

Waiting for a bite, Paul reached for his salt-encrusted boom box and pushed play on his *Boat Mix* tape. To no one's surprise "Blue Sky," Paul's favorite song, thundered out of the distorted speakers, echoing loudly across Vineyard Sound.

Paul called out, "Hey, Mel!" With his hand on his heart he began serenading his true love by singing along to the lyrics.

Mel shouted back, smiling, hand over heart, "That's my man. You're second to nobody, babe."

Paul then sat with his legs hanging over the bow of the boat, bobbing his head in rhythm to the music. The sun shined on the summer freckles that decorated the tip of his nose and then his smile really grew when the guitar solo broke. With his boyish grin, he turned and yelled, "God, this song makes me feel so alive!" And on that day they all nodded in agreement.

Turning his attention from the game, he looked to see what Mel's reaction was to hearing "Blue Sky." Had she remembered? In the middle of a circle of loud, buzzed girls who were gossiping about old boyfriends sat

Mel, white as death, oblivious to the annoying screeches of laughter. She stared into space. Yup, she remembered all right. He knew she was still on that boat, too. And when that same guitar solo played, she jumped from her seat in tears and ran out of the room as the rest of the girls watched with puzzled expressions. Like so many times in the past year, he ran after her.

Slowly opening the bathroom door, he found her sitting on the edge of the tub, face buried in her hands, crying uncontrollably. He sat down and tried to comfort her. Something about her tears warmed him because they at least gave him a purpose, and that purpose was to protect her.

Struggling, she said, "Do you remember that day? The day when we were all out on *Plato's Paradise*? 'Blue Sky' and Paul?"

"I'll never forget it."

She turned, staring into his dry eyes. "Don't ever leave me, Colin. Promise me."

"I'll always be here for you, Mel. Always."

Colin emptied the rest of his beer down his throat. Yup, Christmas break in Dwayne's bathroom was the last time he had spoken to Melissa, and he was now moments away from a face to face reunion. He didn't want to go, but Dwayne had strong-armed him by playing the guilt card. "How long have we known Mel? She needs our support."

Colin sat on one of The Shanty couches. Already starting his night, he grabbed his one-hitter from his pocket, packed it and smoked, repeating the procedure several times until his anxiety softened. He was stoned and finally comfortable. Figuring one more beer was a "genius" idea, he rose from the couch and floated to the kitchen.

The Guinness fridge needs a paint job. He changed his mind and opted for a mixed drink, remembering the bottle of Kappy's Vodka in the freezer. Vodka would hide some of the beer breath. He grabbed a glass and then snatched the plastic bottle of liquor beside an un-opened bag of sea salt and vinegar Cape Cod Potato Chips. Derm had gone shopping.

He laughed, thinking about the unusual habit his big brother picked up when he was a freshman at Northeastern. Of course, he had poked fun at Dermot for putting his chips in the freezer, calling him a freak for the weird ritual that still continued. But Dermot explained the last place drunk college kids look for munchies is in the way back of the freezer, so when the party's over, there's always a late-night secret snack. The irony was that after many years of Colin mocking his brother this past winter he had begun freezing his chips. He would snatch a bag out of his parents' icebox on the way up to his room while drunk, high, or both. Sitting alone, staring out his window at the Atlantic, he would think about Dermot, thousands of miles away in Ireland. He had wondered if things might be a little different if Derm was around—easier.

But now, summer was here and so was Dermot, and the harsh realization was Colin didn't give a shit. Tonight he was just happy to have The Shanty to himself. Filling the glass more than halfway with vodka, he followed with a splash of cranberry juice. No ice needed, it just took up space. Right before he was about to sip, a car horn jolted him. An impatient Dwayne leaned on the horn once, twice more.

Draining the glass in two gulps, Colin wiped his mouth dry and headed for the door while shoving a cigarette between his lips. Slowly making his way to the car, he ignited his smoke.

"What's up, boy," he asked D and slid into the passenger seat. Immediately rolling the window down, he took a drag and exhaled, watching his smoke rise. "Hey, let's not stay any longer than we have to at this *exhibit.*"

He looked to his left and realized Dwayne still sat idled in the driveway, staring at him. He was wearing a sharp blue button down shirt with pressed slacks, making Colin feel a little insecure in his shorts and T-shirt that bore a picture of a drunken leprechaun with his thumbs pointed inward asking, WHO HAS TWO THUMBS AND LIKES TO PARTY?

"What's wrong, D?"

"Where do I start? The shirt for one. This is a big event."

"It's at the goddamn coffee shop."

"I have a Yacht Club sweatshirt in the back."

"All right. I'll grab it when we get there if it will make you feel better. Anything else?"

"Well, yeah. No more smoking in the Lexus."

The Lexus was really an '85 navy blue Buick Skylark riding on American racing rims with tinted windows that Dwayne kept in mint condition. But everyone called it the Lexus and it was his stereo that set the Lexus apart from any other ride in town. People always joked that D's bass was so powerful that when you heard it coming, you still had enough time to mow your lawn before getting ready to be picked up. But tonight, like a ninja and not a friend, D had crept up on him, radio off, leaving him unprepared for the evening.

"You really want me to throw this out? I just lit it."

"Yeah, man. That's the new rule. Even though you keep your window down all that ash blows in my backseat. I'm a little tired of cleaning up after you."

Colin flicked his cigarette onto the driveway and angrily mumbled, "You're ridiculous. Just drive, man." The two headed to Coffee Mania in silence listening to some Miles Davis on volume three. Dwayne clearly was trying to set the mood with some low jazz and it pissed Colin off even more, but he kept his mouth shut. As they pulled into the jammed lot, he reached for his gum but realized the pack was filled with empty cellophane. *Screw it. The vodka probably did the trick.*

"You going to grab that sweatshirt?" D asked when they got out of the car.

"Fuck that. I'm here. That should be good enough."

Dwayne shook his head and led the way. Colin was definitely feeling the effects of the vodka. Cautiously following D to the entrance, but then abruptly stopping, he whistled, "Hey, I need to catch up on my tobacco fix *now*. I'm gonna burn one. I'll see you in there."

Dwayne raised his eyebrows and went inside.

"Fuck him." Colin spat and puffed away on a cigarette while a family shuffled by him, sporting their Cape Cod summer best in matching Nantucket reds. The mother scowled. The father hurried their children through Colin's cloud of smoke. Almost reveling in their annoyance, he continued smoking before finally toeing out his butt and heading in.

It didn't matter how much he had to drink, catching a glimpse of Melissa across the crowded room shocked his system. Four artists were featured and each one had his or her own section, but there was no competition—Melissa's area was by far the busiest.

Slowly making his way to her, he saw that she was talking to Mrs. Holcomb, her high school art teacher. He heard someone call out his name and was relieved to see Eric Chance.

"Eric!" he yelled louder than necessary.

"Hey, Colin."

"What are you doing here, you crazy bastard?" he asked, while messing up Eric's neatly combed hair and then trying to give him a bear hug.

"C'mon, Colin, cut it out. What are you doing? People are looking at us."

"Oh, relax. They love it. What's up with the stylish do? Is that for your girl?" he asked, eyeing Natalie, who was walking around the room with a tray of desserts.

"Shhh, Keep your voice down, man. Calm down, will ya?"

"Calm down? I'm calm, man. She didn't hear me. So, why are you here, Mister Eric Chance?"

Fixing his hair, he answered, "I'm here to support our local artists. Why are you here? Oh, and by the way, nice shirt."

"Yeah, I feel a little underdressed, but it's all good. I'm here because my . . . ah . . . my friend has her stuff on display, so I gotta do my charity work before I can go get my drink on."

"Smells like you already did."

"Ooh, funny boy." Colin tapped him on the shoulder.

Eric backed off. "I'm just kidding. So, who's your friend?"

Colin pointed to Melissa, who was now talking with Dwayne. "That girl over there."

"Oh, you're friends with Melissa Robertson?"

"Ah, yeah."

"Her paintings are amazing. She's the main reason I came down here."

"How do you know Mel?" Colin asked.

"Well, I don't know her personally. I read about her in the newspaper."

"Newspaper? When was she in the paper?"

"I think it was two days ago. Pretty big write-up. Talked about how she took a semester off and switched from Mass Art to some art school in Colorado for personal reasons . . . What are the personal reasons?"

"Personal," Colin fired back. The importance of the event finally registered with Colin and he probed the room for any family members or close friends who could be there. Now he was nervous. A run-in with Melissa's parents or the Hurleys would be awkward for everyone involved.

"Hey, man, I'm almost done with your hat. I should have it to you in the next couple of days. It has taken longer than I originally planned. Sorry for the delay." Colin tried to change the subject.

"It's cool. I'm in no rush. I just appreciate the help."

"I have to be honest, Eric. This could be my finest work yet, but it may be a little hard for me to part with it since I had to get the sewing kit out for you, dude."

"Sewing kit? You sew?"

"Only when the job demands it, then I sew like a crazy madman. I've had some roadblocks with this project, but I'm almost there."

"Colin, I don't know what to say. Thanks a lot."

"Not a problem. But, man, you gotta call me C-Dog. Anyway, I couldn't let you walk around town any longer in that helmet. It looked like you were ready to play football sportin' that brim on your head." He laughed a little too uproariously, and Eric joined in.

"I had no idea you Cape Codders take your hats so seriously. So it was pretty bad, huh?"

"Yeah, it was, but not anymore. Soon you'll look a true Cape Codder-like fisherman, and not some Tennessee trucker. Enough with that talk, how goes the writing battle?"

"It's going well. I just finished a poem that I've wanted to write for a long time and it sure *was* a battle. I think it always is when you're putting your real feelings out there on paper. You know what I mean?"

"I hear you. Well, just keep fighting, man. You only live once. You gotta go after your dreams. My mom always says, 'A nightmare is a dream not pursued.' So keep writing."

"Wow, that's a great line."

"Yup, my Mom is full of 'em. Well, I gotta carry on, my friend." Colin put his right hand on Eric's shoulder and moved in closer, almost whispering. "You keep doing what you're doing, Eric, and don't ever let anyone tell you that you can't do it. Because that's . . ." He paused and Eric hung on for his next line. Then Colin burped before continuing. "That's bullshit if they tell you otherwise. Okay, I have to go deal with something. You take care, and I will see you soon."

He turned to leave, but this time Eric grabbed his arm. "Hold on, man. Before you go take some of these." Reaching in his backpack he pulled out a tin of mints and offered the can.

"Well, Christ, Eric, that's not *too* subtle, is it? But I won't turn them down," he said, laughing and motioned to a busy Natalie. "What, you got these for your girl over there?"

"No, man."

"C'mon. You got the mints for her, right?"

Eric's eyes darkened. "No, man. I always have a tin of mints."

Colin threw some mints in his mouth and chewed them like gum. "I don't know what the hell that means, but it's a good thing you did, because it looks like there are some cute girls around here. I really have to keep moving. Thanks, man, and I will find you when I'm ready to hand over your lid."

"Sure. I gotta head out. I have to work in the parking lot bright and early. Later, C-Dog!"

As Colin crisscrossed through the waves of people, he continued to scan the room for family and friends. His buzz enhanced with the adrenaline rush he got when his eyes met Melissa's. When he approached her, Dwayne stopped talking to her, which put the spotlight squarely on Colin.

He reached in and gave her a feeble hug and then a kiss on the cheek. "Hey, Mel. Welcome home."

"Hi, Colin."

"Well, I'm going to let you two catch up." Dwayne eyed Colin and turned back to Mel to ask, "He's the guy with the dreads right, Mel?"

"Yeah, right over there." She motioned with her hand.

Dwayne made his way to the circle of people Melissa had pointed to, leaving them to talk.

"Your display looks great."

"Thanks," she one-worded him.

"And what a great article in the paper. Looks like your dreams are coming true. You must be so happy."

"Yeah, I am . . . I didn't expect you to come tonight."

"Well, just 'cause you didn't call doesn't mean I'd miss something like this."

"Colin, you are kidding with me right now, right?"

"What? What are you talking about?"

"Me call *you*?"

"I'm just saying . . ." He trailed off because he really had nothing to say.

"I was thinking of letting it go tonight, but seriously, where the *hell* have you been?"

"Here . . . I didn't leave."

"Is that it? I've talked to you every day since the first time you held my paddle in Pollywogs at Stirling Beach. How old were we then? Five? Think about that. Five years old. Every day we've talked since then and now I've gone *six* months and nothing from you. You didn't return my calls, my pages, my letters, nothing. I finally gave up hoping you'd make an effort. I don't have a brother and you don't have a sister, but we always said we didn't need anyone because we had one another. But I guess that's bullshit, huh? I really felt you were my brother. I don't understand . . . I don't get it. Now you show up smelling like booze and obviously stoned and acting like 'no big deal.' So, I want to ask you again, are you kidding me?" She had him on the ropes and he had no clue how to respond.

"Oh, come on, Mel. This winter was such a bitch. My job . . . we . . . ah . . . we're short staffed, so I was picking up a lot of extra hours."

She just looked at him, and he believed his bullshit was working on her because he almost believed it himself, so he continued. "But, why even focus on the past? You know what I mean? You're back for the summer. So, we just need to focus on now. You know, the present. It's all good. Look at all of this." He motioned to her artwork and could feel her eyes on him like a scientist studying a lab rat. And deep down he felt like a rat too. He pointed at the Silver Shores Lighthouse painting.

"I saw this one the other day, Minnesota purple."

"It seemed the only color. You know, Colin, you're right. We have to catch up."

"Yeah, after this thing, let's party tonight."

"I'm . . . Well, maybe. There's someone here I need you to meet first. If you're okay with that?"

"That's fine, Mel. I'm not that fucked up."

"His name is Tad, and we paint together at school. He lives in New York, but came up for the exhibit. It was a surprise. A big surprise, actually." She called over to a tall, lanky kid with dreadlocks who was laughing with Dwayne. The kid, wearing a dress shirt with a red polka dot tie, shorts, and Birkenstocks glided over to them.

The sight of this guy made Colin chuckle. Even though he felt underdressed, he thanked God he didn't look like Tad.

With a big smile, Dreadlocks threw his hand out. "Tad Kazmir. And you must be the C-Dog. It's great to finally meet you."

"Hey, Tad. Nice to meet you, too."

"I've heard so many stories . . . all good, of course."

"Oh."

"Oh yeah, the one thing that I was told when we first got together was that I had to get the approval of the C-Dog before the relationship could go any further." Tad laughed.

"Huh?"

"But, I'm thinking driving four hours to see Mel must get me some points with her best buddy. Am I right?" Tad smiled and squeezed Colin's shoulder.

"Relationship? Approval? What? I'm confused. You guys paint together, right?"

"Well, Tad's also . . ." Mel began, but Tad beat her to the punch.

"I'm Mel's boyfriend. Of course."

Boyfriend. The word shot Colin square in the gut. His confusion turned into anger. Rage.

"Boyfriend? Boyfriend? Mel, what the fuck is this guy talking about?"

"Colin!" Mel snapped.

Tad then took a leap of faith, trying to stem Colin's rage with a wave of his hands. "It's cool, C-Dog. It's cool. I know everything. I know about Mike and Paul. I know how hard it's been fo—"

"It's *Matt* and Paul, you fucking asshole, and don't fucking call me C-Dog."

"*Whoa*, man," Tad said.

"And do me a favor. Take your fucking dreadlocks and get out of my face! I need to talk to my friend."

All eyes and ears were now on them.

"Colin, keep your voice down!" Mel hissed. "Can you give us a minute, Tad?"

"Yeah, sure. I'll be over there." He thumbed over to where Dwayne was standing. He glared at Colin before he walked away. Colin returned the stare down until Tad got to D, who instantly began asking him questions.

Melissa, who was that guy?"

"Okay, that's not how I wanted it to come out, but Tad's my boyfriend."

"No, no, no, no, no." Colin put his hands on the back of his head and rubbed it. "No, your boyfriend is Paul. Paul is your boyfriend."

"*Was!* Colin, what are you talking about? Listen to yourself."

"I mean, yeah. Was. But, I don't get it. You were with me."

"With you?"

"At the beach. You were with me there."

"Wait . . . Why are you bringing that up? That has nothing to do with what we're talking about."

"It does. You know it does! Because you were there!"

"You know what, Colin. If you were *there* for me like you said you were going to be, you would already know about Tad, and maybe this wouldn't be such a shock. But you probably still wouldn't have liked it because . . . well obviously, you can't seem to move on."

"But, I guess you *can*! Shit, ladies and gentlemen, we got the white Oprah here and over there the albino Bob Marley. Let me tell you something, Mel, don't ever think you can stand where you are and fucking judge me. That's the fucking asshole you picked to take Paul's place? Nice work, Mel. Those dreadlocks are *so* cool! God, Paul would be pissing in his pants laughing if he were here right now."

"Someone do something!" a voice in the crowd rang out.

Dwayne took the cue and made his move, clenching Colin's arm. "Hey, dog, let's go grab some fresh air, ok?"

Colin shook his arm loose. "Oh, shit, everyone! Look, it's Chocolate Thunder to the rescue! You know what D, keep your fucking hands off me!"

"Stop being an asshole, man!" Dwayne shouted.

"No, fuck you! You make me come down to this . . . this fucking bullshit. I'm getting a little tired of the big-brother routine, too. I don't need your counseling. I'm tired of it. I'm tired of people riding my ass. You're both fucking liars! You stand there looking me in the face talking bullshit. 'Oh Colin, you need to chill out' or 'I'm concerned about Colin.' Fuck all that noise from both of you. Oh, and Tad, you don't know a fucking thing about anything. You're just a fucking pussy!"

Tad looked at him in shocked anger that only rose when Colin flipped him the bird. Jeff, the manager, suddenly hopped from behind the register, ran over to Colin and grabbed him.

"All right, enough is enough! You're outta here, man!"

"I'm going! I'm going!" Colin barked as he was being ushered out. Pointing to the Silver Shores Lighthouse painting, he shouted, "Hey, Mel, nice painting! It's such a great memory of that night! What's you're next one going to be of? Matt and Paul drowning?"

Gasps rippled across the room.

"Why you!" Jeff's grip tightened and there was even more urgency as he rushed Colin through the crowd that quickly parted.

Colin didn't care. A part of him actually enjoyed feeling something. And it *did* feel good to make someone else feel his pain for a change, especially someone who had abandoned him. He left, unloading one last bullet from his verbal chamber. "He was second to no one, Mel! Second to no one! Yeah, right!" Jeff ripped Colin's leprechaun T-shirt as he rushed him out the front door, tossing him like a cowboy from a saloon.

Once outside and alone, pure anger and adrenaline fueled him to walk and then run and finally sprint until he was back at The Shanty. Nothing mattered anymore. Everyone he knew and loved was now gone. Why even fight it?

Kappy's Vodka!

He grabbed the vodka, the chips, and a few more beers for his cargo shorts before heading to Stirling Beach. With the help of the crescent moon, he drunkenly made his way to The Fighting Chair. Sitting alone, ripping from bottle and can, he watched the glowing, black sea. This was the same sea in which he had learned to swim, and the same sea that swallowed his two best friends the summer before. That painful irony had played over and over for the last year and now it was thrashing around in his foggy skull. Sometimes he just wanted to go far away, where no one would ask him, "How are you?" and then gawk at him with those probing I-know-what-it's-like eyes. But they *didn't* know. How the fuck could they? The whole situation had become a broken record, but deep down if he could allow himself to admit it, Colin did hope somehow he could pick up the needle and turn off the player. And then he thought of Mel, Paul, and Matt, and where it all had begun—the school bus. They were ten years old.

Like every morning, Mel was letting Colin copy her math homework, while also patiently attempting to teach him. Matt hung over their seat and cracked the occasional joke. But then the doors swooshed open and the new kid stepped onto the bus.

"I heard his name is Paul Hurley," Susan Bishop whispered as Paul walked down the aisle.

"Yeah, my mom says he's from Minnesota," Matt said.

"That explains the Vikings purple people-eaters shirt." Colin laughed.

"I heard his dad is a full-of-os-a something professor," Terry Handon whispered loudly, causing Mel and Colin to pick their heads up from their notebooks.

"It's called *philosophy*," Mel said, turning to her, but then froze as her eyes locked on Paul's. That's when the days of tugging on Colin's coat to "go talk to him for me" began, and now, nine years later, as Colin looked out at the Sandy Point Lighthouse blinking its lonely white light in the distance, he realized those days had vanished with last summer's tide.

TWELVE

Colin took multiple hits from his glass pipe, blowing the clouds of smoke out his bedroom window. He watched the gray sea in the distance, which was as still as a mountainside lake. The dense fog beyond covered the Vineyard, but he knew by noon the fog would burn off, and the camps of chairs and towels on Stirling Beach would soon be settled. Right now, the beach he used to man was empty except for two lifeguards in matching red sweatshirts and sweats tossing a Nerf football. And of course, there were the few die-hard swimmers taking their early morning dip. He used to be one of them.

When Dermot and he were younger, these were the mornings they lived for. To them, a deserted, calm ocean was paradise where they could race to the marker and back and not have to worry about bumping into city guys chucking seaweed at one another. Today was a fresh start. He didn't want to think about the marker and took one long last hit before stepping away from the scene and putting on his work uniform.

Now that he was older, the definition of an overcast morning had changed. It meant it would be a chaotic day at The Shoe Fort, crowded with young, screaming kids busting through the doors, tearing sneakers off the shelves, and bickering with their parents about what shoes they wanted. He knew the scene would only add more ache to his hangover, but for now, he was pretty high and feeling damn good. So he decided that today he was going to be like that lifeguard from the year before who taught swimming lessons and was able to coax the most hesitant of children into the water by telling silly jokes or doing belly-flops. Today the crying kids, the perturbed parents, they would all leave The Shoe Fort with smiles on their faces.

While buttoning up his shirt, he ordered to himself, "Keep it together." He pulled on his khakis and laced up his sneakers, and was actually leaving his room with an "attitude of gratitude," as his mom called it, before his half-shut eyes caught the picture on the bureau. He walked over and picked up the light blue frame that was nautically decorated with buoys and sailboats and examined the photo.

Colin, Paul, Melissa, and Matt were all wearing maroon gowns and large smiles displaying their diplomas proudly for the camera. Backward baseball hats on the boys had replaced their tossed caps, and Paul, the prankster, was pointing to a baby-bib he wore around his neck that read I AM THE FUTURE.

How could I ever forget that moment?

The foursome had just walked out of the gymnasium following their graduation ceremony when Mrs. Brennan ran up from behind and caught them by surprise. "My graduates! My graduates! I need you to say, 'Cheese!'"

They had all put their arms around each other and screamed out, "Mrs. B's macaroni and cheese!" and Colin followed by raising his hands to the heavens and screaming out one of his mom's favorite quotes, "Together we can!"

His mother had laughed, "That's right, sweetie!" as the flash from the camera captured their euphoric expressions forever.

A year later and everything is so different now.

His stomach turned and it had nothing to do with booze. He went back and sparked up the pipe, took it all in until, eventually, he felt like he was glowing like a Christmas tree.

"Oh, shit, Eric's hat!" Colin hid his pot paraphernalia in his old trunk while at the same time rifling through it and tossing aside dozens of styles of hats looking for the *Island Ferry* crew one. Then, he remembered around six or so that morning when he got up to get some Gatorade he put the hat in the dishwasher for a final rinse break-in. He was about to shut the trunk when he spotted the sea blue hat with white lettering: ATLANTIS.

"What the fuck?" He wanted to yell, but he was too stoned, so he mumbled instead and quickly slammed the trunk and did the same with the door behind him.

Not today! Today's a new day!

He plodded down the stairs, but a light knock on the door stopped him in his tracks. It was followed by a voice he *thought* he knew all too well.

"Hello? Is anyone home?"

"Hold on a second." Mrs. Brennan answered, while Colin secretly watched from the corner of the stairwell. She unloaded an armful of old toys onto a table and wiped her hands on her pants before opening the door.

"Oh, wow, look who it is. My sweet, sweet Melissa, as my son would say. How are you, dear?" Mrs. Brennan hugged Melissa for a minute. "You're up early."

Colin slinked up the steps to the safety of the shadows.

Holy shit. What the fuck is she doing here?

"Hi, Mrs. B. I know it's early, but I knew I would be able to talk to you without any distractions. Do you have a minute?"

Mrs. Brennan motioned to the box. "Absolutely. This can wait. Come into the kitchen. We can have a cup of tea and catch up."

"Great." Mrs. Brennan led Melissa into the kitchen and shut the door behind her.

Oh shit! Oh Shit!

Colin sprinted to his room and tried to organize his thoughts and process the situation. He paced back and forth. The weed was increasing his paranoia. It felt like his heart was going to bust free from his chest.

What the hell should I do?

He hustled out of his room down the hall, and stopped at the old rod iron grill in the floor. He slid the lever, opening the vent, and then got on his stomach and pressed his ear to the opening. When he was kid, he and Dermot used this technique to hear what Christmas gifts his parents had bought. This was also the same vent he used to spy on his folks while they discussed what kind of disciplinary action they should take on him after the dreaded Miss Shannon called the house.

Today he strained his ear and concentrated on his mom and Mel's conversation. "So, did I see toys in that box, Mrs. B?"

"Oh, yes. I found them in the cellar. I'm getting ready for a big yard sale sometime this summer. It's time to clean out. And I have to say, cleaning is very therapeutic. It makes life easier to balance."

Colin took a deep breath when he heard the tea kettle being filled. He listened to them discuss Mel's first semester in college. Mel described the captivating mountain views that played such a key role in her therapy, and went on to explain that picking up an art brush again had paved her road to recovery. She then thanked Mrs. Brennan for the beautiful card that Dermot had dropped off the night before.

"I'm glad you liked it, Mel. I'm just sorry that Jim and I missed your big night, but we had those tickets for months."

"Honestly, it's fine. How was the play?"

"It was good. But, the Cape Playhouse is all the way in Dennis. I forgot how long a drive that is. And I have to admit, the whole time I was thinking about you."

"Don't worry about it. Jeff is going to keep my exhibit up for the rest of the summer."

"Fantastic! I'm really looking forward to my next cup of coffee. So tell me about last night."

"Well, there was a big turnout and it made me realize how much I *do* love this town."

"That's terrific. Silver Shores is such a supportive community."

"Yeah, it was going great and all, but . . . " She paused. "Colin came, too."

Mel, please keep your goddamn mouth shut.

"Oh that's good. I wasn't sure if he'd go, and I didn't want to push him."

"Well, it actually would have been better if he *hadn't* shown up."

"What? What do you mean?"

Ah, shit, Mel. What the fuck are you doing to me?

"A lot of friends and family stopped in throughout the night, even my old art teacher Mrs. Holcomb popped by and we had a great talk and I was so happy to see everyone, but then . . . "

"Then what?"

"Then Colin waltzed in, or *stumbled* in is more like it, and we got into an argument. A fight really."

"A fight?"

"I was mad because I haven't talked with him since I left for college. I kind of laid into him."

"What do you mean you haven't talked to him since you left for Colorado?"

"Yeah. Christmas break was the last time we spoke."

"I didn't know that. Every time I've asked about you, he has said you were doing great."

"He'd only know that if Dwayne had told him. He's been there for me during the whole time. But, as for Colin, he never returned a call, a page, or my letter. He didn't acknowledge anything. It got to the point where I had to get updates from mutual friends and, as you know, they were never good."

"This is all news to me. Mel, why didn't you ever mention that in your letters to me?"

"I didn't want to involve you and I thought it would eventually blow over. But last night he showed up and he was ... ah ..."

"What is it, Melissa?"

"He was drunk."

"How drunk?"

"Wasted."

No I wasn't. Fucking liar! I was feeling pretty good, but wasted? Jesus, come on, Mel.

"Oh Lord! What happened?"

"He got very angry when I introduced him to Tad."

"The friend you wrote about?"

"Yes. Actually, Tad is more like a boyfriend these days. If Col had stayed in touch he would've have known all about Tad, and maybe it wouldn't been such a shock. When I introduced them, Colin went crazy and said some horrible things to me, and then to Tad, and he also went off on Dwayne. He made a huge scene and Jeff ended up kicking him out."

"Kicking him out?"

"Yup. It wasn't good."

"Oh my God! Oh my God! I'm going to wake him up right now."

Oh shit!

"No. No. No. Please, Mrs. B., don't do that. I feel bad that I'm even telling you. If you bring him down here now he'll never forgive me."

"Well, I can't just let this go, Melissa."

"I know, but please wait until I leave. Please?"

"Alright. I understand."

"I'm sorry, but I thought you should know. I'm worried about him."

"Don't apologize. I'm sorry you had to be exposed to such anger. Honestly, I don't know what to do anymore. We've tried everything and I really thought he was getting better. Now I hear a story like this and I say, 'This is not my child. This is not the boy I know.' And it isn't. I know he's wounded and hurting."

"I miss Col so much." Melissa's voice cracked. "And I need him. There are things I can only talk to him about. Lately, I feel like I lost all three of them."

"I know what you mean. He's so distant. Either he's walking straight upstairs to his room or running out the door to God knows where. He skips out on all family gatherings. Jim and I go days without saying ten words to him. We try to connect with him, but it's getting futile. I look out at that ocean everyday and I ask God why he took them from us. They were good boys and they shouldn't have died so young. No one should die that young. It's just not fair."

The kettle began to scream and Mrs. Brennan quickly shut it off. "Now it's so quiet and it's that damn silence that is louder than ever. I miss Matt and Paul so much. They were like my own. I miss the way the three of them would trip over one another's jokes or each other when we had our movie and homemade macaroni and cheese nights."

"The three stooges, I use to call them." Mel laughed and Mrs. Brennan joined in before Mel continued. "So much has changed. You know, I sometimes wake up in the morning and for a minute or so I forget. I forget they're gone and then it hits me. And the pain hits me all over again."

"I know."

"What are you going to do about Colin?"

"I'm not sure. I've tried everything the Program has taught me. Parents are not prepared for this type of tragedy. I need to talk to his father and maybe also to Dermot. It may be time for another intervention, but the last one didn't work." She sighed. "I really don't know. Jim and I have done a lot of research into Outward Bound. That could be an option."

Fuck that!

"Don't be too hard on him. I know he didn't mean what he said. I know it was the alcohol. I just want my friend back."

"I know you do. And I want my son back. That's where I get confused. Do I show compassion and let him work it out on his own, or is the real compassion tough love? I have no idea." There was a long silence before Mrs. Brennan continued. "I think we need to keep him in our prayers. I'm certain God will show him the way. We need to keep the faith and stay positive. I know that sounds like a corny sentiment, but if we don't have faith we don't have anything. "

It was quiet for a while and then Mrs. Brennan spoke. "Mel, I don't think I've told you, but I have been working part time at Page Turner's bookstore for the last six months and this past spring I attended a book fair in Boston and was able to get an advanced copy of *The Healing Runes.*"

"What's that?"

"I'll show you. Hold on a second."

Colin heard his mother leave the room and soon return. "These are the Healing Runes. Open the bag."

"What are these, stones?" Mel asked.

"Runes. They offer us spiritual guidance. When you have a question or concern— something that is weighing on your mind—you can look to the runes to give you insight. They really have been helping me lately. Would you like to try them?"

"Sure. What do I do?"

This is so ridiculous. Has mom been smoking my chronic, too?

"Think of something that is on your mind and then put your hand in the bag and pick out one rune."

There was a short pause before Mel said, "Okay. Here. This one."

"Alright. Now you look at the symbol on it. Match that symbol to the one that is on the inside of the cover of the book and it will direct you to the page where the definition is."

"Oh, here it is. It says courage and it's on page 101.

"Courage. That's very interesting. Read it out loud."

Melissa began to read. "Courage is faith in action. Drawing this rune indicates that you are being asked to recognize and honor courage and strength of your own spirit. As you do, you will grow in the understanding necessary to continue traveling the road you have chosen, and to face with wisdom whatever challenges life brings you." She stopped to take a breath and continued. "Anyone who has been sorely tested—suffered through the death of a loved one, been critically ill, recovered from an addiction or broken the silence of spousal abuse—knows well the courage it takes to heal. The insight from these transforming experiences gives us hope and teaches us that the reward for courage is wisdom." Melissa stopped reading and her voice cracked.

"It's okay to cry, Mel. God wouldn't give us tears if he didn't want us to use them. Do you want me to finish the passage?"

Mel composed herself. "No. I can do it. Thanks." She continued reading. "Time and again, the true test of courage is to live rather than die, to survive the period of crisis and complete your healing. Take comfort also from this: There is intimacy with the Divine arising from the small brave acts that help us through each day. For some, receiving this rune may be a reminder to reach out and ask for help. Taking the risk of reaching out is one of those brave acts of daily courage. For others, the rune of courage announces that the cycle of sorrow and pain has finally come to an end. Be at peace with your healing. You have walked the path of true courage; now it is time to go out in the world and live the life you were born to live."

As soon as Mel stopped reading she broke down, and the sobs were familiar to Colin. He heard that same thunder of pain the day he told her that her boyfriend and best friend were missing and feared drowned.

"I think about Paul everyday," Mel wept.

"I know you do. I know. And he's watching. And he is very proud of you."

"He was my first love. My only love. He was going to go to Bentley, and I was going to be at Mass Art. That was the plan! I get so mad at him sometimes for leaving me. There is not one single day that goes by when I don't picture his big brown eyes and that pearly white smile. And now I'm seeing Tad and I feel. I feel . . . "

"Don't feel guilty. It's okay to love again."

"But I also need Colin back."

"Don't worry, honey. But you have to continue to stay courageous. Continue to be strong and stay on your journey. As much as you love Colin, you have to think about your recovery too."

"Thank you so much, Mrs. B. For everything."

"You're welcome. Now come out back with me for a moment. I want you to see my meditation garden."

This was Colin's cue. He lifted his head up from the floor, waited for the screen door to slam, and then ran down the stairs into the kitchen. He pulled Eric's dripping hat from the dishwasher and stuffed it into a plastic bag and hurried to the front door. As he reached for the knob, he suddenly stopped and turned around and headed back into the kitchen. He shot a look out the window to see if he was still safe. His Mom and Mel had their backs to him. *Probably meditating.* He picked up the green felt bag of runes off the counter and shook it lightly. Picking a stone out, he gazed at the symbol on it, and looked up the meaning. He scanned the passage quickly and closed the book.

What a bunch of bullshit!

But instead of putting the stone back into the bag, he shoved it into his pocket and rushed out the front door.

THIRTEEN

The first ferry of the day was about to depart for Martha's Vineyard, but with the sun bearing down on him like a hot poker, Dermot felt like he had already put in a full fourteen-hour shift. The seasoned veteran of the *Island Ferry* parking lot had been making several rookie mistakes. The biggest error—a Cardinal Sin for *Island Ferry* workers—was that he was out of uniform. He knew if any of the managers were to come down from the office for a money transfer he'd be in serious trouble. Not too mention it was a two-packs-of-mints morning, and he was still feeling the previous night. Wearing a sweat-drenched, dirty gray golf shirt and khaki shorts also made it difficult for him to convince the customers that he even worked there. His saving grace was an old *Island Ferry* hat he was also wearing that he had found under the La-Z-Boy in the lot's shack. When he pointed to it most people handed over their money, but not all.

"I'm not giving my money to you! You look like a hooligan," an elderly woman snapped.

"Hooligan? What am I, James Cagney in *White Heat*?"

This time, the old movies worked for him. It always did when it came to *old* ladies. After her initial shock at his response, the woman repeated his line to her carload of blue-haired companions, and they all roared with laughter. She then handed him a crisp ten dollar bill, and he shuffled back two ones, sending her on her way to park in the third aisle.

Dermot had recovered in *that* exchange, but soon after lost his fastball with other customers, floundering while figuring out change or fielding the simplest of questions.

"Excuse me. Where's the boat dock?"

"Ah, yeah, it's up the street."

"Well, *yeah*, but how far?"

"A little ways."

It went from bad to worse, and for the past hour and a half, he had sprinted in and out of the shack grabbing the wrong tickets, change, or both for the endless line of cars that beeped before slowly moving forward to fill the empty lot. But the blazing sun and constant bustle of the lot wasn't the real reason he was dragging his ass. The rush was nothing new to him. He usually thrived on the buzz of cars and tourists' questions that flew his way every morning. And how he felt also had nothing to do with Gary Molloy, who, scheduled to work a rare morning shift, called in earlier saying he was running late because he had to a fix a cable power outage in a new development. Sure, that added situation had left Eric and him understaffed and overpowered by clueless tourists, but that wasn't anything new, either. Sometimes, he even had to work those kind of shifts with lazy co-workers.

But lazy wasn't the word he would use to describe Eric Chance. Over the past couple of days, the shy kid had opened up and seemed to have a personality after *all*, and more importantly, he worked his ass off. Normally having a hardworking co-worker like Eric by his side, Dermot would've considered it a challenge for them to get every customer parked and on that nine o'clock ferry, even the asshole New Yorkers. But not today.

He didn't give "three shits," as Molloy would like to say. The excuses were in place, and he wanted to use them and any others he could find to justify why he wasn't on his A game, but deep down, he knew there was only one reason why he felt the way he did.

Ever since he witnessed Miss Tabitha Gutter Mouth and her sloppy make-out session with Chucky "He's All" Dunn, the biggest loser in Silver Shores, he had decided to just shut it down and give up on women altogether. And the best way to do that, he thought, was to go on a two-day bender, which he was now paying for. Big time. He wasn't sure if he was still drunk or hung over, or a little bit of both, but like a wet sponge being squeezed, the booze ran from his pores, making him wonder if he could bottle up his sweat and resell it to underage drinkers.

What a weird-ass thought that is. I must still be drunk.

And if he was still drunk, the hangover wasn't too far away.

Captain Stansfield's boat horn finally moaned relief for Dermot who had just shooed a late car away. "That sound means the boat just left. Next one is 10:30," he said, before staggering away and plopping into his chair.

The ferry's departure should've been a half-hour reprieve before the next rush, but a quick breather was all he could take before going to The Shanty and grabbing his uniform. There was also another reason he didn't have any excuses for his screw-ups and now he had to face it.

"So Dermot, are you going to tell me about what happened this morning?" Eric interrupted his brief sit down.

"What's to tell?"

"Well, you know . . ." Eric waited.

"What? Why I slept in the parking lot shack last night?"

"Well, yeah."

Dermot had come up with what he hoped sounded plausible. "I was in charge of the company beeper and had a late let-out call around four or so."

"Four? Wow. No ferries run that early, so how did they get back from the Vineyard?"

"I don't know . . . Oh, yeah, it was a guy, and he said he came back on his buddy's fishing boat. Had a meeting in Boston he had to get to or something. The thing is my car is still acting up so, I figured if I had to walk here, I might as well stay and sleep in the La-Z-Boy."

"Well." Eric sat down and looked over. "It was a little more than that."

"Than what?" Dermot asked, but he was concentrating more on his head that was beginning to throb. He dragged his teeth along his dry tongue, and felt the sour taste in the back of his mouth. It was hitting him.

"It was more than sleeping. You were like . . . passed out on the floor. I mean, you were gone. Snoring like crazy. It took me about ten minutes to wake you. You didn't even know where you were for like another five minutes."

"How about *like* you forget about what you saw."

Eric wasn't listening. "What I also don't understand is, if you decided you were going to sleep here, why you wouldn't bring your uniform?"

"Wow, I guess the new kid feels pretty comfortable now. About a week ago the kid couldn't even talk and now it's Twenty Questions with your host Eric Chance. Hey, I got a question for you, Eric."

"What's that Dermot?"

"Are you my *fucking* boss?"

"Ah, no."

"You're goddamn right you're not. This is your first fucking summer. You don't bust my balls. I bust yours. You got that?"

"Ah, yes, Dermot. I didn't mean to piss you off. I . . . I . . . Ah . . . I just thought you might have gone out last night and had a good story to . . ."

"I don't care *what* you thought. By the way, where's your hat? You haven't worn it since the first day. You know, that's also part of the uniform. As your superior, I could report that shit. Where is it?"

"A friend of mine is breaking it in and . . ."

"Never mind." Dermot rose. "I need your bike."

"My bike?"

"Yeah, I gotta go home and get my uniform."

Dermot grabbed the ten-speed, kicked up the stand, and hopped on.

"But then I'll be all alone."

"Gee, a moment ago you wanted to run this place. Now's your chance, big boy. Molloy should be here soon. If any of the managers from the office come down here, just say I went to get coffee. Nothing more. You got that?"

"Ah, yes." Eric nodded.

Dermot clumsily pedaled off, changing gears and realizing the last time he was on a bike was on those cobblestone streets in Ireland. He finally gained momentum and had a flashback of days as a teenager playing bike chase with his little brother, Matt, Paul, and Mel. After a rainstorm when there were puddles was the best time to play. As the oldest, he'd chase after all of them, watching their little feet desperately working peddles, and even though he was capable of catching them, he always let them escape. It was more fun to hear their victorious laughter, thinking they outsmarted Colin's big brother.

He tried to turn the memory off, but thought of seeing Mel at the artists' reception the night before at Coffee Mania. Dermot had dropped off a congratulatory card from his mom, so he arrived early in hopes that he wouldn't bump into Mel. But, there she was, setting up her show.

She ran over and hugged him for longer than usual, whispering, "I've missed you, my dreamer, my romantic, my writer, my big brother."

He laughed, and released her from the hug first. He then gave an excuse saying that Tommy was in the car waiting, and they had to go down Cape to a party. Of course, it had been a lie. He hadn't seen Tommy since the lifeguard party. A few seconds later, he was out the door.

"What an asshole I am," he muttered, as he glided down a side street to avoid passing the ferry landing.

When he got to The Shanty, he threw the bike down, lunged through the front door straight for the bathroom, fell to his knees, and worshipped the porcelain god for a good two minutes. After he was done yakking, he washed his face, threw off his foul clothes, wobbled into his uniform, and headed back out the door, literally bumping into his father.

"Whoa, what's up, buddy?" Mr. Brennan asked.

"Oh, nothing Dad. I had to change my uniform."

Mr. Brennan squinted. "Oh, okay. Well, I was grabbing the lawnmower out of the shed and saw you go by doing your *Breaking Away* imitation, so I came over here. I was hoping you had a minute for a chat."

"Oh, sorry, Dad." He headed for the bike. "I have to get back before the ten-thirty rush. I left the new kid alone."

"Oh, okay. So, can I come to the lot a little later?"

"Sure," he replied and jumped back on the bike, "I'm there all day."

"How many guys are working?"

"Should be three by the time you come by."

"Okay, buddy." Mr. Brennan held his hand halfway up in the air.

While he hauled ass back to the lot, he wondered what the hell his dad wanted to talk to him about. It was probably the fact that he was now another year out of school and he still hadn't written anything more than drunken book ideas on cocktail napkins and newspaper paragraphs about missing cats. When he had told them he wanted to be a writer, his parents were really cool. They had raised the Brennan boys with the philosophy that, in life, you have to follow your dreams, no matter what. But they also had warned that you can't just dream it, you have to work at it to make your destiny come true. The simple fact was Dermot had a dream, but he hadn't done shit about it. He had spent all of his winter afraid of following it by staring in the bottoms of lined-up shot glasses, and now he was probably going to get the "it's time to work on your resumé" lecture.

The blackout lights from the night before finally turned on, as he pedaled toward the *Island Ferry* lot. He remembered it all—at least, most of it. He had grabbed a ride from the party to Pucky's, where he hoped to watch old movies with Pucky and tell him about his trip to Ireland, but Pucky had gone to a funeral off-Cape, so Dermot sipped a pint alone. The substitute bartender was an insecure asshole named Rob, a twenty-something-year-old with a closely trimmed George Michael goatee. Rob grinned at Dermot and offered a few free shots of the men's names—Jameson and Johnny Walker. Dermot knew exactly what was behind the generosity. He had watched that bartender's game for a couple of years now. Every night when Pucky was off duty, Rob had a gaggle of fresh, blonde underage girls hanging around the bar. Rob liked to get someone hammered and embarrass the shit out of them by pretending to be smarter than he really was. It usually got him laid by one of the girls.

Dermot had seen it take place a thousand times before, but he had welcomed the role of the drunken guinea pig so he could bask in his Francesca depression. He didn't remember exactly what Rob had said, but he knew it had something to do with the fact the whole town thought Dermot would never get published. He swayed out of the bar, determined to come up with a home run idea, but then realized he forgot his writer's journal at the parking lot shack. So, at two in the morning, he grabbed his key from The Shanty and headed to the lot to write down whatever that idea was.

Now he rounded the corner and Molloy's brown Bronco was parked in the first employee spot. Eric was beside it, tossing an orange cone and trying to make it land upright—the ultimate game for bored parking lot attendants.

"Dermot, come in here for a minute!" Molloy ordered him back to reality, and he walked into the shack.

"Okay . . . Jesus, Molloy!" he exclaimed upon walking in on Molloy, who had his pants halfway down his legs and his right hand under his Tarzan-patterned bikini briefs.

"Sorry, you had to see that, Dermot." Not sorry at all, Molloy grinned, as he cupped his crotch area for a second and then pulled his pants up and zipped them shut. "I was ball bound. I had to fluff the boys up a bit."

"Ball bound? Fluff them up? I don't even know what that means."

"You'd know if you climbed those ladders for the cable company for a living. They get sweaty. They need to breathe now and then. So, where's my coffee?"

"Coffee?"

"Yeah, Eric said you went to get coffee."

"Oh, yeah . . . I . . . ah . . . "

Molloy waved him off. "I knew that was a bullshit story. Something's going on if you're riding the new kid's bike around town. So, skip the BS and get to it. What's up?"

"Well, Molloy, it's this simple. You know we've argued for years about everything from racism to homelessness to whether or not Robin Williams is funny. Actually, we did agree on that one."

"Yeah, my left ball bag is funnier than that guy."

"I agreed with you before about him but even more so after what I just witnessed. Fucking *Tarzan* briefs? Jesus, man. Later on are you going to ask Cheetah if that's a banana in your pants or is he just glad to . . . ? Anyway, I've come to the realization that you are right about something." Dermot opened his old college mini-fridge and pulled out a can of Coke.

"I'm right about something? Right about what?"

After Dermot popped the top and sipped, he took a dramatic pause before continuing, "Deep down all women are whores."

"What?" Molloy's eyes bugged out.

"You heard me. You've said it for years, and you have finally converted me. I'll say it again for the record. Deep down all women are whores."

They had tackled the topic over the years during countless shifts so, as Molloy looped his belt, he was actually speechless.

"Hey, Dermot, your friend Clay is pulling in," Eric yelled from outside, and Dermot headed out to greet him leaving Molloy still stunned. Eric moved another orange cone from the employee spot and Clay squeezed the black Cadillac in between the Bronco and a blue van.

"What's up, Derm?" He walked over with a jackpot winner smile.

"What's up? That's what *I'd* like to know. I've called you a few times the past couple of days and nothing."

"I know, man. I'm sorry. I've been busy. And actually, that's the reason I came by."

"What do you mean?"

"I need four passes for the twelve o'clock boat and free parking would be great, too. I'm going to the Vineyard with Meri, and her sister Natalie and I guess her friend."

"Did you say Natalie? As in Natalie Nazerian?" From out of nowhere, Eric perked up and they both turned to him.

"Yeah, why the Peter Brady it's-time-to-change voice?" Clay asked.

"Huh?" Eric didn't get it.

"Your voice just hit another octave, man." Dermot studied Eric.

"Oh, ah, no reason. She was just in my English class this year. She . . . ah . . . seems . . . ah . . . okay."

Clay and Dermot both exchanged knowing looks. The kid had a crush.

It wasn't missed by Molloy either, who was quick to emerge from the shack and pounce. "Natalie Nazerian." His grin widened. "She works at the coffee shop, right? *No wonder* Eric's been volunteering to make the run on his bike when I tell him I can drive there in like two minutes. So, Eric, does that Armenian grease monkey make your pants rise?"

"Fuck you, Molloy!" Eric snapped, and Molloy burst into laughter.

"Well, that answers *that* question," he said, still howling. "Hey, Dermot might be able to give you some advice. He's got a new theory going about women."

"Come on, Molloy, let it go for now," Dermot said and turned to Clay. "After all, this asshole got to go to his first fire the other night and I *still* haven't heard about it."

"Oh, shit. I didn't tell you about that."

"No, asshole, you were supposed to come by the next day. So, how was it?"

"Okay, all of you have to hear about this. Oh, and before I start, Eric don't listen to Molloy. The last time he got laid, bell-bottoms were in style."

They all laughed, including Molloy.

"So," Clay stood before them as they sat down in their chairs. "Here I was at a party talking to Meri, this amazingly beautiful and sweet girl, and my beeper goes off. I mean, literally. So, I have to leave and I go to the firehouse and they tell me to put my gear on and we go to that old abandoned yellow house by the movie theater. So we get there and the place is in flames. I mean, I'm talking a major fire. So the Chief says to me, 'Pelligrini, now's your chance,' and I'm *like*, 'My chance?' And he's like, 'To see what it's like.' And I'm *like*, 'What what's *like?*' And he's *like*, 'To put out a fucking fire. Now, get your ass in there.' I'm telling you, I couldn't believe it."

"Why?" they all asked.

"Because the place was on fucking *fire*, man. I mean, no little beach bonfire here. It was everywhere and it was hot. I mean fucking hot."

Dermot, Molloy, and Eric exchanged glances.

"What?

Dermot answered for them. "Well, it *was* a fire. What did you expect?"

"Yeah, all right, so anyway, we finally put the fucking thing out, and I go back to the station at about three a.m. or so. And I'm just dead tired, so the Chief says I can sleep there. So I'm trying to get some z's, but I smell like a goddamn campfire. After a while I pass out. But you'll never guess what happened then."

This time it was Eric. "What?"

"Around five thirty the bell sounds and the Chief is like, 'All right, come on.' And I'm like, 'Come on, what?' So he says, 'There's a boat on fire at Swain's Boatyard.' So we go there and it caught on another boat and next thing I know I'm working that hose for about two hours. I was so fucking exhausted."

Again all three laughed and Clay asked, "What?"

"Well, Clay, man, it's not like they can schedule fires from nine to five," Dermot pointed out.

Clay finally realized how ridiculous he sounded and broke into laughter. "Yeah, I know. I just always envisioned being a firefighter more like you guys just hanging out and shooting the shit. Speaking of that, anything new on the hot plate today?"

"Actually, big news," Molloy said. "Mr. 1940s has finally come to believe in my theory that all women are whores."

"Dermot, not *you?*" Clay sounded hurt.

Dermot responded with a shrug.

"Come on, look what's happening with Meri and me. It's like we talked about the other night. It's just like one of those movies you always want to write."

"Yeah, but I haven't. We'll see how that Meri deal goes for you."

"Wow, thanks, dickhead. Hey, but Tommy said you were talking with a cool girl the other night who liked old movies and shit or something."

"Yeah, never mind that. Where's that prick, Tommy, been? Do either of you guys return phone calls anymore?"

"He really hit it off with some girl at the party with big party balloons named Jessica and he actually *likes* her. She seems cool. The four of us went to see *Speed* last night."

"Oh, great. Double dating even," Dermot said. But in the back of his mind, he suddenly realized that because of Francesca he never returned his boys' phone calls the previous summer, and now the shoe was on the other foot.

"So, what happened with the old-movies chick?"

Dermot glanced at his watch. "The second boat rush is going to hit us in about four minutes, so the short version is, she was amazing. We were talking old movies and had a great back-and-forth conversation and then she left the party with Chucky Dunn."

"Chucky 'He's All' Dunn?" Clay gasped.

"Yup." Dermot nodded.

"I've heard you talk about that guy," Molloy said. "Hasn't he been to rehab a couple of times?"

Dermot and Clay both shot three fingers to the air.

"I've also heard of him. I think he's friends with a friend of mine," Eric added.

"Well, whoever that friend is, I'd stay away from him if I were you. Chucky is a big-time loser. But that's what the women seem to love. I bet if I had a fucking restraining order on me I'd have all of the ladies," Dermot said.

"She's just another cock jockey looking to be whipped." Molloy declared. "But Dermot's right. Look at all the serial killers. They get all the bitches writing to them and wanting them and shit. You know what, Dermot? I think you should become the next Ted Bundy," Clay suggested.

"I couldn't do that." He paused. "Too much digging."

They all laughed, and a minute later Clay, with passes in hand, pulled out of the lot just before the rush for the second boat arrived. And did it arrive. But unlike the first boat, now a third guy was on duty to help, and by having an early morning puke session followed by some cold caffeine, Dermot felt he was back on his game. The onslaught of customers made the time fly, forcing him only to concentrate on the moment, and forgetting about everything else. But three minutes after the ferry departed and the calmness returned, a blue '90 Nissan Sentra pulled into the lot and idled beside the lot's shack.

"Hey guys, I thought you might need some iced coffees to keep you all going," Mr. Brennan said, while passing the cardboard tray out the driver's window. A beaming Molloy accepted it and headed for the shack.

"Thanks, Jim," Molloy remembered to say over his shoulder as he went inside.

"Oh, and Gary, in the bag there's some extra cream and sugar and a few donuts."

"Hey, thanks, Dad."

"Yes, thank you, sir," Eric added.

"Oh, Dad, this is the new kid I was telling you about, Eric Chance."

"Nice to meet you, Eric. I hope these guys haven't been giving you too hard a time."

Eric gave a quick glance at Dermot to remind him of what happened earlier in the morning, but then replied, "No, sir. They've treated me like I've been here forever."

"I don't know if that's a good thing, either," Mr. Brennan laughed, but then shifted his attention back to his son. "Hey, I was wondering if we could take a quick spin around the lot, Derm?"

Here it comes! The speech!

"Ah, yeah, sure, Dad. I have to check for spots in the back lot, anyway. We're almost full." He ran into the shack and grabbed the small silver counter, a walkie-talkie, hustled back out, and hopped in the passenger seat.

From inside Molloy hollered, "Wait. You want your iced coffee?"

Dermot leaned over his dad and yelled back, "No, just put it in the fridge. I'll only be a couple of minutes."

As he turned to his son, Mr. Brennan waved his hand in front of his nose. "Rough night with the boys?"

"Huh?"

"You don't just smell like a goddamn brewery, but an out-of-business one. You know—that stale booze smell." Mr. Brennan's foot pressed the accelerator. They headed down the first aisle, took a right, went along three filled aisles, and turned left into the back lot.

"Oh, yeah, I ah . . . forgot to brush."

Pissed for being dumb enough to breathe in his dad's face, he began clicking away on the counter even though he didn't need to; he knew every nook and cranny of the lot, and there were between sixty and seventy spots left.

"It wasn't a rough night, just a late one," Dermot offered lamely.

"Yeah, I know." Mr. Brennan pulled into a spot and turned off the ignition.

Holy shit! Did I see him when I was hammered? I have no idea.

"What do you mean, Dad?"

"Oh, just that I went to the Sea Shanty twice this morning. Once when you saw me and once earlier at seven or so, and your car was parked, but you weren't home. I will say I'm glad to see that you don't drink and drive."

"With that dying piece-of-shit car I have, I couldn't get it up the street to Pucky's, even if I *wanted* to drink and drive."

"Well, I bet when you write that Great American Novel, you'll look back at that car fondly ... Anyway, I'll say this quickly. Just be careful when you're handling the bottle. I thought I had the upper hand on the booze, but then it snuck up on me in the eighties, and it smashed me over the head. You don't realize it at the time, but now, after being sober for eight years, I know there were a lot of factors behind why I drank so much back then. It wasn't just the taste. It was to forget. To escape. You know, your mom was going through her depression and I was depressed, too."

"Really?"

"Oh, yeah."

"It was no secret about Mom, but you? You were 'Mr. Pizza and Movie Night Guy' with us."

"Oh, I never drank when we all watched movies and hung out, but it was after you guys went to bed. That was when I did the damage. You see, back then I was having more and more memories of some of the things I experienced in the Korean War ... things I never told you boys."

"Oh."

"Yeah, you know, no one can prepare you for war. Think about it. One moment, I was playing in the summer league, holding a baseball bat in my hands, thinking I'm the next Ted Williams, and the next minute I'm drafted into the Army and swinging a bayonet like it *was* a baseball bat at other young guys—guys who probably had dreams just like me. The whole thing just didn't make any damn sense. Still doesn't." Mr. Brennan was staring beyond the steering wheel at something his son could not see.

"Dad, we always talk about everything. You always made it sound like the war was like ... like ... I don't know ... Like going to the country club. Why didn't you ever tell us?"

"Well, I promised myself I'd leave that hell on Pork Chop Hill. And when you and Col were born, I decided I didn't want to raise you guys with war stories because it was undeserving of glorification. There's nothing beautiful about it. But then some of those stories began to resurface in dreams. They still do now and then, but now I remember, I didn't have a choice. I was just trying to stay alive. I just wanted to make it home and play baseball in the park again. Anyway, maybe if I had told you it wasn't a bed of roses for me, we wouldn't be here right now."

"Geez, Dad, don't get me wrong. I appreciate you opening up like this, and I'll admit last night I may've had a few too many, but it's not like I'm going down some bad road in life."

"You're not, but your brother is. That's why I'm here."

"Oh."

"I need some fresh air." Mr. Brennan got out of the car, walked to the back, and leaned against the trunk. Dermot got the cue and followed him.

When he looked at his Dad, he noticed something: tears. Not the kind of tears that flowed when he watched *It's A Wonderful Life* every Christmas, and proclaimed he also was "the richest man in town." These tears were a product of inner turmoil, leaving Dermot feeling hopeless. His father was always the one to comfort him, but suddenly, it was the other way around.

Mr. Brennan bit on his knuckle. "I was going to come and talk to you about Colin this morning, but we missed each other. And then I wished myself into thinking I was overreacting about everything, but I just talked with your mom . . . Mel came by just a little while ago and I guess your brother made a big scene last night at her art show."

"Oh?"

"Have you heard anything?"

"No. Nothing."

"Well, Mel was really upset and your Mom was great with her. But she told me she can comfort other kids, but not her own. She is losing the Al-Anon faith . . . Dermot, the program has been so good for your Mom and me, but I understand how she feels. I don't know what to do with Colin anymore. I've tried the tough guy act, and I even threw him out this winter after he got arrested. I think he actually enjoyed being a nomad going from couch to couch."

"What? Wait a second. *Arrested!* I didn't know that!"

"Well, you know how he looks up to you. You're his big brother. He promised me not to tell you, and I said I wouldn't say anything, as long as he cleaned up his act. He did for a bit and we took him back in."

"Let's get back to being arrested. What did he get arrested for?"

"He got drunk one night in February and broke into the aquarium. Why? I'll never know. Officer Jakes found him staring at the shark tank, completely oblivious to the alarm which woke up half the town."

"Oh, man. No one told me about that."

"I don't think it's the kind of thing your buddies would want to tell you. They know how much you love Colin, too . . . Derm, what I just told you about the Army. I told him. I even got into a little more detail. I wanted him to see that I understand the ghosts that probably haunt him, too. It didn't work. He hemmed and hawed as if he were listening to some boring sermon. So I tried to figure out how I could I get through to him and I thought about movies. I raised you guys on movies, so I talked him into watching *Ordinary People*. I hoped it would get him to open up and let it all out and then we could deal with it. You know, just yell and cry in my arms and just get it out. You know that movie, right?"

"Yeah, of course, your man Redford directed it. The brother who survives a boating accident but his brother drowned . . . Wow, he was a swimmer, too. I never thought about *that*—how similar it is to what Colin's going through. So how did he react?"

"He basically got up after the opening credits and said he'd watch it later. That was two months ago. Derm, you know how your mom always says to look for signs in the world to guide you?"

Dermot nodded.

"Well, the other day, I was driving down 6A on my way to teach my film class at Four C's, and I was thinking about the boys and how almost a year has passed since their accident and how much I missed them. I was lost in thought and then it dawned on me that I was staring straight ahead at a fishing boat being pulled by a truck. That alone isn't a big sign. Boats on trailers are everywhere on the Cape, but then I noticed two life preservers tied firmly to the boat's steering wheel. I don't know . . . In my mind I thought it was some sort of sign that Matt and Paul's souls were safe and secure and heading in the right direction toward peace. Probably silly, but my interpretation made me smile because that's what I *want* to believe. I want to believe there *is* something better out there. So I was happy, but then, as I passed the truck, I looked over and noticed another life preserver. This one was not on the steering wheel, but tied to the cleat on the side of the boat, and it wasn't secure at all. In fact, it was flapping wildly in the wind, and I knew it was only a matter of time before it came loose. It was either going to cause an accident or just blow away to the side of the highway. I tried beeping and pointing to warn the driver, but he just looked straight ahead. He didn't notice me at all. He just kept driving. I finally had to pull off at my exit and realized something. That life preserver was your brother. It was Colin. I *know* it was." Mr. Brennan stopped. He wiped his eyes and looked away.

Dermot leaned over and hugged his father. "It's okay, Dad, it's okay. It's just a phase he's going through. He'll be fine. I know he will."

"I just don't understand how it's come to this. We were all pals. 'Love one another and stick together.' That was our motto. And now . . . nothing. Our family is drifting apart. I can't even get you two to watch a baseball game with me."

"What do you mean?"

"I left a note on the fridge the other day to watch the Sox game with me and neither one of you even answered. That never happened before. You guys would at least write back, but nothing."

"Well, Dad, I think I was in a rush or something. Anyway, why would you want to watch a game when the strike is coming and all? Come to think of it, I don't think it's a big deal for us not to answer you."

"But it *is* a big deal, Dermot. You see, you and your brother, *you're* my boys of summer and just like baseball, you're both leaving me....Look, your mom, my God, I love her to death and all, but this co–dependency thing she preaches sometimes can be just too goddamn clinical."

"What are you talking about?"

"I'm talking about the fact I'm asking you to reach out to your brother and talk to him. He stopped listening to me a long time ago. Your mom doesn't want you to get in the middle, but Dermot, you're his big brother and what did we teach you when you were growing up."

"'He ain't heavy, father, he's my brother,' from *Boys Town*." His father nodded and he knew he had to give the whole shpiel. "Spencer Tracy as Father Flanagan and Mickey Rooney also starred in that one."

"That's right. Very good. Instead of staying up late with me when you were kids, I probably should've been making you guys do your algebra homework. Anyway, some might think that's a corny line, but that's how I raised you, Derm. You've been a great brother, but now he really needs you more than any other time in his life."

"Okay, Dad. I'll try to talk to him again. I don't think it'll happen overnight since he didn't listen to me before, but I'll try."

"I think it's more like *you* need to listen to *him*."

"But, he won't talk."

"I know, Derm. I know."

The walkie-talkie crackled to life with Molloy's voice. "Hey, Dermot, how many spots?"

Dermot clicked back, "I'd say about sixty."

"Hopefully, we don't get any carloads of fish heads. 'Cause, you know how those fish heads like to come late in the day, thinking they can park for half price. I don't want to open Siberia," Molloy spat, referring to the overflow lot up the street.

"Fish heads?" Mr. Brennan asked.

"That's what he calls Asian people. He seems to think we get a lot around this time of day, because it happened once about three years ago."

"God, he's unbelievable," Mr. Brennan laughed.

"Yeah, his craziness actually makes him fun to work with, but when the laughs are over for the day I always go home thinking one thing . . ."

"What's that?"

"I wouldn't want him to be my father."

FOURTEEN

It was anger, not sadness that consumed Dermot as he stood inside the parking lot shack and pressed the ink stamp to mark the date on the back of the parking tickets. He was torn up from just seeing his father cry. A part of him wanted to cry, too, but he fought the feeling and instead it intensified and he wanted to punch something or someone.

Mr. Brennan had always been more than just a father to his sons; Jim Brennan was their best friend. He had raised them with laughter and love, but somehow the Brennan boys were turning into royal fuck-ups, especially Colin. After all, Colin was the reason his father was crying. It was Colin who was dividing the Brennan family. Not Dermot.

"Dermot . . . Dermot, what the fuck?" Molloy hollered from behind.

Dermot turned around. "What?"

"What? Well, it's the noon boat we're getting ready for and you stamped like a hundred fucking tickets. We don't even have that kind of space in this lot, and the major rush for the day is over. We never sell that many tickets for the noon boat, you know that."

"Oh, yeah, well excuse the fuck out of me." He threw the stamp on the counter, clanging it against the metal change box.

"Jesus. You've been pissy ever since you and your dad talked in the back lot. Something wrong?"

"Yeah, there is . . . Molloy, did you know about my brother getting arrested this winter?"

There was no sarcastic laugh or line just a simple, "Of course, I did."

"Why didn't you tell me about it or bust my balls?"

"First of all, it wasn't my place to tell you. Second of all, I may be an asshole, but I'm not a *fucking* asshole. You know what I mean?"

"No."

"Well, it was some fucked-up shit he did breaking into the aquarium and reciting lines from *Jaws* to the sharks and shit. It kind of goes beyond funny, you know?"

"What? My dad didn't tell me that part."

"Oh, well, yeah, I guess he thought he was Quint and shit."

"Who else knows about this?"

"The whole town. It was in the goddamn paper. Not the Quint stuff, but, of course, word got out on that pretty quick."

"I can't believe Clay and Tommy didn't . . ."

"Again, Dermot, it wasn't their place to tell you."

"Yeah, I suppose you're right. Hey, I'm going to need to borrow your Bronco this afternoon when the lot's dead. I'll just need it for a little bit."

"Sure, what for?"

"I'm going to go to the Shoe Fort to talk with Colin."

"No problem."

"Oh, my God. Oh, boy!" Eric shrieked from outside. "Dermot, can you come out here quick?"

Dermot brushed past Molloy and hurried, spotting Clay's Cadillac coming down the street.

"What's wrong?" he asked Eric.

"Well, they're coming."

"So?"

"Well, could you deal with them . . . I guess I'm a little ah . . ."

Dermot held off using the word *nervous* to finish Eric's sentence and just nodded, waiting for the Cadillac to stop in front of the shack. Out of the corner of his eye, he caught Eric running into the shack for safety.

"What up, Clay?" Dermot smiled and then leaned on the driver's door. He scanned the passengers: Meri in the front passenger seat, Natalie in the back seat sitting next to . . . *What? What the fuck? Why is he with Natalie?*

Dermot couldn't believe it. There, sitting way too close to Natalie, was the wannabe bouncer from Meri's party, Blue Polo.

"Hey, what's up, Derm. You remember Meri?"

"Yup, hey, Meri."

"Hi, Dermot, good to see you again. You know my sister Natalie?" She thumbed to the back seat.

"Yeah, of course, what's up, Natalie?"

"Nothing much, Dermot." She motioned beside her. "Oh, this is Graham."

"Yeah, I know." He couldn't contain his sarcasm. "We met at the party. He was bouncing. I guess you could call it that. Yup, how could I forget Graham? I'll tell you that kid welcomed us with open arms. Good to see you again." Dermot eyed him and Graham shrank a bit in the backseat.

"Yeah, about that." Graham treaded lightly. "That whole thing was a real big screw up. I already told Clay I was sorry about the misunderstanding and he's cool with it. Time to move on, you know what I'm saying."

Dermot turned his glance back to Clay. "Oh, really. Clay forgave you."

Clay just raised his eyebrows and gave a "what the hell else could I do" look.

"Anyway," Natalie broke in, "Dermot, Clay said you gave us boat passes and free parking, so thanks for that."

"Oh, yeah, about that." Dermot tried thinking on his feet. "Clay, I need to give you the passes."

"Huh? What do you mean? You already gave them to me."

"What I mean is I need to validate them with the date like we do with the parking tickets. So just come in the shack for a minute." Dermot raised his eyebrows and motioned to the shack with what he hoped would be meaningful head movement.

"Since when did you start doing that?"

Molloy hollered from inside, "Clay, just get your wop ass in here!"

Clay finally got the point. They needed to talk to him. He put the car in park and said, "I'll just be a minute."

Dermot lit into Clay, "How can you hang out with that fucking asshole kid?"

"What can I do?" He shrugged.

"Easy. Don't bring him."

"I can't. He's Natalie's date. Oh, sorry, Eric."

Dejected, Eric just watched on from the La-Z-Boy.

"That kid is like nineteen or twenty," Dermot continued.

"Actually, he's eighteen," Clay said.

"Well, Natalie's only fifteen. That's sick."

"She's going to be sixteen in a couple of days. That only makes him two years older."

"Those are crucial years at that age. I can't believe this."

"Geez, Derm, it sounds more like you're the one who likes her and not Eric. Remember, you just said it, she's only fifteen. Seriously, what do you care?"

"I care for him." Dermot pointed to Eric. "And I care for her. I *do* like her. I like her as one of the good girls we always wished we had the guts to ask out. She's a nice kid, but if she hangs out with Graham, well, she'll change. You know she will. We saw it so many times back in high school. You know, how the girls would go through the dating the bad boy thing. I'm confident Natalie will figure out assholes like Graham soon, but right now she's young and naïve and he's going to use that to his advantage. It should be our job to not let it even start. She should be Eric's girl."

"Dermot, Dermot, Dermot."

"What?" Dermot turned, realizing Eric had been saying his name for a while.

"I appreciate you trying to help, but don't worry about it. It's not like I'd have a chance with her anyway. A girl like her . . . I mean, I can't even talk to her."

"That's bullshit thinking, man. That's how I thought all through high school *and* college. It got me nowhere."

"Dermot's right." Molloy had had enough and finally jumped in. "Mr. 1940s spent countless hours bitching about some dream girl he could never get, and last summer he finally strapped on some balls and got Francesca. If you learn that lesson to not give a shit and take chances early in life, Eric, you'll be better off."

Eric couldn't respond because Molloy was already out the door and now talking to the carload of people.

"Oh, shit! Oh, shit! What is he saying?" Eric muttered over and over.

Molloy then shouted, "Hey, Clay, I need you to park, oh, and Eric, I need your help out here."

Clay shrugged and went out.

Eric was in repeat mode. "Oh, shit! Oh, shit! Molloy is going to make a fool out of me."

Dermot grabbed him by his shoulders and said, "Molloy might talk some serious shit with us, but in the end, he looks out for his boys. I promise you, whatever he wants you to do, he won't embarrass you."

"Eric, I seriously, need your help!" Molloy hollered again.

Eric dragged his feet out of the shack with Dermot following and wondering what exactly Molloy was up to.

"Kid." Molloy snapped his fingers at Graham while opening the door. "Get out for a second, will you?"

"Huh?"

"I need you to get out. Come on, hurry up." Molloy clapped his hands.

"Why?"

"You want free parking?"

"Yeah."

"Then get your ass out. Come on, kid." Molloy clapped again, and Graham reluctantly got out of the car.

Molloy snapped his fingers again. "Come on, Eric, hop in."

"Huh?"

"You *do* need Miracle-Ear, don't you? Hop in and show Clay where to park in the back."

"Oh, okay." Eric finally realized Molloy's plan, got in, and sat next to Natalie.

"Oh, I can wait with Grah—" Natalie began, but Molloy tapped the Cadillac and shouted, "Head for the back lot, Clay. Eric will show you where to park."

Clay, finally on the same page, pressed on the gas and took off down the first aisle, took a right, then a left, and headed for the back.

Molloy turned to Dermot and smiled. "You see. It's that easy."

"Hey, I don't understand why you had me get out of the car. I mean . .
." Graham began, but was interrupted by a female voice shouting, "Graham!
Graham!"

Graham, Dermot, and Molloy all turned around and there was a hot
blonde around his age riding her ten-speed on the sidewalk. She skidded
to a stop.

"Graham Stockwell? Please tell me that is you." She walked over and
smiled up at him.

"Yes." He looked surprised, then smiled broadly.

"Oh, my God, Veronica? How are you?"

"I'm fabulous. It's so good to see you."

She hugged him. "It's been what . . . two years?"

"Ah, yeah. You look amazing." Graham smiled while scanning her up
and down.

"You don't look so bad yourself. So you're down on the Cape just for
the day to go to the Vineyard?"

"Actually, no, I'm living here for the summer."

"Oh, that's great. I'm down here for a couple of weeks. Daddy rented
me a house. I'm staying with four girlfriends. It's been so much fun. We
really should get together."

"Yeah, we should." Graham looked over his shoulder to see where
Natalie and crew were.

"You need a pen?" Molloy hollered over.

"What?" Graham looked back annoyed.

"A pen and some paper. You gotta get her number, right?"

"What the fuck, Molloy?" Dermot said under his breath.

"This will work out better than I planned. Keep acting pissed off at me,"
Molloy replied softly, and then said loudly, "I'm just saying. The kid needs
to get her number."

Graham smiled at Veronica. "The man's right. I need that number. Ah,
yeah, sir, could I borrow a pen and paper?"

"Sure, thing." Molloy raced into the shack, hurried out, and gave Veronica
the pen and paper. In loopy writing, she wrote her name and digits and

handed it to Graham.

"Call me sooner than later." She smiled and jumped back on her bike and pedaled off.

Molloy tilted his sunglasses and watched Veronica bike away.

"God, she's got a nice leg on her, huh?" Molloy said, nudging Graham.

"You mean she has nice *legs*?" Graham looked at him.

"No, around here we say nice *leg*. That Veronica girl had a nice leg on her. What do you think, Dermot? Did she have a nice leg or what?"

"Whatever." Dermot shook his head.

"So, you know, kid, you remind me of me when I was your age." Molloy continued his conversation with Graham.

"Oh yeah?"

"Oh yeah. It's good to see some guys still have it. Dermot over there would've pissed his pants and called for his mommy, but you, you're the real deal. You played that nice and cool. Yup, you do remind me of me back in my heyday. I used to get a lot of ladies, but I'm guessing you'd put my numbers to shame."

Graham smiled. "Well, I've been known to rack up a few."

"Whoops, shut up, here they come." Molloy got serious and walked over to the group. "Did Eric help you guys find a spot?"

"Yup," Clay and Meri said.

"Yup, Eric was a big help," Natalie added with a smile.

"Good to hear." Molloy nodded.

Natalie turned to Eric. "Well, I'm glad we talked Eric because I always wanted to tell you how much I like your poems in English class. I've actually tried to stop you, but you always kind of rushed out before I could."

"Oh, you two were in the same English class?" Dermot asked.

"Yeah, Eric likes to write like me. Dermot, you guys must have a great time talking about writing since you work together and all. Eric, I've had so many good talks with Dermot over the years about different authors and styles."

Dermot was about to answer, but was interrupted by Molloy who hit his own head with his palm. "Speaking of writing, Graham, I need that pen I let you borrow."

"Huh?" Graham's eyes bulged at the question.

"The pen. I need it back."

"Oh, ah, yeah." He quickly handed Molloy the pen.

"Why did you need his pen?" Natalie turned to Graham.

"Oh . . . I . . . ah . . ."

"He just met a girl with a nice leg on her. I'm telling you it was a nice leg. So Graham here, not letting an opportunity to go out with a girl with a nice leg get away from him, got her number." Molloy turned his classic smile on, and Dermot and Clay couldn't help but laugh.

Meri punched Clay in the shoulder. "It's not funny."

"Graham, is he serious?" Natalie asked.

"No, I didn't get . . . a . . . Come on, this is ridiculous. We should get going."

"No. No. No," Meri jumped in. "Wait, let me get this straight. You're going to the Vineyard with my sister, and when she's out of your sight for like five minutes you get another girl's number? Tell me this isn't true."

"Of course, it's not true. I don't know what that guy is talking about?"

"What I'm talking about is you got a number in your pocket from a girl with a nice leg on her. You should be proud of that shit."

"Show me your pockets," Meri ordered.

"Meri, he said he didn't get a number . . ." Natalie began, but then turned to Dermot, "Wait, Dermot, did he get some girl's number or not?"

"Yeah, he did. I'm sorry. Natalie, you're a good kid. I don't even know why you're with this guy."

"Fuck you, asshole," Graham grunted.

"No, screw you, Graham. I can't believe I fell for all of that stuff you said to me the other night," Natalie said. "I still want to go to the Vineyard with you guys, Meri."

"Sure, let's go." Meri nodded to Clay, who followed the girls leaving Graham standing with Eric, Dermot, and Molloy.

Molloy laughed. "You still here, kid?"

"What the fuck was that, man?" Graham glared at him.

"Not my fault you didn't see that one coming. Now, get your chicken dick out of here, kid."

"I'm going, and you might think you're all funny and shit, but I still have a number, and I'm still going to get laid while you three circle-jerk one another." He raised the paper in the air, but behind him, Clay appeared, snatched the paper from him, and ripped it up, tossing the pieces to the wind.

"I forgot my wallet in the Caddy," Clay said to the group and ignoring Graham.

"What the fuck!" Graham shouted.

"Get the fuck out of here before I kick your ass," Clay barked, causing Graham to pick up his pace until he was far enough away to hurl his slurs before taking off.

Eric turned to all three of them and said, "Thanks, you guys. That was one of the best moments of my life."

"That's nothing. Wait till she gives you a hand gallop." Molloy laughed.

"Geez, Molloy, do you always have to ruin everything by being so sick?" Dermot shook with laughter, and Clay joined in.

"Hey, Dermot, if we did it your Jimmy Stewart way, the kid would still be inside sitting on the La-Z-Boy crying with his hard on. But now the game is on!"

"You know, Molloy you're a real asshole." Dermot chuckled.

He grinned. "Like I said before, I may be an asshole, but I'm not a *fucking* asshole."

Colin was relieved as he exited the air-conditioned Shoe Fort and headed into the early evening summer heat. Just as he had expected, the day had been hectic, and showing up late hadn't sat well with the usually mild-mannered Larry Furfey. The elderly manager had always taken pride in his position and wanted all employees to follow suit. To Larry, arriving late on a cloudy summer's day was almost as bad as calling in sick. He had taken Colin into the stockroom and laid into him, questioning his "maturity" and "leadership."

After lunch, Larry's cold shoulder routine went to another level, leaving Colin wondering if perhaps he had talked with Jeff or someone else when grabbing his afternoon iced coffee from Coffee Mania. He knew it was only a matter of time before word of the art show tirade spread. He avoided walking past Coffee Mania by crossing to the other side of the street and picking up pace. With the events of last night now racing through his head, plus Melissa's drop-by visit early that morning, another wave of shame and embarrassment toppled him.

I can't believe Melissa. What a fucking sellout. She's had bad nights. She's no angel. I can flip this. I will just say, "An embarrassing thing happened to me last night, Mom, and I really need to talk to you about it." I'll put it on Mel. She's the one who is guilty about Tad. I'll flip it. I have to. I have to make Mom believe me. From this day forward I have to be smarter. Gotta stay out of trouble. I don't want to get kicked out of the house. This time it could be forever.

Crossing the street again, he hopped into the driver's seat and quickly fired up his car and headed for home. "Why wait?" he said to himself. "Let's just get it over with." He turned the stereo up loud and sang along to "The Day I Tried To Live" by Soundgarden. Having a plan and knowing he could charm his way out of trouble lifted his spirits for the time being. With his left hand manning the wheel, he cautiously rummaged around his car for cigarettes. That's when his eye caught the plastic bag staring at him.

Oh, man, Eric's hat.

A smile formed, and instead of going straight home, he decided to make a quick pit stop at the *Island Ferry* to see Eric. There was something about the kid that he liked. There was one problem: Dermot. The last thing Colin wanted was to hear Dermot and his self-righteous bullshit. *If he's there, I'll bail.*

As he pulled in, he saw Eric directing a confused couple driving a car with Quebec plates. The car inched onto Beach Street, and as soon as they drove out of sight, Eric shook his head, put his hands in the air, and yelled to Colin, "Crazy Canadians. Gotta love 'em."

"No you don't," Colin shouted back as he lit up a smoke, making his way over to him.

"What's up, Colin?"

"Not much Eazy-E. Just getting off work. You the only one running the lot?" The two high-fived.

"For now. I can't believe they left me here alone. I was really struggling to keep up with all these cars, but they radioed down from the ticket office, and there's only two more people coming this way, thank God. Man, this job is a lot harder than it looks."

"Bullshit, man. Half the time you guys sit on your ass rating the chicks walking by."

Eric laughed. "Okay, you got a point. Hey, what's in that bag?"

"That, my friend is what you've been waiting for."

Colin grinned, slowly removing the worn and beaten hat from the bag and handing it over to a wide-eyed Eric.

"Wow, C-Dog, this is awesome. I love the brim," he said as he placed it on his head. "This is crazy. It looks like a completely different hat."

Colin smirked. "Kind of my point. You've arrived, bro. It took a little while, but that *is* one sweet hat, man. Cape style, homey."

"I needed this, too, 'cause I was getting a hard time for not being in full uniform."

"Glad I got it to you then. Enjoy it. I gotta run. I'm sure I'll talk to you soon."

"No, C-Dog. Don't go yet. She came in today."

"Who came in?"

"Natalie."

"Natalie? No shit? What happened?"

Just as Eric began telling his story a middle-aged father pushing his handicapped son in a wheelchair walked onto the lot.

"It's Eric, right?" The man stopped, caught his breath, and wiped a bead of sweat from his forehead.

"Yes, Mr. Gomes, right?"

"You remembered. So how was your day?"

"Good. Busy, but good."

The man's eyes shifted over to Colin who was in mid-drag. He realized the situation and flicked his cigarette behind the shack.

"Hi, Eric." The boy sounded younger than he looked.

Eric leaned down. "Hey, Donnie. How did you like Martha's Vineyard? Was it fun?"

With his head cocked to one side and the sun shining down on his young, peach-fuzzed face, Donnie excitedly told Eric about his day, while Colin looked on. "It was awesome! We went to the Flying Circus, and my daddy picked me out of my chair and held me on a horse. I felt like I was riding across the Wild West!"

"That's, right, pal. You were like a cowboy today, weren't you?" Mr. Gomes said, wiping more sweat from his forehead.

"Yeah, Daddy. I was like a cowboy, Eric. And we got some gold rings. It was so much fun. Then after we went to the beach and we saw all these people on mopeds. And my Daddy took me swimming. The water was really, really cold, but it felt good. Then we went to this place for lunch, and I had a cheeseburger with French fries." He pointed with his arthritic hand that appeared almost claw-like to a hat perched on his head that had an image of the MV Black Dog.

"Wow." Eric's eyes lit up and he exaggerated his enthusiasm. "That's a real sweet hat, Donnie. All the kids back home are gonna be so jealous of you. Don't you think, Colin?"

Colin nodded. "Yeah, I bet all the kids will want a hat like that!"

"But you know what?" Eric stopped.

"What?"

"In order to make that hat complete we need to break it in a little, that way you're a true Cape Codder." He turned to Colin and winked.

"What do you mean, Eric?"

"Can I show you?"

Eric took Donnie's hat and replaced it with his, and slowly began rolling the brim between his hands as the father and son watched on. "We just need to work it out a little. We can't have this thing look too stiff on you. It has to be a nice, relaxed fit. Like a baseball glove. Right, Colin?"

"Yup. Listen to this guy, Donnie. He knows what he's talking about."

"I will. His hat is comfortable. Your name is Colin?"

"Yes."

"My name is Donnie. And this is my daddy. His name is Mike, but people like to call him *Mr. Gomes*."

Colin walked over and shook both their hands.

"So, Donnie, do you like baseball?" Colin asked pointing to the Red Sox game jersey Donnie was wearing. For the next few minutes they talked baseball stats while Eric worked the hat over. After sculpting it with his hands, Eric put it back on Donnie's head, adjusting it comfortably for him.

"Now you look like Mike Greenwell, buddy. How does it feel?"

"It feels great. Thanks a lot, Eric."

"No problem."

"Thanks, Eric. You're a good kid . . ." He paused and turned to Colin. "You both are."

As Mr. Gomes pushed Donnie away, Colin said to Eric, "So, I don't quite get it. Are they friends of yours?"

"They are now. I just met them this morning. They're from Springfield. Really nice guy. He's a single father. I got the feeling his wife couldn't take the pressure of raising a kid with problems. "

Colin nodded.

"They missed the ten-thirty boat, so like you just did, we talked for a while about baseball, and, of course, the strike came up . . ." He paused. "You know what pisses me off about this whole strike talk, Colin?"

"What?"

"That kid loves baseball. You should've heard him this morning. He seemed a little tired this afternoon, but this morning he was throwing out Red Sox stats like crazy. I mean stats as far back as the '67 Impossible Dream Team. He just glowed telling me how Mo Vaughn is his favorite player and other stuff like that. And here he is, one of baseball's biggest fans, a kid who can't even play a simple game of catch with his dad, or even run the bases. All he can do is *watch* the game. But now, because of money and egos, in a couple of weeks he'll be up in the Springfield heat and won't even be able to do that."

"I know. It's pretty ridiculous. You were great with him, though. You made his day. You had him smiling the whole time. He really likes you."

"He made mine, and if I were to be so bold, he seemed to put a smile on your face, too. It sucks, though. He's just thirteen. And because of that wheelchair and stuff there is so much he'll never be able to experience. Life sometimes just isn't fair. I see him smile and laugh and I realize, shit, I'm pretty lucky."

"I know what you mean." Colin lit up another smoke. "Hey, why are they parked in the back? Don't you have handicapped parking?"

"Yeah we do, but the older guy I work with gave the last spot to some blonde college girl."

"Let me guess, Molloy?"

"Yeah. You know him?"

"Oh, yeah. I've known him since I was a kid. My friends and I used to come by here on our bikes all the time."

"I can't figure that guy out. He actually helped with Natalie today."

"He doesn't mean any harm. I think he acts the way he does more for show. Let me guess." In his best Molloy voice, Colin said, "Did Natalie have a 'nice leg' on her?"

"Wow, you *do* know him. He actually did say that, but I'll save it for the story."

"Yup. Where is that clown?"

"He's at the far lot."

"Siberia?"

"Um, yeah. He said he wanted to do let-outs of those cars instead, but I think he just didn't want to see the kid when he got back because now he feels like a jerk. And he very well should. No offense, but he's a dog when it comes to women."

"Big time." Colin took a drag from his smoke. "All right, enough about him. I want to hear about Natalie."

"Oh, yeah. Well, she came in with Clay and Meri this morn—" Eric was interrupted by an elderly couple who pulled into the lot beeping their horn and waving him over.

"Excuse me, young man, what time does your first boat leave tomorrow?"

"Oh, man, I can't get a break," Eric said to Colin. "Let me go deal with these people and then let the Gomes's out and then, hopefully, I can give you the whole story. I promise it won't be too long."

"Don't worry, it's cool. Take your time. I'll just wait in here for you," Colin said, motioning to the shack.

"Well, I'm not allowed to have visitors go in there."

"Don't worry, Eric. I'm family when it comes to this place." Colin toed out his cigarette. In the shack, he saw the two La-Z-Boys facing a coffee table, which held a small black-and-white television sprouting a coat hanger for an antenna. This was where he and Dermot had played countless hours of Tecmo Super Bowl on rainy summer days and slow autumn weekends. It had been over a year since he had seen the inside, but the interior hadn't changed much. The décor was still Molloy. Above the old and abused metal time clock hung a poster of Anna Nichole Smith blowing a kiss, wearing red lipstick that matched her short satin nightgown. *Damn, that woman's fine.*

After snatching a Coke from the mini, Colin reached under the loveseat and pulled an old *Playboy* that featured the Girls Of The ACC from Molloy's stack. As he did, he noticed something sticking out of the seat cushion. He got up, turned around, and pulled the cushion off to reveal a five-subject notebook. Colin *had* to read the first page because someone had attempted to hide it.

"The Color Red," by Eric Chance.

Colin took his eyes off the paper and peeked out the window to see what Eric was doing. He was now talking with Mr. Gomes and Donnie, so Colin knew he was safe to read on.

I took out my piece of lead
as my third grade teacher said—
"I want you to write about the color red."
"No, no, not red!
I hate that color," I shook my head.
"But, Little Eric, how can you hate the color red?"
"Please, just let me write about green instead."
"Is that what I said?
No, young man, I want you to write about the color red!
For example," she said, "red is the color of a fire truck."
If I knew the word I would have said, "So who gives a fuck," BUT I JUST

plead, "Please, please, I want to dream about green instead!"
"No dream!" She again shook her head.
"Another example of red is that's the color of Santa's sled,"
said the kid beside me, who, for the purpose of this rhyme, we'll call Ted.
Oh, not red, red, red I hate red, I thought, but said—
"You know, red is also the color of a stoplight."
"Yes, yes, Eric, that's so right!"
She smiled bright patting my head.
"I know that because it was red, red, red but the drunk driver still drove
through it and struck my daddy and then he bled, bled, bled until he was
like your favorite color, yes, he was good and red and of course forever dead.
So for once can I dream about the color green instead? Or teacher, will it
always have to be red, red, red?!!"

Colin sat in stunned silence. He read it again and all he could hear was
Eric's joyous voice in the background talking with the Gomes family.

"Well, it was nice meeting both of you. And I hope you come back soon.
Drive safely, and, Donnie, remember you're a Cape Codder now. . . Hey,
Colin, get out here!" Eric yelled.

Colin shoved the notebook back in the chair and popped his head out
the door just in time to see Donnie yell out the window, "Bye, Eric. Bye,
Colin. See you next year."

"I look forward to it. Bye, guys," Eric shouted back, but all Colin could
do was give a weak wave. His mind was on the poem. He hurried back to
the loveseat, picked up another *Playboy*, sat in the La-Z-Boy, and flipped
through it trying to act natural as Eric walked into the shack.

"All set?" Colin asked.

"Yeah, man, I really like those two. Found Molloy's stash, I see, so you
must really be family."

"Yup."

"So, are you ready to hear about one of the best days of my life?" Eric
asked, slapping Colin on his outstretched leg, before plopping down in the
adjacent La-Z-Boy.

"I'm all ears, Eric."

For the next five minutes Eric recounted the events that had transpired earlier that day—his short car ride with Natalie, their conversation about poetry and how great it was to be sitting next to her. But it was the part about Molloy that they both got a good laugh from.

"C-Dog, I couldn't believe how he hooked me up like that. I didn't know he had it in him."

"Well, again, that's Molloy, a complete enigma. First, he gives away a handicapped spot to a chick, and then he turns around and does a good deed for the little man. Don't try to figure that guy out, man."

The whole time Colin couldn't shake Eric's poem from his head. He looked at this kid who was smiling from ear to ear and he couldn't believe how happy he was.

Will I ever be that happy again in my life?

"You know what the best part was, Colin? Once she found out that jerk Graham got a number, she didn't let it ruin her day. She still went to the Vineyard with Clay and Meri. Strong and beautiful. What a combination." He stared into space.

"That's awesome, Eric. I'm happy for you. That guy Graham sounds like your typical summer asshole. Natalie is a good girl. She needs to be with a good guy."

"Yeah. You're right. That's what that guy I work with, Dermot, said. He was pretty instrumental in making it happen. He kept saying she's a good girl who should be with a good guy."

For a second Colin considered telling Eric who Dermot was but decided it would just slow down his pep talk, so instead he said, "Well, that Dermot guy is right. So the question is, are you that good guy?"

"Um, I don't know."

"C'mon, Eric. It's time to man-up. You know she's single. Plus, you have a lot in common *and* she even complimented you on your writing. What else do you need? Ask her out."

"I don't know, C-Dog. I'm not a ladies' man."

"It doesn't sound like she's looking for one. Listen, I struggled when I was your age, too. But if I knew then what I know now, it would have been a completely different ball game. Let me tell you a story that, hopefully, will change your mind."

"Okay, cool."

"Her name was Jenny Mosley. I was a sophomore and she was a year older. She had moved from Arkansas. She was absolutely stunning with long blonde hair and blue eyes that entranced me when she'd talk with that southern accent. I had never seen anyone so gorgeous before."

"Really?"

"Really. Every time I saw her I would get those butterflies and turn numb."

"Yeah?"

"Yeah, man, everybody's been there, Eric. It's part of growing up."

"So what happened?"

"Well, one night I talked with her at a party after a swim meet. I told some jokes and made her laugh and after talking with her, I felt very comfortable, because she was so damn funny."

"You were on the swim team?"

"Yeah. Why are you surprised?"

"Well, you smoke cigarettes, for one."

"Yeah, but I didn't then."

"Why do you smoke now?"

"Eric, can I just please tell you my story."

"I'm sorry, man."

"It's okay." Colin paused. "All right, where was I?"

"You became friends."

"Right, we became friends, good friends. We would go out for dinner or go grab ice cream. We rode the bike path a lot. Just hung out and laughed. It was great, but the whole time I realized something. I was in love with her."

"How did you know?"

"It was beyond the looks. It was something my brother once told me."

"You have a brother?"

"May I go on?"

"Yup. Sorry."

"My brother said to me, 'You know you're in love when the girl you like makes you feel comfortable. She makes you feel cool.' That's how Jenny made me feel when she laughed at my jokes. The only problem was there was another side of me that felt like Duckie in *Pretty in Pink*."

"Who's Duckie?"

"*Pretty in Pink.*"

"Still don't know."

"It's a movie from the eighties, you should rent it sometime. Anyway, I fell into that friend role, but, Eric, I was head over heels in love with this girl. She was all I thought about night and day. I'm sure you can relate to that."

"Oh, yeah. So what did you do about it?"

"Absolutely nothing. I spent so much time with her but in those two years never told her how I really felt. Then after she graduated, she went to college in Ohio, and we talked on the phone a couple of times, but that was about it. Her parents moved back to Arkansas and I never saw her again. We don't even talk anymore." He paused and sighed deeply. "Thank God I had my friends back then because I was so heartbroken. I really loved her and never did a damn thing about it."

"Wow, that's sad. I'm sorry for you, Colin."

"Hey, it is what it is. But I tell you this story because I don't want *you* to live in regret. And don't listen to Molloy and his bullshit about getting laid or anything like that. It's not about that, not even a little bit. It's about being with someone who makes you *feel*. I mean really feel. You like Natalie. You need to let her know."

"But what if she's not interested?"

"That's a chance you have to take, but at least then you will know. And I think you have a shot. Remember, Natalie is beautiful, but she's like Jenny— she's a good girl who just wants to be with a good guy. And if you're not going to do it for yourself, do it for me. Think about the pain I had to go through because I didn't say anything. Not knowing is the worst. Trust me, bro, you don't want that pain."

"Okay, okay. I'll try. But you have to help me, Colin."

"Don't worry. We'll work together on this one."

"Thanks, C-Dog. You're a hell of a guy."

"Yeah, I know," he said, laughing. Colin walked out of the Shack and headed to his car with Eric following. Before opening the driver's-side door, he prodded his young friend. "All right, we're gonna do this, right?"

"Yeah, I guess."

Colin grabbed Eric and put him in a playful headlock and started lightly slapping him on the head. "What do you mean, you guess? You're going to ask out Natalie Nazerian if it's the last thing you do. You understand me, Eric Chance?

Eric laughed and said, "Okay, I promise, Colin, I'll try. Just let go of me."

"No, man." Colin kept him in a headlock and their momentum brought them back to the shack. "No trying. I want to hear, 'Yes, Colin, I will!'"

"Yes, Colin, I will . . . try."

Just then their play-fighting was cut short by the sound of a screeching Bronco bulldozing into the lot. It startled both of them, and Colin let go of Eric and looked up and instinctively said, "Molloy?" But it wasn't Molloy who jumped out of the Bronco and grabbed him, and threw him against the shack. No, it was his brother in a fit of rage.

"Keep your fucking hands off him, asshole!" Dermot screamed in his face.

"What the fuck is your problem?" Colin automatically pushed back. That's when Colin was caught by a right hook to his mouth, slamming his head against the shack's shutters. He fell to the ground. At first, more stunned than hurt, Colin felt his jaw and instead of punching back, stared up at Dermot, who was looking down at him with both fists ready to go.

"What are you doing?" Eric screamed.

"What am I doing? He was hurting you?"

"No, he wasn't. We were just playing. He's my friend. What's wrong with you, Dermot?" Eric screamed.

"Yeah, well . . . He's my brother and he's a fucking loser!"

Colin, still in a daze, got to his feet and walked past Dermot, not saying a word. Dermot had never hit him before and he was in shock. "Well, if he's your brother, why the hell are you punching him?"

"Don't worry about it, Eric. Dermot always assumes the worst when it comes to me," Colin said as he wiped a small trickle of blood from his mouth.

"Don't make yourself sound like a fucking victim here. Dad told me about the Aquarium. You have turned into a townie loser, Colin. A complete fuck-up. I should've punched you months ago!"

"That's kind of hard to do since you were all the way in Ireland crying in your Guinness over some whore who owned you."

"You son of a bitch!" Dermot lunged at him again, but this time Eric held him back.

"Cut the shit, Dermot! You guys are brothers. Family! This isn't right."

"That's right. We *are* family, so mind your own business," Dermot said, composing himself. "Just get the fuck out of here, Colin. Go find Chucky or some of your other loser friends. I can't even look at you. You make me want to puke."

"Thanks, Derm. Yeah, I guess you're right. I sure got a lot of friends these days. You know, you're one hell of a brother. Thanks for always being there for me, *Champ*."

"What does that mean?"

"It doesn't matter. Nothing matters anymore." He stared long and hard at Dermot, then got into his car and drove off.

FIFTEEN

Dermot, holding a long pole given to him by Captain Stansfield, appropriately had the song "Medicine Bow" by The Waterboys still blasting in his head as he waded through the thigh-high water flooding the back of the *Island Ferry* parking lot. A few minutes before, he had been in the shack, warm and dry, stretched out in one of the La-Z-Boys listening to his Red Rain Mix tape on his Walkman. Molloy had kicked back on the couch. With the baseball strike underway, he was ogling and grunting at the cleavage treats that flashed across the muted Spanish channel.

"God, they taught me Spanish all wrong. If they had only shown us these bitches back in high school I would've changed my name to Jose Molloy and would've become the goddamn mayor of Mexico!" Molloy bellowed as Dermot tried to escape to his mix-tape world.

But Dermot's comfort left him when the captain's truck barreled into the lot. It zoomed up and down every aisle and before Dermot knew what hit him, he had lost a Rock, Paper, Scissors game with Molloy. And because of that loss, he no longer had his Walkman on and was no longer warm and dry, but he was cold and drenched trudging through the slashing rain and booming thunder and lightning that lit up the dark afternoon. His job was to use the pole to poke around in the far back corner of the lot until he found the clogged storm drain. When he found it, he had been instructed to use the pole to push the drain open so all of the water could then rush down into it. Before he continued to the back lot, which resembled a rising lake, he turned around, cupped his hands, and shouted to Stansfield who was parked at the edge of the flooded area.

"This is pretty deep! How bad's this storm going to be?"

From the warmth of his truck's cab, the captain leaned out the window and hollered back, "We've canceled the next two boats, but the storm's supposed to pass in a few hours or so. Be careful when you open it." He paused and then laughed. "You don't want to be sucked down the drain. Oh, and you also might want to hurry up because it looks like that lightning is getting closer."

"Huh?"

"Brennan." Stansfield pointed at the pole. "I know you're used to having a rod in your hands but that one is metal."

Dermot flipped him the bird. "Whatever, Captain Valdez."

Stansfield loved it and grinned. "You know what, Brennan, Captain Moore is going to do the last trip, which means I'm off for the rest of the day and a drink does sound like a great idea. I think I'm going to take my oil tanker and get the hell out of here!" The truck peeled off, spraying more water all over Dermot.

"Asshole," Dermot muttered.

Normally, unclogging a drain that was always covered with whatever random trash that had floated into the corner would've been a rookie's job, but when the rain arrived that duty changed. Business had become so slow that someone had to be released early, so he and Molloy decided to send Eric home with strict instructions: "Strap it on and go to Coffee Mania to ask Natalie out."

Eric had breathed hard, nodding and sounding like a minor leaguer psyching himself up to face Nolan Ryan. "This time I will. I have to. I know I will."

"Yeah, you will, Eric. We know you will," Molloy and Dermot agreed, but when Eric rode his bike out of the lot it was obvious what they really believed. Molloy laughed for a while.

"No way in hell that kid asks her out this summer."

Out of spite, Dermot considered betting him, but wasn't a sucker. Eric had made that same statement about twenty shifts in a row. Now that it was out in the open about his crush on Natalie Nazerian, Eric talked about her constantly to Molloy and Dermot, plotting how he would ask her. They all came up with some great ideas, but as far as actually doing anything about it, Eric remained gun shy. They reminded him often it wasn't an impossible mission. He definitely had an "in" with her. Now, whenever Eric went to the coffee shop, Natalie asked how his writing was going and one time she even said, "Sometime I'd like to show you some of my poetry."

Eric's reply had been a stutter. "Yeah, maybe."

Those two words entertained Molloy for a whole week. "Yeah, maybe! Shit, kid, that girl was throwing you a lifeline to hook up and you didn't grab it. Yup, it's official, you *are* worse than Dermot. You know what, I'm going to start calling you Mr. 1930s."

"God, it would really make my day if he did ask her out," Dermot said to himself, but then drifted to another thought as he watched two kids laughing with one another, furiously pedaling their dirt bikes through the puddles beside the sidewalk. He thought they resembled gray ghosts riding off into the mist.

"This sucks!" he yelled at the top of his lungs to the sky as he worked the pole around hoping to hit the jackpot.

If the drain hadn't clogged, it would've been an easy day for him. He could've just sat on his ass while another hangover faded away, bullshitting with Molloy or zoning out to the beat of the drops against the shingles. But, it did clog and if it wasn't fixed soon, water would rise to car windows and eventually seep into those cars and then all hell would break loose. He had to stop daydreaming and act quickly. As he fished with the pole along the concrete for the grates of the storm drain, a part of him was actually relieved he *was* getting wet and doing something active, not zoning out because the Red Rain Mix had been forcing him to think of things he didn't want to think about and they all depressed him—Francesca, Tommy and Clay now having girlfriends, not writing, and Colin.

Lately, the last topic depressed him the most. It had been about a month since he had the fight with his brother, and he still felt sick about it. Nothing he had promised his dad about reaching out to Colin had happened, in fact, he had done just the opposite. Thinking about the fight again, Dermot slammed the pole into the water and against the concrete shooting more spray. He had never punched his brother before that day. Dermot was sorry Eric had to witness that.

"Colin's been great to me and you have, too, Dermot. You know, I'm an only child and I guess . . . I think . . . Well, you guys are so lucky to be brothers. I wish I had a brother," Eric had told him after Colin had left.

"You call having that fuck-up for a brother being lucky? You don't know shit, Eric."

Dermot had walked away, regretting his words immediately but at the same time refusing to take them back. It was easier to embrace the rift, so he handled his situation with Colin with true Irish resolution. He gave him the silent treatment. And it was evident that Colin was doing the same. Of course, to avoid any family meetings, they had an unspoken pact of fooling their parents by playing the old game of exchanging pleasantries around Mr. and Mrs. Brennan: "Hey, man, how was work?"; "The baseball strike is coming"; "See any good movies lately?" But when their parents weren't around it was ice between them; each pretended that the other didn't exist.

Dermot slammed the pole down again into the puddle. More water. This time he didn't wipe his face.

"I think Colin's getting better again," Mrs. Brennan had told Dermot a few weeks after the fight. His Dad had repeated the same feeling. Colin had confessed to Mrs. Brennan about how embarrassed he was about the fight with Melissa, and the parents took that as a sign that Colin was coming around. Dermot knew better. That was pure grade-*A* Colin Brennan BS. If Colin really felt guilty about everything, he would've apologized to Melissa before she left for New York for the rest of the summer to do an art museum internship and be near her new boyfriend. Acting remorseful to his parents was Colin's best strategy to avoid getting his ass tossed out on the street. It certainly hadn't meant he had quit drinking or doing drugs. That's for damn sure. Dermot still heard the whispers. Too many whispers.

"Finally," he said to himself after he felt the pole lock into the teeth of the grates.

Like a weightlifter, he bent his knees and crouched down. He was about to push down on the pole when he heard the foghorn. It sounded closer than it had all day. The last time Dermot had really listened to the foghorn was on that night the previous summer, and nothing had been the same since then. A line then came to him: the foghorn was more like a questioning moan of futility and not a warning call to the travelers of the sea . . .

"I'll have to ask Eric if he thinks it's worthy of anything or if it's just a piece of shit." Dermot pushed down on the pole. Along with living vicariously through Eric when it came to his crush on Natalie, the one thing Dermot really liked about working with the young kid was that they both had the same interest in writing. Talking about that interest had made this summer's shifts go by faster.

For many summers Dermot had been stuck with Johnny Towers, a seventy- something-year-old former high school football coach. He was a guy who knew only three jokes involving either rabbis or priests walking into bars, and after he told those, he would spend the rest of the workday recounting every play of every game he had ever coached. It was sad. *Will I be like that? Always living in the past?*

"I'm like that now!" And he hadn't accomplished a damn thing. At least Coach Towers had that Division Four Championship team back in '73. "Fuck it." He pushed down on the pole as hard as he could. The drain then creaked open just enough and like a whirlpool the water around him began to swirl, and in seconds, it rushed for the hole. The force of the wave almost knocked him over, but he held on knowing if he let go the drain would close and he would have to start the whole process over again. He desperately fought to keep his balance while he pushed down on the pole. It worked. After about five minutes, the back lot was water free. He scanned the cause of the blockage and saw fast-food bags, a turned-over deserted shopping cart, and scattered baby diapers.

"Some people," he spat and headed back toward the Shack to grab a trash bag, but he stopped walking when he saw Molloy on the phone in the doorway. Dermot stood in the falling rain because he didn't want to interrupt Molloy, who he figured was talking on the phone with his girlfriend (known only to Dermot), not his wife, but then Molloy gestured to him.

When he hesitated, Molloy put his hand on the phone and shouted to him, "It's your mom!"

"Oh." He picked up pace.

"Did you fix the flood?" Molloy asked, handing him the phone.

"Yeah, don't worry. You can stay nice and dry and learn more Spanish," he said to Molloy before turning his attention to the receiver. "Hi, Mom. What's up?"

"Oh, hi honey. Did I hear you say Mr. Molloy is learning Spanish?"

"Ah, yeah, sure."

"Well tell him that a desire to learn is a great quality."

"Yeah, sure, Mom, I'll tell him. So, what's up?"

"Well . . . it's . . . I have some news . . ."

"Is there something wrong with Colin?" he blurted out.

"Why would you say that?" she replied.

Why wouldn't I say that? "No reason. What's wrong?"

"Well, there's nothing wrong . . . it's just that . . . well . . . I just got the mail and you got a postcard from Italy. It's of the Leaning Tower Of Pisa."

Italy! The Leaning Tower Of Pisa! Oh, my God! Francesca! She wrote to me!

Mrs. Brennan continued, "I didn't read the card. I just saw it was addressed to you and thought you might like to know."

"Ah, yeah. Thanks, Mom!"

"I have my book club coming over for tea, so I can bring the card over to The Sea Shanty and put it on your desk or when your dad comes home he can drop it off to you."

He thought for a minute and realized he couldn't wait that long. He had to know what Francesca wrote. "No. No. No. Mom. Actually, can you read it to me?"

"Are you sure?" she asked.

"Yes, I'm sure. I need to hear it. But, please read it straight through."

"What do you mean?"

"Well, I mean don't stop to analyze what she's writing."

"Okay."

In his mind he could see Francesca's handwriting probably in purple pen. *How could I have been such a fool? I need you! I miss you! I love you! Please come to Italy!*

That was not what he heard.

In Mrs. Brennan's sweetest voice she read non-stop and verbatim: "Dear Derment, remember how we say bad girlfriends are bitches. I came to place where they are not no bitches. They nice girls who like me. The picture on card is not me! My little Japanese friend in pants is not leaning! He is flying straight and happy since I meet girl named Angela with a big tit on her as you tell me in pub. I hope you still no cries in beer! Please come to Italy! Your Japanese friend, Kaz." The confusion in Mrs. Brennan's voice faded as the realization hit both of them.

"Classy guy." His mom tried to break the ice.

"Yeah, he is." And Dermot then laughed so his mother could. After explaining to his mom who Kaz was, he hung up the phone and faced Molloy, who doubled over with laughter. The laughter increased when Dermot explained the postcard's contents.

"Oh, my God," Molloy said, trying to wipe his eyes dry. "I can't believe it! Margaret Brennan actually uttered my line about a girl having a big tit on her."

"I know. Don't remind me."

"That's a classic! But, Dermot, know what the kicker is?"

"What?"

"What are the chances that you get a postcard from *Italy* and it's not Francesca! Wow, God *really* is out to fuck with you, huh?"

"Yeah." Dermot forced more laughter but inside was making his plans for the night. *I'm going to Pucky's and I'm going to get fucking hammered.*

After his shift, he threw his drenched *Island Ferry* shirt and khakis into the laundry basket and, even though it was still thundering and lightning, he headed for an outdoor shower. He didn't care; he wanted to tempt Fate. *Maybe I'll get struck and killed. That would be a good way to go. No one would ever forget me if that happened. Yup, that would show Francesca, too! The guilt she would have to live with would be worth it.* Like a scene from a bad romantic movie, within twenty minutes, the sun broke through the clouds. Dermot did not feel sunny; he was more focused on his mission than ever. Wrapping the towel around his waist, he walked into The Shanty, opened the Guinness fridge, and grabbed the first beer on the line, a Keystone Light.

Keystone Light? If fuckin' Colin is leaving his underage shit here and drinking it later I might as well . . . He sucked it down and actually liked it, and then went into the other room and threw the empty can up into the fan. It was a tradition that he, Clay, and Tommy had before girlfriends came into the picture. The fan grabbed the can and launched it, slamming it up against the overhanging poster, slicing a slight hole in the armpit of Ian Astbury, the lead singer of The Cult, before continuing on its wild path, finally landing snuggly on the empty bookshelf beside the tattered copy of *The Old Man and The Sea.*

Dermot stared at the book for a long time. He then turned around and went into the other room, grabbed another beer, drank it down just as quickly, and underhanded it up at the fan. This time the fan shot it back in his direction making him duck and almost lose his towel.

"I guess not," he said and then got dressed and headed across the street for Pucky's. He was about to cross onto the Wiffle ball field when he spotted Tommy leaning against the fence.

"TK? TK? Is that you?"

Tommy turned. "Oh, hey Dermot, what's up?"

"What's up? You tell me. I haven't seen you all fucking summer, man."

Tommy pushed off the fence, wiped his wet hands on his jeans, and walked over.

"I know." He smiled slightly. "Sorry about that. Been real busy with the girlfriend."

"Justine."

"No, man, Jessica."

"Oh, sorry, it's just that you thought her name was Justine the first night you met her. You know, when we used to hang out. Remember, I had to remind you?"

"Vaguely." Tommy shrugged.

"But how would I know her name? You haven't even stopped by The Shanty or the Shack to introduce me."

"No, man, that's not true. I've come by a few times, but I just keep missing you." Dermot didn't want to argue, and he really could use a drinking partner for the night, someone to get his mind off Francesca and everything else.

"Well, you're here now and I'd like to know all about the love of your life."

"You would?"

"Sure, TK. Why don't we go to Pucky's and throw a few suds back and you can tell me all about this Jessica chick with the party balloons who's rocking your world."

"Oh. Well . . ."

"Well what?"

"It's just she's my girlfriend now and I don't really like talking about her like that. You know what I mean?"

"Oh, Jesus, whatever. I'll keep my questions PG for you. Let's go." Dermot began cutting across the park.

"Um, well, Derm, I really can't," he said and raised his voice. "You see I'm supposed to meet her after she gets out of work."

Dermot turned around. "I thought Clay told me she worked at the movie theater."

"She does."

"So what's that, 11:30?"

"No, midnight."

"Even better. It's like quarter of eight. We can put in a full night of drinking before you have to hang out with her."

"I know, Derm. It's just that I don't feel like drinking tonight."

"What?"

"You heard me. I just don't feel like it tonight."

"I don't get it. You don't *feel* like it? Then, why are you up the street from my house leaning against the fence staring out at nothing?"

"Oh, no, it wasn't *nothing*. Did you see the clouds break and that sunset tonight?"

"Huh?"

"The sunset? Did you see it?"

"Ah, no."

"Oh, man, it was something. There was this heavy pink-colored sun that went down just about five minutes ago. I swear the horizon flashed green when it happened. It was absolute poetry in motion."

"Wait. Wait. Wait. Wait." Dermot was trying to wrap his brain around what he was hearing. "So you're telling me you walked down to my neighborhood not to hang out with me and drink beers but to see the sunset?"

Tommy didn't seem to hear the contempt in his voice. "No, actually I was planning on taking a long walk down on the beach. You see, I was watching the news earlier, and I guess there are going to be a lot of stars out tonight."

"So?"

"I don't know," Tommy pondered out loud. "I just thought I might walk the beach and try and grab me one. I also don't want to get loaded before meeting up with Jess."

"Sunsets? Stars? Grab me one? Keating, what the fuck are you talking about?"

"Come on, Derm. You're a man of words. You know what I mean. I just want to take in the night and appreciate where I live. You know, we never stop to take a deep breath and say, 'Wow, I'm so lucky to live on Cape Cod.' So you wanna come with me? It'll be fun. I can tell you all about Jess, and you can tell me how your summer has been."

"Could we hold hands, too?"

"Huh?"

"Nothing. You go and have fun, Stargazer." Dermot smiled, but as he walked away he mumbled under his breath, "What a fucking loser." *Please tell me I wasn't that pathetic last summer?* He knew the answer to the question and didn't want to acknowledge it. Every day he was feeling more and more like the Molloys of the world, losing who he was and letting the bitterness slowly overtake him. It scared him, but what scared him the most was he really didn't care. The whole world was changing around him anyway, and as he continued along crossing through the empty section of the park which had been his Wiffle ball field, he remembered an example of that change, something he had witnessed on his way to Pucky's a couple of days after the baseball strike began. He had seen three kids rest their bikes against the fence and then trade baseball cards with one another. The sight made him remember when he was their age and how he loved doing the same thing until he heard *how* they were trading the cards. There was no chatter about favorite players or teams or ballparks. It was all about how much they speculated each card would be worth in the future.

Now, thinking about it again, Dermot realized what he had witnessed was a story he could write about the loss of innocence, but he quickly put the idea aside when he grabbed the brass handle to Pucky's and walked inside. After five pints of Guinness, the idea was back, and he scribbled it down on a stray Samuel Adams coaster and tucked it in his back pocket. After two more, he got up from his barstool, broke the seal, and then swayed from side to side to the sounds of The Scarlet Begonias, a Grateful Dead cover band made up of semi-talented, late-twenties Silver Shores fishermen. Dermot normally wouldn't have acknowledged their music since the Scarlet Begonias always acted like they actually wrote the songs they played. However, he was feeling pretty buzzed and decided to let bygones be bygones and bobbed his head while sipping his beer in the corner beside the small sound table run by the lead singer's shaggy-bearded burnt-out father.

Staying rapt for two songs, he was about to go back to his stool when a short, chunky blonde in her late fifties wearing a flower child tie-dye shirt and matching skirt grabbed his free hand and pulled him into the crowd.

"You look lonely," she hollered above the music into his ear and then spun him around causing half his pint to splash onto the circle of sweaty dancers.

Even though they were doused with half a beer, everyone kept jumping around, except a college-aged girl who seemed a little too clean to be with the rest of the group. She glared over at Dermot, but being in the moment, he threw her a peace sign forcing her to change her facial expression from angry to apathetic and her stare pierced right through him. He knew she probably realized since she was playing hippie for the night she couldn't act pissed. Hippies are about love, and as he squinted over at the chunky blonde draping her beefy arms over his shoulders he knew one thing: *she* was also about love . . . loving him. Dermot wasn't sure what to do about that.

After they bounced against one another to a "Touch of Grey," Dermot made his decision and motioned over to the bar. She nodded, grabbed his hand again, and led him through the crowd. The dying sober voice in his head warned him not to let people see her holding his hand, but he knew he would be quieting that voice soon, so he held on.

Pucky, who was in his sixties, as weathered as the old buoys that hung above the bar, beckoned Dermot by waving his bar rag. "Hurry up, man. I've had to shoo away half the bar from your stool. That must've been some piss."

"Sorry, Puck."

"No, problem," he said flipping the Guinness tap on, but then noticed Dermot was holding the woman's hand. "Oh, geez, Dermot, I see you have met Marsha."

Dermot sensed that Pucky's tone was far from enthusiastic, but ignored it by turning to the woman. "Yeah, well, not officially. Nice to meet you, Marsha."

"Nice to meet you, Dermot." She shook his hand and her plump figure shook with it.

I know I'm hammered, but I need to get blind drunk if this is going to work.

"What are you drinking, Marsha?" Dermot ushered her to his stool and stood above her. Now he was close enough to really check her out and realized one thing: he needed more booze.

She suggested, "How about a couple of shots of Jagermeister and a couple more beers?" He was eager to accept.

"Coming right up." Pucky eyed Dermot before going to work.

Dermot downed the shot in seconds, but then stared at his Guinness for a while.

"What's wrong?" Pucky asked.

"Are you sure you poured this right? In Ireland they let it settle for about two to three minutes or so."

"Just like clockwork." Pucky threw his hands up.

"What is?" Marsha asked still smacking her lips from her shot.

"Every night, Dermot will plow down about eight to ten pints and only after that he'll start asking me if I know how to pour a pint. It happens every night. He just doesn't ever remember."

"That's not true," Dermot said doubtfully.

"It is true, Derm. It's your segue way to talk about the fact that you went to Ireland this winter and then will lead into the reason you went there which is what you really want to talk about."

"So why *did* you go to Ireland?" Marsha moved closer.

"Here we go . . . To get over a girl," Pucky answered for him.

"What the hell, Pucky?"

"Derm, I'm not saying anything you haven't said for the past three nights in a row. In fact, let me help you with what you'll want me to do next." Pucky picked up a remote control turned around and aimed it at the TV. A few seconds later, the VCR light went on followed by the movie *Casablanca*.

This part he did remember and Dermot couldn't help but smile. "Thanks."

"Hey, follow your problem." Pucky shrugged and then wiped down the bar.

"What do you mean by that?" Marsha asked Pucky.

He looked at her and then at Dermot. "Can I be brutally honest?"

"Go ahead." Dermot took a small sip and added. "I know it's coming."

"You see, Marsha. This past winter Dermot was dumped by his first real love. So he went to Ireland to get over her, maybe even drink her out of his system. But guess what?"

"What?" she asked.

"I love the kid and all, but, before he left for his trip, for a whole week he'd come in here and get blind drunk and beg me to watch *Casablanca*. And you know what, he's been back all summer and he's doing it again, so I guess the trip didn't work."

Marsha rested her chin on her hand and stared at Dermot. "Well, you have to admit, Pucky, it is one of the most romantic movies ever made, if not the most."

Dermot then pointed at Pucky. "See! I told you! Thank you, Marsha." He clinked glasses with her and Marsha, smiling, said, "No problem, honey."

Pucky shook his head. "Look, I've said this before, and I'll say this again, since we now have an audience. *Casablanca* is an amazing movie, and Rick is considered such a cool guy in it, but in real life he would've been looked at as a fucking loser. A fucking loser, I tell you!"

"A loser?" Marsha asked.

"It's so simple. He let the woman he loved leave him. Bye, Bye Richard,

I'm going to live my life with Victor Laszlo and sire his children as you fish in a fucking desert, no less, with Sam. Play it again, and again, and fucking again, Sam. And Dermot, you've been playing it again, too. Over and over." Pucky left them to serve the waving hands at the other end of the bar.

"Wow, he's bitter about that movie." Marsha gestured to the TV.

"And me. I think hearing about my love life became to Pucky what the song 'Margaritaville' is to all the bartenders on the Cape. It was good the first thousand times he heard it, but after that he wanted to shoot himself or me." Dermot took a gulp.

"And do you want to shoot yourself?"

"No. I just want to 'shot' myself. How about some Tequila this time?"

"Sounds good to me." She smiled and Dermot noticed her crooked teeth and knew Tequila was the perfect choice.

They drank and drank more, and Marsha told him stories about how she traveled across country in a VW bus from California when she was eighteen, almost forty years ago, to settle in Vermont before eventually moving to the Cape. Dermot's drunken math had her age at thirty-eight. *Not too old*. Then it began—his Francesca how-they-met-to-how-they-broke-up story. "So she calls me right before her Christmas vacation and says she has to talk to me. So I'm driving down to Providence and it's blinding snow, and I know she's going to break up with me. I just know it. But I'm still driving. And, of course, she does break up with me in the same fucking brown Volvo where she had said she loved me."

Marsha massaged Dermot's hand as he sat in the barstool beside her. The bar was practically empty by then, except for the band breaking down their equipment.

"Please tell me you didn't give her the Christmas gifts you bought her and the poem you said you wrote."

Dermot took a sip of his beer and didn't say a word.

"Wait. I'll be back. I have to pee." Marsha got up unsteadily from her stool and left.

He then glanced up at the black-and-white screen and saw Rick driving Ilsa in the French countryside and he thought again of the blinding snow, and Francesca standing beside her brown Volvo in an empty parking lot.

"I'm sorry, Dermot. It's not me. It's my father. He says you wanting to be a writer is a fool's dream."

"But what do you think, Francesca? You believe in me, right?"

"It doesn't matter what I think. He won't pay my tuition if I keep seeing you. He wants more for me in life."

In the bottom of his glass, he could see that day so clearly. He had tears and snowflakes clouding his vision, but he still went to his car and retrieved the leather backpack he bought for her trip to Italy, the one they had planned on taking together. It was filled with Christmas gifts and the love poem he wrote that he no longer remembered the words to, just the pain he had while writing it, knowing she'd probably be reading it after they had broken up. He could see himself walking away and hearing her in the distance say, "A part of me will always love you. I'll never forget you, Dermot. Never."

"Finish them up!" Pucky barked to the stragglers, and Dermot was back in the present.

Pucky was at the door helping usher people out, so he didn't notice Dermot reach over to grab the bottle of Tequila and, instead of filling his shot glass, he filled his pint glass halfway. He drank it down like it was lemonade on a hot August day. It didn't taste like it, though. When he was done, he shivered it through his system, but then the glow came. The one he was trying to achieve all night. He could barely see straight and that was the vision he wanted. He saw Marsha come out of the bathroom and he staggered over to her, and without needing to ask he began sloppily making out with her.

In the background he could hear Pucky say, "Oh, Jesus, Dermot. No. Don't do it! You'll regret it in the morning."

But, he wasn't listening. They felt their way out the door still mashing tongues.

"I want to kiss you everywhere." Her hot breath warmed his ear.

"I don't want to go to my place."

"I can't go to my place." She stopped and pointed to a dumpster. "How about behind there? I have plenty of condoms."

Dermot stared long and hard at the dumpster. *Should I? Of course, I should. I'm never going to feel love again. This woman wants me. As Molloy would say, "Don't be a pussy."*

"Come on, baby, I'm going to rock your world." She began hiking up her skirt as she made her way behind the dumpster.

Dermot finally decided to follow, but then he heard a booming sound in the distance that stopped him. *Is it the foghorn? No, there's no rain. It's a clear night now. It makes no sense.* The sound got louder and louder, and suddenly he realized it was a car's bass speaker pumping. He turned around and the car screeched to a stop in front of him. The music was turned down by the driver who leaned over and popped his head out the passenger window.

"What the fuck? Is that you, Dermot?"

"Huh?"

"Dermot, it's Dwayne."

"Huh?" Dermot said again with the booze now totally shutting him down.

"You know, Colin's buddy. Chocolate Thunder."

"Oh, shit, Dwayne. What's up?"

Dwayne was about to answer, but was interrupted by Marsha who came from around the dumpster.

"Come on, baby. I don't have forever here. I got a sitter watching my grandson, and I can't be out all night."

"Oh, yeah, sorry, honey," Dermot managed and then turned to Dwayne. "Hey, good seeing you Thunder, but I'm a little busy here."

"Holy shit!" Dwayne's mouth gaped.

Marsha wrapped her arms over Dermot and giggled. "Yeah, we *are* a little busy here."

Dwayne hopped out, hustled over, and ordered to Dermot, "It's time to go home, man. Come on, let's go."

"Go home? What are you talking about? We're going to party."

Dwayne pointed, "No. The party is over, man. Get in the car."

"But I don't want to go."

"Yeah, who the hell are you to tell him to go home?" Marsha used her left hand to slap him on the shoulder.

Ignoring her, Dwayne yelled, "Dermot, get in the fucking car now!"

The force in his voice awakened Dermot just enough from his haze to listen.

"I guess I gotta go, baby. We'll hang out again." Dermot leaned over to kiss her, but Marsha pushed him away.

"Fuck you. If you're going to be ordered around like a little kid you can go fuck yourself. I'm going to find me a real man who can handle this."

"Well, next time, Grandma, find one that is sober enough to know the mistake he's making." Dwayne grabbed Dermot's arm, opened the passenger door, and ushered him into the Lexus.

"Fuck you, asshole!" she shouted as Dwayne sped off.

When they were in the clear, Dwayne turned to Dermot. "What the fuck was that?"

"Huh? What do you mean?"

"What do I mean? Do you know who that was?"

"Yeah, that was my friend Marsha."

"How long have you known her?"

"I don't know, three or four hours. She's nice. She bought me some drinks."

"Dude, she has like five kids from four different guys. I seriously think she's like close to sixty years old. What the fuck were you thinking?" After pulling into the seashell driveway in front of The Shanty, Dwayne turned and faced him.

"No, man. I think she's like forty."

"If you think that, you must be wasted. No chance."

Dermot shook his head. "No, I'm telling you she's not that old. She's like forty. Didn't you see her blonde hair?"

"Yeah, one of the worst dye jobs ever. Dermot, listen to me. I used to work with her when I bussed tables at the diner when I was a kid. The woman is ancient."

"She's not that bad."

"Look, I'm not going to argue with you when you're drunk. You can thank me later." Dwayne motioned with his head to the door for Dermot to get out.

"You want *me* to thank *you*? I was going to get some."

"Yeah, get some from an old lady behind a dumpster. That's fucking nasty, man."

"No, man. It's all good, as you guys like to say." Dermot fumbled with the handle and finally opened the door and was about to get out when Dwayne stopped him.

"No, man, wait a second, will you?" he said.

"What?"

"It's *not* all good. In fact, it's all bad. I've heard you're drinking a lot this summer. You gotta stop this shit, Dermot."

Dermot just gave him a blank look.

"Do you even know what I'm talking about right now?"

"Yeah, sure. I had too much to drink. I get it. It happens."

"It's more than that."

"Huh?"

"Your brother."

"Oh shit, that fuck-up? Why are you bringing up that fuck-face?"

"Fuck-up. Fuck-face. I've never heard you talk about him like that before. You love that kid. You always have. But people have been telling me that's what you think of him now. That he's a fuck-up."

"Why wouldn't I think of him that way? Fucking selling shoes and shit for a living."

"Hey, if we want to talk about fuck-ups he wasn't the one about to screw the old woman who lived in a *shoe* behind that dumpster."

"Fuck you, Dwayne!"

"Just like your brother you can tell me to fuck off all you want, but let me get this out before I go."

"All right, go then." The sooner Dwayne was done the sooner Dermot knew he could have his nightcap.

"He needs you, man. You escaped to Ireland while he was here to deal with it. And, you know how he's dealt with it. He gets fucked up every night and I know he's on his way to take it to the next level."

"Next level?"

"I won't lie to you. I've smoked pot with him, but I've quit that shit. He's doubled the usage, and I know the next level will be even harder drugs.

Look, he's got no one to turn to for help. His best friends are dead. Mel moved and then you left for Ireland. As for me, I've tried to talk to him, but he needs his big brother. He looks up to you and you are gone."

"What do you mean *gone*? I've been back all summer."

"Have you, man? You still seem gone to me calling your brother a fuck-up."

"Well. Back to shoes. If the shoe fits."

"You don't fucking have a clue. You know what, I gotta go. Get some sleep, man. Your head is going to hurt like shit in the morning."

Dermot didn't say a word. He just got out of the car, slammed the door, walked into The Shanty, and headed for the refrigerator. He popped open a beer, walked through the beads and went over to his mix-tape collection and rifled through it, while he mumbled to himself, "Who the fuck is Dwayne to be giving me advice?"

He found his *I Drink Alone Mix*, put it on, and listened to the Bodeans' "Far, Far Away From My Heart." That set the mood he was looking for: depression. Like so many other nights, he wanted to bathe in his sadness, and he remembered the book *The Old Man and The Sea*. He took it down and opened the front cover avoiding the handwritten inscription. All he wanted to see was his one and only remaining picture of Francesca, which was always tucked away in the first chapter. It was a picture of them from the previous summer at the county fair. He studied it like it was the first time. Francesca was smiling, holding the teddy bear Dermot had won after knocking milk cans over with a baseball, and he was laughing while displaying the Jim Beam mirror she had won at the shoot-the-squirt-gun-in-the-frog's-mouth booth.

Dermot thought about that night as the music segued into the clear sounding sadness of Dave Herlihy's voice, front man of the Boston band O-Positive, singing "Holding Onto You." It was one of the best nights of his life. Although a few minutes before they posed for the picture, he hadn't felt that way. He had been annoyed with Colin, Matt, Paul, and Mel. The four were also at the fair and just happened to follow him and his date to the bumper cars where they proceeded to get the couple in the corner and ram them over and over again. Dermot was pissed, but Francesca had been a good sport and told him to lighten up. A few minutes later, they were both posing for Matt, who snapped their smiles on his new camera.

Looking away from the photo, he tried to think just of Francesca and losing her, but this time when he opened the book he allowed his eyes, for the first time in a very long time, to make their way to the inscription:

Dear Dermot,

I found this book and remembered how you spent a whole summer tutoring me on it, and I don't think I ever thanked you. Well, I just wanted to thank you for that and all the other things you've done for me over the years. I know your Colin's big brother but I always like to think you're mine too!
—Matt

P.S. Here's the picture from the fair. I thought you might like to have it, and here's another I found that might bring back some memories. Remember the bike in the background?

"Remember the bike?" Dermot asked himself and then followed with, "Another picture?"

All he ever remembered looking at was the picture of Francesca, but as he thought about it, he realized he had only read the inscription that one time, the day Matt left the copy of *The Old Man and The Sea* at The Shanty. He had read quickly because he was late for work. It was two days before it happened. And since then, he had never dared to look again at the inscription and now he wondered about this other picture, and where was it? He flipped through the pages as the acoustic version of "Tears" by The Chameleons UK snuck into the background.

He shook the book and suddenly a picture fell out and fluttered to the floor. He picked it up and what he saw brought him back in time.

It was Colin, Paul, and Matt around fifteen years old wrapped in beach towels with the white marker bobbing in the ocean in the background. In the foreground was Dermot's blue Schwinn ten-speed and Matt was showcasing it with one of his hands, while keeping the other on the towel.

"That's right," he gasped. "After Matt wrote the paper for summer school I gave him my bike."

It all came back to him how thrilled Matt was to get the bike and how he bragged to everyone that Colin's big brother had given it to him.

Dermot stared at the picture for almost an hour. No tears or laughter. Just straight staring and then he made a decision. He went through the beads, opened the refrigerator, and got himself a bottle of Poland Springs water. He came back into the room, got out his notebook, took out the coaster with his idea, and decided it was time to write.

SIXTEEN

C olin woke to a light knock on his bedroom door. "Hey, pal, you awake?" Mr. Brennan asked quietly from the other side.

Opening his eyes slowly, he replied, "Yeah. I'm . . . ah . . . I'm up, Dad." He answered before realizing his clothes along with his sheets were wet. *Not Again. What the fuck?*

"Okay. I just didn't want you to be late for work. I can make a pancake for you if you want?"

"Um . . . all right. I gotta shower and get dressed first."

"No problem. Take your time. I'll get everything ready." Mr. Brennan said cheerfully before trotting back down the hall to the stairs.

Wiping the sleep out of his eyes, Colin sluggishly rose to his feet. The taste of booze still lingered in his mouth. Last night he hit the bottle hard, real hard, and now his head and stomach were paying the price. Pulling his sheets and comforter off, rolling them in a ball, he stuffed them under his bed along with his wet clothes. He needed to get high, but he was out of weed. So, he scraped his pipe and collected a ball of resin, which he smoked, helping him to ease his hangover. After a long, hot shower he gargled intensely and then brushed his teeth. Putting on his work uniform he was trying to remember last night, but no luck.

Before leaving his room, he sprayed a can of air freshener to cover up the smell of stale alcohol and urine. He walked downstairs and stepped into the kitchen where his father was waiting for him, reading the paper.

"Have a seat, big guy, and I'll get one going."

"Okay. Thanks, Dad." A plate and utensils along with a large glass of milk were on the table. Colin drained the milk in seconds then wiped his mouth and yawned.

"Tired?"

"A little."

"How come? You were in bed before the eleven o'clock news."

"Yeah. Yeah, I know. Um, I had trouble falling asleep."

"Oh, that's a pain."

"Yeah, tell me about it."

"It's been a while since I've made you one of my world famous pancakes."

"Yeah."

Colin recalled the mornings that he, Matt, and Paul sat at that same table. When he was a kid, the boys knew that the best part of a sleepover at the Brennan house was the pancake breakfast the following morning. Mr. Brennan would put on a very feminine apron, doing his best Jim Backus impersonation from *Rebel Without a Cause*, with Colin as James Dean, grabbing at him and painfully saying, "Dad . . . dad . . . stand . . . don't . . . I mean you shouldn't . . . don't." He'd hurl the dishtowel to the floor. "What are you?" Then dramatically, Colin would leave the room to the hysterics and applause of his two best friends.

He yawned again. Today, there were no impersonations. There was no laughter or applause and, as Mr. Brennan scraped a pancake off the frying pan onto his plate, Colin suddenly lost his appetite.

"Throw that baby down," his father said with a proud grin.

"Thanks." He took a couple of bites before saying, "Great as always, but I gotta go."

"Really?"

"I know. I'm sorry. I don't want to be late. I'll see you later. Thanks." And he was out the door.

As Colin trekked down the brick walkway, he glanced at the kitchen window and saw his father, now sitting at his place looking down at the plate. *I'm sorry, Dad.* Making his way to the driveway, he saw several tables set up on the front lawn holding knick-knacks covered with price tags. *Oh yeah, Mom's finally having her yard sale today.*

He stopped at one table giving a quick survey of the items. There were some movies: *Meatballs, My Bodyguard, Creepshow 2, Red Dawn. I loved Red Dawn!*

His eyes shifted farther down the table to some paperback books. He read a few of the titles: *Huckleberry Finn, The Call of the Wild,* and *Paddle to the Sea,* a favorite of the Brennan boys growing up. They spent many nights falling asleep to their father's tranquil voice reading to them, and they'd dream that the Indian, Paddle, would someday land his canoe on the shores of Stirling Beach. He then spotted his old saxophone and shook his head.

Man, I haven't touched that since junior high.

He walked on until he was stopped dead in his tracks. There, gawking at him, almost mockingly, was his Aquaman figure wearing a price tag of seventy-five cents. He snatched it and stuffed it in his pocket before jumping in his car and peeling out of the driveway.

At the shopping center, Colin was walking to the back of the Shoe Fort when he heard someone holler to him.

"C-Dog! C-Dog!" Holding an iced coffee, Eric skidded to a stop on his bike.

"Hey, man, what's up?"

"Oh my God! Oh my God! You'll never guess what just happened."

"What? Is everything okay?"

"Everything is great! I just asked Natalie out! And she said yes! Can you believe it?"

"Seriously? No kidding around?"

"I'm serious. I wouldn't joke about this. Oh my God, I can't believe it! It's all because of you, man. I just went there and thought about Michael Jordan and said, 'Just do it,' and I asked her."

"Were you nervous?"

"Heck yeah, I was nervous, but I did it and she said yes!"

"That's awesome!" They high-fived.

"Where are you gonna take her?"

"Well, I asked what she wanted to do, and she said we would figure it out. I'm still in shock."

"You gotta plan something romantic. Show her you're different from other guys. If you need any help, I'm here for you."

"Thanks, Colin. It's because of your pep talk, it gave me strength. I've been thinking about if for a while now. God, I can't believe this! All right, I gotta go. Gotta get back to work. I can't wait to tell the boys. I'll talk to you soon." He rode off smiling.

I love that kid! Colin lit up a cigarette while walking the loading dock behind the store. His whole body ached and the early morning sun added to his dehydration. Pulling out the Aquaman figure, he inspected it carefully. It seemed so much smaller. He shot a look to the dumpster but couldn't muster up the nerve to throw it away, so he put it back in his pocket. He took another drag off his cigarette and smiled, thinking about Eric and how happy he was. It had been a long time since *he* felt that way. And then a piece of last night came back to him, his run in with After Midnight, and his smile disappeared.

He had walked out of 7-Eleven with his bag of necessities, which included cigarettes, Rolaids, a pack of Big Red, and stepped right into the path of Terry Handon. He hadn't seen her since he wet her bed, and now there was no way of avoiding her, so he did his best just to make small talk.

"Hey, Terry, what's up?"

"What's up? You tell me, Colin. The whole fucking town is under the impression we had sex!"

"Oh, man. I don't know, Terry. Dwayne must have said something."

She gave a sarcastic laugh. "You know, Colin, that is so like you, passing the buck. Trying to sell out Dwayne, when I know for a fact you said all kinds of shit the other night at the power lines."

"Huh? What are you talking about?"

"Susan told me everything. She heard you saying to Chucky and a bunch of other people how you were so drunk and I basically 'raped' you," she said, throwing up air quotes.

"What? No way. Susan's lying. Don't believe that shit." *I don't remember that. Power lines? What night was that?*

"No, Colin. You're the one who is lying. You've turned into a real fucking drunk. You know what the worst part is? That night, at Susan's party, I brought you inside because I felt you drank too much, and I hate seeing you like that. I just wanted to put you to bed because you looked so pathetic lying in that lawn chair. I know you're still hurting and I wanted to help you."

Unable to look Terry in the face, Colin's eyes stared at the handicapped symbol beside his car.

"I just wanted to be there for you, like you were always there for me. I tried putting you on the couch, but you headed straight for my room and you were mumbling a bunch of gibberish about Matt and Paul and then you just passed out. I didn't want to leave you because I was afraid you might puke in your sleep, so I slept beside you. I watched you throughout the night. And then my thanks—you end up pissing my bed, but I didn't tell anyone, Colin, because I felt bad for you. I would never want to embarrass you or make a joke of you because you're my . . . well, you *were* my friend. But you showed me this is how you thank people who try to help you."

"Um . . . well . . . let me say . . ."

"No, Colin. You've said enough." She pushed him aside and walked into 7-Eleven, leaving him standing alone.

Now, the following morning, a mass of guilt festered, and the ache in his stomach grew rapidly until he couldn't take it any longer. He ran behind the dumpster and heaved. First the liquor and bits of pancake shot out of him, resembling a geyser with the syrupy yellow bile soon following. The familiar burn in his chest almost comforted him as he relieved his insides of the pain. He tapped his chest and after a minute or so it subsided. His eyes watered and his nose ran and the last thing he wanted to do was deal with little kids. Drying his mouth clean he heard a voice from behind.

"Colin, what the hell are you doing out here? It's almost 9:30 and you're scheduled for 9:00. I thought we talked about this," Larry Furfey barked.

"I'm sorry, Larry, I'm just a little under the weather this morning."

"And, I'm sure it's self-inflicted. Get yourself together. Fast! I got a kid in there screaming like crazy who refuses to put his foot in the measurer. Cameron doesn't have the experience like you do. So hurry up and get your butt on the floor."

Colin shoved a piece of gum in his mouth and entered the building. He hoped the cinnamon would mask the smell of alcohol as he slowly made his way through the stock room. He stopped and inhaled deeply as he heard the sobs of a child. He pushed the swinging doors and saw Cameron Perry doing his best to calm down a four-year-old boy. Cameron was a seventeen-year-old summer kid working his first job at the Shoe Fort. He resented not being able to spend his time at the beach and it showed in his work.

"Hey, Cam."

"Colin, thank God you're here. Can you take over? I don't know what to do," he asked, flustered.

"Yeah. Don't worry about it."

"Thanks, man."

Colin got on one knee and looked up at the crying boy. "What's wrong, little guy?" He turned to his mother. "What's his name?"

"It's Ryan. I'm sorry. I didn't know he was going to react like this."

"There's nothing to be sorry about, ma'am. It happens all the time." He turned his attention to the boy. "These measurement things can be a little scary, can't they, buddy?"

Ryan nodded.

Somewhere behind him, Colin heard the familiar voice of an older woman. From where he was, he was unable to see her, but it was impossible to ignore what she was saying. "You would think parents would be able to control their children. When I was growing up that type of behavior would never be tolerated, especially in a public place. There's not enough discipline these days. That's the problem."

Larry responded, trying to be polite. "Well, Miss. I think the boy is a little frightened having his feet sized. A lot of kids get that way. I'm sure he'll be fine. I have my best employee assisting them."

"Well, it's very annoying this early in the morning. Now, sir, I need a comfortable shoe. I have a wide foot, so I need something that isn't going to be too tight. I'm on my feet all day, and the last thing I need is to be walking around in pain. Do you understand what I'm saying?"

"Yes, and I am going to do my best to satisfy you today."

Colin could detect Larry's irritation. He peeked over his shoulder trying to steal a look, but a display of Tevas made it impossible to make out who was behind the voice. It made him feel uncomfortable, so he did his best to block out the conversation and focus on his young customer.

He stretched to his feet and removed one of his own shoes and placed his foot in the measurer. "See, Ryan. It's not going to hurt you. All it does is measure the size of your foot." He pointed down. "I have a size ten. Let's have you try it."

"No, Mommy, I'm scared. I don't want to do it." The tears started again as he clutched his mother's leg.

Colin looked at the woman. "What have you done in the past?"

"This is his first time. Ryan has an older brother and he's always had hand-me-downs, but now his foot is growing too fast and nothing fits." She exhaled. "I'm sorry," she said, squinting to see his nametag, "Colin. We'll just come back another day. Thanks, anyway."

"No, no, we can do this. Let me ah . . . let me try something else," he said before going to the back. He soon returned with a lollipop and a Barney sticker, waving them in front of the boy, but nothing changed, and the child's tears persisted.

"I don't blame you, Ryan. I'm not a big fan of Barney, either."

He was running out of ideas, until he remembered something. Aquaman.

"Okay, Ryan. I have a special gift, only for you. I think you're going to like this."

The boy wiped the tears away. "A gift?"

"Yup." Colin slowly pulled Aquaman from his back pocket and placed it in front of Ryan's face. The tears and hysterics immediately came to a halt as the boy reached for it.

"Can I see?" He smiled.

"Not so fast, my little friend. I will make you a deal. See, Aquaman needs a new home and I'm pretty sure you can give him what he needs, but I need you to do your part first. I'm willing to give him to you, but I want you to put your foot in here, okay?"

Without hesitation, Ryan jumped off the bench and kicked off his sneakers. Colin grabbed his foot and worked it into the metal measurement tool until he was able to get a good read.

"Okay, Ryan. Looks like you're a three."

"Oh, thank God," Ryan's mother said, relieved. "All he needs is a reasonably priced plain white sneaker."

"No worries. I can take care of that for you." He turned to Ryan. "I'm proud of you, buddy. You did a good job. Now, this is for you." He handed over Aquaman. "Aquaman really meant a lot to me when I was a kid."

"Really?" Ryan said with wide eyes, inspecting the action figure.

"Yeah. My friends and I played with him all the time. We used Aquaman to help us search for the lost city of Atlantis. Do you know about Atlantis?"

Ryan shook his head.

"It is a magical underwater city."

Ryan then turned to his mother in amazement. "Do you know about Atlantis, Mommy?"

"I do, honey. And I'll tell you all about it in the car."

"Okay!"

"I'll be right back." Colin went to the back room and returned with a pair of Reeboks. He put them on Ryan's feet and they were a perfect fit.

He looked up at him. "How do they feel?"

"Great. They feel nice."

"Fantastic. And how much are they, Colin?" Ryan's mom asked.

"They're on sale for $29.99."

"Perfect. We'll take them. Can he wear them out?"

"Certainly. I will put his old ones in here and you can just give the box to Cameron at the register," he said, smiling. "Is there anything else I can help you with today?"

"No. You've been amazing, Colin. Thank you so much. You're incredible with kids." She smiled. "Wait a second. You're mother isn't Margaret Brennan, is she?"

"Yeah . . . yeah that's my mom."

"I know her from Page Turners. She mentioned her son worked at the shoe store. She's a great woman. I see where you get it from."

"Yeah, she is. Thank you."

"And, it's okay that he keeps that toy?"

He rubbed the top of Ryan's head. "Of course he can. I think Aquaman has found the perfect home."

"You're something else. Ryan, say thank you to Colin."

"Thanks, Colin."

"You're welcome, pal. Now take good care of Aquaman, okay?"

"I will." He walked away with dry eyes and a wide smile, gliding Aquaman through an imaginary sea.

As Colin watched the little boy, Larry put a comforting hand on his shoulder.

"That's the Colin I know. And that's the Colin people love. Nice job, kid."

"Thanks, Larry. Hey, who was that woman who was complaining?"

"Oh, she was a real pill. Where did she go?" He scanned the crowded room and then pointed. "There she is, the woman walking out the door."

Colin looked toward the exit sign. "Oh my God."

"What's wrong? Do you know her?"

"Yeah. Yeah, I know her. Larry, I need five minutes, okay? I'll be right back."

"Okay, sure. But hurry. Today is going to be crazy. I can feel it."

"No problem. Thanks."

Colin hustled to the exit, opened the door, and followed the woman to a Lincoln Town Car in pristine condition. He had been waiting for this moment for so long, but what would he say? His heart pounded, and the palms of his hands got clammy. He had second thoughts about confronting her, but he pushed through his reluctance.

"Excuse me, Ms. Shannon?"

The elderly woman turned around quickly. She didn't appear as threatening as she was when he was a child, but he was still tense.

"What? I paid for these shoes. What's the problem?" she snapped at him while closing the trunk of her car.

"Oh, I know you paid for those shoes. The problem? Where do I begin?" He gave a bitter laugh.

"Who are you? What do you want?"

"It's me, Colin Brennan."

"Colin Brennan." She studied his face for a bit. "Colin Brennan. Of course, I remember you. You were a little troublemaker, always in my office. What do you want?"

"Troublemaker? I was a kid. I was a kid who struggled with school. I wasn't a troublemaker."

"You were in my office because you misbehaved. In my book, that makes you a troublemaker. Now, I have to get going. I don't have time for you." She turned away.

"No. Don't turn your back on me."

"Excuse me, young man?"

"Don't 'young man' me. I'm nineteen. And you're gonna look at me. You did a lot of talking when I was young and you know what? Now, it's my turn to talk. I had trouble learning when I was a kid. I struggled, but I would go after school for help all the time and you knew this. I tried so hard but that was never good enough for you. You shamed me, even though you knew I was trying. Then, in high school I was diagnosed with ADD and put on medication. It was like the fog had been lifted and I was able to focus and have success in school. That's why I didn't do well when I was young. But you always told me I would never amount to anything. You called me stupid. Why would you do that? I was just a little kid."

"Let me ask you something, Colin Brennan."

"What?"

"Do you work here part time or full time?"

"Full time."

A smile crossed her lips. "A shoe store. You work at a shoe store full time. That's what you've done with your life. So I guess I wouldn't say that you've amounted to too much. Now, if you'll excuse me I have more important things to do." She opened the driver's door, slid into her seat, slammed the door, and moments later drove off. Just like when he was a child, Miss Shannon once again left him paralyzed and feeling like a loser.

SEVENTEEN

Dermot's old dying car refused to start, but it didn't upset him, as it would have in the past. Instead, he chuckled and headed down the street towards work. For the first time in a long time, his head was clear and he was a half hour ahead of schedule.

He hadn't had a drop of alcohol since he had started replacing his wine with water. He laughed at this thought. It happened after the night Dwayne had rescued him from Old Lady Marsha. When the haze lifted, he used his pen to uncork his bottled-up emotions. Soon the blank pages of his notebook were filled and the chirping birds followed by sunlight that had once been hangover torture were now an almost heavenly like reminder that he was a writer who had been in an all-nighter flow.

But was that flow good enough? He wondered, seeing in the distance the blue and white *Cape Cod Times* newspaper dispenser anchored to the curb in front of the *Island Ferry* landing. The editor at the *Cape Code Times* seemed to think so. Dermot saved the message left on his answering machine the previous afternoon. "Oh, hi, Dermot, this is Mr. Tate. I'm one of the editors of the *Cape Cod Times,* and we received your article and well, quite frankly, we all really related to it, and, more importantly, we think our readers will love it, too. I am waiting to see an outcome of a couple of other stories so I can't say for sure, but we may be running it in tomorrow's paper. But the newspaper business *can* be tricky, so if we don't run it, I still wanted to call and tell you to remember something. You've got a talent to move readers with your words. If you ever have doubts remember, you *are* a writer and the best advice I can give you is that writers write. So keep writing. Have a good day."

Dermot picked up the pace walking along his old bus route. He saw himself in '78 jumping down the school bus steps and sprinting for home to watch the rest of the one-game playoff between the Red Sox and the Yankees. That day he was so excited because he was going to see the Red Sox finally beat the hated Yankees, until his dreams were dashed when a Punch-and-Judy hitter named Bucky Dent somehow lofted a three-run homer over the Green Monster, devastating the Sox fans for yet another year.

The next day Dermot wore his baseball cap to school, with what was viewed by his classmates as the scarlet letter *B* on it. At recess, he defended his team to the turncoats on the playground by promising with raised fists, "Wait till next year!"

He reached into his pocket for a quarter to buy the paper. He didn't want to be that little kid on the playground hoping for next year. He needed that victory *now*. He needed his little essay to be published because that would give him some hope and strength, and if he knew he possessed those two things, he could move forward and work harder on his dream of becoming a writer. If he didn't get that sign from the writer gods, he also knew he probably would give up on the dream once and for all. It was that simple, and it was for that reason he clutched his shiny quarter as if it were his last, contemplating putting it in the dispenser like it was a slot machine in a Vegas airport.

"All right, let's do this thing," he said to himself.

Just as he decided to insert the coin, a loud car horn from behind startled him. He swung his head around and eyed Captain Stansfield who was giving him the finger, gunning his truck past and into the captain's spot. Stansfield hopped out of the truck and grinned. "I scared the shit out of you, didn't I?"

"Whatever, Captain Valdez," Dermot said and turned his attention back to the dispenser, but Stansfield shouted back, "You already used that one. Brennan, get over here. I need your help."

"With what?"

"I need you to carry something from my truck."

"Can it wait?"

"Nope."

Dermot shrugged, put the quarter back in his pocket, and walked over.

"It's in the passenger seat." Stansfield sipped from his extra large 7-Eleven coffee cup.

Sulking a bit, Dermot opened the door and saw a bound bundle of *Cape Cod Times* newspapers. Dermot looked up confused. "Is this for the boat?"

Stansfield laughed. "No. You know how I get up at the ass crack of dawn every morning?"

"Yeah."

"Well, this morning I went into 7-Eleven and I hear two old bastards talking while they were scratching their lotto tickets about some great article they had just read about the baseball strike by a guy named Dermot Brennan. So I pick up a paper and sure enough your article is right smack beside our ad for the moonlight cruise."

"Oh my God! So they published it! They published it!"

"You're damn right they did," Stansfield said, while pulling out of his pocket a folded-up newspaper and handing it to Dermot. "Check B14."

He opened it up and his eyes raced along the title. "Sadly, the boys of summer have all gone home" by Dermot Brennan.

"Good title," Stansfield said.

Dermot looked up, smiling. "Yeah, I like it, too. He did a great job."

"What do you mean, he?"

"Mr. Tate." Dermot went back to perusing the article and didn't see that any major changes had been made.

"Who the hell is Mr. Tate?"

"He's the editor. He probably came up with the headline." Dermot didn't look up as he read the short bio at the end to himself. *Dermot Brennan is a graduate of Northeastern University and lives in Silver Shores.*

"Oh . . . well, you wrote the rest of the shit, right?"

"Oh, yeah."

"Good. 'Cause that whole goddamn bundle in the truck is for you."

Dermot looked up. "It is?"

"Yeah, after I read it I figured I better start kissing your ass now in case someday you make it. Now grab that stack and go down to the lot and open up. I saw a couple of assholes already parked out front and one was a camper."

"Okay."

"And tell the douche bag he can pay double, that is, if you can even fit him in."

"I will." Dermot was beaming while grabbing the stack of newspapers. "And, thanks, Captain. That was really nice of you."

"Oh, fuck off, Brennan. It's no big deal. I figure if you pass them out you can also promote tomorrow night's moonlight cruise while you're doing it. Now I gotta go blow out the bathroom in the ticket office before the ticket girls get here."

Dermot took his time heading down to open the lot. He wanted to savor the moment. When he arrived, he noticed the camper had left, but there was still a line of about eight to ten cars waiting to park. *Sorry, people. This is my day!* He decided before he unlocked the gate for them that he'd slip into the shack and cue his Morning Blend mix tape on the player. It opened with U2's "Red Hill Mining Town" and went to an even-higher level of rock bliss featuring Eddie Van Halen's magical pick in Van Halen's "Little Guitars." A few moments later, Eric arrived, and to the annoyance of the early customers who were still parked along the street, he and Dermot talked about the article for a few minutes before finally opening the gates.

Dermot enjoyed Eric's positive feedback, but he felt out-of-this-world after the second boat departed when his mom and dad came by with coffee and donuts and beamed.

"We are not just proud of you, we are happy for you," his dad said.

"Yes," his mom added, "because you finally took the first step in what you want to do in life." They were right. Now more than ever, he knew he wanted to be a writer. The praise gave him a high like no drug he knew. He *was* a writer. It was Dermot's best day in a long time, but he still felt there was something missing: Colin.

They had grown up sharing their ups and downs with one another, and when there was a victory like Colin winning a meet or Dermot being picked Best Writer his senior year at Silver Shores, the other brother also felt he had won. There was never any of that sibling jealousy bullshit, just pride for one another. That connection and feeling was now gone, and Dermot wondered if Colin would even read the article and, if he did, would it have any sort of impact on him? He allowed himself to stay upbeat while several friends like Clay and Tommy popped in throughout the day to tell him how much the article meant to them.

When the morning rush passed and things died down, Dermot realized that after Eric's initial compliments about his piece, he had been pretty quiet. He settled into his lawn chair beside Eric and asked, "Is everything okay, man? You seem distant today."

Eric looked over at him. "Yeah, I know. My mind has been elsewhere all day. I keep thinking about my date with Natalie. You know it's tomorrow night?"

"Yeah, I know. You're taking her to the movies, right?"

"Yeah."

"So, what's there to worry about? If you're nervous then going to a movie is always a good first date because you don't have to talk that much. It's perfect because you can't blow it. So seriously, what's the problem?"

"The problem is what you just said. It's a standard date. Dermot, I might have one shot at taking out the girl of my dreams, so I'm wondering do I really want to do the normal date thing? I mean, come on, will she really be impressed if we go mini-golfing or go see another lousy comedy starring Brendan Fraser like *Airheads*?"

"*Airheads*?"

"Yeah, it's either that or a remake of *The Little Rascals* or *Clear and Present Danger*, and I certainly *don't* want her to see that one."

"Why?"

"'Cause for two hours she'd be staring at a guy who's ten times better looking than me."

"I haven't been keeping up with my movies these days. Who's in *Clear and Present Danger*?"

"Harrison Ford."

"Ouch. I see your point."

"I don't know, Derm. I've been thinking, and maybe I should just take a chance on life if you know what I mean?"

"No. I don't know what you mean."

"I want to take Natalie on a date that she'll remember. I mean, even if she never goes out with me again she can still say to her grandkids someday, 'You know, back in '94 I went on a very romantic date, but I didn't even realize it at the time.'"

Dermot laughed. "Now I know why Molloy is always saying how similar we are. What you are suffering from, my friend, is a disease called John Hughes syndrome. He writes about that hopeless romantic feeling a lot in his movies."

"So, what do you think?"

"From experience, I think it's a big risk. Girls always *say* they want a romantic guy, but then when they get one and he does all of that romantic stuff, he often ends up looking like some kind of freak. But with a girl like Natalie, it may be different. You might have a chance. She reminds me a lot of my girlfriend . . . I mean my ex-girlfriend. Anyway, Natalie may be one of those special ones."

"I know she *is*, but I also know it's a risk. Remember, Derm, we've been working together all summer. I've picked up a lot from you and Molloy."

Dermot checked his watch. "Speaking of Easy Shift Molloy, he's running about ten minutes late."

"Never mind him. Are you going to help me plan my perfect date?"

"Sure. But if it backfires, don't say I didn't warn you."

"I won't." He smiled.

For the next twenty minutes, they batted around ideas, but none of them seemed to stick. They stopped their conference when Molloy's brown Bronco bounded past them. He parked it beyond the Shack, but kept the engine running as he lumbered out of the driver's seat while a black woman in her early forties hopped out of the passenger side and walked over to them. She had a big smile on her face.

Dermot couldn't help but notice a sweatshirt tied around her waist as she smiled back and said, "Hi."

"Hi, you must be Dermot. I'm Kimberly. I'm the voice on the other end of the phone when I call here looking for Gary."

"Nice to meet you, Kimberly . . . Oh, this is Eric." Dermot pointed at his co-worker and tried to recover from the shock of Molloy bringing his girlfriend to work.

"Oh, I know. He's the boy with the crush on the girl at the coffee shop," she said, shaking Eric's hand. "Gary tells me all about you guys. You're like his little family."

"They are hardly that, honey," Molloy said to her and then turned to Dermot and Eric. "Sorry, I'm late, fellas."

Fellas? No jackasses or assholes. But fellas. "No problem." Dermot covered his confusion.

Molloy waved his hands from side to side. "Okay. I know what you're both thinking, 'Is Molloy fucking nuts! He brought his girlfriend here.'"

"Please don't use the f-word, Gary." She frowned.

"I'm sorry, baby. I'm working on it." He took her hand.

"Girlfriend!" Eric almost choked on the word.

"Yeah, *girlfriend*. What's the problem, Eric? Is it because she's black? Are you racist or something?" Molloy asked.

"No, no, it's just that you're . . ."

"Married," Dermot filled in the sentence.

"Oh, yeah. That little fact. Well as of this morning's mail I'm legally divorced."

"Divorced? You didn't tell us you were getting a divorce."

"I know. I had to keep it quiet until Kimberly and I were both divorced. Hers went through last month. So I'll tell you it's a damn good day." Molloy squeezed her hand and gave her a quick peck on the cheek.

"It *is* a great day." Eric got out of his chair, went inside the shack, and came out with the paper and handed it to Molloy. "Check this out. Dermot was published in the *Times*."

Molloy glanced at Dermot before he and Kimberly read the article silently. When they were done, Kimberly was the first one to look up.

"Wow, Dermot, that's a really great story. Gary told me you had a lot of talent."

"He did?" Dermot asked, but Molloy jumped in.

"Yeah, kid. I know you'll have a book published someday."

"Really?"

"Yeah." He laughed. "They'll sell it at Buck-A-Book for fifty cents. Of course, it will be twenty five cents with your autograph."

"Gary!" Kimberly swatted his shoulder with her hand.

"Babe, Dermot knows I'm just busting his balls," Molloy said, and she glared at him. "I mean nuts." She continued to glare and Molloy tried again. "Stones?" Kimberly shook her head, and Molloy finally went with "Dermot knows I'm just giving him a hard time."

"That's better." She nodded and Dermot and Eric both laughed.

"I like you, Kimberly. You're the only one I know who can tame Molloy." Eric grinned.

"Well, I don't know about that, but I'm at least going to give it a try," she said and turned to Molloy. "And, on that note, remember, no fried food today. Order a salad if you get hungry." Kimberly gave him another kiss, said goodbye to all of them, and drove out of the lot in Molloy's Bronco. It was silent until she was out of sight.

"Holy shit!" Dermot laughed.

"I know. That was awesome!" Eric joined in.

"What?" Molloy said.

"Well, if we are talking about balls or nuts or stones, she just took yours. Don't you agree, Eric?"

"Oh, yeah, as you would chirp to us Molloy, 'It looks like you're whipped.' And speaking of that, I'm confused about a couple of things." Eric paused.

"What's that?" Molloy flashed his toothy grin in spite of himself.

"You say all that racist stuff all the time and . . ." Eric waited.

"And she's black," Molloy filled in the sentence.

"Well, yeah." Eric nodded.

"How many times do I have to tell you guys, I hate everyone *equally*?"

"I guess so."

Dermot smiled. "Or in this case, you *love* everyone equally."

Eric picked up. "Okay, fair enough, Molloy, you're not a racist. But on my first day of work you gave me this whole speech about the sweater trick.

You know, that women wear a sweater or sweatshirt around their waist to, you know . . ."

"Hide their monster asses is what I think I told you," Molloy added.

"Well, yeah, and Kimberly had . . ." Eric stopped.

"A sweatshirt tied around her big ass."

"I don't know about the big-ass part. I just meant . . ."

"Oh, she does have a big ass. Anyway, I have a question for you, Eric."

"Yeah."

"Did you really believe me with all that shit I told you?"

"Well, yeah. I've tried to take notes on that kind of stuff, so I'll know what's right and all."

Molloy laughed for a long time. "That was just bullshit talk to pass the day. You want to know what's right, kid? In the end it all comes down to how a woman makes you feel. My wife never made me feel good about anything. She made me feel like a loser. I could never please her. With Kimberly, she makes me feel good."

"Am I in the *Twilight Zone* or something? Of all people, I can't believe I'm hearing this from Gary Molloy!" Dermot exclaimed.

"I don't care anymore. It's the truth. Now, what's going on here other than Dermot getting published? Oh, and for the record, that was a nice piece of writing." Molloy handed back the paper to Dermot.

"Now compliments? What's going on here? But thanks . . . Well, Molloy, since you are now Mr. 1950s, you can help us. We are trying to think up the perfect date for Eric and Natalie."

"Really?"

"Yeah, he doesn't want to do the standard take-her-to-the-movie thing. So you got any advice?" Dermot asked while scanning his article for the hundredth time of the day.

"Advice?" Molloy rubbed his chin. "Let's see . . . How 'bout this. Take her to a French restaurant, order a nice meal, and, when in doubt, put her hand on it and say, 'Oui! C'est Boner for you.'"

"I take it you flunked French class, too," Dermot said.

Eric laughed. "Molloy, that kind of talk would've worked yesterday. But you just showed your true colors."

"Literally." Dermot chuckled keeping his eyes on his article and then he noticed something else in the paper. "That's it!" He jumped from his chair. "I've got it."

"Got what?" Eric and Molloy asked.

"The perfect date! I know exactly where Eric can take her."

"Where?" Eric asked.

Dermot ignored his question and turned to Molloy. "But, I'll need your help."

"No problem. After all, apparently you two assholes are like family to me."

Dermot smiled, and for the rest of the day they planned Eric and Natalie's perfect date.

EIGHTEEN

Dermot really *was* on top of the world as he was locking up the lot for the night, but then he heard a horn honk.

"Come on! I need to park!"

"We're closed," he said, turning around before realizing it was his friend Eddy Monahan.

"Eddy, holy shit!"

"What's up, man?"

"Nothing. I haven't seen you all summer. What's up, bro?"

Eddy, in a red, sweat-drenched shirt with blue stitching that read GILLIGAN DISTRIBUTORS, hopped out of his delivery truck, walked over to him, and slapped hands.

"I know, Derm. I've been working my ass off. I probably put in ninety hours a week doing beer deliveries all over the Cape and the South Shore. But I figure in the end this shit is going to pay off. So how are things with you?"

"Pretty good. I had an article published in the paper today."

"No, shit. That's great. What's it about?"

"Well, it's about the baseball strike, but there's a little more to it than that."

"Oh, symbolism and all that kind of bullshit?"

"Yeah, actually, you could say that."

"Well, cool, man. That means you're in a partying mood. I have one delivery and then for the first time in like three fucking weeks I have the night off. So do you want to hoist some? I know that Boston band Cliffs Of Dooneen is playing at The Irish Embassy in Falmouth. There should be a shit load of party balloons floating around."

"Nah, I'll have to take a raincheck. I need to write tonight."

"Write? Can't you write any night?" Eddy looked at him.

Instead of getting pissed at the question, Dermot decided to use a little psychology. "Eddy, you're the only one who could understand this. If I want to get where I want to be in life, I have to sacrifice some of these fun nights, too. Just like you busting your balls all summer while everyone else is having a good time. That's what I have to do. Writers write. You know what I mean?"

"I hear you, man." Eddy shook his hand and backed off. "Well, it was good seeing you. I gotta burn and make this delivery, but maybe we can hang out in the fall when it slows done for both of us?"

"Sounds good."

"By the way, what are you working on?"

"I think I want to write a kids' mystery book about Cape Cod," Dermot responded, having no clue where the idea came from, but he liked the thought of writing for kids.

"Hey, that sounds pretty cool. God knows there are a lot of mysteries on the Cape." Eddy jumped back into his truck and revved it up. "Well, good luck, bro."

"Thanks for understanding."

"No, problem." He pulled the gearshift and was about to back out. "When I see your ex, I'll be sure to tell her that you're writing a fucking . . . What are those books called? Newbury Award winners? Yeah, that's it. Dermot's writing a fucking Newbury Award winner."

Dermot didn't hear the second part of the sentence because his mind was still focused on the first part.

"Whoa," Dermot put his hand up. "Wait! Hold up!"

"What?" Eddy worked the gearshift back in park.

"What do you mean my *ex*?"

"Well, Francesca. She *is* your ex, right?" Eddy looked at him, puzzled.

"Yeah, I know that part. What I'm saying is what do you mean you'll tell her when you see her?"

"Well, when I see her at the Yacht Club?"

"The Yacht club?"

"Yeah, the Sea Breeze Yacht Club. It's down Cape."

"Down Cape?"

"Yeah, man, in Chatham. I see her there a lot since she's in charge of the events and all."

"In charge of events? Eddy, what the fuck are you talking about? Francesca is in Italy."

"Italy? What?"

"Yeah, she's been there all summer." Dermot felt his pulse quicken.

"Italy? No, man, the question should be what the fuck *are you* talking about? I just saw her yesterday when I was doing deliveries there. I dropped off forty-five cases of beer for a couple of weddings they're having this week."

Dermot's mind was racing. "Are you sure you saw her?"

"Yeah, man. I'm sure 'cause I even talked to her."

"You *talked* to her? Eddy, you're not fucking with me, are you?"

"No, man. I'm *not* fucking with you. Why are you freaking out? I mean, we even talked about you. She said . . ." Eddy stopped in mid-sentence.

"She said what? What!"

"Oh, man. Oh shit, I get it." Eddy blurted.

"*Oh, shit,* you get *what?*"

"Dermot, awe shit, man, I'm sorry. I didn't realize that you didn't know she was living in Chatham for the summer. I would've told you all of this in a better way. Aw, fucking A! I'm so fucking stupid!"

"Why, *Eddy?*"

"Well, you see, I asked her if you guys ever talk 'cause I knew it was a bad deal for you when it went down and she said, 'We talk now and then.' She said it was totally cool between you two. But, since you didn't even know she's down there, I guess she was lying to me, huh? Right?"

"Yeah," was all Dermot could utter, but his mind was screaming, *Nice deductive reasoning, fucking Sherlock Holmes!*

Eddy sat helpless behind the wheel for a moment watching Dermot's pained expression not knowing what to do. He finally leaned over, restarted his truck, and said, "Hey, I gotta go drop off this order. I'm really sorry, man."

While his insides were crumbling, Dermot flashed one of the worst fake smiles ever. "No, problem, man, it's not your fault. You didn't know. It doesn't really matter anyway. I was just a little surprised. That's all." He was literally *dying* to ask more questions, but he bit a hole in his lower lip. There was only one person who could really answer them, and she was fifty miles away. He had to go see Francesca. There had to be some logical explanation of why she hadn't contacted him. At least, an explanation other than the one that was in the back of his mind. That one he wasn't going to listen to.

Dermot waited until the Gilligan Distributors truck rolled down the street before beginning his brisk walk home that quickly became a full sprint.

When he arrived at The Shanty, he was drenched in sweat and breathing heavily. He crouched over and placed his hands on his knees. "What the fuck? What the fuck? She's *supposed* to be in Italy." The tiny part of his brain still functioning properly suggested taking a hot shower and changing before driving to Chatham, but it lost to the out-of-control side that made him go inside, grab his keys, and hop in his car. "You better fucking start, you piece of shit!" He turned the ignition and, to his surprise, the engine fired to life.

He thumbed through his assorted mix tapes on the passenger seat until he found the *Leave Me Alone Mix*, which was named after the fifth song on the tape by the British-synth group New Order. He popped the tape in, turned the volume up to ten, backed out, and drove down the street.

As his car passed the beach, Dermot watched the light pink sun slip behind the white marker wobbling about in the strong current. He turned his attention back to the road and for the next forty-five minutes he listened to songs like, "I'm Allowed" by Buffalo Tom, to "Pieces of The Night" by the Gin Blossoms, to another New Order song called "Every Little Counts." With each song came more depression for him to bask in.

He fast-forwarded past Robert Smith, who was saying goodbye on a night like this. *What am I going to say to her? What is she going to say to me?* He took his finger off the fast-forward button when he heard a snippet of the next song: "I Burn for You" by The Police, a song he had also used on his *Francesca Mix.* When it came on, it threw him back in time to the previous summer.

It had been the perfect night that began with dinner at the Brennans. Around a table covered with several Chinese food containers, Dermot introduced Francesca to his parents. He was nervous about his parents meeting her. Mr. and Mrs. Brennan were some of the nicest people in town, but when it came to their boys dating, they always cocked a critical eye. Fortunately for Dermot, Colin had eased the tension by breaking into impersonations of movie stars, his Dad making pancakes, and local characters like Chucky "He's All" Dunn flexing his muscles. Dermot sat back, enjoying the moment and loving his brother for it. The laughter continued when Francesca answered Mrs. Brennan's question of how she met Dermot.

"Well, Mrs. Brennan," Francesca replied, making eye contact with everyone at the table, "Derm was wearing a T-shirt with a picture of Cindy Brady on it and I was like, I *have* to go meet this cheese ball because I secretly love *The Brady Bunch.* Of course, I would never admit that publicly and, I guess that's what intrigued me. Dermot didn't care what everyone else thought. He was going for the laugh."

"Chip off the old block." Mr. Brennan laughed.

"Blockhead," Mrs. Brennan added to the old routine.

"That's what he tells me. I mean, not the blockhead part." Francesca giggled and continued. "So after we met and chatted for a while we played a little *Brady Bunch* trivia. And I have to admit, he won by knowing the Brady girls' cat's name was Fluffy."

"They had a cat?" Colin asked.

"It was mentioned only once in the first episode," Dermot said.

"You see," Francesca gave Dermot a love tap. "That's when I knew this blockhead was the perfect guy for me."

Everyone howled.

"The funny part is," Dermot added, "I was only wearing that T-shirt 'cause it was an old one of Clay's and he said he'd give me twenty bucks if I did. Come to think of it, I never did get that twenty."

"Well you know Clay," Mrs. Brennan beat everyone to the punch. "He only has three dollars to his name."

The jovial atmosphere had continued for a couple more hours, and when Dermot was leaving with Francesca, Mrs. Brennan not only gave Francesca a bag with the leftovers, but she also gave her a hug of approval and said, "I like you. You have personality."

When they got to his car, Dermot planted a long kiss on her soft lips.

"This night is not over." He smiled and opened the passenger door for her. In the backseat, he had packed a bottle of wine and a beach blanket. They drove along listening to "I Burn For You," glancing at one another as the lyrics translated their thoughts. When they got to the lighthouse, they climbed down the stairs and maneuvered up and over the jetties that hid their secret beach below the cliff.

Dermot spread out the blanket, and they sat watching the skies turn purple before them, eating egg rolls, and drinking cheap wine. It was at that moment the midnight rain fell bringing with it the foghorn's warning moan. Dermot rose from the blanket, suggesting they should probably leave before the downpour, but Francesca grabbed his hand with force, pulling him back to the blanket.

She loved me! She said it to me over and over again! What happened? I have to know! Like the angry surf on that fateful night, the thoughts pounded him as he took his eyes from the yellow line on the road to a sign to his right and mouthed, "Welcome to Chatham." Holding onto the wheel with the right hand, he nervously rubbed his chin with the other, directing the car to where he thought the harbor might be. He knew he was on the right track when he spotted a green sign with bold white lettering: SEA BREEZE YACHT CLUB. Underneath it was an arrow pointing straight ahead.

"Oh, God," he gasped, finally realizing what he was doing. He really *was* going to face her.

He encountered two more arrowed signs before pulling up to the big gray weather-shingled building overlooking a dozen or so Nantucket-style yachts tied to their slips. Dermot turned off his tape so he could watch and listen to the scene before deciding what to do next. The place was bustling with activity. White lights barely shadowed the laughing figures milling about on the top deck while the sound of tinkling piano keys spread its warmth in the background. He took in the scene, and when the smell of scallops wrapped in bacon also wafted his way, it told him one thing: wedding reception.

The car remained idle as he contemplated what to do. He checked his watch: 9:17.

This thing could last till eleven or twelve. He might not have been thinking straight, but he was still sane enough to realize he couldn't just burst into the reception and yell, "Where is she?"

Scanning the parking lot beside the club, he saw it was packed with a who's-who of luxury vehicles, so he decided to drive out back. When he got there, he noticed the quality of the vehicles diminished significantly from BMW's, Mercedes, Jaguars, to Civics, Chevys, and Sedans. He saw a hastily painted red EMPLOYEE PARKING sign hanging in the far back corner near the dumpster.

Dermot thought he spied a couple of openings in that area between the dumpster and a white truck with blue lettering on its side that read CHEF ROLAND'S PRIME CUT CATERING, so he continued and that's when he saw Francesca's brown Volvo. It had been hidden in the spot directly adjacent to the dumpster.

He slammed on the breaks and closed his eyes. Even though it made no sense, in the back of his mind he had hoped that Eddy was somehow horribly mistaken or was playing some cruel joke. It had been a ridiculous hope to have. When he opened his eyes and looked at the Volvo with the sunroof now closed, Dermot realized the only joke was *him*.

Francesca *was* back and she had never called. He frantically swiveled his head around expecting to see her watching, but there was no one there, just laughter in the distance. He was alone and now he really didn't know what to do. "What kind of sign is *this* one, *Mom*?" he growled to himself, realizing the only open space was between the Volvo and the catering truck. He lurched the car forward and then considered driving away, but, at the last second, he threw the gearshift in reverse and nestled the Pontiac between the catering truck and the Volvo. Then he waited.

Sitting in his car, his eyes were transfixed on the steps a couple of hundred feet in front of him. They led up to a landing that was outside the kitchen door. A fluorescent white floodlight and a yellow bug zapper that crunched in between the DJ's song intros lit up the words SERVICE ENTRANCE.

When she is done working she'll have to come out that door.

At 10:20 p.m. he listened to Kool and the Gang celebrating with the groom's family.

At 11:06 p.m. it was the bridesmaids screaming to anyone who would listen that they were family, too.

At 11:31 p.m. everyone and their grandmothers were going down to the YMCA.

And at exactly 11:50 p.m., with the summer wind, the DJ gently ushered people from the reception, promising an after-hours party at the maid of honor's hotel suite.

Dermot had hours to reconsider and drive back home, but he had spent the past seven months grappling with the reason for the break up. If he left now, he would spend another seven months or more wondering why she lied to him. He continued to wait as the cars of revelers zigzagged from the lot and the catering truck and DJ van packed up and drove off. There were still a few cars in the lot, but the night was still except for the zapper, which was now working overtime.

Dermot had played mix tape after mix tape and was leaning over about to grab another one when the spring of a screen door creaked open before slamming shut.

He snapped his head to attention. He gulped at the sight, and his pulse raced. The floodlight shined down on Francesca Giordano as if she were an actress on a stage.

Instinctively, Dermot shrank in his seat, but then remembered his car was under the cover of darkness, so he propped up and studied her. She looked exhausted, stretching in her Yacht Club pink polo shirt emblazoned with a sailboat logo. Under the floodlight, her movements defined the outline of her breasts, and all he could think of was the lighthouse's halo on that rainy night from last summer. It had revealed her soft, glistening figure every few seconds as they made love that night for the first time.

But, that was then . . .

She pulled the tucked shirt from her khaki skirt that showcased her tanned legs and pulled her black hair out of the loose bun, shaking it as it fell past her shoulders. At this point, Dermot couldn't take it anymore. He opened the door and walked across the seashell driveway, but Francesca didn't notice him. She was leaning over tying one of her pristine white Topsiders. Her ankles were slender and brown, and Dermot was compelled to stare. They were small, perfect ankles. He realized he had stared at them and beyond to the summer of '93, as he heard her voice in the distance.

"Dermot! Dermot!" He looked up. Francesca had finished tying her shoe and her dark eyes were bearing down on him. "What are you doing here?"

"I, ah . . ." He began thumbing behind him and remembered why he was there and his anger resurfaced. "What am *I* doing here? What are *you* doing here is the question?"

"I work here." Keeping her eyes on him, she reached into her pocket and calmly pulled out a pack of cigarettes. She took one out, lit it, and puffed away.

"You smoke?" He pointed.

"Huh?"

"You smoke?"

"What do you mean?" She looked at her cigarette.

"I mean, since when did you start smoking?"

"Since . . . I don't know . . . a few years."

"A few years. You didn't smoke last summer."

"I guess I was taking a break. You didn't answer my question. What *are* you doing here?"

He ignored her and said, "You're supposed to be in Italy."

"Oh, yeah, that. Well, as you can see, I never ended up going. I ah . . . Wait. I'm going to ask you one last time. Why are you here? I mean, don't tell me it's to find out why I didn't go to Italy."

Dermot moved one step closer. "Well, yeah, that and why you lied to me."

She exhaled before replying, "Lied to you?"

"Yeah, you've been here all summer and you didn't call me."

"Not calling you isn't lying." She took another puff.

"Okay, whatever you want to call it. Just tell me why you are here."

"Well . . . Right after we broke up I got to thinking how much I loved the Cape, and near the end of the second semester, I decided I wanted another summer down here. So, I just told my dad I didn't want to go to Italy and, as luck would have it, I met a guy at school whose uncle was on the board of trustees of this place."

"You're telling me you met a guy right after we broke up. What the fuck? I can't believe this shit!" His anger was rising at her cavalier attitude.

"Calm down. Will you? He's gay, for Christ's sake. He's just a friend who got me a job."

Thank God. At least, she's still single. "I don't understand." He moved up another step.

"What's so confusing? Dermot, we broke up. End of story." She took the last drag and threw the cigarette to the ground.

"End of story?"

"Look. I don't mean to be harsh. Really, I don't, but it didn't work out. It happens."

"It didn't work out because of your father. That's the only reason. You couldn't stand up to him, and now you're telling me you did stand up to him with not going to Italy. I could still . . . "

"Oh, that," she broke in while toeing out her cigarette.

"What do you mean *that*?"

"Hey, Francesca," a male voice hollered from inside.

"Yeah, I'm out here, Greg." She returned the holler over her shoulder.

What the fuck is going on here? She's acting like she has no feelings for me! We're in love!

A moment later, a guy with a blond crew cut and a muscular frame wearing the club's work uniform emerged through the screen door carrying something. "You forgot this." He handed her the leather backpack that Dermot had given her for Christmas.

Greg turned and smiled at Dermot. "Hey, what's up, man?"

"Hey," Dermot managed, but kept his eyes on the backpack. Francesca took it, unzipped it, and grabbed her keys before slinging it over her shoulder. *That backpack is supposed to be in Italy!*

She handed the keys to Greg. "Can you start up the car? I'll be right there."

Greg looked at them both and said, "Sure. But be quick. We have that after-party."

"Yup, it'll be just a minute."

Just a minute! Is that all she has time for to talk about our love! A fucking minute!

He tried to regain his composure and waited to hear the Volvo roar before talking. "Is that your friend, the gay guy?" Dermot motioned over to the car up two more steps.

"Who, *Greg*?" She laughed. "Far fr—" She stopped.

"Shut up. I don't want to hear it," he stressed.

"I'm sorry, I didn't mean to . . . We're just hanging out. That's all."

"Kind of like us last summer. Is that what it was? Hanging out?"

Francesca looked down at her Topsiders.

He climbed the final step and wanted to grab her and shake her, but instead tried with his words. "You told me you loved me! And, that night . . . That night on the beach. In the rain . . . We were in love. We gave each other our . . . our . . . virginity."

"Jesus Christ, Dermot, grow up and *wake* up, will you?"

In their months together, she never talked down to him as she was now and her venom stung him. He could hear the bug light zapping, accentuating her words.

"I'm sorry. Really, I'm sorry. I tried the nice approach last time but now I have to be honest. The truth is, I made up that virgin talk just so it would be special for you since you had held out so long and it was your first time. You always wanted everything to be so romantic. I wanted to give you that. As for my dad's objections, it *is* true he thought you were living a fool's dream."

"So last summer was all a lie?"

"No. I had feelings for you. Of course I did. And I always will, but,

Dermot, did you really expect for us to stay together at our age? We're young. We have to 'seize the day' like that movie you were always talking about. The Poet something."

"*Dead Poet's Society*," he answered out of habit.

"You always did know your movies. And I have to say that might be your problem."

"*My* problem? Are you listening to yourself?" He rubbed the back of his neck with his hands trying to hold it in.

"Yes, and I make sense. What doesn't make sense is that you're in your work uniform. But I'm guessing Eddy probably went by work and told you I was here and you jumped into your car and drove like a madman, listening to sad mix tapes to capture the mood. Am I right?"

"Fuck you, Francesca! You fucking bitch!"

"Good. Good." She nodded. "I'd rather you hated me than to put me on some pedestal. I'm not a perfect person. I never was, and I never will be, and Dermot as much as I loved being with you, you're not perfect either. You try to live life like it's a script. Life is not a two-hour movie with a happy ending . . . I gotta go. I'm sorry."

His eyes were moist; hers were dry. "Yeah, me too." He moved to the side, and she brushed by him. She skipped the steps and walked along, jumping the shells, hopped into the passenger seat of the Volvo, and a moment later was gone. He refused to cry, so he fought the tears, standing in silence as the shifting cool breeze moved on to ring the bell buoys in the harbor. After five minutes, he walked to his car and, in a subdued autopilot state drove for home. His scattered mix tapes remained on the passenger seat. He couldn't allow thoughts. He was broken and numb and just wanted to get back to the Shores. But halfway home, he couldn't take the stillness of the empty highway since the thoughts were creeping back into his head, so he turned on the radio.

Dermot wished he could escape to the voice of Jerry Trupiano calling balls and strikes of a Sox west-coast game, but as his article had pointed out that morning, the boys of summer had all gone home. Spinning the dial, he momentarily bumped into the late night DJ Delilah talking some dumped trucker off *his* ledge of loneliness.

"Fucking loser!" Dermot spat at the man who was babbling on about how much he missed "Sharon," but the truth was, he was really cursing himself.

The next station offered him a dose of Brandy, so he quickly moved on knowing it would take him back to a time at Pucky's when he serenaded Francesca during karaoke night.

"Wait. I'm near Four C's," he exclaimed, actually perking up thinking the Cape Cod Community College radio station would come in. "This will be good." College radio could be his short-term cure. *I could go for some Ramones like "Bonzo Goes To Bitburg," or The Cult's "She Sells Sanctuary."* He turned the dial just as the female DJ, who was trying hard to put some smoke in her voice, said, "This next song is by a guy who's one of my favorites. If you don't know him, his name is Jeff Buckley, and his band is the Jeff Buckley Band. This is from their new album *Grace." Thank God. No old memories with this song.* The DJ continued, "It's a beautiful ballad called, 'Last Goodbye.'"

"You gotta be shitting me," Dermot blurted and was about to change the station when the opening slide guitar riff caught his attention. It was followed by the drumming of a bass guitar and then came the words that floored him. The song chipped away, and as he tried to focus on the taillights in front of him, his vision blurred. The tears came freely. Not only were there tears, but the pain that had been way down deep rose to his chest. He couldn't hold it in anymore. He tried to wipe his eyes dry, but his hand couldn't keep up with the drops. He could barely see the road. Jerking the wheel to the right, he heard a honking car horn sound its annoyance. He pulled the Pontiac over to the breakdown lane where he slowed and shifted to park. He buried his head under his folded arms and leaned against the steering wheel.

As the song ended, it came to him. He never really *did* know Francesca at all. It was a fun summer romance, but he had built her up to be something she wasn't, and he knew that wasn't completely her fault. He should've taken a longer look at the situation and he might have realized that not only did she *not* love him, but he didn't love her. Francesca Giordano had simply been the diversion from the real pain. When they broke up, he made himself believe he was mourning her. In two days it would be the anniversary of the accident. With the tears still falling and his forehead resting against the steering wheel, he asked, "Why Paul? Why Matt? Why did you leave us? And why, God? Why did you take them?"

NINETEEN

Just as the entire year, the summer had been a blur for Colin. He was on a roll, never missing a party, even after he told himself to stay out of trouble—and by his standards, he *had*. Tonight he was tired, exhausted. It might have been the constant raging or maybe the energy he used to shield it from his family. It had been two months since his blow-up at Melissa's art show, but with some good acting, he had convinced his mother it was just a misunderstanding and nothing like that would ever happen again.

Since then, every night he would come home by ten o'clock and join his father in front of the television to catch the end of Sox games. However, with the baseball strike now official, Jim Brennan entertained himself eating microwave popcorn while watching and reciting lines of classic movies on AMC. Shoveling the kernels into his mouth like a POW, he would use his shirt to catch any morsels he missed. Once the bag was devoured, he would cautiously rise from the couch, holding his shirt full of crumbs, and walk out to the front yard, shaking himself clean. "A little something for the birds in the morning," he would always say when returning inside. As soon as this ritual took place, Colin knew it was time.

After brushing his teeth, sometimes in front of his dad for extra effect, he would kiss him on the forehead, say, "Goodnight," and head up to his room. Once inside, he would wait another twenty minutes before jumping out his window eight feet to the ground below, then dash to the basketball court where Chucky was waiting with a case of beer and a party destination.

Sneaking out of his house wasn't new to him. As a kid, he would bail out that same window, landing on piled cushions from lawn furniture to break his fall. After getting up and brushing himself off, he'd grab his pole and tackle box, which lay hidden under a cluster of rhododendrons. He'd skip straight to Stirling Beach where Matt and Paul were waiting for him at The Fighting Chair with *Plato's Paradise* beached on the shore. It was the adventure that made those evening fishing excursions so exciting, and even though he now was sneaking out for different reasons, that feeling of adventure was resurrected.

It felt like he had hit a hundred parties in fifty days, but now the cries of "C-Dog" had become less enthusiastic when he showed up at a bender with Chucky at his side instead of Dwayne. The last time he talked with D was at the art show; he was beginning to feel like he was losing everyone he loved. Tonight, standing alone on the deck of Billy McCarthy's house, he watched Vineyard Sound and listened to the waves smash on the shore while holding a beer with his right hand; with his left hand he clutched the rune, thumbing the etching. He carried the stone everywhere, every day.

It was eight o'clock and already dark, a sign that autumn was on its way. The foghorn sounded in the distance, blowing a warning to any vessel that might be on the open sea. In the distance the Silver Shores Lighthouse stood tall, the gray haze blocking the intermittent light that chased his melancholia.

He couldn't believe it was already mid-August, and in a couple of days, it would be a year since Matt and Paul died. Life was so different now and there was no chance it would ever be the same. He raised the bottle to his lips, but stopped, and squeezed his eyes shut.

Earlier that night Colin left his house, just before seven o'clock, and headed for Stirling Beach. The plan was to meet Chucky and Tabitha before Billy's party for a little pre-game joint, but he wanted to get there early enough to spend some time alone on The Fighting Chair. When he got to the seawall, he noticed someone fishing on the jetty, but it didn't deter him. He took his sneakers and socks off, and jumped down to the beach. Dangling his sneakers from his fingers, he treaded softly across the sand towards the shore. It was dusk, and the moon and sun were competing for center stage. He started laughing to himself as he got to the jetty and then shouted out, "Are they biting?"

"C-Dog! What's up, man?" Eric Chance replied. "They *are* biting, but I haven't hooked any yet." He stood holding his fishing rod in his right hand. His smile was wide and the salt-stained *Island Ferry* hat he wore had been faded by the sun's rays, giving him a true Cape Cod appearance.

"What are you using?" Colin asked as he got closer.

"Pogies."

"Nice. They love the pogies."

"They sure do. You weren't kidding about this spot, either. I caught two keepers here last week."

"I wouldn't steer you wrong. But don't tell anyone. We don't want this place getting crowded." Colin put his sneakers down and began poking around Eric's tackle box.

"Don't worry. I won't tell a soul." There was a short pause. "Guess what?"

Colin looked up. "What?"

"I had my date with Natalie last night."

"No way!" He wiped his hands clean on his shorts. "How did it go? Tell me everything."

Eric hollered to the sea, "I'm in love!" He then turned back to Colin. "I've been walking on air all day, man. It's hard to put into words, but easy to write." He laughed. "Of course, I already documented the whole date in my journal, so I wouldn't forget anything."

"Well, where did you take her?"

He pointed to the Silver Shores Lighthouse in the distance. "I took her there."

"Huh?"

"You know that private beach . . . the one right near the lighthouse?"

Colin nodded. "Yeah, I know that beach well."

"I got there early to prepare myself because I was nervous, and I figured I should try to calm down a little, but she was already there, waiting for me. I couldn't believe it." He shook his head. "You should have seen her, Colin. God, she looked so beautiful. She was wearing a light blue sundress and her skin smelled like citrus, which made my heart race faster. I thought I was going to faint. I had these crazy thoughts that she was going to cancel on me or just not show. But, she did show *and* she was early."

"She likes you."

Eric smiled. "I had bought some Italian food from Ascensio's and packed it into a picnic basket along with a radio and some other stuff. I used a flashlight to lead her down this path that's overgrown with brush and briars, but after about a hundred feet it opens up to a clearing right below the lighthouse. Once we got there I lit a fire, spread out a blanket and broke out a bottle of sparkling cider . . ."

"Whoa, hold up a minute. How did you know about that path? And how did you get a fire started?"

"Your brother. He said he took his ex-girlfriend there last summer. And as far as the fire, Dermot *and* Molloy set that up for me."

"Molloy, too?"

"Yeah. That guy keeps surprising me. So, when we arrived all I had to do was strike a match. Once I had the blanket down, I put on a mix tape of slow songs Dermot had made me. I mean, it was flawless. It was something straight out of a movie."

"Wow, it does sound perfect. That's a night she won't forget."

"That's not all, Colin. After we ate, the fireworks for Illumination Night on Martha's Vineyard went off. We had the best view from this side of the Sound and *that's* when I reached for my poetry."

"Look at you. What the hell were you so nervous about? Sounds like you're a true Casanova."

Eric laughed. "It just felt so natural being with her, so right. She makes me, you know . . . *feel*. Like with you and that girl you liked in high school, Jenny?"

Colin smiled and nodded.

"So, I read some poetry to her and then she recited some to me, from the hip, Colin. God, she's the girl of my dreams."

"That's deep."

"The light of the fire captured her beauty and it kinda froze me, but then she gave the sweetest smile I'd ever seen telling me it was okay, so that's when I went in for the kiss."

"Oh, you devil. You got a kiss, too?"

"Yeah. Now, I've kissed a girl before, but it was spin the bottle, it wasn't like this. This was different. Perfect. I had been imagining that since the first day I saw her in my English class." He paused. "You know what? It's because of you. If you didn't give me that pep talk none of this would have happened. Your words have stayed with me all summer. I really appreciate everything you've done for me."

"Don't mention it."

"You've been such a good friend to me. You and your brother."

"I think you're a great kid, Eric. I'm happy I could help." He gave him a soft pat on the back. "So, when are you going to see her again?"

"Tomorrow night. She's cooking me dinner. I can't wait."

"Well, have fun. But for now you need to concentrate on reeling in some fish. And I have a party to go to. I'll talk to you later."

"Okay. Thanks again, C-Dog."

Colin picked up his sneakers and started to make his way off the jetty, but quickly stopped. The question had been weighing on his mind ever since that day. He needed to know. He turned back.

"Hey, Eric?"

"Yeah?"

"I need to ask you something."

"Sure. You can ask me anything, you know that."

"Do you remember that day when I brought you your hat? The day we were talking with that handicapped boy?"

"Donnie? Yeah, of course. What about it?"

"Well, when I was inside waiting for you, I stumbled across your notebook of poems . . . I wasn't trying to be nosy. I was looking for one of Molloy's *Playboys*."

"Okay."

"Well, I read one of your poems."

"That's okay, C-Dog. I don't mind. You're my friend. Which poem did you read?"

"'The Color Red.'"

"Oh." His demeanor changed. "That one."

"Yeah." There was a long pause. "Is it true, Eric? Did your father die in a car accident?"

"Yes. When I was in the fourth grade he was killed by a drunk driver."

"I'm so sorry. I had no idea. That's horrible."

"It's okay. I'm not going to lie. It wasn't easy. I was devastated, but it really affected my mom. She started drinking a lot after my father passed. We had some tough years at my house, dark years. But, thank God, she's sober now."

"That's great."

"Yes, it is. Because honestly, after my father died I felt like I lost my mom, too. It's amazing to have her back again and to see her smile and laugh. That's why we came to the Cape. My mom needed a change . . . we needed a change. She's been sober a little over a year. Now we have a chance at life again."

"I'm happy for you both, but I have to ask . . . I mean . . . you seem so happy . . . you're always so upbeat. How do you do it? With your father being gone?"

"As I said, C-Dog, it wasn't easy. I always wonder if the light had been green for the drunk driver and not red my dad would have been stopped and that driver would have barreled into no one. That kind of thought can drive you crazy, but I made a vow that I wouldn't let my father's death define me. My dad was a great guy. He was a very loving person. I try to think that his spirit now lives through me and I have to do something with it. You know what I mean?"

"C-Dog. Yo, Colin . . . Hello . . . Paging Colin Brennan. Are you there?" Billy McCarthy said, waving his hands in front of Colin's face bringing him back to the moment. He looked around the deck.

"Oh, sorry. How are you, Billy?"

"You okay? You look out of it."

"Yeah, I'm fine. Sorry. I was just thinking about something. How've you been, man? It's good to see you. It's been awhile." Colin smiled.

"Yeah, probably about a year."

"Yeah."

"I'm happy you came by. It wouldn't have been summer without having a good laugh with you." He patted Colin on the back.

"Thanks, man."

Billy rested his arms on the railing. "I finally met your brother Dermot. I crossed paths with him at a party at the beginning of the summer. He's a good dude. I see the connection."

"Fuck him!"

"Huh? I thought you two were tight."

"We *were* tight. Past tense. But let's not waste time talking about stupid bullshit."

"Okay. Sorry, man."

"It's cool."

"Um . . . so . . . what are your plans for the fall?"

"Same shit. Just work." Quickly changing the subject, Colin motioned to the Sound. "I gotta say, Billy, your parents have one hell of a house. On a clear night you must have the best view of the Atlantic. Typical, rich summer kid."

"Oh, come on. You know I don't take it for granted."

"I know. I'm only kidding. I'd never put you in that category. I always liked you. You're good people."

"I feel the same way about you, man. We sure had some fun summers lifeguarding. I miss seeing you down at the beach, probably not as much as the kids, though."

"Yeah, right. I'm sure they're fine."

"No, man, I had a lot of depressed kids this summer. When they found out the C-Dog wasn't coming back there were some sad faces."

"Really?"

"Hell, yeah! Remember little Kevin Walsh? The redhead who wore the floaters on his arms? Well, until you taught him how to swim."

"Yeah, of course."

"He cried for a week when he heard you were gone. He didn't even want to go into the water. He said swimming lessons weren't the same."

"No shit?"

"Yeah. All the kids miss you, man."

"Yeah, I miss them, but my days in the ocean are over, Billy. Time to try something else."

"I understand. But, maybe someday you'll change your mind and get back to doing what you do best."

"Yeah, I highly doubt that."

"Never say never, Colin." There was a long pause before Billy continued. "Hey, C-Dog, you didn't bring Chucky Dunn, did you?"

"Yeah, why?"

"Well, no offense man, but that kid's a loser. I didn't even know you were friends with him. He's not gonna start any shit, is he?"

"Billy, you're my boy. I wouldn't let him do anything disrespectful to you or your home. That's a promise. And if he starts acting up, I'll get him out of here, but he won't, so don't worry. He's not that bad when you get to know him."

"Please don't tell me that clown is driving."

"No, he's not that stupid."

"Are you driving?" Billy asked concerned.

"No man. That girl Tabitha is driving us. She's Chucky's girl. Don't worry, everything is cool. Everyone just wants to get twisted and have some fun."

"All right. Because this is really the last party of the summer for me. A lot of friends are leaving to go back to school, so I want tonight to be memorable. No problems, you know what I'm saying?"

"It's all good."

"Cool. As long as you say it's okay that makes me feel better." The two high-fived. "You want to go inside and grab a beer?"

"Billy, you read my mind."

He directed Colin through the house, passing friends and strangers on their way to the kitchen. Once there, Billy marched straight to the refrigerator and reached for the handle, but stopped. "Hey, C-Dog, remember this?" he said, pointing to a picture magnet of a group of smiling, tan lifeguards, with Billy and Colin in the front row raising their fists to the sky.

Colin squinted as he took a closer look. "Holy shit. Yeah, I remember that. That was the day of the beach meets."

"Yup. We kicked everyone's ass. Those were the days," Billy said as he handed him a beer. Colin remained silent, quickly twisting off the cap and taking a large gulp.

"Thanks, man, always good to wet the whistle."

"Hell, yeah. Listen, C-Dog, I gotta go make the rounds. I don't want to be a bad host. Make yourself at home and we'll catch up later?"

"Definitely."

Billy pushed through the swinging doors and strutted into the living room leaving Colin by himself. He took another look at the picture on the fridge. His hair was much shorter then and his body more toned. *Yup, those were the days.*

He leaned against the warm dishwasher, and sipped his beer while staring at the flashing *12:00* that repeatedly lit up the screen on the microwave. His deep trance was broken when a beautiful brunette with striking brown eyes walked into the room carrying the faint smell of CK One, a unisex fragrance that his boy Dwayne Peters also wore.

"Hey, stranger. How are you? Long time no see." She stood on her tiptoes and gave him a warm hug that surprised him. It felt nice having her in his arms. She seemed so fresh and clean and possessed—an uncanny resemblance to Francesca, Dermot's ex-girlfriend.

"Hey, how are you?" he asked. *Who is this? She is the most beautiful girl I've ever seen.*

"I'm okay, but what's up with you? How was your summer?"

"It was okay. How was yours?"

"Pretty good. A lot of work." She rolled her eyes as she opened the fridge and pulled out a bottle of cranberry juice and poured herself a glass. "I took those summer classes at Four C's I was telling you about. What a pain, but I got two A's and that's what matters. It will raise my GPA, so I'm pretty psyched. I just can't believe I have to go back to school now. Why does the summer have to be the shortest season?" She frowned.

He answered with a shrug.

"I really thought I would have seen you sooner than this. How's the shoe store been?"

He nodded his head. "Same as always, I guess."

"Yeah?"

"Yup." His behavior and short answers spoke volumes.

"You don't remember me, do you?"

He laughed. "Um . . . well . . . no, I don't. I'm sorry."

"Wow. Um, well," She reached out her hand. "I'm Sofia. We met at the beginning of the summer."

"Really? I can't believe I forgot meeting someone as pretty as you," he said as he shook her hand. "You're absolutely gorgeous. It's a pleasure to meet you, Sofia."

"Oh, you're still a charmer. I can't believe you forgot, either. It's nice to meet you *again*, Colin."

"Did I sell you some shoes or something?"

"Wow, this is really unbelievable. No. We met at my house."

"Your *house*? When was this?"

"It was after Memorial Day, probably sometime in early June. I had just gotten home from UVM for the summer, and I was having a party and, out of nowhere, you waltzed in."

"Who was I with?"

"Nobody, you were flying solo."

"Solo? What was I doing?"

"You thought you were at another party and then realized you were at the wrong house. But you jumped on the Beirut table with my friend Henry and won, like ten games in a row. You ended up staying for a while."

"Really? Jesus, I don't remember that at all."

"Well, you *were* pretty drunk."

"Yeah, I guess so. Did anything bad happen?"

"Bad? No, why?"

"No reason."

"No, you were hilarious." Her petite frame shook with laughter. "You were doing some hysterical *Jerky Boys* impersonations and had everyone dying."

"Seriously? Are you making this shit up? Did Billy tell you to screw with me?"

"No, not at all. I wouldn't do something like that. You don't remember any of this?"

"No," he shook his head.

"Oh, that's too bad. So, it's safe to assume you don't remember our conversation on the porch?"

"Nope. What did we talk about?"

"We talked about how summer was the best season, but way too short. You told me growing up it was your favorite because it was an escape from school and your time to be free. And, I told you how I spent all my summers in education programs. I guess someone blacked out." She winced.

Colin replied, "Well, ah . . ."

"I probably shouldn't have been giving you all those Otter Creeks. You also promised me you were going to take me fishing. You said you had the best spot in town. And then I never saw you again, until now." She grimaced. "Broken promises, I guess."

"Really? What an asshole I am. Let me make it up to you. You know, it's still high tide. We can cast off the shore right now." Colin opened the fridge and began pulling out beers, shoving them in his pockets.

"Come on, Sofia. No broken promises here. Let's go reel in some stripers."

"No, it's too late now. I'm here to hang out with my friends tonight. You had your chance. I shouldn't even talk to you since you left me all alone that night."

"Left you alone? What do you mean?"

"When we were on the porch we were having a very serious talk and Henry came up and asked if you wanted to smoke a joint, and you were gone. It's too bad."

He pulled a bottle of Southern Comfort from his back pocket and took a blast. "Sorry about that, Sofia. You want a rip?"

She waved her hands. "No way. That stuff is nasty."

"Wow. What are you, like straight-edge or something?"

"No. I like to have a couple of drinks, but I don't overdo it."

"To each his own. So what was this serious talk we were having? Were we planning our wedding?"

"No." Her tone became more serious. "You were telling me about your friends."

"My friends? What friends?"

"The boys that passed away last summer."

Boys that passed away . . . How many times had he heard that in the past year? The phrase stung and there was no remedy for the pain. It had become too much for him to bear. His face flushed crimson. *I told her about Matt and Paul? Why would I tell her about them? I barely know this girl. What the fuck was I thinking?*

"Oh . . . well that . . . that was . . . ah . . . that was last year. That's in the past now. There's no need to talk about that."

"I was only saying it because . . ."

"Forget it. Let's get back to the fishing." He shook the topic and changed direction. "I can go grab some rods and gear out of Billy's garage, and we'll walk down to the beach. It will be nice."

"You had your chance. And I think you're a really nice guy. I really do." She rubbed his shoulder. "I hope things get easier for you. Just like summertime, life is short. We need to do the best with the time we have." She flashed an empathetic smile. "Take care of yourself, Colin." She walked out the door leaving him puzzled. He didn't remember any of that night, but apparently he shot himself in the foot and that pissed him off.

In an attempt to drink the embarrassment away, he wrapped his lips tightly around the bottle of Southern Comfort and finished it. The syrupy liquor coated his insides and temporarily concealed his shame. Again, he caught sight of the picture magnet on the refrigerator. Friends. Smiling faces. The beach. He walked over to it and pulled it from its place, firing it across the room. Taking a deep breath, he tried to compose himself before going back into the party.

With a beer in each pocket, he headed out to the living room where the music thumped. He spotted Chucky and headed his way until someone grabbed him from behind and said, "What's your deal, man?"

He turned around and saw Josh Baker staring with an annoying smile smeared across his face. "What do you mean, Josh? You always seem to creep up on me. What do you want?"

"Jesus, relax, Colin. Did Larry tell you I came by the store last week?"

"Yeah, he did. And my dad told me you called, and my mom also said that you came by the bookstore and talked with her. And the answer is still no. I don't want to be on your goddamn swim team. Why don't you concentrate on yourself instead of harassing me and my family?"

"Harassing? Don't be so fucking dramatic. I'm trying to help you. I've been telling Coach you just needed some time, but, now we're going into another season."

"Talking to the coach? Figures. You were always such an ass kisser."

"You're a real asshole, Colin. At first, people felt sorry for you, but now it's old. It's been a year. Matt and Paul were my friends, too. You know what? Don't worry about me *harassing* you anymore. Just like everyone else, I'm done with you." He turned around and disappeared into the crowd.

Colin felt the rage building. It formed in his toes and traveled up his legs, hitting the pit of his stomach and then shot through his arms. He clenched his fists and gritted his teeth. His first instinct was to pounce on Josh like a rabid dog and tear him apart, but he had to refrain. The conversation with Billy lingered in the back of his head. Instead, he pushed the anger back inside and added it to the heap of festering pain, something he had been doing for a year.

Brushing off his remarks, he hurried over to Chucky. "Dunn! Hey, Dunn!" he barked loudly. Chucky raised his index finger indicating he would be a minute. He was busy describing to several wide-eyed summer kids that it was he who broke into Tex's Super Lube and changed the sign.

"The owner of the Super Lube, Tex, is born-again or some shit. He's been sober for fifteen years. Always preaching the Bible and junk like that to all the guys in the pit. You've seen the messages before?"

"Yeah, I always check to see what's posted," one boy responded.

"Okay, so the other day he put up 'One Who Follows the Footsteps of God Lives a Life of Honesty.' The typical stupid shit he always writes. So, after he fired me, I figured I'd make him look like a fool. I broke in that night and wrote 'Alcoholics Anonymous Is for Quitters!'"

They all laughed and one said, "Yeah, it is. Shit. That is hilarious, man. You're awesome."

Tabitha grabbed his arm and pulled him away. "Honey, you don't know those kids, and Tex didn't press charges on you for that. If he hears you're making a mockery of him, he might change his mind."

"Those kids aren't going to say anything. Plus, I have so many charges right now, let him add that shit," Chucky assured her.

"Don't say I didn't warn you. I gotta take a piss." She stormed off.

Chucky shrugged and turned to Colin as he approached.

"Hey, Chucky, you want to puff a joint? I'm feeling claustrophobic in this place."

"Yeah, that sounds good. I'll be out in a minute after Tabby pisses."

"All right. I'm gonna go smoke a butt. I'll meet you outside in five."

Chucky nodded, and Colin walked to the sliding glass door that led out to the deck. As he reached out his hand to open it, chants of "Chocolate Thunder" echoed throughout the room. He peered over his shoulder and saw Dwayne walking into the party. The two exchanged a quick glance.

You got to be fucking kidding me. How much worse can this night get? He snubbed his old friend and broke for fresh air passing two kids wearing popped-collared polos, who were shooting the shit while smoking their cigarettes. He glided down the steps to the lawn, unzipped his jeans, and relieved himself on the swaying beach grass.

What the fuck is Dwayne doing here?

After zipping up, he remained on the grass and listened to the conversation above him.

"So, Graham, when are you leaving for school?"

"In a couple of days. I can't wait. South Beach is going to put Stirling Beach girls to shame. All the bitches down there look like Pamela Anderson sporting her C.J. Parker look. I hope to land myself a part-time lifeguard gig and take my game with me because it's been good this summer."

"Graham the Man. How do you do it?"

"I have the gift, bro."

"I guess so. How many did you take down this summer?"

"Guys like me, we don't keep numbers. I would need to carry a goddamn calculator in my back pocket. You know what I'm saying?" He laughed.

"Yeah, you do have a quite a rep, but what happened with you and that Armenian chick from the coffee shop?"

Colin perked his ears up.

"What do you mean what happened with her?" the other kid said.

"I heard she told you to get lost. She wasn't into it."

"Get lost?" He laughed. "She had to say that. I popped her cherry and her older sister found out. I just had to hit it and quit it. But that didn't stop that little freak. I nailed her last night, too."

"No shit?"

"Yeah. A girl like that is nothing but a cum-dumpster. She'll be stuck in that coffee shop her whole life."

Cum dumpster? With his adrenaline pumping rapidly, Colin stormed up the stairs and spotted the two kids in the corner of the deck. He ran over to them and shouted, "Which one's Graham?"

The surprise of Colin's arrival silenced them.

He repeated, "I said, 'Which one is Graham?'"

Clenched by fear, the smaller of the two quickly thumbed to his right, selling out his friend. Colin studied the pretty-faced boy before striking him in the mouth with a right hook. Graham's head snapped back. Stunned by the punch he lost his balance, but Colin grabbed his polo shirt and pulled him upright. He threw another jab, blasting him in the nose, exploding it like a tomato. Graham fell on his back, reached for his face and tried to stop the flowing red tide, but Colin jumped on him and held his arms down with his knees. "Don't you ever talk that way about Natalie, you fucking liar!" He cursed as he jack-hammered him with repeated blows to the head. "Do you like that, you piece of shit? I'm gonna kill you!"

There was a maddening smile on Colin's face. He *did* want to kill him. All the fury, all the rage he had bottled up boiled over. He was in a trance. If felt good to go off. To release. His frenzy was cut short when someone grabbed his left arm, pulling him away. On instinct, he turned and threw a vicious haymaker connecting with the person's chin. The figure fell back, tripping over a chaise lounge. That's when Colin realized who he had hit.

"What the fuck!" Dwayne yelled from the floor.

Colin was back in the moment. He rushed to his friend's aid. "Oh shit! Sorry, D. I didn't know that was you." He extended his hand and tried to help him up, but Dwayne swatted it away, rising to his feet. "Fuck you, Colin," he said, massaging his face. "You know what? I'm done with you. You wanna go? Let's see how tough you *really* are!"

Colin backed up and waved off his invitation. Most of the crowd had shuffled out onto the deck to see what the commotion was, including an

irate Billy who jumped in front of Dwayne. "Easy, D. Relax." He turned
to Colin. "What the fuck is wrong with you? I ask you to keep an eye on
things and you beat up my friend?" He turned to Graham who was now
sitting up and holding his head back. "You okay, Graham?"

"I think so. That kid is crazy. Get him out of here," he grunted.

"Oh, don't worry about that." Billy turned back to Colin. "Dude, get
the fuck out. Now!"

Chucky came running out of the crowd like a madman, ripping off his
shirt, firing it to the deck. "You want some, bitch? Huh? You wanna dance
with the devil?" he yelled in Billy's face. "I will fucking end you *and* you," he
said, pointing to Dwayne. "Come on bitches. Throw a punch. I'll spill your
blood quick-fast." He circled them like a wild animal toying with its prey
until Colin grabbed him.

"It's fine, Chucky! It's okay, man! Let it go!"

"No. Fuck that shit! These guys wanna fuck with you, then they're
gonna fuck with me," he said, pounding his chest like Tarzan. "I'm a fucking
animal! I'll eat you!"

"Thanks Chucky, but let's let this one go, please. Can we just get out
of here?"

"Are you sure that's what you want?"

Colin looked around at all the faces ranging from disappointed to
disgust. These were the kids who used to yell for him but now they were
yelling *at* him. As much as Graham deserved what he got, Colin knew he
was wrong, again. "Yeah. Yeah, that's what I want."

"Then posse up." Chucky pointed to Billy and Dwayne. "You two are
lucky. If you ever want to continue this shit, let me know." He cupped his
crotch and spit on the ground. "This is what you bitches lack."

Dwayne was obviously pissed. His nostrils flailed, and his breath was
heavy. It was clear he wasn't intimidated, but he didn't pursue it. Chucky
picked his shirt up off the deck. "C'mon, C-Dog. Let's roll. Grab the cooler."
He called out for his girlfriend, "Tabitha! Tabby!"

She pushed herself out of the crowd. "Yeah, babe?"

"Let's go. We're outta of here!" Taking hold of her hand, he led her away
from the scene.

Colin gazed at his friends. An awkward silence lingered until Colin spoke. "I'm sorry, guys. I really am," he said and walked out.

No one in the car was sober, so Tabitha took the beach route to Chucky's apartment. Colin sat silently in the back seat and peered through the window at the fog floating above the ocean. The only real friends he had left now turned their backs on him and his only companion was a local thug. He wanted to tell Tabitha to turn around and bring him home, but he was unable to muster up the words.

"Man, I should've fucked both of them up, babe," Chucky said to Tabitha. "Goddamn, I was ready to drop bombs. I'm always ready to fight, always!"

"Of course you are, honey. You're a real man. Those two are just faggots."

"Fuck them. Fuck all those pussies. And, you know what, C-Dog? Fuck that Peters kid. He ain't nothing but a stupid nigger."

"Whoa, Chucky." Colin lunged forward. "Don't ever call him that."

"C'mon, C-Dog. He's an Uncle Tom. He wasn't even that good at hockey. I've seen him play. Chocolate Thunder? Fuck that shit."

"I appreciate you having my back and all, but don't ever let me hear you say that again. You got it?"

"Yeah, whatever."

Colin thought about a conversation he had with his father when he was sixteen. One morning the two sat at the breakfast table and, out of mere curiosity, Colin asked his dad what it was like to be sober. The lighthearted Mr. Brennan became serious. He looked at his son long and hard and said, "The best high in the world for me is living sober. I got tired of always having to apologize for things I did when I was drunk. You know what, Col? I didn't get into trouble every time I drank, but every time I got into trouble I was drinking."

Chucky whistled from outside the car, breaking Colin from his trance. "Yo, C-Dog, we're here. It's time to gas some beers, motherfucker," he said, carrying the cooler in his hands.

Colin kept quiet and stepped out of the car following the couple down a rusty bulkhead into Chucky's apartment. His "apartment" was actually his grandmother's musty basement that he called home after being kicked out of his parents' house for the second and final time three years ago.

As soon as Tabitha opened the door a rancid stench traveled up Colin's nose and burrowed itself in his nasal passage. Chucky flipped a light switch revealing his room. The walls were made of cheap wood paneling, covered with posters of nude women and mildew stains. The seven-foot ceiling was a maze of exposed intertwining brass pipes that dripped every few seconds.

"Babe, do we have any ice? I wanna make myself a 'boat drink,'" Tabitha said as she opened the door to the kitchen, which also stored a washer and dryer and a mountain of dirty laundry.

"Yeah. In the freezer, genius."

Chucky and Colin continued onto the front room, which was furnished with a bed, love seat, two metal folding chairs, a beat-up coffee table, and a mini television. Colin plopped down on the old grimy loveseat that looked as if it was salvaged from the town dump. He lit a cigarette as Chucky handed him a beer from the cooler, taking a seat on a chair next to Colin.

"I stole a case of beer from those fuckers early in the night. Now, I'm *really* glad I did. Fucking assholes," Chucky said.

"Nice work."

"Crazy night, huh?"

"Yup."

"So, what do you think? Should we really party?"

"What do you mean?"

Chucky reached into his pocket and pulled out a small plastic bag of white powder and tossed it on the coffee table. "That's some jet fuel right there. Got it in New Bedford from some little Rican. I think after what we went through we deserve a pick-me-up. Sound good?"

Colin hesitated. He was buzzed, depressed and overwhelmed. Chucky had offered cocaine before, but he always had the will to turn him down. But tonight was different. He figured there were no consequences left. "Yeah. I'm game. Fuck it. Let's do this thing," he said, forcing a smile.

"Nice. I'm gonna lay some fuckin' caterpillars, boy."

"Caterpillars?"

Chucky laughed. "Fat lines. You'll see." He stood up and walked into the kitchen and yelled over the sound of a blender. "We got no clean plates, what the fuck?" He returned with a paper plate and dumped some coke on it, crushing it with his Massachusetts I.D. "Tabitha hasn't cleaned the dishes." He then hollered to her, "You better clean those dishes soon, Tabby, and make yourself useful."

She shouted back, "Fuck you. Clean them yourself. You're unemployed. You have the time."

"Calm down, baby. I'm only playing."

The blender stopped, and he lowered his voice. "She's moving in with me permanently. Told her old man she needed a year to figure out what she really wants. Not sure that college bullshit is for her."

"No shit? How do you feel about that?"

"I don't care. She can be a real bitch, but, C-Dog, it's the best ass I've ever had. She was a coke virgin, didn't even touch the shit until she met 'All Dunn,'" he said with a menacing smile. "Now, she loves it, so we're a good match. Now I get what the hype was about Studio 54. Sometimes we just get a gram or two and spend the whole night banging. I'm a goddamn porn star on this shit and so is she. She's my dream girl."

"Wow, that's awesome, Chucky."

"Yeah, it is."

"Hey, man, you got any music?"

"Of course. Here take this." He handed Colin a hollowed out pen that was cut in half. "That's the best snorting utensil. You always see people in the movies using dollar bills or straws. Fuck that. They don't know shit." Rising from the seat, he left three large lines on the plate as he switched on his clock radio. "I only get one station. Not the best reception down here."

"That's all you have? Where's your stereo?"

"It broke the other night."

"Broke?"

Tabitha walked in the room carrying a mudslide. She jumped in the conversation. "Yeah. Fucking asshole. I bail him out of jail and he comes home drunk and pissed and smashes the stereo."

"Don't worry, babe. I'll pick one up somewhere." He looked at Colin. "I had a bad night."

"Hey, it happens." Colin sighed.

"You better get another one. All we have is that fucking thing," Tabitha said, pointing to the alarm clock that was singing "Live for Today" by the Grass Roots.

"Colin, bang that line down. Let's get this party started."

"Oh. This is so exciting. Is C-Dog about to do his first line?"

"He sure is." Chucky put his arm around Tabitha and looked on like a proud father.

Colin fought through his reluctance and leaned over the coffee table with the pen in hand and dove in. After the cocaine shot up his nose, his eyes bulged. A little had trickled down into his throat, so he coughed into his fist. "Whoa!" He wiped his mouth and rapidly blinked his eyes, taking in the room. Everything was brighter. All the depression, all the gloom was suddenly replaced with a feeling of euphoria that surged through his body. The alcohol buzz disappeared and a smile emerged on his face.

"That's my boy! Man, you just took that shit down like a champ. I guess I should have laid out some Route 28s instead."

"Yeah. You're a fucking pro, C-Dog!" Tabitha shrieked, put her drink down and clapped her hands. "But pass me the pen, it's my turn."

She snorted a line. With her index finger she slid some residue off the plate and rubbed it on her teeth. "Oh, fuck yeah. I gotta have my *numbies.*"

Then Chucky stepped up to the plate. Without hesitation he blasted his line. "Oh, fuck yes. I told you that was the *fire,*" he said rubbing his nose.

Colin was feeling energized and was now ready to party. "Hey, Chucky, you got any whiskey in this place?"

"Yeah, I got a half bottle of Jim Beam in the freezer."

"Cool."

"When you're in there check out my arrest in the police log. You still haven't seen it, have you?"

"No, I don't read the paper."

"Well, it's on the fridge. It's awesome."

Colin stood up and headed towards the kitchen. He grabbed the whiskey and ice and poured himself a drink. While sipping his cocktail, he scanned the police log pinned to the fridge by a Red Dog beer magnet: DUI, minor in possession, possession of a Class D substance, destruction of private property, breaking and entering.

Nothing new here, he thought to himself. But then he saw "possession of a stolen town vehicle."

He walked back into the room. "Stolen town vehicle. That's a new one."

"Oh, you like that?" Chucky asked.

"So, let's hear it."

"Well, Tex, that asshole, fires me because I didn't show up for two days. I mean, what the fuck, C-Dog. He fires me for that?"

"Did you call him?"

"No. But he didn't have to fire me. And he could've called *me*, he usually does. So, I went there after they had closed. You see, I had a set of keys made for myself." He chuckled. "All I wanted to do was change the sign. Nothing too crazy. But there was one of the school's retard vans in the parking lot, and I figured why not take it for a joyride and go see Stevie Garrison. I knew he would piss his pants if he saw me roll up in that shit and he did. So we started partying. He had some beers and a bottle of Jägermeister and of course, we took some hits off the six-footer. I mean I was fucked up, son. So driving back to the shop was no easy chore. I was almost there. I was *so* close and then I fuckin' hit something. I thought it was a fuckin' dog or some shit, so I stopped." He started laughing hysterically. "But it wasn't a dog, it was some fuckin' statue. You know, like one of those little elf fucking things. With the white beard?"

"You mean a gnome?"

"I guess so, man."

"What the hell was a gnome doing in the middle of the street?"

"Well, that's the fucked-up thing. I was in some dude's backyard. So I grab this fuckin' little guy and buckle him into the passenger seat 'cause I had to get out of there."

"Whoa, whoa, whoa. What? You buckled him up. Why would you buckle up a gnome?"

"Man, at the time I was so fucked-up, I wasn't sure if the little guy was real or not."

They burst into uncontrollable laughter as Tabitha said, "Yeah, it might be funny now, but you may be looking at some jail time."

Wiping tears from his eyes Colin asked, "Yeah, how did you get caught anyway?"

"Well, that's the thing. I was planning on leaving. But I passed out behind the wheel and woke up to some old bastard in a blue bathrobe threatening me with a garden hoe and two seconds later, the fucking cops show up. Then I was cuffed and stuffed, end of story."

"I hate to say it, but Tabby's right. You might do some time."

"Yeah. Maybe ninety days, I'm not too worried. I'm more upset that I got my second DUI. Who knows when I'll get my fucking license back."

Colin suddenly had a flash of his first meeting with Eric Chance in the coffee shop and then his conversation about how Eric's father was killed by a drunk driver and now it wasn't so funny and he stopped laughing.

"Wow, Chucky. That's one of the craziest stories I've ever heard. You're lucky you didn't kill anyone."

"I know, dude. I love it. I'm a fucking celebrity. Everybody's talking about it. It definitely overshadowed your brother's article."

"My brother's article? What are you talking about? Dermot got arrested?"

"No, dude. He had some gay little thing in the paper the same day."

"What? What was it about?"

"I don't know. I didn't waste my time reading it."

Tabitha butted in. "I read it. It was a nice piece, Colin. It was about the baseball strike. He mentioned you in it, too. He's an excellent writer. I met him earlier this summer at a party. He's a really nice guy."

"Do you still have the paper?" Colin asked.

"I threw the rest of it out. It might still be in the trash," Chucky said as he cut up more lines.

Colin hustled back into the kitchen and yelled out, "Dude, there's three trash bags in here. Which one?"

"It's not gonna be in one of the bags. Those are old. Look under the sink, in the barrel. You're gonna actually pick through the garbage?"

Colin dragged the barrel on the floor. He reached in, pushing empty Chinese food cartons and beer cans aside until he saw sections of the *Cape Cod Times*. He pulled it out. The paper was out of sequence. As he thumbed through it, wiping crumbs away, he found the sports page and, right there on the front, he saw the headline: "Sadly, the boys of summer have all gone home," by Dermot Brennan.

Wow. Derm made the front page of the Sports section. That's awesome.
He proceeded to read the article:

In a week or so, the loud school bus engine will replace the singing ice cream man's bell. The baseball glove that has finally been broken in will be tossed into the cellar, and replaced with a football. Autumn is coming, which is always a sad time for baseball lovers because they have to face the fact: summer is over.

Earlier this summer, as I walked to Stirling Beach, I saw two little boys playing Wiffle ball. Memories from when I was that age flashed through my mind when a watch wasn't needed to tell the time—only a mother's call.

My little brother Colin and I would play our Wiffle ball games as if we were cast for *The Natural*, while his friends, Matt and Paul, watched on cheering him to beat his big brother. I would step solemnly up to the plate, which we designated with our sneakers (dress shoes on Sunday mornings).

In the background we had our own play-by-play team. Paul would burst into his Sherm Feller impersonation, "Now batting for the Red Sox. The leftfielder, number twenty-four, Dermot Brennan. Brenn . . . an."

Then, it was Matt's turn to add the color commentary. "This kid had just finished feeding chickens on his father's farm in the Berkshires when he got the call to the 'Bigs,' and with only a pair of pants and three dollars in his pocket he headed to Fenway and he's about to make his major league debut."

The goal of every neighborhood kid was to hit the Crescent Road sign on the fly in the deepest part of our field. Colin and I would play for hours and sometimes I'd let him win to the enjoyment and praise from his friends.

"I can't believe you beat your big brother!" They'd tussle his hair, hug him, then, of course, pepper him with noogies, the ultimate sign of adolescent friendship.

When we got home two glasses of lemonade were never enough, and the real fun came when Colin would recount his win to Mom and Dad.

You see, deep down, I knew I would never make it to "The Show," but

I could always fall asleep to the dream. I wasn't in love with *who* won as much as *how* it was won. I loved the beauty of the game, the players who were truly characters, and the mystique of the ballparks.

I remember Dad taking Colin and me out of school early one June day. At first I was upset because I had my paper route money tucked away and was planning to buy a fishing rod from a classmate at the end of the day. But Dad promised us both, "You'll never forget this night as long as you live."

As our station wagon made its way onto the highway, I had no idea where we were going. All I knew is it was far. After a man with an orange flag directed Dad where to park, Dad turned to me and said, "Hold onto your brother's hand and don't let go." I gripped Colin's little hand and we followed Dad as he walked up to a brick building that read *Fenway Park*.

"Oh, my God! Oh, my God!" Colin and I hopped around yelling with excitement while Dad laughed and handed us our tickets. We walked up the ramp and the first thing I noticed was the white bases. I had never seen anything so pure. For the first two innings my brother and I were mesmerized by the atmosphere—the lush green grass, the Green Monster sent by the baseball gods to say, "You have to earn it, son!" We loved it all: cracking nuts, crunching popcorn, the white-haired ushers brushing the chairs, vendors with their carnival chants. "Hot dogs *here!*" The "ooh" and "ahs," the "yeas" and "boos," and the sight of cigar smoke slowly rising into the June lights out to Kenmore Square.

I took out my wad of money and volunteered to buy all the snacks, but I remember somehow several green bills magically appeared in my piggy bank the following day.

I don't know if the Sox won that night, but I do know it was one of the best games I ever attended. It was a night I will never forget—a night that every child should experience.

But it was a different time—a time when contracts took a backseat to fulfilling a dream; when a player's uniform wasn't clean the entire game. There was Dwight Evans's shoestring catches and golden arm. Fred Lynn sacrificing his body to stab one in deep center, and clutch hitting from Carlton Fisk, who chewed, spit, and stretched as he lumbered to the plate just before unleashing one into the netted night.

This was a time when players didn't run to the media lights when they were in a fight. They settled it in the locker room with their own version of noogies and made up by patting one another on the back while the manager gave the reporters a "boys will be boys" chuckle while answering questions.

The players didn't wear jewelry; they wore grease under their eyes. They weren't walking billboards, and they didn't charge twenty bucks to sign a little fan's glove.

The other day I made that same walk to Stirling Beach and this time saw two boys resting their bikes on our homerun fence. I studied them for a minute. One pulled out some baseball cards he had just bought. I noticed he was chewing the hard, chalk-covered gum, and remembered how I once lost a tooth that way. The other kid peered over his shoulder as he thumbed through his cards.

"Oh, boy, you got Roger Clemens'," he said to the gum chewer. I figured he must be a fan and smiled, remembering my jealousy when Colin would get a Hobson or a Tiant.

"Yeah, what's the big deal?" asked the card owner.

"I read this card's gonna be worth some big money in a few years," replied the future businessman.

"Yeah, well I wish I had the bucks he has now! I hear he has a mansion with three swimming pools!" the other added.

I walked away from the two businessmen and looked at the Crescent Road sign. I was thankful Colin and I never did hit it on the fly. I strained, hoping to hear the voices of Matt and Paul doing their play-by-play, but all I heard was the two little businessmen still talking about Roger Clemens' real estate. Then a sharp chill went up my spine. I realized it was the season for sweaters, hot chocolate, and football because "the boys of summer" had all gone away, and nobody knows if they'll ever come back.

Dermot Brennan is a recent graduate of Northeastern University and lives in Silver Shores.

After Colin finished reading, he put the paper down and let his eyes wander around the room. *What am I doing here? What am I doing?*

Chucky hollered, "You done reading?"

"Um. Yeah."

"So, you ready for another line, bro?"

"Yeah. Just give me a second." Colin walked back from the kitchen. "I left my weed in Tabby's car. I'm gonna go grab it. I'll be right back."

"Sounds good. We can pack a bowl and sprinkle some coke on it. Get real fucked up, dog."

"Um . . . yeah . . . okay." Colin marched up the bulkhead steps. When he was outside, he inhaled the clean air. From a distance the foghorn bellowed, calling him home. He started to walk but soon picked up his pace and ran the two miles without stopping. It was well after midnight when he arrived at his house, and he was sobering up. He walked inside and stopped in the kitchen, grabbed a trash bag, and headed upstairs to his room. He opened his bedroom door, and hit the light switch. Out of habit he turned on his stereo and pressed the shuffle button. "Blackhole" by Beck quietly played.

He lifted open the wooden chest and plucked out all of his marijuana paraphernalia and tossed it into the garbage bag. Then he rummaged through his things, opening chapters of his life he thought he had closed for good. He flipped through old photo albums, birthday cards, and old copies of *Fangoria* magazine. He studied the 1966 Roberto Clemente baseball card Dermot had bought him for his twelfth birthday, which was still in mint condition. It brought a smile to his face. Near the bottom, beyond dozens of baseball hats, neatly wrapped in plastic covering, was the program from his first game at Fenway. As he leafed through it, he stumbled upon the scorecard from that evening—Kansas City 6, Red Sox 2. Dermot's article had brought him back to one of his fondest childhood memories. Derm had reminded him how fortunate he was to have such a great family. How did he stray so far from that little boy who idolized his big brother?

And, then the answer hit when he saw the sea blue hat with its white lettering that read ATLANTIS staring up at him. He took the hat out and traced the lettering with his finger. He flipped it over and read the inscription under the brim: "Matt Sweeney Swain's Boatyard." He walked over to the window and looked out at the lighthouse and thought about that morning.

He had awakened with a sudden start. There was a fluttering sound in the distance. *What is that?* he wondered. He looked over at the clock, which read 5:47 a.m. He jumped out of bed and walked to the window. Several boats dotted Vineyard Sound, and in the middle a Coast Guard helicopter hovered. Its quivering blades churned the water into boiling foam.

The next sound he heard was a knock on the door. He turned around and saw his parents, whose expressions told him all he needed to know. His father started to speak, but all Colin heard were bits of what he said. "They took *Plato's Paradise* out last night . . . The storm was bad . . . The boys are missing."

TWENTY

Dermot buttoned up his white Oxford and ran past the wall calendar marked with the notation he had written months before, to remind him that the one-year anniversary memorial mass for Matt Sweeney and Paul Hurley was scheduled for 6:00 p.m. at St. Peter's Chapel. He briefly analyzed the fact that he had written the boys' last names on the calendar as if they were strangers to him.

How detached have I been? Throughout the past couple of days, that disconnected state had ceased, and it had felt cathartic to finally face the pain of losing two kids who were, in essence, his little brothers. Once he finally grieved, he decided, whether Colin listened or not, he had to talk to him, but when he went looking, Colin was nowhere to be found. He prayed his brother would show up for the service. "Oh, man!" he groaned, seeing the numbers on his clock radio click 5:59 p.m. He rushed to the bathroom, and grabbed from the doorknob the navy blue pre-knotted tie his dad had left for him, tightened it around his neck, and checked his teeth in the mirror.

"Good enough," he said while wetting down his hair.

He hurried back to his closet, slipped on his blue blazer and asked himself, "What am I forgetting? Oh, keys!" He scanned The Shanty and found the keys resting on the quarters table, snagged them, but stopped at the sound of chiming church bells in the distance. "Oh, man," he said again, this time more quietly, realizing the moment ahead, and also knowing he was definitely going to be late.

Suddenly, a flash of anger surged through him. This was not what he had planned. It was a humid day and he intended to leave work early so he could take a shower to cool off. After that, he hoped to walk with his parents and maybe even Colin to the chapel, but his plans changed when a customer's car broke down right in front of the Shack just as the afternoon boat unloaded, causing a massive back-up. He wondered if *his* car would also break down when he turned the key and the engine coughed a few times before sputtering to silence. He wasn't surprised. The last couple of days the Pontiac had been working overtime for him. He pumped the gas pedal and tried it two more times. Nothing. He was flooding it, so he stopped and tried to regain his composure by taking a deep breath for a minute.

"Okay, Matt and Paul, I need your help, guys." He turned the key again. The Pontiac roared to life. "How do you like that?" He smiled, backed out, and headed around the corner for the chapel.

When he pulled up, there was a line of cars parked in front, so he turned down the side street and rolled onto the road in the back of the church, which ran parallel to the harbor and parked. He jumped out, briefly glancing at the bench Melissa donated to the town in Paul's memory, which overlooked a half dozen moored sailboats. It was adorned with both fresh and dead flowers, as well as two weathered teddy bears beside it keeping guard.

His attention shifted when he heard Father McDaniel's voice filtering through an open stained-glass window, so he sprinted to the front of the chapel and opened the sea blue painted door. He thought he could sneak in, but the door's creak caused everyone to snap their heads his way. The eyes he first met were Mel's. She was sitting up front with the Hurleys, but leaned into the aisle and craned her neck back. She was wearing a white sundress that made the purple ribbon in her hair stand out. In that quick second before she turned her attention back to Father McDaniel, Dermot read her expression. She looked excited, but then when she saw him, her expression changed to disappointment. After scanning the pews, he understood why: Mel had been expecting Colin to bust through those doors.

His eyes then met his father's; he was also up front. Then Dermot scanned the back corner where his mother was standing with the choir, and both his parents' expressions confirmed Colin was a no-show. Dermot ducked into the first available pew while Father McDaniel finally resumed addressing the congregation.

"As I was saying, tonight's mass is in memory of our young friends, Matt and Paul. I was fortunate to know both boys because, let's face it, you couldn't know one without knowing the other." Father McDaniel's tall, seventy-plus frame leaned over the lectern and he smiled at the audience. It was a cue for light laughter, which he received.

"Yup, they were all . . . I mean, those two were like brothers." He patted his thumbs against the wood and it was obvious to everyone he was lost in thought.

"Um," he cleared his throat, "someone once asked me, 'What is the hardest part about being a priest?' And, really folks, it's moments like this one. A year has passed, and I look out at the faces tonight, especially the young ones looking up at me, and I know they are still asking, 'Why? Why did this happen to two great kids?' And, here we are a year later, and I still can't give those faces the answer they need, and, to me, that is truly the toughest part of being a priest. But if you will listen, I will give you the answer. Simply put, God has a plan. I know. I know. I know. In your heads right now, some of you are probably groaning and using some of those words you admit to in confession, and I don't blame you. I have done the same thing myself over the years, but every time I do I try to think as tragic an event as this was, still something good has to come from it. And if we can't find it, we have to *make* it good. Tonight I think that good is the lesson we are all taught, for each and every one of you to live every day with that joyful spirit that Matt and Paul possessed and be the person you were meant to be in life. You see, in their short time here in Silver Shores that's what they taught all of us, even an old curmudgeon priest like me. They taught us to live life. So please all of you, live life. Thanks be to God. In the name of the Father, the Son, and the Holy Ghost." Father McDaniel blessed himself as everyone followed his lead and then replied, "Amen."

"Now, I would like to ask Bob Hurley, Paul's dad, to come up here. He'd like to say a few words. Bob." Father McDaniel waved him up.

Dermot hadn't visited Mr. or Mrs. Hurley since he got back from Ireland. The guilt hit him when he saw Mr. Hurley's appearance as he adjusted the microphone. Mr. Hurley, in his late forties, was once lean and scholarly-looking, but now he was merely thin and his hair, once black with specks of gray, was now completely gray.

"Good evening, ladies and gentlemen," he said awkwardly into the microphone, to which everyone replied by mouthing, "Good evening."

"First of all, I would like to thank Father McDaniel for his kind words and also for allowing us the church for an evening mass in the summer. I know summer evening weddings are big business." Mr. Hurley laughed, and Father McDaniel chuckled loudly, which elicited laughter from everyone, even Dermot.

"But seriously." Mr. Hurley waited as everyone quieted. "Morgan and Erin Sweeney and Lindsey and I wanted to have a memorial mass during the early evening because this was always the boys' favorite time of day. It usually meant the beginning of high tide down at Stirling Beach, so with fishing poles in hand they, along with Mel and Colin, would head down to begin a night of fishing. So it is my hope that we can all begin a night of remembrance. You see . . ." He paused and his voice cracked. "Last year I didn't have the strength to stand up here and remember my boy . . . *Our boys* . . . Tonight the Sweeneys asked me to speak for both families, and I am honored to do that because as Father McDaniel said, 'You couldn't know one without knowing the other,' and there is no statement truer than that one. I always thought of them as both being only children whose passion for fishing brought them together, but I also think what Father McDaniel said is true. There *was* a bigger reason. There *is* a bigger reason. They were meant to spend their last moments on earth together that night. I used to be haunted by that thought, but I now try to use that as comfort . . . I would like to admit something to all of you. Last year I couldn't talk at the funeral because I was angry at God. I hated him. And I hated myself. You see, we moved from Minnesota to Silver Shores so I could take a job as head of the Philosophy department at Cape Cod Community College. I remember the day I told Paul. He was not happy at all because he was a Vikings fan and he said there was no way he'd ever root for the 'lousy Patriots,' as he called them." Mr. Hurley paused to allow for more light laughter.

Dermot looked to the left and his eyes met those of Clay's and Tommy's. The young men nodded at each other, and then Dermot's gaze moved down a few pews in front of them, and he saw Dwayne. He hadn't seen Dwayne since his drunken night and realized that must be the reason the nod he threw Dwayne's way was only returned with a cold stare.

He saved my ass that night. I'll have to talk to him and clear things up.

"Paul actually refused to get in the car that day," Mr. Hurley picked up, "but then he asked if there was ice fishing on Cape Cod. That's when I told him not only could we go ice fishing in the ponds in winter, but we could fish in the ocean all summer long. After I said that, it didn't take him long to hop in the car. I remember throughout the whole drive from Minnesota, I made up stories about the ocean off Cape Cod and, being a philosophy professor, I told him about a place called Plato's Paradise. Most of you have probably heard Paul over the years talk about Plato's Paradise, but for those who never heard his stories, Plato's Paradise is what Plato called the Lost City of Atlantis. Ever since that car ride, the boys would make up stories about that lost city and now I've come to why for so long I have blamed myself . . ." His voice cracked again and everyone waited for him to continue.

"Not only did I give him that sense of adventure with my stories of the sea, but I also gave him his boat *Plato's Paradise*. For a long time after the accident, I thought maybe if I didn't feed that adventurous soul and maybe if I didn't give him that boat he loved so much that he and Matt might still be here. But what I've finally come to realize, and what Father McDaniel reminded us all tonight, is if I hadn't done that the boys wouldn't have fully lived the way they loved to live. I look out at all of you tonight and realize I am a fortunate man to have had Paul as my son and for him to have Matt as his brother, because that's what they were to me and to all of us. I'll miss my boy, but I can go to sleep at night knowing that somewhere out in that sea he is with his brother Matt, two boys of the sea searching for that lost city of Atlantis. And if I know those two, they've already found it. They're just waiting for us to come join them. Someday we will, boys. We will. Thank you." Mr. Hurley let his shaking jaw surrender the battle. His cries reverberated off the stained-glass windows and moved on from pew to pew. Father McDaniel gently put his hand on Mr. Hurley's shoulder. Nodding to the priest as he left the altar, the grieving man buried himself in the arms of his sobbing wife.

As Dermot's tears fell, he wished his brother had been with him not only to hear the message, but also so he could hug him and tell him how much he loved and missed him. He knew he had failed Colin and that knowledge was almost as painful as what he had just witnessed.

The organist took the slight nod from Father McDaniel as a cue to begin playing. Dermot focused on the choir, particularly his mother, who with tears in her eyes, sang "A Gaelic Prayer":

Deep peace of the running wave to you,
Deep peace of the flowing air to you,
Deep peace of the quiet earth to you,
Deep peace of the shining stars to you,
Deep peace of the gentle night to you,
Moon and stars pour their healing light to you,
Deep peace of Christ the light of the world to you.

He bowed his head and wept. When the song ended, he felt a presence standing beside him, and he looked up to see his father. Mr. Brennan had walked from the front of the church to the back to be with his older son.

Mr. Brennan leaned over and whispered between his own sobs, "I miss your brother. I miss Colin so much."

Dermot reached over and hugged him tightly. "I know, Dad. Me, too."

When the service ended, Mr. Brennan returned to the front to talk to the Hurleys and Sweeneys, but Dermot stayed in his pew, silently praying to God until a hint of purple outside one of the open windows caught his eye. Melissa was holding her ribbon and it was rippling in the wind. In true Mel fashion, she had let her hair down the moment she left the church. He exited through the side door and followed Mel as she crossed the street and sat on the bench staring out at the harbor. He didn't want to sneak up on her and was about to say something when he heard her voice crack. At first he assumed she was crying, but the sound that came from her reminded him of the times when Mel and the boys used to ambush Dermot with snowballs.

"Excuse me, Mel," he said and she turned her head as he continued, "I didn't mean to . . . Are you laughing?"

She nodded her head and patted the bench for him to sit beside her. He did and listened to her laugh for a minute before he continued.

"What's so funny? I mean, you are laughing, right?"

"Oh, I'm laughing all right." She caught her breath. "I'm all out of tears and can't do anything *but* laugh . . . Look at those teddy bears, Dermot." She pointed at the two filthy bears he had noticed earlier.

"Pretty sad looking, don't you think?" she said.

"Yeah. They could use a bath."

"The reason I was laughing is because I was remembering when I dedicated it last fall to Paul and the head cheerleader, Dakota Gamble, showed up with them to put beside the bench. Of course, the bears were white then and she was bawling her eyes out."

"So, what's so funny about that?"

"Two reasons. One, what the hell is the significance of teddy bears at Paul's memorial site? Action figures, sure. God, how you guys loved your action figures. But teddy bears? C'mon. Paul hated stuffed animals. The second reason is that Dakota knew Paul since the day he moved here and God she probably knew Matt since the sandbox days. But she was always too good to talk to either one of them. Yet, she had the balls to show up here, wearing mascara that instantly ran down her face, I might add, holding those two goddamn bears. She kept telling anyone who would listen to her how much she was going to miss Paul and Matt. Pathetic. I'm telling you, Dermot, the girl has balls and on that day that's exactly where I wanted to kick her."

They both laughed for a minute.

"And then she had the nerve to ask me in front of a few people why I only had the bench inscribed to Paul and not Matt."

"That is a little 'uncouth' as they say. I always figured it was just because Paul was your boyfriend."

"Yes, that's the main reason, but there's a little more to it than that. I mean, I loved Matt like a brother. But, when I was thinking of donating this bench, I thought about the fact that they never found the boys' bodies. But, at least for the Sweeneys' sake, they found Matt's ATLANTIS hat, you know, the one Paul gave him for his sixteenth birthday? He wore that thing day and night."

"Yup," Dermot said, remembering. The day of the accident, even though he knew it was futile, he drove Colin around town searching for the boys. "They haven't found *Plato's Paradise* yet. Maybe they beached it and are just sleeping," Colin said over and over again, and Dermot knew the only thing he could do for his brother was drive until Colin told him to stop. That command finally came in a whisper. "Just go home."

But on their way home, they spotted a Coast Guard boat docking, so they parked and hurried toward it, desperately hoping for good news. A young Coastie appeared and walked down the gangway holding the soaking wet ATLANTIS hat. That's when they knew. Dermot's eyes filled at the sight, but Colin's face was expressionless.

He whispered again, "They're dead. Let's go home."

"Dermot? Dermot?" Mel said, and he broke from his thought.

"Oh, I'm sorry. What were you saying?"

"Don't worry about it," she began. "I know the feeling. My mind is haunted by memories all the time. At first I fought them, but now I realize the memories are the gifts and no one can ever take those from me . . . Anyway, I was saying the Sweeneys had the hat, so I wanted to give the Hurleys something that they could have to remember Paul, so I picked this place for the bench. I figured I'd put it here since they are churchgoers and can listen to the bells, but if you look over there . . ." She pointed to the red building in the distance whose white sign read SWAIN'S BOATYARD.

How many times did I visit Paul and Matt while they worked at Swain's gassing up the boats? So many laughs . . . "Yup, this is the perfect spot."

"Well, I was considering another spot, but because of what happened there I didn't think it would be right."

"Huh?"

"The Fighting Chair. I was going to have a bench placed overlooking

Stirling Beach, but thought better of it." Mel looked away.

"I'm confused. What happened at Stirling Beach?" Dermot asked.

She turned back to him and this time she had tears in her eyes.

"Colin, didn't tell you did he?"

"Tell me what?"

"Why would he? We never talked about it ourselves. The only time Colin did talk about it was the night he was drunk at my art show. I mean, I never even told your mom, and we wrote several letters back and forth. Now that I think about it, it was so unfair of me to not tell her everything since she was trying to help me deal with it. I mean, how could she help when she didn't have all the information?"

"Mel." Dermot tried to restrain himself. "I'm sorry but whatever you're trying to tell me you're talking around it. What are you trying to tell me?"

"I'm trying to tell you, Dermot, that Colin and I were supposed to be on the boat that night."

"What?" He squinted. "What are you talking about?"

"That night Matt and Paul wanted us all to go fishing. The problem was Colin and I both had other plans, so we told them we'd meet them at The Fighting Chair at eleven. It was going to be fun. They were going to pick us up and we'd drop anchor by the lighthouse for a couple of hours. You know, just hang out, cast a few, and laugh and stuff. I remember getting there after Colin, and when I sat on The Fighting Chair beside him I instantly had this terrible feeling in my gut. I couldn't explain it but I told him, 'They're late. I think something is wrong.' He said he also had a bad feeling. But we waited for a little while longer and then it began to rain and pretty soon it was a full-blown storm. I should've listened to my instincts, but at that point, we both second-guessed ourselves and came to the conclusion that Paul and Matt heard about the storm coming and probably just turned around. And since they always worked that early morning shift at Swain's, we figured they were sound asleep in their beds. At the time, it made so much sense to us. It really did. Why did we think it made sense? It's a question I ask myself every night right before I fall asleep."

"Oh, my God," Dermot closed his eyes. "So all this time you both have kept this from everyone."

"Yes. As I said, Colin and I didn't even talk about it, so how could we tell anyone else? The first person I told was my boyfriend, Tad, a few nights ago when I was breaking up with him. He's a really nice guy and he was trying to help me through everything, but the truth is I wasn't ready to love again so soon. I had to face this tragedy head-on. After today's service, I realized part of facing it is to talk about it. My hope today was Colin would show and we'd sit right here on this bench and talk about that night. Then we'd tell our family and friends, cry in their arms, and we could finally move on. But he didn't show."

"No, he didn't."

"But you did, Dermot."

"Yes."

"I can't help but think of what your mom always says about signs. It's a sign for you to sit here because I know you're the one who has to find Colin and make him face it and realize it wasn't his fault. There was nothing he could do . . . nothing *we* could do. Ever since he could talk he's worshipped the ground you walk on. He'll listen to you. I know he will. You're his big brother." Mel wiped her tears away, smiled slightly, and leaned over and gave Dermot a light kiss on the cheek. He hugged her tightly and she whispered in his ear, "And remember something, you're not just Colin's big brother. You're mine, too." She wiped her eyes one more time, rose from the bench, and walked back across the street to the groups of family and friends huddled in conversation in front of the church.

Dermot stared out at a flock of ducks gliding along with a Beetle Cat sailboat that an elderly man was guiding toward the mouth of the harbor headed for the open sea. *Does that man know how lucky he is to have lived so long?* With his free hand, the man gave Dermot a friendly wave. He realized the question really should be, *Do I know how lucky I am to be alive today? And does Colin?*

He got up from the bench, went over to his car, got in, and looked at the mix tapes lying on the passenger seat beside him. He thought about that morning after Francesca trampled his spirit. He woke up thinking it was time to throw out all of his mix tapes. Then he realized he couldn't let her dictate what kind of man he should be. He was a romantic and he *did* want happy endings in life, so he had made a mix tape for Eric's date, and it turned out to be one of the best nights of Eric's life.

He eyed the other tape he had made that morning: *The C-Dog Mix*. It was a tape with all types of songs that he hoped would remind Colin of Matt and Paul and even him. He picked it up and popped it in as he tried to start the car. The engine turned over and then died.

"I know I have to let you go." He patted the dash. "But, please, just start for me one more time." He turned the key, and this time the engine barely came alive. "Thank you, God." He looked at St. Peter's Chapel and blessed himself as he pulled away.

Dermot knew he should just drive the car home, but he also knew if his brother wasn't off partying with Chucky trying to forget everything there was one place he could be. He guided the car to the hilly road that lead to Stirling Beach. He fast-forwarded *The C-Dog Mix* past Donovan's "Sunshine Superman" and bands like the Beastie Boys, U2, and The Police until he came to a song called "Feel Us Shaking" by the college band The Samples. The mood of the song offered him hope and the lyrics represented his youth, growing up with his brother, the boys, and Mel on Stirling Beach:

Gentle thoughts meander through the sand
as the ship made currents reach the land
the omniscient sun paving through the sky
and when it's done all the seabirds fly

The car had almost reached the top of the hill, but then the engine began to stall.

Dermot tried to ignore the sound. With tears in his eyes, he sang softly with Sean Kelly, the lead singer, "I'd like to stay but I couldn't stay with you. I have to go, but I have a lot I want to do. Pleasure be waiting by the sea with a smile for all the world to see." The car made it to the peak of the hill, but then the engine died completely and so did Sean Kelly's voice. In that brief second, Dermot had the ridiculous thought his car would roll backwards, but then, like those many days riding around on his ten-speed, the Pontiac rocketed forward down the hill. He steered to the side of the road to an empty spot that overlooked Stirling Beach.

The music of The Samples may have been silenced, but it was still playing in his head and got louder when he looked across the beach and saw his brother, dressed in a blazer and tie, sitting on The Fighting Chair staring out at the sea.

The red sun colored the early evening sky, and the dark blue ocean sparkled as Colin, loosening his tie and unbuttoning his top button, sat on The Fighting Chair. He looked around the beach, which was almost empty except for an older man hovering his metal detector above the sand in search of lost treasure. Beyond him was a typical urban family from the city trying to squeeze in every ounce of beach time before they had to head over the bridge and off Cape. He pulled Matt's ATLANTIS hat from his back pocket and pushed his hair back before positioning it over his golden locks. It was a perfect fit.

A few days earlier he got a call from Mr. Sweeney and Colin promised he would say a few words in Matt and Paul's memory. He had every intention of honoring that promise. So when 5:30 rolled around, he started out for the chapel, but when from afar he saw the crowd pouring in, panic gripped him. He took a deep breath, which snapped him from his paralysis and then he detoured to Stirling Beach. Now, alone on the jetty he pulled the healing rune out of his pocket and stared at the engraving for the thousandth time. The marking, which looked like a bent letter *F*, almost resembled an arrow. Even when he wasn't looking at the etching, it, along with its meaning, crept into his head. He quickly shoved the stone back into his pocket.

As he watched two seagulls dance through the sky, he thought about the last time he saw Mr. Sweeney. It was last November and he had just started working full time at the Shoe Fort.

One cold, quiet morning, while stocking snow boots, Larry interrupted him.

"There's someone here to see you. He's out front."

Colin made his way to the floor and saw Mr. Sweeney standing near the exit sign holding a small plastic bag.

"Hi, Mr. Sweeney."

Mr. Sweeney turned around. "Oh. Hi, Colin. Listen, I hope I'm not getting you in any trouble."

"No, not at all. It's fine. What's up?"

Mr. Sweeney sighed. "Well. I just wanted to stop in and say good-bye."

"Good-bye?"

"Yeah. We finally passed papers. So it's official. The old house is sold. I'm on my way up to New Hampshire now to our new place."

"Oh. Okay." Colin looked over him. "Where's Mrs. Sweeney?"

"She left two days ago. She wanted to say good-bye, Colin, but she couldn't . . ." He paused "Every time she looks at you, well . . ." Mr. Sweeney caught himself and handed over a piece of paper. "This is my phone number. If you ever need anything, anything at all, please don't hesitate to call me."

Colin looked it over. "I won't. Thanks."

"There's one more thing," he said tapping the plastic bag against his leg.

"What?"

"Rebecca and I want you to have this." He handed the bag over. Colin opened it and his heart skipped several beats which was followed by a wave of nausea. He stepped back and thought he was going to faint. The last time he had seen Matt's ATLANTIS hat was the day he found out his best friends were dead. He quickly tried to hand it back.

"I can't. Thank you, but I just can't."

"You have to . . . For us. Please . . . Wear it for Matt."

Colin kept his eyes on the floor. "Okay."

Mr. Sweeney wrapped his arms around him and hugged him tightly. With a broken voice and his eyes welling up, he whispered in Colin's ear, "Continue to chase your dreams, C-Dog." He released his hug, turned around, and walked out of the Shoe Fort.

That was eight months ago, and Colin had completely lost track of his dreams. He wasn't running towards anything, just running *away* from everything. Scanning the sea, he spotted a long piece of driftwood inch closer to the shore. He stood up, took off his blue blazer and draped it over The Fighting Chair before slipping off his penny loafers. The driftwood moved closer to the shore, so he cuffed up his khakis and jumped off the jetty onto the sand. He waited for the waves to bring the wood to shore, but every time it came closer, it would then float out of his grasp. He wanted that wood. He needed it.

He walked into the incoming surf, and the cold water shocked his system, but he continued on even as the water rose over his cuffed pants. He reached out and grabbed the wood and thought of when he was a kid and he would've pretended it was a pirate's wooden leg. He walked to a smooth area of sand that the breaking waves couldn't quite reach. Like a woodcarver, he began working the sand for a couple of minutes until he heard a voice.

"Nothing like a farm."

Colin looked up and saw Dermot.

"Nothing like fixing things." Colin managed a smile and continued. "Roy Hobbs says that to Pop in *The Natural*. That's one of Dad's all-time favorite movie lines."

"Yup, he would be proud that you knew that one . . . We missed you at the mass," Dermot said.

"Yeah, I know." Colin dropped the driftwood and began walking back towards The Fighting Chair to get his shoes.

Dermot followed him onto the jetty, and just as Colin was reaching down to grab his penny loafers he said, "I talked to Mel. She told me everything."

"What?" Colin turned around.

"About that night. She told me you were supposed to be on the boat. Why didn't you tell me?"

"I don't know, Derm. I just couldn't."

"What do you mean you couldn't? I'm your brother. You know I would've been there for you."

"*Would* you?" Colin's voice was edgy, ragged.

"Of course, man. You know that. I know what you're thinking, but you can't beat yourself up. You probably think, 'Why am I alive and not them?' You have to stop being angry and forgive yourself."

"You see, that's the reason I couldn't come to you."

"What do you mean?"

"It wasn't just me I was angry at."

"I don't understand. Who else? Not Melissa?"

"You just don't get it, do you, man?"

"Get what? What are you talking about?"

"You! I was angry with you, Derm."

"Me? What the hell did *I* do?"

Colin looked away. "That night I was supposed to meet them, I was late. I just knew they had been here. But I was late. I just missed them. Probably seconds. I should've figured out they were in trouble and called someone. I was so stupid and I missed them. And, you know *why* I missed them?" Colin's voice rang out.

Dermot just shook his head.

"That was the night you introduced Francesca to Mom and Dad."

"Oh."

"If I didn't stick around doing those fucking stupid impressions, Matt and Paul would be here today."

"You don't know that. If you didn't do those fucking stupid impressions maybe *you* wouldn't be here today, either."

"Are you fucking kidding me? Do you know what kind of swimmer I am? I'm the best lifeguard this town has ever seen. Why the fuck do you think they called me 'Aquaman' when I was little? Why the fuck did I become the C-Dog to everyone? I can't do a lot of things, Derm, but I can swim. And if I was with them that night, I would've told them to stay with the boat, and I would've swum my ass straight for that fucking lighthouse." His finger stabbed the horizon.

"And I would've reached it . . ." He stopped, his voice cracking. "And a few minutes later, they would've been on a Coast Guard cutter wrapped in blankets cracking jokes. But no, I was trying to help you get laid!"

Dermot lunged over and grabbed Colin's shirt, but then looked down at his white knuckles and released his grip. "I'm sorry. I shouldn't have grabbed you. I knew you've been pissed at me ever since that night I saw you here last winter."

Now it was Colin's turn to ask questions. "What do you mean?"

"I knew you didn't remember. Right before my trip I was walking by the beach in the middle of the night and I heard someone shouting. I came over here and it was you screaming incoherently at the sea. When you saw me you got even worse and punched me in the eye."

"I did? I don't remember."

"I know you don't remember because the next day you asked me how I got the black eye. I told you, Mom, and Dad it was from wrestling with Clay. I figured I was leaving and why get into a family drama. I hoped all the drama would be over by the time I got back. And that's why I'm sorry for running away when you needed me the most. But, Colin, I'm not sorry for what-ifs because that's not real life and that's what *you* have to realize."

Colin looked straight ahead for a long time before answering. "You're right, Derm. It's taking me a whole year to realize that you can't live life with the what-ifs, but I'll tell you I've gone through a lot of shit to come to that conclusion. You see, Matt and Paul are everywhere. They're here." He tapped his forehead. "And they're right here." He tapped his heart, but harder, and then began to cry. Dermot reached out and took his brother in his arms and held him.

"Derm, it hurts so much. It hurts so fucking much. And I don't want to hurt anymore."

"I know, buddy. I know. I know you don't. But you know Matt and Paul are at peace with the sea."

"It's good to finally cry," Colin said after a few gasps and let go of the hug. "And let it all out. Because I have no idea who I am anymore or what I've become. The only thing I ever think about is getting completely fucked up to numb the pain. It first started off with having a couple of drinks in memory of the guys and then it became drinks to *forget* the guys. But as I told you, they're always with me. Man, I've done some things that I never in a million years thought I was capable of doing. And I'm scared. I don't want to be that person anymore. I want to be like that kid who used to love the beach. Growing up, the summer was my favorite season because we both know I was never good in school, so the beach was my escape. And that ocean out there was my sanctuary. But then last year that all changed. Do you realize I haven't been in the water since the accident? And now when I look out my bedroom window, I hate what I see, and I have the same feeling when I look in the mirror."

"Can I say something to all of this?"

"Yeah."

"At the mass tonight, Father McDaniel admitted he wished he could give an answer to why this happened, but he said the one lesson we can learn from Matt and Paul's lives is to live our own lives fully and to use their joyful spirit as our example. You are right, Colin, this beach *was* your escape, but it was also the place that taught you who you truly are meant to be. You have such a good soul, and I know deep down it's still there. I know that. It's time for you to embrace it again. You have so much to give, but how can you give anything if you're not being who you're truly meant to be? You have to enjoy what you are, the C-dog." Dermot stopped and looked out at the white marker bobbing in the distance and smiled. "But wait, I just figured out the first step of how you can get back to that person."

"How, Derm?"

"Just like when we were kids. Remember when you were little, and I taught you to swim over your head? The first thing you wanted to do was race me to the marker. I beat you by *miles*, but kept looking back to make sure you didn't quit. And you didn't. You got there. Every time we raced, I always beat you, but then the day came when you left me in your wake, and I just watched you with the pride of a big brother knowing his younger brother was something special. And you are. So are you up for it?"

Colin smiled. "For the first time in a long time, I think I am." He placed the ATLANTIS hat on The Fighting Chair and they both walked to the shoreline.

Dermot laughed. "I sure as hell hope you're wearing boxers and not a pair of Molloy's bikini briefs. Race you to the marker!"

"You just worry about trying to keep up with me, old man." Colin took the rune out of his pocket, glanced at the symbol, and skipped it, watching it cut through the top of the ocean.

"What was that?" Dermot asked.

"My past." Colin nodded, stripped down to his red boxers, and took a racing dive plunging into the waves. Beneath the sea, he pushed through and then opened his eyes.

He instantly pictured Matt and Paul on either side of him, and he smiled, realizing they were no longer ghosts haunting him. No, he now knew his friends were spirits who would always be there to guide him. When he resurfaced, he did the crawl with the same urgency back when he was racing in swim meets, and when he reached the marker first, he hugged it before turning around to look for his brother who was nowhere in sight.

A second later, Dermot's head popped out of the water, and he casually made it to the marker grabbing the other side and holding onto it. "Wow, the water is cold," Dermot said and shivered while looking at Colin.

"I know. It feels good." Colin nodded and, with his right hand, leaned over and held his older brother's arm.

"I love you, little brother," Dermot said.

"I know. I love you too, Derm."

Colin treaded water and thought about the rune of Guilt he had drawn with his driftwood in the sand. He smiled. He knew high tide would be coming soon, and with it, so would the running waves sent to erase that symbol forever.

ACKNOWLEDGMENTS

We would like to thank the wonderful people of Cape Cod where so many talented and supportive people reside.

Our mom, Margaret A. Murphy, who has never given up on us, this book is a result of her knowledge, guidance, and faith in her boys' dreams.

Our dad, James F. Murphy, Jr., our in-house editor, our greatest writing teacher, our comedian on a rainy day, and most of all, our best friend. You make us strive to become better men.

Our four sisters, Nina, Joanna, Sarah, and Courtney, we are so blessed to have sisters that truly have been our buddies in life. You are all so talented and so "wicked natural" at what you do. We love you!

We would like to thank John Furfey because we can't pay him. Thanks Furf for not only creating CapeCodWriter.com and TheRunningWaves. com, but fixing every Murphy electronic system over the last twenty years. Your sarcastic wit and loyalty is endless.

We would like to thank Jeremy Townsend and her awesome staff at Publishing Works, Inc. for turning our "overdressed manuscript" into a novel.

Gerald Hagerty and Jeffrey Wolf, thank you for having our backs.

A special thank you to everyone who has joined our FACEBOOK fan page www.therunningwaves.com and has spread the word about our book! If you read the book and like it please join and tell everyone you know. If you don't like the book, please just keep it to yourself.

We would like to give a shout out to our publicist Marci Tyldesley who will be promoting our book. Oprah, you can contact her at marci@ capebeachcomber.com

Being co-authors, there were some very long nights on the phone so Seton would like to thank Vanessa Andrade for dealing with it by being "a cool girlfriend", and T.M. Murphy would like to thank Vanessa for being "*his* cool girlfriend." Thanks Vanessa for always laughing at my bad jokes, and never giving up on me during the downtimes. P.S.

Finally, there are too many friends to list here, but please read our blog Journey of The Running Waves on TheRunningWaves.com because there are so many more people who deserve recognition.

ABOUT THE
AUTHORS

SETON AND T. M. MURPHY.
PHOTO BY AMY STEELE.

T.M. Murphy, featured in the book *101 Highly Successful Novelists*, is the author of the several books for kids. Murphy spends his time teaching creative writing at Boston College, touring schools to motivate young people to write, and also teaching writing during the summer at The Writers' Shack in his hometown of Falmouth, Massachusetts. *The Running Waves* is Murphy's first novel for adults, but not his last. For more information about T.M. Murphy check out his websites capecodwriter.com and therunningwaves.com.

Seton Murphy lives and works outside of Boston, but grew up in Falmouth, Massachusetts, in a family of writers. He is a graduate of Bridgewater State College. His influences include Dave Chappelle, Chris Rock, Tom Brady, Beck, and his parents. This is his first book.